Rich
Women

BILL ADLER

Rich Women

BART

NEW YORK

ISBN: 1-55785-86-0

First Bart Books edition: March 1989

Bart Books
155 E. 34th Street
New York, New York 10016

Manufactured in the United States of America

PROLOGUE

In her bedroom, Hayley Prescott Welles brushed her long auburn hair in front of the cheval glass until it assumed the sheen of burnished copper. She studied her classic curves and flat stomach under the diaphanous peignoir, then turned for an admiring profile view.

The sight of her trim silhouette brought a smile to her lips. She loved the way men's eyes riveted to her as she turned sideways and away from them.

Not bad for a woman in her late thirties. A nice tan, too. Tennis and golf did wonders for her.

The squat, stocky man steered the Ultralight over the ten-foot-high, electrified chain-link fence. He banked, pushed forward on the throttle, and brought the aircraft down for a landing on a grassy glade behind a thicket of pines, on the Scobie Hills estate of the Prescott family.

The rolling, bumpy terrain jammed the man's coccyx and sent shudders up his spine as he taxied behind the pines. Suddenly one of the Ultralight's small rubber tires struck a rock, flipping the aircraft to the right, onto the tip of its fifteen-foot wing.

Unhurt except for the tingling up his backbone, he cursed his sloppy landing, unbuckled his harness, removed his helmet, and inspected the wing tip for damages. If the Ultralight could not fly, he was dead meat. There would be no escape.

The wing appeared to be all right. The Ultralight seemed able to fly him and the woman out.

He had to move quickly. The sound of the aircraft's engine might have alerted one of the security guards prowling the perimeter of the estate.

The man rolled the Ultralight among the pines to hide it from the casual glance of any patrolling guards, withdrew the Uzi machine pistol braced under the pilot's seat, and sprinted up the hill toward the sprawling mansion.

At that moment, a burly security officer in a Jeep drove into view. The running man spotted him and hit the ground. The guard drove around the hill, out of sight, without noticing anything out of the ordinary.

The man looked up at the mansion above him and made out the figure of a woman passing a lighted third-story window. He knew who it was, and he knew where the room was located from the floor plan he had made from a magazine article.

The onset of dusk helped conceal his movements as he mounted the hill and reached the mansion's massive mahogany front door.

He paused, caught his breath, screwed a silencer onto the muzzle of the Uzi, and tried the door. It did not surprise him that it was unlocked. The tight security around the estate gave the inhabitants a false sense of safety within the guarded perimeter.

The man smiled crookedly and edged into the entryway of the mansion. He reached the foot of a sweeping marble staircase and, at that instant, heard an unwelcome sound.

He stiffened, turned his head, caught sight of a dumbfounded butler, aimed the Uzi at him, and cut him down. The scores of bullets, whispering through the air, sounded oddly like corn popping.

The man had to move quickly. Somebody might stumble onto the dead butler any moment now.

He climbed to the third floor and bolted down the corridor to the room directly over the front door, the room where he had spotted the woman. He twisted the doorknob and walked inside.

Nonplussed, Hayley Welles stood beside her bed in her wispy negligee, her eyes on the stranger and the lethal-looking machine pistol he aimed at her.

"Jesus Christ," she said.

Her heart thumping with fear, she managed to hold herself in check while she surreptitiously slid her foot along the parquet floor to where she knew the secret button that would alert the security forces was located. From her present position she could not reach it. She stepped closer.

The man leered for an instant at the sight of her breasts, visible through the white negligee, then said, "Let's go."

"Go where? Who *are* you?"

She stepped closer to the button and simultaneously broke into a cold sweat.

"Over here, not there," the man barked, jerking the machine pistol toward the door behind him.

Hayley stretched her toe and depressed the button, then reluctantly walked toward the door, feigning helplessness. She would bluff it out now to see what would happen.

"Who do you think you are?" she demanded, trying to occupy the intruder's mind.

"Shut up, or I'll kill you where you stand. Now, move it!"

Hayley moved circumspectly toward the door. She knew she must not let him read her fear. He could be a psychotic. The least little thing might set him off.

Through the open door behind him, she could see the welcome sight of a security guard stealing into view and taking up a position in the doorway.

"Who *are* you, anyway?" she demanded again, to keep his attention focused on her.

"Shut up, you rich whore!" the man hissed. "Just be glad your husband will give a fortune to get you back!"

"Drop it," said the security guard, crouched in place, his service revolver drawn and trained on the intruder.

Startled, the man swung around to confront the guard. In the same movement, he squeezed the Uzi's trigger, and the slugs flew in a parabola as he moved.

The first two shots of the guard's .44 magnum revolver blew off the back of the man's skull before the Uzi had time to complete its arc toward the guard's vitals.

When the man fell on the floor, his trouser leg rolled up and revealed the letters P.O.W. tattooed on his calf.

"Who is he?" asked Hayley, grimacing at the blood spattered all around. "A nut?"

"P. O. W.," read the guard, looking at the tattoo.

"What did you say?"

"On his leg. See it?"

Hayley saw it, shuddering as she did so. "What does *that* mean?"

"Prisoner of war? P.O.W.? Probably not." The guard shook his head. "Just another scumbag psycho."

"Certainly must be. Clean up the mess and get this gutter trash out of here. And keep this quiet as much as you can. I don't want anybody *else* getting the idea and doing an encore!"

BOOK ONE: NEW YORK

CHAPTER ONE

Abbey Prescott Martin stood on the window's walk of the Prescott mansion, high atop the Scobie Hills estate, surrendering herself to the luxury of the cooling afternoon breeze. At nineteen, she was hardly the proper member of the Prescott family to be pacing the widow's walk—that portion of a New England home reserved for grieving ships' officers' wives—but widow or not, she loved the feeling of height and weightlessness here on the most elevated spot of the compound.

· She shook back her head, letting her long corn-yellow hair play in the wind. From this vantage point she could see *everything*—the Hudson River, winding between its banks; the woods surrounding the Prescott estate; the tiny village of Scobie Hills below; the highway from New York City to Albany, cutting through the valley; and even the thin strands of the New York Central's railroad lines traveling along the lip of the riverbank.

The widow's walk had been an afterthought on the part of the designer when the original Prescott had ordered the Colonial structure built, just before the turn of the century. It dominated the entire structure, because the tower atop which it was erected rose six feet higher than the main portion of the mansion.

This was Abbey's hideaway, the place she came when she wanted solitude and space. Space! There was plenty of that. Miles and miles in every direction. She felt better after even a moment or two on the walk. Her psyche needed airing out. Her mother and father were in a bitter mood with each other, and with her. And she—she was restless and moody. The enclosed and protected world of Smith College was fine for some people—not for her. It was summer vacation now, and she wanted some—oh, some *action!* Was that too much to ask?

According to her dear mother and darling father— yes, it was. She was her mother; he wasn't really her father. She hadn't seen her real father for months. He was making television commercials in a loft in New York. Dumb, to have given up all that Prescott money for his own independence—or was it so dumb?

She leaned against the white, painted timbers that formed the border of the widow's walk: *X*'s joined together with a post and secured with a rail along the top. She could even see the main gate of the compound, and the drive that wound up to the entrance of the mansion. Around the estate, the perimeter road followed the electrified fence. Regular checks were made by the Prescott security forces.

As she looked down, she could see a big, heavyset uniformed man about to climb into a Land Rover with the Prescott crest painted on its side. It was Charlie Garnet—the head of Prescott security. She had known him all her life. He was almost part of the family. As he gazed about before leaning over to open the door, he spotted her up on the top of the mansion and waved to her.

She saw him and waved back. There was nothing wrong with Charlie. He knew about school and about parents and about the Prescotts. She wished her own mother and father knew as much about people as Charlie did. Maybe he could teach them.

Charlie Garnet seated himself comfortably in the Land Rover and flicked the ignition switch. He had been employed by the Prescotts most of his working life—first as swimming pool maintenance man, then on the interior security staff, and finally as head of exterior security. He knew every one of the Prescotts by sight, as with Abbey Martin, both from a distance and close up. By now, he was familiar with most of their more intimate friends—although, of course, they really had few "intimates" in the true sense of the word.

As he drove the Land Rover away from the main gate, he glanced back in the rearview mirror to spot-check the man in charge of the entryway. He was a handsome, black-haired young dude, typical of the kind of help the Prescotts preferred. Not too macho, but not too pseudo-Ivy League either, he was just right—in-between, low-profile American. A limousine came sliding to a halt as the young guard moved to the chauffeur's side to check the invitation.

Garnet lost sight of the main gate as the Land Rover rounded a curve in the perimeter road—a road that was exactly two miles and three-tenths in length according to his odometer. The road bordered two hundred acres of land enclosed by a ten-foot-high chain-link Cyclone fence topped with two strands of electrified wire.

He settled down to a routine drive as he executed another curve around an outcrop of rock. Through the chain link fence he could now see the end of the tennis court. Still too far away to hear any noise, he could nevertheless see movement as someone drew back to smash a return over the net. Now Garnet could see the rest of the tennis court, the swimming pool beyond, and a corner of the mansion itself.

More people became visible, disporting themselves on the grounds of the sumptuous estate. Keeping those grounds in the proper trim cost a mint of money, Garnet knew. The Prescotts demanded and got the best in upkeep, and no one with a tendency to sloppiness lasted long, particularly on the mowing team. It took six men working full time with six of the latest-style gang-mowers to keep those lawns in mint condition.

Garnet chuckled at the extravagance. And yet, was it extravagance? The Prescotts were worth, it was said, billions. They had been here at Scobie Hills since before the turn of the century. Members of the fourth generation of the original Prescott family were now in charge. There were five cousins who actually held the reins of the Prescott fortune—but at least a score and a half of their relatives were multimillionaires in their own right.

The road wound through a stand of jack pines and came out into brilliant sunlight. Here the chain link fence overlooked a rather steep slope, which bottomed out into a small pond that was fed by a trickling stream winding through the trees. Garnet stopped the Land Rover and sat there a moment, relaxing. It was restful and beautiful, even to a member of the stolid proletariat. Staring lazily at the bucolic scene, he lit a cigarette and waved out the cardboard match before bending it and inserting it into the dashboard ashtray.

A man moved out of the woods and stood looking at the pond. Garnet started. He took the cigarette out of his mouth and made a movement to switch on the engine to move on—he did not want to be caught eavesdropping—but then he held back. Who was this one, anyway? He did not immediately recognize the rather lithe figure; the suppressed tension underlying its movements; the smooth, almost feline grace of its progress as it began to walk toward the shadows of the trees by the pond.

Garnet removed the field glasses from the dashboard compartment. They were heavy Zeiss binoculars, capable of bringing objects from a great distance up to well within viewing range. He focused the lenses on the figure that was now bending over and facing him. Garnet sat upright. Now the figure was undoing its trouser belt.

He let a smile cross his lips, canting the cigarette at an upward angle. The old swimming hole. For years the Prescotts had used that pond as a place to take a dip out of sight of the mansion and the servants. It seemed that this unknown person must be a guest . . . .

The powerful lenses caught the face now. Garnet could see it clearly, and as he did so the name leaped out at him. There was a book kept by security with mug shots of every guest who had ever come to the Prescott estate. Many in The Book, as it was called, never came again. Others did. The Book was part of the Prescott legend. And this was a new face in it. This, in fact, was the first time for Mead Brookhaven III. Garnet prided himself on his accurate memory and on his quick recall.

Although no Prescott, Brookhaven worked for Carney Welles—more properly known as Cornelius Welles—the husband of Hayley Prescott Welles, the number one Prescott of today's cousins. The Prescott dynasty had met the day before, holding their yearly family reunion in order to discuss the various financial problems arising from the multitude of companies, foundations, conglomerates, and business groups controlled by Prescott money. Today, the day following the family meeting—limited to Prescotts and spouses (excluding those divorced out of the family) —the compound was thrown open to friends and associates not invited to the tight family meeting.

Garnet frowned. Brookhaven looked exactly like his picture. He was in his late twenties, perhaps, with an athletic build that was not that of a football linebacker, but more that of a world-class runner. The face was even-featured, topped by curly light-brown hair, and highlighted by very-blue eyes and an easy smile. Garnet was suspicious of easy smiles.

Off came the slacks, then the shirt. Garnet focused on it as it lay on the grass, carelessly tossed aside. Expensive, he concluded. Designer sports shirt, definitely the real thing. And the slacks, too. Tailored. Well draped. Tight in the ass. And they fit the wearer, too. He had the trim hips and bottom demanded by the designer.

Now Brookhaven was fiddling with his jockey shorts and off they came, to be plopped inelegantly on top of the expensive shirt and slacks. Off with the shoes and socks, quickly now. As he stood there, poised to jump in the pond, Garnet studied his body. He was nicely built, nicely muscled, nicely kept in shape. Who couldn't be, at age twenty-odd? Garnet wondered with the regret of an aging ex-athlete.

The smooth tan was something else. Garnet noticed that it did not stop at the hips. That meant Mead Brookhaven III was professionally toasted—doubtless at a private suntanning salon. Again Garnet frowned. There was something fake—

His thought was interrupted as a second figure appeared quite suddenly in the sunlight that stabbed through the trees at the edge of the pond. Garnet's breathing halted. It was Hayley Welles—the leader of the flock! He flicked the glasses onto her face to take in her reaction. Here was a naked young buck about to jump into the pond. It was Hayley's pond, as Garnet knew. He had seen her use it privately during her days home from college, and during interims between her marriages. And now . . .

Not a hint of shock or dismay penetrated her usual calm and laid-back expression. Her lips moved slightly, but Garnet could not lip-read. He turned to view the young man's face. He was, oddly enough, smiling at something. His eyes were traveling up and down Hayley's body, much in the manner of a rutting college jock. In astonishment, Garnet flipped the glasses back to Hayley's face, seeing her expression darken just a trifle, and then relax. He saw her eyes narrow.

By now Garnet was frowning in bewilderment. What was this? A prearranged meeting? If the scenario had played out the way it should have, she would have ordered him to dress and leave the estate immediately. There would be a phone call to the main gate to assure his departure—or an order to come up and get him to escort him out.

There was some more talk between the two, with Hayley facing the young man, and with Brookhaven turned to face her. He seemed interested in her, Garnet thought—at least his *body* was beginning to respond. Garnet chuckled. The woman was gazing at him full-on, and *she* knew what his body was telling him—and her. But there was no immediate reaction from her other than to continue what had to be an inane conversation.

Nerves of steel, Garnet conceded. I'd hate to come up against that ball-breaker in fair combat, he told himself. She was a real Adam-smasher, as his young son called strong women. My God, he murmured to himself, what the hell were they talking about? It was no rendezvous. It was in no way pre-planned. What in *hell* were they saying to each other?

Infuriating—that was what it was, if you had to put a word to it. Hayley Welles had been wanting to throw something and break it ever since she had heard Carney's profit-and-loss report for the previous year at yesterday's rundown of the Prescott fiscal situation. Cornelius Welles Associates was the *only* investment that had not shown an increase in profits! That made her look twice the fool—for financing his public relations enterprise *and* for being married to him.

But there was more to her anger than a simple reaction to Carney's failure to have a big year. Their marriage was on hold. It needed *something* to bring it back to life. That was the reason she had suggested the Beatrix Fontaine project and had put the two of them together on it. But maybe, she now thought, *that* had been a mistake, too!

By instinct Hayley was heading through the woods toward her favorite wailing wall—the pond on the northern slope of the estate. There she had managed to overcome the various traumas, reversals, and irritations in her life, either by plunging into the bracing

water buck naked—doe naked, in her case—or by
leisurely sunbathing in a swimsuit. Today's upset had
occurred too quickly for her to prepare her costume;
perhaps she would just sit by the pond and let it all
seep out of her skin.

It wasn't only the bad financial statement of Welles
Associates and the Beatrix program that bothered
her. She had to admit that Beatrix herself, whom she
had met at least a year before and had *liked* then, was
beginning to give her bad vibes. The brilliant French
cosmetologist was sultry, classically beautiful, keyed
to sexual encounter in the *au courant* Gallic way—
and likable almost to a fault. She had Carney wrapped
around her little finger, damn her! Not that it *meant*
anything. Hell, Carney wasn't your usual stud rear-
ing to plunge into carnal action. It had been months,
in fact, since he had *touched* Hayley where it counted.

Beatrix bore close watching, Hayley decided, pushing aside the branches and stepping out into the
clearing that was so familiar to her. And there she
halted in dismay. She was not alone as she had
expected to be. Someone was sharing her hideaway.
But her dismay was overlaid with shock, and then
with amusement. Her unknown companion was a
man—a young man, in his twenties, perhaps. She
couldn't tell about age anymore. He was muscled and
fit and deeply tanned in the well-to-do manner of the
affluent and bodily pampered.

The shock came from the fact that he was stripped
naked. Hayley had been approaching too rapidly and
too angrily to halt her precipitous emergence from
the woods. And now she stood there, temporarily
speechless. Who was this clown who stood there like
a ninny, with everything—but everything!—hanging

out? And who had told him he could come here, anyway? This was Hayley's private domain.

And yet—he was a guest. She had it now. He was that young, upwardly mobile kid Carney had hired some months back to be his roving assistant. She had never met him until that morning, and then she had only seen him in passing. Mead Brookhaven III. Silly lout. Nobody used Roman numerals any longer. Was she Hayley Prescott II? Hell no, in spite of the fact that her maternal grandmother's name had been Hayley.

"Who are you and what are you doing here? This is my pond!" Hayley always believed attack was preferable to retreat.

Ordinarily a man without clothes on would turn away in modesty or shame. This one simply stared at Hayley, almost challengingly, or perhaps encouragingly. "Mead Brookhaven," the kid said. "We met this morning."

"Did we?" Hayley responded lightly. She cast an eye on the pile of clothes behind him. "Oh, yes. Now I see the *real* you more clearly." Her eyes came back to his face with force. "You're Carney's new troubleshooter."

"Sorry if I've invaded your private space." If he was sorry, he was making no move to pick up his clothes and split, Hayley realized grimly. The young man spoke again. " 'Oh! the old swimmin' hole! . . . How pleasant was the journey down the old dusty lane!' "

Quite suddenly, Hayley knew the truth. He had planned this, damn his hide! Although he continued to maintain a calm and ordered reserve, his body was fighting him in the most obvious way. Any other man would have blushed, but this one continued to stare at her out of a pair of very probing blue eyes.

"I *do* admire a man who can recite poetry," Hayley said smoothly. "Even James Whitcomb Riley's, but not when—" Suddenly she lifted her chin and roared with uncontrollable laughter at her pun. "Not when he's *in a rut*!"

That broke the tension. He gave her a smirk and turned to pick up his clothes, slowly slipping into them while she stared at him. Her own good humor had dissipated as quickly as it had come.

"Get out of here," she snapped at him. "I want to be by myself." She was watching his graceful yet masculine movements as he dressed directly in front of her. Finished, he tucked his sports shirt into the belt of his slacks and studied her. His eyes wandered up over her skirt and the light sweater she wore over her blouse to the beads around her tanned, slender neck—one of the most attractive features of her body— and lingered then on the outline of her breasts under the soft sweater.

"I'm going."

Her temper flared. "God damn it! This is Prescott property! How dare you come slipping through the trees into *my woods!*"

He moved slowly toward her. She had not advanced from the point where she had emerged from the trees on the sloping ground that dipped into the pond. He was only inches from her when he stopped; she would not have budged now if bulldozed.

"I wanted to make an offer you couldn't refuse."

She snorted with contempt. "You call yourself God's gift to women? Bug off, buster!"

He smiled. "Now you know what you'll be missing."

"The *audition* is over." She eyed him, feeling the heat from his body enveloping her, smelling the sub-

tle aftershave lotion he wore, experiencing that familiar old *frisson*, as if someone had placed a warm
hand directly on her crotch.

He smirked and turned to leave.

"Don't call us," Hayley said as a parting shot.
"We'll call you."

He moved off jauntily and turned to face her. "I'll
be ready when you are."

He vanished.

She stood there, finding herself suddenly trembling.
There was no question about it, he certainly *would* be
ready. And the ironic thing was—she was ready
now. But of course, no one knew that—not even she
herself on the conscious level. But her unconscious
certainly knew. And her body ached. She perspired,
and suddenly contracted in a familiar intimate spasm.

She sank down near the pond and stared sightlessly
at the water as it rippled slightly in the light breeze.
Damn him! How did he *know?*

Charlie Garnet bumped along the perimeter road,
thinking back on the amusing scene he had just wit-
nessed between Hayley Welles and her unembar-
rassed guest. He had an affection for Hayley; there
was a bond between them that nothing could break. It
was on Charlie's first day on the job at Scobie
Hills—he was at the swimming pool then—that Hayley
had been born in the mansion. It was just two years
before the birth of his oldest girl, Arlene—the one with
the bad leg, the one who had turned his life upside down
by becoming the first runaway in the Garnet family.

Over the years, he had watched Hayley grow up.
He had seen her older sister Megan grow up, too,
and others of the clan—but it was Hayley whose life
interested him the most.

In many ways she was the most intelligent of them all, the most resourceful, and the most exciting. Now into her third marriage, she might easily break that up to create another, if she felt like it; or she might go on with Carney Welles for the rest of her days, in great peace and contentment.

"Hey!" shouted Charlie, grinding the Land Rover to a halt and killing the engine. "What are you kids doing there?" He had come upon two youngsters from the village. They were at the bottom of the slope, engaged in doing the usual: peering through the chain link fence and trying to figure out how to scale it without being roasted alive. They stood in simple defiance as Charlie opened the door and clambered out of the car toward them.

"Just lookin'," said one of the lads.

"Just looking isn't allowed," snapped Charlie, standing over them, his stance making the Smith and Wesson revolver very evident as it rode on his hip.

"Why not?" the other youngster asked.

"Because it isn't! Now get out of here! I don't want to have to call for reinforcements."

The kids were already moving away from the fence. "There's nothin' in there anyway," said the first one, casting a lowering glance at the fence.

"Bunch of rich bastuds," said the second with a giggle.

Charlie hesitated. He almost grinned. "Bunch of *very* rich bastuds," he corrected.

The boys laughed and ambled into the brush alongside the road, headed for Scobie Hills Village.

Charlie started back to the Land Rover, glancing through the fence at the scene spread out below. He could see the swimming pool clearly, and the tennis courts beyond, with the mansion in the distance.

There were very few people in swimming. In fact, it was a fairly cool day, and no one except a Californian or a Floridian would even think about going in the water. But there were two women sitting in deck chairs near the small dressing room that contained showers and private stalls for bathers.

With the glasses firmly in hand, Garnet gazed through them and adjusted the focus. He could see the profile of one of the women, apparently in her late thirties. A much younger woman was seated beside her. Funny, he couldn't place them. The older woman turned her head to talk to the other, and he could make out her features. It had been the bathing cap binding up her hair that had prevented instantaneous identification.

She was Beatrix Fontaine. Her picture was new in the Prescott book. But Garnet kept up with *The Wall Street Journal*—it wasn't only the Prescotts who put their money into stocks and bonds—and knew that she was the phenomenal Frenchwoman who had started Beatrix Cosmétique on a shoestring only five years before and who was now challenging the supremacy of the Coco Chanel empire and others in the cosmetics industry.

He had checked her in at the front gate early in the afternoon. It was the hair that gave her distinction; unlike the typical Frenchwoman, her molasses-colored hair grew thick and long. Her eyes were a strange yellowish brown—the kind you could almost call "golden." She was certainly well built and had kept herself trim: witness the rounded breasts, the slim hips, the long thighs, and well-shaped legs.

He was not conscious that he whistled to himself as he shifted the glasses to her companion. He recalled her as well—Thérèse Maupin. She was in her twenties, he guessed. He knew nothing about her at all, except that she had simply stared straight ahead of her while the Fontaine woman had chatted briefly and amicably with him—her accent was a delight—and then had driven on. Her daughter? Possibly—married and with another name. Or her younger sister?

The young woman leaned toward the older one and kissed her on the side of the face. Beatrix laughed and shook her head. Garnet's eyes narrowed. Damn it! He was going to have to take up lip-reading after all!

Since there was no one around, the two women were speaking in French—one slowly, her once-slovenly provincial accent now trimmed into vintage Parisian, and the other with her anti-establishment jargon from the Left Bank pared down only slightly.

"It's an embarrassment to these people!" Beatrix was telling her companion. "In Paris, no one would blink an eye. But here, if anyone walked in, the Prescotts would have the vice squad on us."

"But they've given us separate rooms!" wailed Tessie. "We can go in the dressing rooms," she suggested suddenly, with a glint in her dark eyes.

Beatrix stared at her lover. Tessie Maupin was an angular, awkwardly constructed young woman, with very flat breasts and wide hips. Her face carried out the theme of angularity that clung to the girl. Her eyes were snapping black, with heavy brows. Even with lipstick properly applied, Tessie was far from pretty. She was, in fact, almost ugly.

But who needed beauty when she had such a singularly exciting sexual abandonment? Beatrix knew she was lucky to have run across Tessie after a series of lackluster male lovers, mixed in with several so-called lesbians who were interested only in their own weird satisfactions.

"I don't think I want to right now," Beatrix sighed. She glanced over Tessie's square shoulder into the woods that surrounded the swimming pool. "Is there someone out there watching us?" she wondered aloud.

Tessie turned to look. "I don't see anyone."

"My imagination," Beatrix said, shaking off a small tingle of apprehension.

Tessie leaned toward her again. "I'm terribly horny, Trish. The flight over, I guess. All that jouncing and sliding. I don't want to have to go in and do it alone."

"How about a cold shower?" snapped Beatrix, suddenly annoyed at her lover's somewhat inappropriate and hazardous suggestions. "Maybe that'll straighten things out."

Tessie sank down in the deck chair, her face tight in an angry pout.

After a moment Beatrix relented. "Baby, I'm sorry. It's just that I've been so concerned about this trip. It's so important for Beatrix Cosmétique to get off on the right footing with Welles Associates. And I don't want to ruin everything before we start. Don't forget, this is an entirely new image for Beatrix. Conventional. Moderate. Middle-class. Solid. We *must* tap that important middle market—and that's where the prudes live, my dear."

"*Merde!*" growled Tessie, jumping up from the deck chair and running into the dressing room alongside the pool deck.

Beatrix leaned back, her eyes closed. There was no substitute for Tessie, but she was becoming a damned bore. Her incessant needs were beginning to exhaust even Beatrix. Of course, if it was necessary, she could always dump the girl. But her presence was serving a double purpose. Not only was she Beatrix's sex outlet, she was also the best copywriter Beatrix had ever hired for the company.

The company was the reason she had made this important trip to America. To meet Cornelius Welles and to work with his people, preparing for the eventual launching of the new Beatrix Cosmétique. She couldn't lose Tessie now. But frankly, no matter how good she was at making love, she was beginning to get on Beatrix's nerves. And when that happened—

Beatrix shivered. She *needed* the damned girl. Sitting there thinking about her had worked her up into a sudden and urgent need for psychic and physical release. She shoved up off the deck chair and slipped swiftly across the deck into the dressing room.

Tessie stood there in the shadowed semi-dark of the shower room, the water cascading down her back, sliding along her long black hair, plastering it to her shoulders, her tiny breasts and rounded belly. Her nipples were erect, looking huge and pink and inviting, and she was gazing straight at Beatrix. Her hands, Beatrix saw, were at work between her legs. Now they stretched out toward Beatrix, shining and wet, as Beatrix moved quickly toward her and wrapped her own arms around the square, strong, vibrant naked body.

Beatrix's close-fitting swimsuit slipped to the concrete floor, and Tessie's fingers went to work in their skilled, breathtaking, ecstatic fashion.

Beatrix's eyes closed tightly, and her lips drew back against her teeth when the warmth spread through her and convulsed her as the two of them slid down sideways onto the concrete with the water smashing down onto them from above.

*   *   *

Rocketing along the roadway above the Hudson River, with the railroad tracks of the New York Central below him, Charlie Garnet shot up an incline and once again had the mansion in full view. He could see the tower and the famous widow's walk. Abbey Martin was gone now.

Absently, Garnet wondered how Abbey got along with her stepfather, the public relations mogul Cornelius Welles. Now there was a guy who had made it big on Prescott money—big in a way that was obviously hurting some of the more conservative Prescotts. But you couldn't knock his success. He had made tiny personalities into big, impressive forces in industry and—most especially—in entertainment. Movie actors, rock stars, groups, Broadway stars— you name it, he had made them.

And of course he was a bed bunny, too—as active as the late Jack Kennedy. Hayley knew it, and so did everyone else in the Prescott clan. She put up with it; they put up with it. It was all part of the game he played. Odd that he and Hayley had never had children. Yet it was probably just as well. Abbey was enough to handle.

As soon as she was in the house and out of sight, Abbey Martin headed for the "wreck" room on the floor just below the widow's walk. Of course it had originally been called the recreation room—but nobody in the Prescott family felt any need to conceal their thoughts about it. There were several television sets in various states of usefulness along with an expensive stereo set built into one of the walls, and there were two VCRs. In addition, there was a bar built along one side of the large room. The most impressive thing about the wreck room was the number of floor-to-ceiling windows. In fact, it seemed to be an outdoors room without actually being outdoors.

Abbey was dying for a toke. Her throat was dry and her hands were sweating. What she had was Panama Red, but with her parents quarreling about Welles Associates' profit-and-loss sheet and Beatrix Cosmétique and everything else that was falling apart, she really needed a stronger rush—like Sensimilla—but this would do in a pinch.

There was a large storage closet at the end of the bar. The earlier Prescotts, with their fascination for the British way of life, called it a "lumber room," but Abbey never bothered to name it at all. There were bottles of expensive liquor in there, along with some cheap table wines that were not stored at the bottom of the mansion in the deep-down wine cellar.

She opened the door, pushed past some huge cardboard boxes containing seltzer water and quinine, and settled down on a crate of brandy pushed against the back wall of the closet. There, with the door closed against any intruders, she lit up a fine Panama Red she had been saving for a special occasion.

The sweet, penetrating smoke knifed into her and calmed her within minutes, and she leaned back drowsily against the wall, letting the smoke slide in and out of her lungs. Another summer at Scobie Hills, she thought. Could she stand it?

Quite suddenly she was aware of someone talking nearby. It was a voice that was unfamiliar and—

It was a television announcer! He seemed to be reporting a race of some kind. Of course, a horse race. But the set had not been on when she entered the storage closet. Someone must be out there. She leaned forward, a bit nervously, trying to hear more clearly.

She stubbed out the roach and put it carefully in a small handkerchief she carried in her skirt pocket. Then she moved to the door and unlatched it noiselessly, pushing it just slightly open.

It was her mother!

Quickly Abbey began waving her hands about, flapping the stench of the marijuana somewhere else—but it wouldn't go away. The atmosphere in the closet was permeated with the sweetish, overpowering, languorous smoke of the weed. Shit!

She stopped flapping her arms and moved to the slit between the door and the jamb, peering out at her mother. She was standing indolently in front of the set, watching with a half-smile on her face and listening to the announcer.

Now Abbey could focus on the words . . . and she had it. Her mother was watching the race to see how Starfish was doing. Starfish belonged to Austin Bush—and Austin was Abbey's stepfather, just like Cornelius Welles was. Austin Bush was Hayley's Number Two husband.

Abbey had never known him very well, because he had never been home when he was *in loco parentis*. He was always out at the track. The guy had a thing about horseflesh. But he was one of the real horse lovers—not a fake like some of the jet-setters. And he could play polo like a demon!

The marriage had fallen apart quickly because Hayley would not put up with a half-marriage. She wanted a man around the house—not around the stables. Besides, he didn't really pay all that much attention to her, and Abbey's mother never really forgave anybody who *ignored* her.

Suddenly Abbey saw Hayley's head turn. At the same moment, a string of incomprehensible sounds overrode the announcer's voice. Abbey moved slightly and could see that there was someone else in the room with her mother. She recognized the Frenchwoman she had been introduced to earlier that afternoon. Beatrix Fontaine.

She seemed to be urging on the horse the announcer was talking about. Hayley turned her gaze back to the set without even acknowledging the presence of the newcomer. But then, finally, probably thinking about her overall persona, she turned once again toward the intruder and smiled ingratiatingly.

"You like horse racing, Mademoiselle Fontaine?"

"Beatrix, *s'il vous plait*. It is not horse racing I like, it is a particular horse."

The accent was easy to follow. Abbey had heard Frenchwomen no one could make out. But Beatrix was one you could get along with . . . unlike the curious little frump that traveled with her—the one who was supposedly a copywriter. Abbey had her own ideas about *that* one.

"You know Starfish?" Hayley seemed surprised.

"Oh, I know the horse. But I know better the driver."

"The jockey?" Hayley was trying to understand the point Beatrix was making, obviously with little success.

"Oh, the owner. I mean, the man who has the papers on the horse. The man who feeds him. I like him."

Hayley smiled; her eyes narrowed slightly. "You *know* Austin Bush well?"

Abbey was in a position where she could see both women. She watched the Frenchwoman stiffen momentarily. Then she turned her face toward Abbey's mother, made a most Gallic moue, and said in a very soft but even voice:

"Once." Her lips pressed together primly. Then her eyes sparkled. "Or twice. Or perhaps three times."

"More than that for me," Hayley said, her face softening slightly.

"But of course. You *were* in marriage to him."

"Only for a *coup d'oeil*."

The Frenchwoman laughed.

"Maybe four times all told." Hayley sighed.

The two women watched the screen as the announcer's voice rose in pitch and excitement and—

Beatrix shrugged in indifference. Hayley shook her head. "Just like Austin. Always fades in the stretch." Then, remembering her manners, she turned to her guest. "Drink?"

Beatrix hesitated, then nodded. "*Merci*. Please."

Hayley strolled over to the bar and rustled around behind it, bringing out some gin and tonic. She poured the drinks, broke ice out of the bucket, and mixed the drinks.

"Cheers," she said, lifting her glass. "To Beatrix Cosmétique."

"To Cornelius Welles," said the Frenchwoman.

"To men in general," Hayley laughed.

"I prefer men in the particular," smiled Beatrix.

Hayley looked at her guest across the bar. "That surprises me somewhat."

Beatrix frowned, gesturing vaguely into the distance. It was obvious she was referring to the young woman she had in tow somewhere "out there." "A momentary aberration," she said.

"Of course. To *individuals* in particular."

Beatrix smiled and sipped at the gin and tonic. "How did you know I liked the British affliction?" She glanced down at the drink in her hand.

"Research," said Hayley and lifted a thick sheaf

of papers from the shelf behind the bar. "Under the *F*'s." At Beatrix's amused expression, Hayley went on. "The Prescotts never leave anything to chance."

Beatrix had moved back to the television set and was gazing absently at the screen. She frowned momentarily and lifted her head.

Hayley put her glass down on the bar. "Something wrong?"

"I thought it might be Thérèse." She had walked over to the door to look into the corridor. "But, no."

"ESP?" Hayley wondered as she came out from behind the bar to pick up her drink and rattle the ice.

"Pot," said Beatrix, pronouncing the *o* just a trifle broadly. "She likes a stick now and then."

Abbey began perspiring. If they found her now—

"Hayley!" cried a familiar voice. "And Mademoiselle Fontaine!" It was Abbey's father. Stepfather. Saved by the bell!

She could see his tall figure through the crack between the door and the jamb. He was older than her mother, but not much, and he had a way of carrying himself that made women look twice at him.

"I told you before, Monsieur Welles—it's Beatrix! Not Fontaine. Please!"

"Oh, *oui*," laughed Carney Welles. "Mind if I join you?" He moved behind the bar and banged the bottles around. "Hayley, what's happened to that sister of yours? She's late again. Christ, I thought they took the damned Concorde so the Count would be on time for once."

"She'll arrive," Hayley said softly, switching off the television set. "She always does—eventually."

"Viewing Austin's nags?" Carney wondered vaguely.

"Ah, you are familiar with Austin Bush?" Beatrix asked, her eyes flirting.

"Distantly. We share the same concerns." He glanced at Hayley significantly.

"A great lover of horseflesh," said Beatrix.

"Why limit it to the flesh of the horse?" wondered Hayley, and she sloshed her drink around as punctuation.

Giggles.

Beatrix placed her empty glass on the bar and nodded her head toward Hayley. "Now I must go. I have things to do before dinner."

"Copy to supervise?" Carney asked, with an innocent expression.

Beatrix stared at him. "Something like that." And she moved out of the room into the corridor.

Hayley came over to Carney and glowered slightly. "She's a switch-hitter."

"What else, with a body like that?"

"Just keep your hands to yourself," Hayley warned him.

"Oh, I can control my *hands*." He laughed. "It's just sex *talk* with her. Don't worry. The French are like that."

"There's no language barrier there," Hayley groused. "Play it straight, Carney. I'm warning you."

His face flattened out, the planes ugly now. "Or?"

"Don't be nasty. You know what I mean."

"Wouldn't it be a joke if it turned out I wasn't interested in her at all—except in an economic sense?"

"Wouldn't it?" snapped Hayley, turning on her heel.

Carney Welles leaned against the bar and finished off the drink he had mixed for himself, his face slightly red. Watching him from the closet, Abbey was sorry for him. God, her mother was a castrator! And yet she could sympathize with her mother's problems. Carney was a stud all right—in public. But in bed . . . Abbey wasn't sure. Maybe he degenerated into a pussycat. She had never thought too much about it. But she knew her mother was acting raunchy again—and that meant she wasn't getting any within the confines of the marriage contract.

Jesus. It was bad enough growing up and being in need, but when you were an *adult* and you couldn't get any—that was goddamn scary!

There were no crises during the remainder of Charlie Garnet's perimeter check, and when he returned to the main gate he sent his assistant back to the security office to fill out his report for the afternoon.

Garnet had barely settled down when a long black limousine rolled up to the gate and an electrically operated window rolled down on the driver's side. A grim-visaged rent-a-chauffeur in a *de rigueur* cap scowled out at him.

"What do you want, Mack?"

Garnet smelled ex-cop and bristled. He could be called a cop, too. Who did this punk behind the wheel think he was?

"Just checking the I.D.," Garnet said neutrally, keeping his own simmering anger under control.

"This is the Count and Countess della Camarra," said the chauffeur, trying to hide his glimmer of disbelief and disdain. "Brought them up from Kennedy."

Garnet flipped through The Book. There they were. Of course, he knew them by heart, but it didn't do to play it that way with one of these turds in the driver's seat.

"Okay," said Garnet, peering in through the window into the back seat.

Megan Prescott Tarantino and Niccolo Ariosto

Tarantino sat on opposite sides of the rear seat of the long limo, each with arms folded across the chest in active and intimidating silence. Garnet studied them much more leisurely than he usually did and then, finally, stood up.

"Okay," he said. "You can go through." He made a pencil mark in his book.

"Where do I dump the baggage?" asked the rent-a-driver.

"They'll take care of you up at the house," murmured Garnet happily. Sure, they'd take care of him—and he'd be carrying the bags himself into the main guest room. There were one hundred and ninety-seven steps up to the main *floor*. Lovely, lovely.

"Thank you," said the driver, not meaning it. The limo was off like a shot.

Garnet watched the dust rise and laughed out loud. What in hell was eating the fucking Count and Countess, he wondered. They were usually lovey-dovey and sucking up to each other like romantics out of a Barbara Cartland novel.

Megan Prescott Tarantino, the Contessa della Camarra, was smouldering with impotent fury. When The Tarantula—as she was known to her Italian servants—and many associates on her own level—smouldered, she usually erupted. And once the security chief was out of hearing distance, she unleashed her frenzy on the silent figure seated opposite her.

"The absolute pits, Niccolo—the worst trip yet. Forty-five minutes more to get from Kennedy to Scobie Hills than from Paris to New York! I should never leave any of the details to you. You simply cannot cope."

She stared out the window of the limo, watching the woods zoom by.

"Oh, I know you used the same chauffeur service as last time—and that was a dream drive—but Christ! We're hours late. And I didn't want to get Hayley in an uproar."

She glanced at her lanky husband, sedated by an inner languor, his aristocratic profile turned for maximum approval from his consort.

"Take down that driver's name, will you, *carissimo!* If we ever get him again, it's the flaming end! You hear me?"

The sleepy eyes stirred slightly. Megan leaned forward, turning slightly so she could view him more clearly. Was he asleep? The lout! But, no. She knew him better than that. He was simply in one of his language-barrier moods, when he pretended not to understand *uno verbo* of English.

She leaned over and slammed her elbow into his ribs. "Hey, Nicky!"

"*Cara mia*," he said with a brilliant smile, turning toward her with that capped-teeth grin that had enchanted Megan from the beginning. *"Bella veduta!"*

You shit! thought Megan, sliding down into the expensive leather seat and letting her fury mount a notch or two. She had five years on Hayley, and she was plumper, more matronly. Her face, which had in her youth evoked the oval planes of the original Prescott physiognomy, was a little rounder than it had been when she was in her prime. Although, technically, she *was* in her prime now, it was true that the Prescott personality and presence had lost something in the past few years.

She had put on a little weight, unfortunately more on the bottom than on the top. The breasts were still holding up, thank you, but the bottom was hanging—well, not hanging, actually, but somewhat bigger than formerly. It was enough to bring a wry comment now and then from the keeper of the bedroom keys. "Fat Ass," he called her sometimes. "Get your fat ass out of my face."

Oh yes, he could speak perfectly good English when he chose to. But during moments of stress he lapsed into Middle Italian—a kind of local dialect he had picked up in his youth in the Della Camarra villa outside Florence.

In spite of the added weight and the shortening of her temper, Megan considered herself as good as new—maybe a little tempered in the crucible of time, but still a good horse in the long run. The man in the saddle had never objected, and that was odd for an Italian aristocrat with a title and a family history of satyriasis.

It wasn't screwing around that was ruining Niccolo Ariosto Tarantino; it was gambling. And that was the real reason Countess Megan was jawing at him now, chewing him out on the way to the Prescott place. She was mad as hell—not at the Concorde that had flown them on time from Paris to New York—but at *him*, damn his eyes, for blowing the assets of the bank, the Cassa Fiorentina di Risparmio, on the gaming tables at Monte Carlo!

"Hey," he said in her ear, "we'll make it up."

She opened her mouth to give him another shot, but his hand touched her thigh and she came apart inside as she always did. Not for nothing had the family Tarantino been known for its expertise beneath the sheets—or furs, or skins—all the way from the fall of the Roman Empire, through the Dark Ages, the Age of Reason, and into the Nuclear Age.

He was only of medium height, but he carried himself well at all times—even seated in a limo or at a dining table. Brought up with a handful of money still in the coffers of the Tarantino family, he had been privileged from birth and had learned always to expect favors from others without being obligated to pay for them.

He had, unfortunately, gone through the remaining fortune within two years of his matriculation from the University of Milan. He had also gone through his allocated number of women friends—both those on a social level comparable to his own and those on that considerably lower level. Megan Prescott was his lucky charm.

Once secured to her through marriage, however, he had settled down. He had sired their two children— the boy now at the University of Milan, and the girl attending the Sorbonne in Paris.

The limousine pulled up in front of the mansion and the Conte della Camarra eased his frame gracefully out of the back seat, extending his hand to help his wife, the Contessa della Camarra, into the fading afternoon sunlight.

"Lee!" cried Megan in delight, embracing her Hayley, who had been alerted by the front gate of their imminent arrival.

Over Megan's shoulder, Hayley and Niccolo exchanged a quick look of intelligence, and then Hayley smiled and kissed Megan on the cheek.

"Cheek only, dear! AIDS, you know."

Hayley threw her head back and laughed. "Megan, you're priceless."

Megan frowned in puzzlement. She never knew what Hayley was laughing about. And, hell, AIDS was a very big problem amongst the upper classes.

"But in Hollywood they've given up kissing—and they almost invented it. With the help of the Italians." Megan giggled. "Hayley. We've got to talk." She glanced at her husband warningly. "Seriously."

Hayley eyed the count and said, "Not again."

Megan sighed. "This is not a repetition. This is worse. Much worse."

"So my spies tell me," said Hayley, tight-lipped. "You didn't escape anything by not appearing at the family board meeting yesterday, Meggy."

"We were in Rome, trying to straighten a few things out."

Hayley took Megan in one hand and the count in the other and started up the steps. "You'll only make it for dinner if you hurry."

When the alarm bells rang in the security center in the basement of the mansion and also at the front gate, Charlie Garnet leaped to his feet in astonishment. The alarm bells never went off unless the chain link fence had been breached, or someone had crashed the barricade at the entryway. Obviously nothing was wrong at the main gate; where was the trouble?

He was on the hot line immediately. "Where is it?"

"Not where is it. *What* is it?" the voice on the other end shouted. "The radar says we've been breached *everywhere!*"

"Everywhere?" Garnet exploded. "What's wrong with you? Give me the coordinates on the fence and I'll—"

"It's not on the fence, Mr. Garnet! It's—all over."

Well, he had made plans for this kind of thing. Ever since the attempt had been made to kidnap Hayley Welles a month ago, Garnet and his group had been working on Plan Survival. This was it!

"How many men you got there? Four? Send them all out with the Uzis. Don't take any chances!"

"Execute Plan Survival?"

"Christ, yes. Surround the house. Don't let anyone near the place. Try to round up the guests as fast as you can. And use those Uzis."

Garnet frowned. "Use." "Uzis." It sounded dumb.

He hung up and wrenched open the door of the Land Rover, jumped in, flicked the ignition, and drove through the open gates. Once on the inside, he pressed the remote control switch attached to the dashboard and the gates clanged shut with a firmness that sounded grim with finality.

He gunned the engine and drove madly up the winding roadway to the house. And then, as he finally rounded the last turn, he saw what had activated the radar guarding the perimeter fence. It was a chopper, high in the air, approaching from over the Hudson right down onto the estate itself. He remembered now that Roger Prescott, of the generation preceding the current one, had been a pilot in Korea and had flown his own chopper occasionally. A landing pad had been constructed in a clearing on the highest bare portion of the estate. It was toward this pad that the chopper seemed to be heading.

But Roger was dead. Nobody in the family now flew a chopper. The security men who flew were not in the habit of using the pad. It *couldn't* be one of them; Charlie Garnet would have been notified. Hell, they understood the need for security. This was like that nut last month.

The Land Rover turned off of the road to the house just below the circular drive and followed the service road across the open fields between the swimming pool and the tennis court. Dust clouded up behind the four-wheeler, and rocks shot out from each side as it bounded up the slope toward the chopper pad. And none too soon.

Garnet pushed on the gas pedal as he saw the craft coming in lower and lower toward the pad. At least the damned thing wasn't armed with .50 calibers, he thought as he made a quick scan of the ship. It looked to be a Sikorsky passenger job, pretty new, pretty sleek. It didn't look like the kind of thing terrorists would rent for a foray like this.

You never knew.

Garnet could see the pad now. Dirt was beginning to stir on the surface, fanned by the tremendous whir of the chopper blades as the ship descended toward the landing target. The Land Rover slammed to a stop in a huge cloud of dust, which swirled about angrily like a tornado on a wheat field.

Garnet grabbed the semiautomatic long-range rifle from its rack behind the front seat and jumped out of the Land Rover. He choked on the dust, unable to see a foot in front of him. Then the swirling cleared momentarily, and he staggered back into an area that seemed to have less dust boiling up.

Now he could see his men. One was crouched behind a stand of scrub brush, gripping the Uzi machine pistol in his hands, looking out in a tense but confident manner at the cloud of dust that surrounded the chopper.

Garnet yelled, "Up, goddamn it! Up! Show them the weapons!"

The kid understood and, looking less happy about the occasion now that he had been ordered to show more balls, he rose and aimed the Uzi at the shape of the aircraft emerging from the clearing dust cloud.

Finally most of the dirt settled, and Garnet strode

across the ground toward the door of the chopper. He was holding the semiautomatic at port, and as he reached the aircraft, he swung it into position, aiming at the oval door itself.

"Come out of there with your hands up!" he shouted, using a throat mike and a loud-hailer strapped to his shoulder. Although the blades of the chopper were still turning, the engines were off, and a modicum of silence was descending over the pad. Garnet turned. What he saw gladdened his heart.

His four men were approaching the aircraft with their Uzis in position, pointing them at the chopper's door, exactly as Garnet was doing.

Now they stood in a semicircle, covering the door so that no one could hope to escape death, even if the one inside came out shooting. Garnet tried to see inside the craft, but he could not. However, he did make out the shadowy silhouette of a figure who seemed to be working at the inner latch.

The door shuddered.

Garnet tightened his trigger finger to the weapon in his hands and squinted one eye.

He waited.

Hot damn! thought Kirby Miles as he eased in the throttle and began circling for the approach to the pad. He could see it in a clearing below, near the mansion. Now wasn't this going to be a gigantic surprise for the Prescotts! Well, according to the way he saw it, the Prescotts *needed* some kind of a surprise once in a while. They were getting too damned placid and too preoccupied with honing their "do-good" and "lovely people" image with busy work.

Of course, it would have been a little more by the book if he could have phoned ahead to alert the

Prescott security folks to the fact that a helicopter was going to land on the pad that afternoon—but he had only accepted the chopper that morning. He didn't have *time* for the amenities.

Besides, a Miles did things differently. A Miles played it by ear and let the chips fall where they might. A Miles was something special! And, fuck the Prescotts, who had money when the Miles were still in Ireland cutting peat with sickles and wondering where the next side of beef was coming from. Now the Mileses had the money and the clout, and—hell, yes—*this* one was a real live United States senator!

Barry Goldwater wasn't the only senator who could fly. Hell, Kirby Miles had learned how in the service, and now he was making prime use of that knowledge. What good was money if you couldn't show off a little with it?

"Hey, Lynn!" He called out to his wife, who was sitting with him in the noisy cockpit. "There it is, baby!"

"Uh huh," said Lynn Barclay Miles. "If you put us in that river down there, I'll break your jaw."

"That's the Hudson, you ignorant Hollywood hick! Now, watch this!"

Miles put the chopper through a leveling-off maneuver that made Lynn's stomach come up to grab her tonsils. She turned green. "I'll upchuck on your jacket if you don't stop that nonsense! Can't you ever act like a human being?"

Kirby Miles laughed good-naturedly. This dumb model and would-be singer he had married didn't know how lucky she was to be a real senator's wife. But she'd learn soon enough. Or maybe she wouldn't. She wasn't the smartest kid on the block. But she could carry clothes. Man, did she look good when she came down the stairs with him, or walked through the lines in Washington. Did the eyes of those aged politicos bulge out when she came shimmering up at them? You could see a few ancient whangs coming alive inside their expensive threads for the first time, perhaps, in years.

"How about that! Won't the Prescotts remember this? A real live chopper dropping in for a visit!"

Lynn looked at her husband with a freezing glance. "Sometimes I don't think you've got all your marbles, Miley."

"No, but you find out later that I *do* have them, don't you, baby?"

She yawned. "Oh, those old things. Are you going to drag them out again?"

"Not before we get on the ground, kitten!" Kirby chuckled and executed a turn toward the pad.

Sons of bitches, he thought as he came in toward the estate. The Prescotts had never accepted invitations to the Mileses' place on the Cape. They'd never accepted invitations to the New York apartment. The third generation of Prescotts had cut his old man's balls off in several Wall Street deals and piddled on the corpses left after the massacres. No friendship was lost between the families after that. But now that this Hayley bitch wanted a little Washington clout, *now* she was inviting the Mileses in for "afternoon tay," for Christ's sake!

"Get ready to cheer, you stuck-up horses' asses!" Gleefully, Miles reversed the blades, and huge gouts of dirt shot up from the ground below, boiling up past the cockpit and shooting off into the sky all around them.

He lowered the ship gracefully to the pad and cut the engine.

"Now, kid," he told Lynn, "here goes a grand-stand entrance that these stuck-up boobs will never be able to forget!"

He rose from his seat and reached out his arm to lift Lynn up from her seat.

"Oh, shit."

She was bent over forward, sick as a dog, her face green, her clothes covered with vomit.

So, for Christ's sake, it was up to him. Kirby Miles moved over to the hatch and cracked it. The door shuddered and swung open. The ladder folded down to the ground. The senator looked up and out through the doorway at the assembled welcoming party and smiled his famous smile.

"Oh, shit," he said again.

Five men with tommyguns out of some late-late movie stood waiting for him. Christ, had he landed in Nicaragua by mistake? What in hell—?

The man at the head of the pack of what resembled armed insurrectionists blinked and closed his eyes briefly. He returned Kirby Miles's salutation with a not-too-original response of his own.

"Oh, shit," he said with feeling. His face assumed a martyred expression. "Welcome to Scobie Hills, Senator Miles."

The senator responded automatically with a reproduction of his famous wide grin and extended a hand in politician's friendship. "Certainly a pleasure to see you, sir. Now, if you could help my wife a bit? She seems to have had some kind of accident in the seat of the chopper."

CHAPTER TWO

O f all the various activities surrounding a dinner party at the Prescott mansion, the one that always grabbed Abbey Martin the most was the gathering for cocktails before the grand entry into the famed banquet hall. She always made sure she was dressed and ready before the first guest appeared at the head of the big staircase and began to descend to the main room below.

This moment—when each Prescott and each guest made his or her appearance at the top of the stairs— sent immediate signals to anyone in the know. No one who was anyone ever appeared at such a dinner party in a dress or suit that was not brand new. No one allowed the slightest ruffle to be out of control, even one hair to be out of place, or the slightest trace of bloodshot eye or trembling hand to be evident.

Abbey had gone to Antonio Ravell for her dress. Ravell had parted company with Galanos some months previous, after a bitter argument over necklines. Abbey selected Tonio because he was younger—closer to her age group—and, in a way, because her mother stayed with Galanos. She was anxious to compare her dress with her mother's.

The procession started, traditionally, with the appearance of the host, and sure enough, at precisely eight, Cornelius Welles strode across the carpeted landing at the top of the stairs and began his descent. Abbey watched him with awe. The two of them were far from close—he was simply her third father. But she had always been struck by the elegance of his handsome face, with its even features and its strong jawline. He carried himself like an athlete, his muscular neck and wide shoulders filling out the dinner jacket to perfection.

"Hi, kitten," he said, taking her by the shoulders and kissing her on the cheek as she reached the foot of the stairs. He smiled. "Can I get you a drink?"

"Please," she said, on his arm as he moved over to the long bar that had been set up along the paneled wall. "Rob Roy," she told him with a smile. What else could she say? It was the traditional drink for any Prescott at a Prescott party.

He smiled, gave the order to the rent-a-bartender, and glanced up at the top of the stairs. It was Aunt Meggy now, Megan Tarantino, attired in a rather tight-fitting gown with what Abbey thought was just a little bit too much lace at the throat. Nevertheless, it was a French creation, Abbey could see, and not the usual Italian frock that her Aunt Meggy favored to keep peace in the Tarantino family. It must be, she thought, a concession to Hayley. And it meant she wanted something from Abbey's mother.

Uncle Nicky, the Count, appeared at Aunt Meggy's side, took her arm, and the two of them descended. Abbey smiled as her father handed her the Rob Roy, sipping at it en route.

Uncle Nicky always exuded a kind of animal vitality, even though he rarely displayed any vitality or color in his speech or actions. It lay there, simmering below the surface. The word was, of course, that before marrying Aunt Meggy, he had bedded some of the most famous women in European royalty. Abbey had to admit that in his white tie and dinner jacket he still looked every inch a count.

Megan kissed Abbey on the cheek, saluted Carney in the same manner, and waved her husband over to the bar for her drink. Uncle Nicky ignored her commands and gave Abbey a squeeze, admired her dress with his eyes, and then brushed her cheek with his. He had given up kissing the wrist, Abbey noted approvingly. She glowed. Her uncle certainly knew how to make a woman come alive inside.

By now the guests were arriving quickly, with Beatrix Fontaine and the French copywriter and Mead Brookhaven III coming down together. The French cosmetics executive—who, everybody claimed, was a direct challenger to the late Coco Chanel's undisputed supremacy in the field—was dressed in an exquisite creation that set off the color of her eyes and hair. It flowed over her figure in a subtle enhancement that brought out her slimness, her elegance, and her taste, in a personal statement of health and beauty.

As for the lesbian companion, Abbey took a deep breath and passed her by, passed her by for the third of the trio. Abbey was always attracted by the kind of wind-blown masculinity that her father's new young troubleshooter displayed. He had the unruly hair—just rumpled enough to appear natural—and the fine-tuned, superfit body that any athlete would envy. There was intelligence there that belied the campus jock image: Abbey perceived an innate canniness that did not usually go with the muscular frame of a college running back.

The guests surged into the room now, and there were greetings and kisses and hugs and all kinds of laughter—giggles, whoops of joy, snickers, guffaws, and noiseless convulsions. Senator Kirby Miles appeared with his wife Lynn, and they began their descent, to the interest of more than a few members of the waiting crowd below. He was just about what Abbey had expected—a good clotheshorse, with a roguish, outdoorsy face and definitely a roving eye. She had heard plenty about his amours—much of the information peddled by hopefuls who had never been approached, but some broadcast from the horse's mouth by ex-lovers. Nobody had ever figured out why he had married Lynn Barclay, but Abbey could see that she had a kind of indestructibility about her that might appeal to a man of Miles's temperament.

"The decline of the West," said a voice at her ear.

Abbey turned quickly. It was Mead Brookhaven. She relaxed, a warm feeling sweeping over her. She found herself smiling impishly, flirtatiously. That low-profile intelligence was there, after all, she thought. She had been right in her estimation of him.

"I mean," Mead said as he studied Abbey, whose face was just slightly flushed from her reaction to his nearness, "to think that the famous chamber of Adams and Calhoun would be reduced to the cockpit of Kirby Miles."

"Oh, I *know* what you mean," Abbey smiled. "*She's* the one who fascinates me more than him."

The tanned face turned from her, and the blue eyes contemplated the lovely face and the busty figure that was enhanced by an expensive gown from some exclusive Rodeo Drive boutique. "See all evil, hear all evil, and speak all evil."

"But she's lovely."

"So is an MX missile, in an engineering sense."

They stood in companionable silence while Abbey continued her surveillance of the crowd of guests.

"What *is* this drink?" Mead asked after a moment. He frowned, trying to distinguish the taste. "Gin? Brandy?"

"Scotch," said Abbey. "And vermouth. Essentially, it's a Manhattan without the rye."

"Any particular significance? I noticed everyone drinking one and simply said I'd have one of the same."

"Family tradition," said Abbey with a moue. "The original Prescott—the one who built that railroad and forged a new real-estate empire on the West Coast—was named Robert Roy Prescott."

"And the drink's a Rob Roy!" said Mead in sudden enlightenment. "Good God! Did they name the drink after him?"

"I cannot tell a lie. They did not. Rob Roy was a famous Scottish Highlands outlaw centuries ago. The use of Scotch in the drink rather than anything else . . . you savvy? The drink is traditional at a Prescott weekend, when the family gets together to talk about money." Abbey's eyes were narrowed. She never relished *those* days, but the parties afterward were something else again. She faced him directly. "Daddy tells me—"

But she never got the sentence finished.

A gasp went up from the assembled guests, and every eye was immediately directed to the top of the long circular staircase. Abbey gasped, too. It was her mother. She was standing at the top of the steps, resplendent in a truly dangerous Galanos original—a thing that would take anybody's breath away. Sheerness. Extravagance. Glitz. And yet . . . simplicity. Definitely Hayley Prescott Welles.

She stood there a moment, savoring the attention, then smiled briefly and started down the steps. No applause broke out, but Abbey could sense the tremendous electrical charge that seemed to pass through everyone in the room. Abbey had always known her mother was lovely, but at moments like these, she knew that she possessed, in addition to her loveliness, a kind of *presence* that only a few actresses and celebrities ever achieved. When she entered a room, everything stopped and everyone—but *everyone*—looked at her.

As she swept down to the end of the steps, a line seemed to form almost automatically, with the women guests kissing her on the cheek, and the men saluting her one way or another—holding her fingers, shaking her hand, embracing, hugging, kissing. She swept through the room, grasped a Rob Roy that materialized in the atmosphere magically, and greeted each guest personally and with varying degrees of warmth.

"Let's look at you," she said finally as she came up to Abbey. Mother and daughter stood at arm's length and surveyed one another. Abbey could feel the blood rushing to her face. It was as if she might be five years old, or her mother's favorite rag doll. "I knew Tonio had no smarts," Hayley said in a low voice. "He's got that neckline much too low, and the hemline too high. You simply have to pay more attention to your clothing, Abigail."

She thrust Abbey away, viewing her from the side.

"Your pantyhose line shows, baby. Take a longer look at yourself next time before you come down to us."

And she was gone.

Abbey gritted her teeth in utter humiliation. Had anyone heard that exchange? But no—her mother was more intelligent than that. Mead Brookhaven had moved away from Abbey and was now talking to Hayley. She had spoken the words for Abbey's ears only. The rebuke had been delivered in a masterful manner—typical of Hayley's bone-crushing style. Abbey still smarted from the blow. Damned if she would go in and check her backside in the bathroom mirror. She'd brazen it out.

Something was happening now between her mother and the young man from her father's office. Hayley was standing close to him, smiling at him as if some marvelous secret were laid out in the open between them, and Mead was giving her the definite masculine response. It was incredible, Abbey thought. Hayley was old enough to be his *mother!*

"You carry your own thundercloud around with you?" asked a male voice in back of her. She turned directly into her Uncle Nicky.

"Just like Charlie Brown," she said, with a short laugh. "Really, does it show?"

"Every bit of it," Nicky said, watching her through those well-known, heavy-lidded bedroom eyes. "Whatever male turned you down was a fool, Abbey."

"Oh, you always put it on a personal level." Abbey frowned.

"Everything *is* on a personal level," the count assured her. He too was sipping at a Rob Roy. "*Life* is on a personal level."

"Not in Prescottland," Abbey said sourly. "Here everything's on a *financial* level."

The count shrugged. He looked a bit haggard. "Let's not go into *that*. At least, not at present."

Abbey smiled into her cocktail glass. She had heard rumors about the troubles at Nicky's bank in Florence. "How's Tina?" That was her cousin Caterina. "And Frankie?" That was Francesco.

Uncle Nicky brightened considerably. He launched into a long and rambling description of the various enterprises and activities both Tina and Frankie were involved in at school, and Abbey found her mind wandering. She had never hit it off all that well with her European relatives. Actually, she liked her aunt, and she liked her uncle. But their kids were, frankly, a couple of stuckup prigs.

"What an extremely attractive woman," said the count, breaking off in the middle of his son-and-daughter roundup. "Is that— ?"

"Beatrix," nodded Abbey. She had been watching her stepfather deep in conversation with the French-woman, and she wondered if anyone else noticed the degree of intimacy that seemed to have sprung up between them. Carney's free hand had moved from Beatrix's waist to her backside, where it rested in a kind of silent approval while the two of them continued to talk in an animated manner.

At that moment, the Frenchwoman happened to turn slightly and catch the eye of Uncle Nicky. It was the queerest thing, Abbey thought. It was almost as if Beatrix *knew* Uncle Nicky! Certainly it wasn't Abbey she was interested in. What do you know about that? Abbey thought. Wheels within wheels.

"I suppose it's the makeup she uses," Uncle Nicky said with a smile. "Beauty on the outer level only. But," he grimaced, "she's certainly got *that!*"

"Love's labors lost?" Abbey suggested lightly.

The count might have been a financial fool, but he

was not a linguistic one. "Of course! The other Frenchwoman—the younger one."

"Young? She's in her late twenties!" snapped Abbey.

"I mean—younger than the cosmetician. But she certainly doesn't strike me as being at all unalert to male interest. I mean Beatrix."

"I guess she blows whichever way the wind blows," Abbey said, tossing off her drink.

Uncle Nicky stared at her a moment as if he had not heard her correctly. Then he covered his knowing smile with a sip at his drink and raised an eyebrow.

"You're growing up, *cugina*."

At that moment the bells rang for dinner.

The Prescott dining room, which had once been featured in a fourteen-page spread in a hard-to-find collector's copy of *Architectural Digest*, had been designed with a keen eye to baronial splendor. While Victorian fussiness had been exaggerated into gingerbread and clutter in most American houses, the Prescott dining room had aimed more at an Edwardian sedateness, with huge expanses of polished oak paneling, with an exaggeratedly high ceiling, with designs and curlicues painted into the bond between ceiling and wall, and with the main feature of the room being enormous and overbearing oil portraits of early Prescott forebears.

From the vaulted ceiling—done in a light bluish-gray that made the height of the room seem infinite—hung three ponderous but magnificent chandeliers. Their bronze branches were adrip with millions of sparkling crystalline teardrops, with facets that sent streams of light shooting off in every direction. These chandeliers hung just above the top of the enormous trestle table, which was carved out of huge live-oak timbers. The table could seat up to forty people at its main section; with other additions, carried in by the sweating and exhausted servants, the dining room could seat seventy-five.

But it was not the table, nor was it the chandeliers, that dominated the room. It was the imperious portraits that hung on the paneled walls, each lighted by concealed electric bulbs mounted in the frames. The frames themselves were complicated swirls of curlicues, executed in plaster of Paris and gilded cleverly to simulate fussy borders of worked gold.

A massive full-length painting of Robert Roy Prescott hung on the north wall. The trestle table ran north and south, with the head of the table under Rob Roy and the foot of the table—the Number Two spot—under a portrait of Rob Roy's wife, Eleanor Bierce Prescott.

He was dressed in a stiff-necked shirt and conservatively cut raven-gray suit, and posed against a background of dark, typically boardroom paneling. His stern visage—beetling brows, flashing dark blue eyes, bristling mustache, and curly black hair— matched the startlingly large hands and muscular body. It was the portrait of an unabashed tyrant.

Eleanor Bierce Prescott was dressed in a lacy bodice that displayed her bountiful bosom and white shoulders. The bodice sagged with circlets of matched pearls and obsidian beads. She was seated in a chair that resembled a straight-back secretary's chair, holding her hands in her lap as she surveyed the world behind the painter. Her eyes were brown, her dark hair coiled in a kind of beehive on her head, and her lips creased in a disappointing attempt at a smile.

These two autocrats perpetually glowered at one

another across the huge room below them, lending a kind of mute but constant hostility to even the brightest, most convivial of gatherings below.

On the east and west walls hung other Prescotts, male and female. These came from a later period, and the painting style was more relaxed, less "tight" —in the artistic sense. They all had the same Prescott look. It was a look that appeared even in the fourth-generation Prescotts, who now began taking chairs at the huge dining table sparkling with crystal goblets, expensive china plates, and gleaming silver carved with the Prescott crest: two capital P's, with the first reversed, and sharing the same vertical.

Hayley took her place under Rob Roy Prescott's portrait, with her husband at the opposite end. She had seniority rights, since she controlled the fortune. Megan came second, as the second heir to the largest of the Prescott holdings. The three other fourth-generation Prescotts—Stephen, Downey, and Ralph—had great clout on the outside, but little inside the family. It was almost as if Hayley had taken it upon herself to introduce women's liberation into the Prescott family by taking over its control under her regime.

When everyone was seated, Hayley rang the tiny silver bell and the food began to arrive. Compote. Followed by soup. Followed by shrimp risole. Followed by braised beef. Followed by salad. Followed by baked Alaska. Followed by coffee. Followed by liqueur.

On Hayley's right sat Nicky. On Hayley's left, Senator Miles. On her husband's right sat Megan. On his left, Beatrix. Abbey was midway down the table, with Mead Brookhaven directly across from her. While the conversation languished at first, it very soon picked up and quite quickly became total babble, with each guest only able to talk intelligently with either the person on the left or on the right.

"What's this I hear about your money troubles, Nicky? You're a prudent investor. *Che a accaduto?*"

"Inadvertent reverses, Hayley. One of those emerging nations fellows has some of it stashed in a Swiss account while he's living the life of Riley in Monaco."

"I've got a proposition for you, Meggy."

"Carney! Anytime you want. Just name the place."

"I'm planning a series of parties I'd like you to throw for me."

"Where?"

"All over Europe. For the crowned heads of state."

"Not many left."

"And the movers and shakers."

"Plenty of them."

"Plus the celebrities and jet-setters."

"Ugh."

"Image-making, Meggy."

"It's about taxes, Senator Miles."

"I hate them myself, Mrs. Welles."

"Hayley, Senator. It's the bill to eliminate tax shelters on charitable foundations."

"Kirby, Hayley. Do I feel fingers scratching my back?"

"Only where it itches—Kirby."

"Perhaps you'll tell me where yours itches?"

"Later. And, possibly, in another place."

"Image-making, it's called. And it's imperative that the image be the correct one, Mademoiselle Beatrix. On that the entire concept depends."

"And what exactly *is* to be the image, Monsieur Welles?"

"Middle-class morality."

"That is indeed an interesting perception, Monsieur Welles. Decadent, but understandable."

"What line of work are you in, Mr. Bookmaven."

"Brookhaven. Mead Brookhaven III."

"Ah! Three? Are you in—let me guess. Banking?"

"Sorry, wrong number."

"Stock-brokering?"

"Wrong number again, Mrs. Miles."

"So you recognized me."

"Who wouldn't?"

"Tell me, don't you think Mrs. Welles is a startlingly individual and unconventional woman?"

"I'm counting on it."

"Whatever do you mean by that, you naughty boy?"

"Slip of the tongue."

"I hear he's balled every woman from the Boston Common to Alice's Restaurant."

"And I hear *she's* dined on just as many from Laguna Beach to Anaheim, Azusa, and Cucamonga."

"Her third husband, isn't he? He doesn't *look* like Orson's son. Is he?"

"Hell no! No relation. But he's Number Three. And from what I hear, there'll be a Number Four before long."

"What's happened?"

"They say she's wearing him out where he lives."

"What a way to go."

* * *

"Something about the Vatican. They've got investments everywhere. And the word is that the count's
bank dropped thirty-seven million."

"Lire?"

"Shit no! U.S. dollars!"

"No, it's *not* true that Senator Miles's brother has
AIDS. And it isn't true that his sister's oldest son has
cancer of the bladder. Where do you *get* these
rumors?"

Thérèse Maupin winced as she sampled the mush-
room sauce that had been liberally applied to the
beef. Not even as good as the cheapest stuff you
could get in Paris. The Prescotts ought to be ashamed
of themselves. But then, she reasoned, maybe they
didn't even *know* their caterers were doing a number
on them. What a bunch of stupids.

Correction. Not so stupid. Her eyes narrowed as
she looked toward the foot of the huge table, where
Carney Welles leaned over toward Beatrix Fontaine.
She could feel the blood rising in her neck. Where
was his damned hand? He had it on her knee—*that's*
where he had it! And she pretended to hang onto her
napkin. Was she feeling his joint? She gave a disgusted sound.

Her right-hand neighbor turned to her with a quirked
eyebrow. "I beg your pardon?"

"I am so sorree; I have no Eengleesh. I do no
speak so good."

"I think you're doing remarkably well," said Mead
Brookhaven III, "considering you're bluffing."

She was shocked into remonstrance. "How'd you
know that?"

"Come on. The Prescotts would never invite anyone to their table who can't speak the language."

"Why not?"

"Trust me."

"You work for Welles Associates, don't you?"

"And you're with Beatrix?"

"Yes. Temporarily." She shot a malevolent glance at Beatrix and Welles. "You know France?"

"Not intimately. You know New York?"

"A little. You know Gay Paree?"

He looked at her intently. "I know one when I see one."

"Eh, bien!"

". . . And my husband was right in the middle of the speech when this red-headed lout rose in the middle row and—thunk—tossed a huge cabbagehead right into his chest! You never know what you're going to get on the campaign trail!"

"The parents were killed in an airplane crash in Spain. He was a Prescott; she was a MacNabb. *She* brought all the MacNabb fortune into the Prescott shelter."

"And so *he* controlled the Prescott billions?"

"Through the weight of his wife's money. Right. Until the plane crash. Then it went to Hayley."

"She was the oldest daughter?"

"Nah. *Megan* was the oldest. But *she* married an Italian aristocrat. A count. The stallion over there."

"How come she didn't inherit control? Christ, she's a countess."

"The parents cut her out of control in their will. The job went to Hayley. They didn't like Italians."

"What about this Welles chap?"

"Kind of a queen's consort, don't you know?"

* * *

"Probably one of the sharpest chemists in France. A child prodigy. She finished some of the most technical courses in college when she was barely eighteen."

"So she's no salesperson. She's the *developer* of Beatrix Cosmétique."

"You'd better believe it."

"She's got great bones."

"The second husband was a blue blood, I guess she got tired of trying ordinary people when Number One turned out to be just one of the boys. Number Two was Austin Bush. Not the beer Busch. Not the veep Bush. *Austin* Bush. The man who is to horses what Paul Newman is to racing cars."

"And then?"

"When the Bush thing died she tried rehabilitation. The rehabilitation required a new image. She hired Welles Associates, a small, struggling firm in Manhattan. He gave her a new image. And—the image was *him!* He landed the big one. Ever since, she's been helping *him* out. But it's really on hold now. Welles is still making images, and Hayley's still making money for the Prescott foundations."

"How'd it be to get in bed with that one, anyway? She's a beautiful woman."

"Like fucking a buzzsaw, if you ask me. I'm glad I'm a woman and she's not after me."

Abbey Martin glanced up to see Mead Brookhaven III talking to the little French lesbian at his side. She wanted to catch his eye. The lesbian looked up and saw her trying to attract his attention, but ignored her. In fact, the woman smiled.

Damn her! Abbey turned her attention to her mother

at the head of the table. She was leaning over close to Senator Miles. My God! Was she going to fall into line with millions of other American women and slide beneath the sheets with the Cape Cod Cock? Then she saw her mother glance down the table and zero in on Mead Brookhaven. It wasn't Miles. It was Mead. *That's* who she was going to bed down! Damn her eyes. And Mead was looking back at her with that intent, slightly brooding, dumb look he had. The look she'd give her ass to get!

"What in hell are you staring at, busboy?" Lynn Miles could barely keep her voice from rising to an almost hysterical level. "You got hot rocks?"

The elderly waiter who had been frowning in perplexity at Lynn Miles stiffened and went on his way, trying to act as if nothing had happened. The man sitting next to the senator's wife turned to her with curiosity.

"I've never seen one of the Prescott staff slip like that before. Interesting."

Lynn was perspiring. It was interesting, all right. And it was also damned scary. Her neighbor sensed something out of the ordinary. It was best to divert any suspicion immediately.

"You fuck?"

The man stared at her. "On occasion."

"So do I. And this isn't the occasion."

"Later?" The man seemed intrigued by the dialogue, if not the direction it was taking.

"Sorry. I have a headache."

The man burst out laughing. A moment later he was frowning into his coffee cup and wondering what he had been thinking about before the senator's wife had put on her little show. After a moment he shrugged and turned to his other neighbor.

Carney Welles leaned back in his chair and moved slightly toward Beatrix Fontaine. "I've planned a business meeting tonight, later on."

"That will be wonderful."

"You. Hayley. She's kind of my partner. Mead."

"And Thérèse?"

Welles turned to Beatrix and their glances locked. "Perhaps that would be a very good idea. She'll have to know sooner or later."

An amused smile crept onto the Frenchwoman's lips. She began to laugh in a soundless way. "Image-maker!" she scoffed. "The truth of the matter is, nothing is ever what it seems to be."

"That's the secret of public relations!"

They laughed together. Carney's hand crept along the soft flesh of Beatrix's smooth thigh and she turned toward him, receiving and welcoming his interest.

Hayley laid down her napkin and stood. The dinner was over. The patron and patroness continued to glower at one another as the servants hustled about and tried to clear off the expensive china, the crystal, and the silver with a minimum of breakage.

CHAPTER THREE

Beatrix Fontaine was the first to arrive at the strategy session Cornelius Welles had called for later that evening. The room in which the meeting was to take place was the Prescott library, a comfortable room with floor-to-ceiling shelves of books on three walls. The fourth was a huge picture window overlooking the sloping lawns, trees, and the Hudson River in the distance.

She was thinking about Welles as she stood there, her arms folded across her breasts, her legs apart, and her eyes searching the scenic distances visible from the window. He was a part of this enormous empire of money-makers, and yet he somehow seemed, at the same time, to be apart from it. She knew that his wife was a formidable woman—intelligent, successful, ruthless, and as cool and cutting as a diamond.

He was coming on to her. What was he after? The rumors had it that the Welles marriage was in neutral. With a track record of three marriages, the prognosis for Hayley Prescott seemed quite evident. Was *she*, Beatrix, Welles's target? Or was Welles simply seeking to understand his client more completely, so he could build up the proper image for the proposed network of health spas?

And how did Hayley Welles fit in all this? After all, *she* was the one who had suggested that Beatrix sign on with her husband's firm. Beatrix and Hayley understood each other: each was strong, shrewd, and smart. No sense getting embroiled in conflict over a man!

No matter. Welles was an attractive individual—vital, masculine, exciting. A woman would have to be a fool to pass *him* up. Why did all this have to happen when the most important thing for her now was to get this gigantic new enterprise off the ground?

Welles entered the library breezily, waving a sheaf of papers and thrusting it onto the middle of the large conference table that dominated the center of the room. She greeted him equally, and he seated her next to him at the table, pawing through the papers and glancing impatiently at his wristwatch.

Almost on cue, Hayley appeared, followed by—interestingly enough—Mead Brookhaven III, and then Thérèse Maupin. There were murmurings of greetings, a lot of chair scraping, and soon silence reigned.

Welles took over. He rose from his seat, strolled over to a cabinet built into the book shelving, opened it, checked the multitude of dials and knobs, turned one, and closed the cabinet doors.

"Ladies and gentlemen, I've activated the tape recorder. What we say here tonight will be transcribed later for your files. Use it as backup for future discussions or think sessions." He gazed around briefly before sitting down. "Any questions?"

There were none. He slid into his chair. The meeting, titled "Beatrix Project I," began.

EXTRACT FROM "BEATRIX PROJECT I":

WELLES. Let me open this first strategy session with a rundown on the overall subject of the Beatrix Project. You are all aware of the fact that Beatrix Fontaine created and built into a gigantic success story the business she calls simply "Beatrix Cosmétique." From a single shade of lipstick, she escalated the business into a score of shades, and then into eye shadow, hair tint, deodorant, shampoo—to create a wide and diversified line of cosmetics.

But Beatrix Cosmétique is a concern that doesn't believe in standing still. In addition to cosmetics, Beatrix has become interested in expanding the look of beauty into the euphoria of beauty—in other words, into the health business. Building a bridge between *looking good* and *feeling good* is the purpose of this brand new enterprise. That's what we're here for.

The overall physical structure will resemble a Club Med operation, with health spas located all over the world. You check into a Beatrix camp, and you get a full course in cosmetics—all of them manufactured by Beatrix, oddly enough [a light spattering of laughter] —along with a full course in body toning.

Note I did not say "body building." Contrary to the weight-lifters and the muscle-flexers, Beatrix does not intend to add muscle to the frame. Beatrix wants you to look good and feel good—*as you are*.

Any questions or comments so far?

BEATRIX. Monsieur Welles is much too kind to this mercenary woman executive. It is not because I can't stand relaxing that I want to move forward. It's just that I want to make more money. [Polite laughter] I think we can do it. Health and beauty have run hand in glove through the centuries and can, I believe, run together now. *Merci*.

WELLES. Okay. Now, to the second phase of this operation. Once the original idea is considered, it becomes obvious that the first important concern in launching a brand new concept, as this one is, must be the name of the product. In this case, the name of the organization becomes a primary consideration. Club Med would never have succeeded if it had not been an original concept—*with a memorable name*.

Consequently, I've had my market-research people and my creative heads working on the *look good/feel good* idea and what it should be named. The first consideration, of course, was the name "Beatrix." But of course, since you are developing a new look, you don't want to use the old name. For awhile, we worked on that angle—abandoning the name Beatrix entirely.

We came up with "Sleeping Beauty," which isn't bad—but which doesn't really tell the right story. Although getting good health and beauty while you sleep, is a terrific idea—the name didn't include the idea of exercising for the sake of your health. We thought of "Club Belle," but that didn't quite jell—and please excuse the inadvertent poetry. Our experts concluded that people might mistake "belle" for "belly."

We had a lot more suggested names, but they were awful. It was about this time that we decided that maybe Beatrix was a natural name to keep—something to add something else to. The "something else" would red-flag the basic idea. The name "Beatrix" has a lot going for it. It's an odd spelling for Beatrice, and for that reason, it's memorable. Our researchers pointed out that the first three letters are the same as the letters of the word "beauty" itself.

HAYLEY. It's the last four letters that are the trouble. "Trix" makes the health spa sound like a hooker's heaven. [Laughter]

WELLES. My wife is a frustrated Borscht Circuit comedienne. Anyway—we tried putting other words with Beatrix and finally came up with two or three that proved to be the most attention-grabbing. "Beatrix Cosmétique." "Club Beatrix." "Beatrix la Belle." "Beatrix Beautique." What do you think?

THERESE. I think they all stink. But I also think "Beatrix Beautique" is at least cute.

WELLES. It's nice to have honest opinions expressed here, Mademoiselle Maupin. In fact, it is refreshingly different from the typical corporate presentation.

HAYLEY. In other words, cast your vote and can the comments.

BEATRIX. I think I like "Beatrix la Belle."

HAYLEY. Except for that confusion between "belle" and "belly."

MEAD. Where's the beef?

BEATRIX. *Le boeuf*?

WELLES. Mead means, where's the mention of exercising? Frankly, the damned exercise portion causes most of the problems with the name. Keeping fit tends to hint at hysteria. We just threw up our hands.

HAYLEY. Why don't we take a straw poll here and see which one wins.

WELLES. "Beatrix Cosmétique"? None. "Club Beatrix"? None. "Beatrix la Belle"? Two. "Beatrix Beautique"? One. Not exactly a decisive sweep.

BEATRIX. *S'il vous plait*, Monsieur Welles, you are the chief executive officer of the company that is being paid to determine the proper name, are you not? In that case, I would like to know which of the names you prefer.

WELLES. Actually, you don't quite understand the corporate system in America. It is best, sometimes to—

HAYLEY. Don't weasel, Carney. Lay it on her.

WELLES. Actually, I rather prefer "Beatrix la Belle." I disagree with my experts. I doubt that anybody would confuse "belle" with "belly." And if so, what would it matter? Maybe a nice bare belly button would help rather than hurt the image.

Hayley Welles was quite aware of the erotic by-play that was going on between her husband and Beatrix Fontaine. For anyone who knew Carney as well as she did, it was rather obvious to the eye. He was coming on to her.

But then, Carney was an ambitious man, a hard-working executive, a person who threw himself into his work with abandon. It was all part of his method of "getting inside the skin" of the person he was supposed to "imagize." At least, so he had always said to her.

He wasn't kidding. He had certainly gotten inside the skin of Hayley Prescott when she had hired him to "imagize" her. Had he ever. Was the same thing going to happen with Welles and Beatrix? It would serve Hayley right if it did; putting Beatrix and Carney together was *her* damned idea!

That was the conflict. Hayley *wanted* Welles to succeed and make Beatrix the biggest money-maker in the history of cosmetology. But at the same time, she *didn't* want him to devote himself exclusively to Beatrix and give up on Hayley.

Christ, it wasn't the sex! She could get that anywhere. It was the *principle* of the stupid thing. Damn
Welles! He was going to do a good job on Beatrix—
just the way Hayley wanted him to do. And *that* was
making Hayley come out all over warts and pimples!

She could feel a warmth in her thighs. Without
quite being conscious of it, she realized that Mead
Brookhaven had shifted himself just slightly in his
chair, so that he was touching her with his leg. When
she glanced at him, she found that, overtly, he was
watching Welles attentively. Nevertheless, at the next
pause in the conversation, he was staring at her with
open invitation in his eyes.

She tossed her head at him and fastened her gaze
on Thérèse Maupin.

Welles was explaining how the Beatrix la Belle
international network of health spas was going to
work. It would be a franchise operation, with local
money financing the spas and Beatrix supplying the
cosmetics and the formulations for the exercises. There
would be a videocassette made, along the lines of the
Jane Fonda and Linda Evans productions. The spas
would be in all kinds of locations in strategic places
around the world.

EXTRACT FROM "BEATRIX PROJECT I":

WELLES. What we will be building to from now
on is the grand opening of the flagship Beatrix health
spa. In order to make the most of this grand opening,
we will have to obtain maximum media coverage.
And to get maximum media coverage, we will have
to provide the media with something to cover. I'll go
into that later.

As for the location, I've had my marketing experts

and my media people taking polls all over. Since Beatrix la Belle is to be international in scope, it seemed obvious that the flagship spa should be somewhere famous for its international clientele. We came up with a group of places.

Maui, in the Hawaiian Islands. Acapulco, in Mexico. The Isle of Capri, in Italy. Disconcesson, in the Greek Isles. Monte Carlo, in Monaco. Nice, on the Riviera. Aix-les-Bains, in southern France, one of the great holiday spas. Baden-Baden, in Germany. Bath, in England. And so on.

What we finally decided on—and this location can certainly be changed if something better comes up— was Nice. Why Nice? They've got a marvelous Mardi Gras festival there. There's a Battle of the Flowers during Carnival Week. They burn a huge thirty-foot King Carnival on Shrove Tuesday. There are giant papier-mâché figures, cavalcades, masquerades, masked balls, and other merriments. *Everybody* comes.

Nice, for many years, has been considered as *the* watering place for the rich, for the aristocrats, for the jet-setters—for exactly the kind of people we want to attract to Beatrix la Belle.

HAYLEY. Just whom are you trying to attract, dear? I get the impression one moment you're after the jet-setters and big-spenders, and the next I think of the solid middle class out there that exercises to Jane Fonda.

WELLES. I'm taking up this subject later, when I deal with the image-making facet of the operation.

BEATRIX. You have decided on Nice?

WELLES. With your acquiescense.

THERESE. If you want the right people, you aren't going to get them to come to Nice. It's a crush at Carnival. At this point, I think it has a sense of

affluent decadence about it. Too much money, too
little taste.

WELLES. We can always handle the lack of taste.
What we can't always handle is the lack of money.

HAYLEY. Alley Oop for Wall Street.

Mead Brookhaven could hardly keep his mind on
the boss's words. Nor could he keep his eyes off
Hayley Welles. She had played along with his
come-on. Now she seemed to be moving in on him.
It was as if he had stepped into a trap that had been
set for him and he was simply waiting to fall into it.

But watch out for this Maupin creature. He knew
exactly where she was coming from. She had never
wanted Welles Associates in the picture at all. She
knew she was losing her control over the Big Mamma
Bee, and she seemed in a fighting mood. Didn't the
boss see it? He was practically making love to the
Fontaine woman right at the table in front of them,
and the French dyke was ready to eat him alive. Yet
he went on playing his tunes as if there were no
tomorrow. Correction: no tonight.

As for Hayley, he could feel the pressure of her
thigh against his, and it was all he could do to keep
his hand from reaching over and groping her breast in
the full light of the Prescott library. Wouldn't they
ever get out of here?

He tried to keep his mind riveted to the words of
his Fearless Leader as he wandered from one point to
another. Welles talked about getting all the best people to the opening. He talked about a series of pre-
liminary parties that would be hostessed by Countess
della Camarra, Megan Prescott, whose continental
parties were the "in" thing for the aristocracy of
Europe to attend. He talked about the presence of

Senator Kirby Miles, who had kindly consented to be there. And with *him*, of course, would come all the media celebrities that ran with the Miles stable—and that included just about everybody the magazines covered. Miles money may have been dirty, but it certainly collected a record number of fellow travelers with celebrity and clout.

He talked about the need to get a big actor or actress to attend the gala. Mead had been the one to suggest this, and he found himself nodding as the old points were gone over again and again. Hayley was stirring against him and . . .

EXTRACT FROM "BEATRIX PROJECT I":

HAYLEY. What about security at this grand opening? You'll be competing with the Palestine Liberation Organization, the Irish Republican Army, and God knows how many terrorist groups. Have you thought of that? My God, even our security here was breached recently. Some nut got into my bedroom, killed one of our butlers before buying it himself, and in passing, scared the shit out of *me*. Carney?

WELLES. That's why we figured Nice would be the best place. There is a good police force there; they're used to crowd control. We can get the help of the French government to keep the place clean. In fact, the security is the one plus that isn't overridden by the huge and uncontrollable crowds that usually descend on any typical resort.

THERESE. One man with a bomb can blow your grand opening to bits.

WELLES. Well, we'll have to take a chance on that. We can't cancel our opening shot just because the woods are full of crazies.

BEATRIX. I agree. But Tessie's right. France is not like the United States. These groups are everywhere. They love to break up something big to get their names in the paper.

WELLES. I'll make a special note of it, Mademoiselle Fontaine. Now, to get to the most important part of this whole strategy session. The making of the image.

BEATRIX. [Coyly] My image is me. How can I change?

WELLES. You're perfect. It's the way others see you that is important—at least, from a public relations point of view.

HAYLEY. Yeah, Miss Fontaine. It's not who you are, it's who they think you are.

WELLES. [Breaking in] Let me go on. It's really a matter of market analysis that convinces me that the image must be constructed carefully. As Hayley wanted to know, who's our target consumer? We think that target is composed of a very specialized group of people.

One: It is a person who has plenty of money to spare, a person who can take two weeks off to go to a health spa without pinching pennies.

Two: It is a person who is not *too* rich—as if anybody could be *too* rich! [laughter]—because that too-rich person may have his or her own personal health attendant.

Ruling out—Three—the masses without a lot of discretionary capital, we come back to the profile of the Beatrix la Belle consumer.

Item: It is a person of the solid middle class who is high enough in the financial hierarchy to pay the bills. Now, this includes the traditional white-collar executive.

Item: It includes the woman worker and executive.

Item: It includes the hitherto excluded blue-collar professional or factory worker whose wife probably works, too.

In analyzing this profile, one thing becomes clearly evident. The consumer in the bull's-eye of the target is a middle- to high-income person who is probably not too sophisticated and is probably very conservative.

THERESE. Reactionary.

WELLES. Quite likely. Therefore I think you can see what I am getting at. The image of Beatrix la Belle must be an image of solid middle-class respectability.

THERESE. Oh my Christ.

WELLES. But there it is.

THERESE. I won't say *merde*, but it is exactly that.

WELLES. It may be a bad dream for you, but it is the ultimate truth. And that leads us into contemplation of the proper posture that will construct an image attractive to the respectable middle-class consumer.

Thérèse Maupin was steaming. The son of a bitch was talking about her, for Christ's sake! He was talking about her affair with Beatrix. The bastard was going to force Beatrix to dump her. Dump her, after all the work she had already done on the new setup. She knew it was coming. Oh, the rotten turd. Yes, she was *really* steaming.

She could see the glances going back and forth between Hayley Welles and Beatrix Fontaine. She could see the snide smile on the lips of that little asp at her boss's bosom: Mead the mole. Damn it!

EXTRACT FROM "BEATRIX PROJECT I":

WELLES. I want this image to be so absolutely correct that you, Mademoiselle Beatrix Fontaine, can be used in the heavy advertising that will accompany the initial phases of Beatrix la Belle after the opening salvo at Nice. I want your face to be as familiar to the public as the face of the Helmsley woman whose color photograph is used constantly to advertise the Helmsley hotels in New York in the magazines and newspapers. I want your face to become as instantly recognizable as Frank Perdue's when he sells a chicken. I want you to be as up-front as Orville Redenbacher and his popcorn. Do you see what I am getting at?

HAYLEY. You want Mademoiselle Beatrix Fontaine to be Mademoiselle Beatrix Fontaine.

WELLES. Exactly. And I want her to be as visible to the public as a movie star. I want her to be a part of the life of every consumer who has the money to spend on her international network of health and beauty spas.

BEATRIX. [Loudly] You are telling me I no longer have a private life of my own?

WELLES. That's right. Mademoiselle?

BEATRIX. [Silence. Then:] Ah. So be it.

THERESE. [Upset] Trish, you bitch! *Au revoir, mes ennemies*! I go now!

BEATRIX. [Whispering] We talk later. Sit down, Tessie.

WELLES. Don't leave now, Mademoiselle. Things are just getting interesting.

THERESE. Oh, what the hell! I sit. I listen.

WELLES. [As if nothing had happened] We have the Beatrix Fontaine we want. Now we need her biography.

BEATRIX. Oh, Mon Dieu!

WELLES. Don't panic, Mademoiselle Fontaine. I'm talking about your life.

BEATRIX. I don't even know—

WELLES. You aren't listening. I want to know every detail of the up-front life of Mademoiselle Beatrix Fontaine. I want to see a biography that molds you into the proper type to head this international network of health and beauty spas.

MEAD. Most Hollywood biographies are made up of one-tenth truth and nine-tenths fantasy.

BEATRIX. Oh. You want—

WELLES. We want to project the image of middle-class respectability. We want to know how Beatrix started out at the bottom of the ladder in Paris. We want to know how she faced desperate circumstances from her early years, and how she eventually overcame all odds, learned her trade, and then started her own company, building it into a smashing success of prodigious proportions.

BEATRIX. Ah. You want the story of Cinderella.

WELLES. Exactly. Now, Mademoiselle Maupin. You have done excellent work on this project from the beginning. I want you to continue. It is now most important that you and Beatrix Fontaine sit down together and come up with a biography that will fulfill what we need here to create an image attractive to our middle-class customer.

THERESE. We ignore the fact that Mademoiselle Fontaine is a bastard without a known father, and we construct one?

BEATRIX. [Mortified] Tessie! For the love of God!

THERESE. I just want to find out what Mr. Welles *wants* from us, love. *Is that it?*

WELLES. [Curtly] That's it.

*   *   *

Cornelius Welles was stunned. Somehow his researchers had not come up with the fact that Beatrix was born out of wedlock. Moreover, from the way the lesbian spoke, there was no indication as to *who* her father was. What a hell of a thing, considering the fact that the final image was supposed to be so low-profile and sedate.

Yet the way the mores tilted today, it might be a real plus—a kind of exotic background for a Princess of Beauty. Could he trust the young Frenchwoman to turn out the right kind of stuff? Or should he have his boy Mead "Three" get into the act? *He'd* know how to do it. The kid was a complete fake-o from toe to tonsure.

He glanced at his troubleshooter and saw him eyeing Hayley. Hayley's face was slightly pink, almost as if she were inwardly excited about making another million dollars. Or perhaps in a quick orgasm? He recognized the look. What in hell—?

EXTRACT FROM "BEATRIX PROJECT I":

THERESE. Then I propose we tell the truth. I had, of course, researched the background of my employer before I went to work for her. Her real story is far more exciting than any you might be able to dream up.

Did you know, for example, that Mademoiselle was born in a tiny village in the vast countryside of the South of France? That, indeed, her mother was seduced at the age of thirteen by an aristocratic Frenchman from Indonesia, who was, actually, a Eurasian of some means?

Mademoiselle was visited by this rich Eurasian

during the early years of her life; it was he who paid for her upbringing. When, finally, he was killed on a Swiss ski run, the money stopped coming in, and Mademoiselle's mother moved with her child to Paris, where she lived with a cousin—in abject poverty. At that point, Mademoiselle made the most of what little life she had, educated herself on scholarships, got a job as a chemist, went to work for one of the biggest cosmetic firms in France—and the rest is history.

WELLES. Jesus H. Christ.

HAYLEY. [Clapping her hands] Very good thinking!

MEAD. Mademoiselle is *vite* on the feet!

BEATRIX. [Subdued] You make a mockery of my life, Thérèse.

THERESE. I was *asked* to, love.

WELLES. Write it up. It sounds exciting already.

MEAD. Just like a novel.

THERESE. [Laughing] *Formidable!*

Abbey Martin heard the meeting in the library break up at about eleven. She kept herself carefully out of sight, but knew, by the sound of the footsteps along the corridor, exactly who was passing the small storeroom in which she waited: the young Frenchwoman; her father, the cosmetics queen with him; her mother a little more slowly—and finally, Mead "Three." Unless Abbey was mistaken, she heard her mother and her father's troubleshooter whispering together.

When she came out of the storeroom, she followed to find her mother hurrying upstairs toward the apartment where Aunt Meggy and Uncle Nicky were quartered. Her father's young trainee loitered in the hallway and then walked downstairs into the main room, where a few of the guests still lingered.

Making it look as casual as possible, Abbey slipped

around to a side entrance and gained admittance to the room, within six feet of him. He was standing there looking over the flock of guests, considering his move. He saw her and his face lit up. "Hello!"

She tried to quell her rising excitement. "I thought you were discussing strategy."

"It's all discussed."

She was smiling. "And so where do we go from here?"

"Beatrix Cosmétique?"

"You and I."

"Did you have something special in mind?" He was watching her shrewdly. Was there just a hint of nastiness there?

"The moon's out. There's a nice walk around the estate. You can see the Hudson River."

"Can you, now?"

"Uh huh."

"Well, I seem to have lost my program and don't have a thing to do." He crooked his elbow to let her take his arm. "Let's go!"

It was cooler outside the mansion. Abbey wound her way skillfully along the path to the tennis courts, made the linkup with the circular pathway, and the two of them continued along in the pitch dark, with only the moon and the stars overhead.

"It's light out in the dark," he said with a laugh. "I never knew that!"

"City type."

"Urban," he admitted. They were walking side by side, not touching. "You're what? Nineteen?"

"Oh, in years, maybe. Ancient, really."

"You were born here?"

"Yes."

"What's it like to be a Prescott?"

She looked up at him. "There's no way of knowing. I mean, I've never been anything else, so I can't compare."

"Dumb question."

She shrugged. "Everybody asks it."

"Your mother is a very exciting woman," Mead said tentatively. "I'm talking about seeing her in action. Of course, your father is damned sharp, too."

"Stepfather. My mother is a steel trap with huge claws."

"She *can* handle herself."

"And everybody else," Abbey observed ruefully.

"You get along?"

"Reasonably well."

They walked on in a friendly silence.

She stopped and turned to him. "What do you think of me?"

He halted and frowned. "I think you're something very special."

She moved toward him, putting her hands up to his shoulders. "Kiss something special, Mead Three."

He responded instantly. She could feel his hands moving along her sides and down to her waist. She crushed herself against him, feeling his lips on hers, his hands on her ass.

Then he was gone. He was still holding her tightly around the waist, but he was watching her with amusement and not lust—damn it all! "That was something special, Abbey."

"Oh, shit!" she said. *"That's* nothing special. That's a goddamned rejection! Why are you afraid of me?"

"I'm not afraid of you, love. I have a curious regard for my own survival."

"What are you talking about?" She was so infuriated she was beginning to weep.

"I don't know you very well, Abbey. What's the point of getting involved so damned quickly—and so damned deeply?"

"You're afraid of me!" she said again, in fury.

"Even a yuppie has a code, baby. What's the point of deflowering a virgin on a moonlit night on the Hudson River? I could get my balls cut off for that!"

"Who said I was a—a virgin!" Her voice shook.

"Research, angel. Research. Now, let's get back to the mansion. I think the hounds are slowly trotting down the steps after us."

Silently, she turned back with him.

"Who's there?" a rough, no-nonsense voice spoke out of the darkness.

She took a deep breath. "It's me, Mr. Garnet," she responded firmly. "It's Abbey."

"Hi, Abbey. Just keeping track."

She said not one word more, all the way back to the mansion. When Mead Three gripped her by the hand to turn her to him for what might have been a good-night kiss, she pulled away. Damned if she would let him see the frustration in her face.

What a fool he must think her! What a damned fool!

CHAPTER FOUR

Megan Prescott Tarantino sat at her bureau mirror in her room, brushing her hair before going to bed. She paused and peered at herself more closely in the shining glass oval. *Maledetto!* she fumed inwardly as she studied the brush. Her hair was falling out at a much more rapid rate than it had been even a year ago. Alfreddo in Florence had assured her that the power of his rejuvenation shampoo was irresistible. *Eh bene!* Alfreddo, like most of the Italians she knew, was full of it.

She stared ruefully at her hair—light brown; slightly frizzy, and cut short because of its thinness, so it could never be styled in any fanciful manner. Why couldn't she have hair like Hayley's? Hers was thick, red-gold, and shiny—nothing like this frazzled mess of froth assigned by a toss of the genes to her. She sighed, shaking her head. What was the use in moaning? Hayley had been standing first in line when they passed out the winning lottery tickets: brains, looks, smarts. Megan? Always an also-ran.

Well, at least she had Nicky. She leaned forward,

flicking at her eyelid to remove a piece of lint—or worse, dandruff?—then stared into her hazel eyes. Yeah. She had Nicky. And where was Nicky now? In the goddamned *cucitore*, that's where!

There was a brief knock on her door and a low call of ''Meggy,'' then the door opened. Megan's heart sank. For a moment she watched Hayley's approach in the mirror without being able to turn around. The brush was frozen in midair.

''Silver threads among the gold?'' Hayley remarked, coming up behind her. ''I throw all mine away. *Nobody* knows.''

Megan bristled for all the wrong reasons. ''Not a streak of white!'' she snapped. ''Granted my hair hasn't the *body* yours has, but it's holding up, thank you!''

Hayley laughed. ''Meggy, your skin gets thinner every year.''

''And your mouth gets meaner!''

They were standing facing one another now, Megan almost white with fury, and Hayley beginning to stiffen in reaction.

''We've got things to talk about,'' Hayley said in an even, rational voice. ''*Then* we can pull each other's hair.'' She turned and strolled over to a chair near the window. ''Now. Shall we sit?''

Megan wilted. She knew her fury was all show and no substance. She was scared silly. Meekly, she followed her younger sister and sank into a second chair positioned in conversational range. She couldn't help but notice how good Hayley looked in that latest Galanos she had ordered. She'd managed a whale of a dinner, had probably run the meeting Carney had held, and God knows what else—and she looked as if she'd just stepped out of her dressing room, ready to take on all comers.

"Did you bring the papers?" Hayley asked in an equable voice. Megan could see it was taking an effort for her sister to keep herself cool and aloof.

"No reason to. The accountants haven't completed their work." Damn! Megan felt like she was six and her mother was giving her a tongue-lashing.

"You said it was bad. Fourteen million?" Hayley's eyes were dangerously alight. She wouldn't abide evasion—Megan knew that. Yet there was no way Megan could tell her the facts when the facts weren't yet available.

"Yeah. About that." Megan felt queasy "Fourteen six, maybe. One of the *contabili* mentioned fourteen six five. Give or take a couple thou."

"Don't try to show off your Italian to me, Meggy. I know you flunked it in college, and after twenty years in residence you probably still speak it like a foreigner."

Megan ignored Hayley's thrust. "The point is, no one can find out exactly where the bulk of the money went. There are a number of portfolios that are completely in shambles. Investments have been traded, transferred, and cancelled almost indiscriminately. Nicky thinks some of his staff are playing footsie with Mgatto, the head of an emerging African nation. Actually, Nicky lent him ten million—I'm talking U.S. dollars, Lee—but there's a chance one of the Mgatto ministers took it with him when he decamped two months ago. Mgatto isn't answering any phone calls. *I* think it's in some Swiss bank account. We'll probably never see any of it again."

Hayley was considering, her green eyes moving

about as if she were looking into a vast distance. Finally, she turned her attention back to Megan.

"Surely you have insurance."

"Nicky says yes, but there are clauses."

"What clauses?" snapped Hayley, becoming flushed at the evasiveness of her sister's responses.

"I don't know," Megan admitted. "You should be talking to Nicky—"

"Meggy, this is Prescott money, damn it! You *know* Prescott money built that damned bank. The Foundation has millions invested—and I don't know what you've been doing with it."

"*I* haven't been doing a thing with it!" Megan flared. "It's the *bank* that's in charge of the money."

"But you're in charge of the bank! You've got to keep an eye on it. I mean, technically you're not in charge, but it's Prescott money that made that bank and that keeps it going. And if it's gone, *I've* got to replace it." She was storming now, her green eyes as frosty as the bottom four-fifths of an iceberg.

"There was never any trouble before," Megan observed in a soft, put-upon voice.

"That Italian stallion you married has gambled it away, Meggy." Hayley gazed at her sternly. "Don't you think *that's* the real story?"

"I sent him to that Gamblers Anonymous clinic. They told me he was cured." Megan was wringing her hands now. She felt awful. In a moment, she would be going into the john to throw up.

"It's your problem, Meggy," said Hayley grandly. "When you think of some solution, you come to me, and I'll see what I can do to help you."

Megan felt fire consuming her breast. "How come everything is *my* fault all of a sudden? When that money I had in your goddamned Foundation grew wings and flew away in the Chilean revolution, that was some deus ex machina thing that 'just happened' way off there somewhere. It wasn't *your* fault for backing the baddies. Oh, no!''

"Fortunes of politics," said Hayley with a faint smile.

"And now, when Nicky's bank puts the money where it's suddenly gobbled up by gangsters—then it's *my* fault!"

"It's your fault because it's Prescott money and it went into the bank you built for Nicky," snapped Hayley. "By God, Mom and Dad were right about Nicky. They never did like Italian titles."

Megan tried to hold back her tears. By rights, *she* should be holding the purse strings on the Prescott money. Their own parents had held the majority of the Prescott fortune, with their mother's money—the MacNabb millions—making their portion larger than anyone else's in the family. When Megan married Niccolo Tarantino, both Daniel and Dorothy—Dan and Dot Prescott—had changed their wills and left Hayley, the younger daughter, in control on their death. And then they had died in that miserable air crash over Spain five years ago. So now it was Hayley who controlled the largest fortune in the world—not Megan. And it was all Nicky's fault; because Mom and Dad were *right* to cut the stupid Guinea off from control of the Prescott money.

She straightened up. "I'll set it to rights!" she cried.

"You've got the fourteen six five to plug up the hole in the sinking boat?" Hayley sneered.

"I've got my own *personal* funds."

"Nothing like fourteen million, Meggy." Hayley had come down a bit off her high horse.

"No." Megan was now fighting back a flow of tears. Her face was screwed up like a small child's. "But I can borrow some. *Some* people still like me."

"All the crowned heads of Europe!" Hayley rejoined mockingly, waving her hands in the air to indicate endless space.

"Oh shut up, you foul-mouthed bitch," Megan sobbed, pressing her plump wrists against her cheeks to dry her tears.

"Throw a party!" yelled Hayley, springing up and marching around the room. "The biggest rent party in history! Bring your millions to fill up Megan's empty coffers! Her husband lost his way to the gaming tables and ended up at the cleaners." She paused and glared at her sister. "Why not? You're the hostess with the European clout!"

"Jealous?" whispered Megan disconsolately.

Hayley was shaking her head. She crouched down on the floor beside her sister. Megan felt her warm arms around her shoulders. "I'll help you, of course. We'll do a little investment manipulation. I'll get it for you." Megan felt her sister's lips on her cheek and burst into tears. "Brace up, Meggy. Things could be worse."

Jesus. She felt like a real jerk. But unfortunately, Hayley was right. Nicky was a dope. A *pazzo*. A *sciocco*. That was the trouble with Italian. The words made everything bad *sound* good!

"Meggy," Hayley pleaded. "Dry your tears. It's all over. For now, anyway."

Lynn Miles hastened along the hallway toward her room. She had been unnerved when that older waiter had stared at her during dinner. Hell, so far nobody

else had tumbled at all. Nobody. And yet *he* had.
She even remembered his name. Barton Greene.

She turned the corner and ran straight into Hayley
Prescott. *Now*, of course, her name was Hayley *Welles*.
Lynn froze absolutely stiff. Hayley's eyes looked
tired, the lines around them pronounced. Lynn thought
immediately of emotional fatigue after a quarrel. With
her husband?

Hayley managed a brittle smile. "Hello, Mrs.
Miles."

Lynn managed a smile. "Hello, Mrs. Welles."
And then, just for effect: "It's such a lovely weekend!" Liar!

Hayley nodded absently. "Thank you." And then,
as a kind of afterthought: "It's nice having you here.
The senator is one of my favorite people." A per-
functory smile. Liar!

Damn her hide, thought Lynn. Hayley *loathed*
Miley!

But before she could come up with a fitting comment, Hayley had taken herself off and was hurrying
downstairs.

By God! Lynn thought triumphantly, Hayley hadn't
tumbled! She *didn't* recognize her! The waiter had
remembered—but not Hayley. And Hayley was the
smart one. Of course, Lynn's hair was blond now,
and she'd had her teeth done, and she'd had that
bone graft on her leg to correct the limp. But Hayley
hadn't tumbled!

Lynn was almost laughing as she continued on her
way. Although she had wanted to make the Scobie
Hills visit all along, she had been terrified lest she be
identified. It was Hayley she had worried about the
most. She'd been so worried, she'd been sick in the

chopper. What a dumb thing to do—upchuck all over the controls!

Suddenly, in the same hallway, she found herself smack in front of the *only other person* at Scobie Hills who could wreck the sanctity of her incognito: Charlie Garnet. For a startled moment they viewed each other. The man's eyes seemed to narrow in thought as he regarded her.

Lynn almost fainted.

"Mrs. Miles." Garnet smiled, his tanned, weathered face relaxing into the semblance of a smile. He was thinking of the pictures in The Book, Lynn realized.

Pop! she cried out inside. You don't *know* me! Pop, she almost whispered aloud. It's little Arlene! Your gimpy daughter! The one who ran away. Pop!

He didn't really *see* her. But everything about her was different now. When she had run off, she'd had red hair, freckles, a round face, and a fat butt. She'd managed to trim everything up a little, so no one would recognize bumbling little Arlene Garnet ever again.

She would have come home a long time ago, but she knew it would bring up the same old arguments about the goddamned Prescotts and Pop's job and how beholden to them he was—and all that bullshit!

"Feeling better?" her father asked her, not knowing who she really was, not *dreaming*. "After the plane ride?"

Oh, that. "Yes. Thank you. I'm feeling much better."

He nodded and passed on down the hall.

She wheeled to watch him, wincing a bit at the slowness of his walk, the defeated, bent-over "ancient retainer" attitude he had always thought was so proper in his position at Scobie Hills. Tears came to her eyes. She wanted to talk to him, to talk about Mom, whom she knew was dead now, and Ricky, and Estelle, and Danny. But she couldn't. It wouldn't be right. And it wouldn't be smart.

Because, she still hadn't done the number she wanted to on the Prescotts.

Pop! Forgive me, Pop!

The moon was high. Hayley Prescott Welles strode along the woodsy path, driven by a disconcerting blend of blind determination and psychic exhaustion. She hated emotional confrontations—particularly with her sister. Megan, the damned fool, loved her, and she always seemed to be begging for psychological support or physical help. And she loved Megan, of course. But—really!

And then, in the hallway, when she had run into Senator Miles's busty little wife, she had had that weird and sudden déjà vu, and the whole thing with Megan merged into some unpleasantness way back in her past, when she and her sister were still kids at Scobie Hills, long before their parents were dead, and—

Who the hell *was* this Lynn Miles, anyway? Just some dumb kid the senator had picked up—one of his political workers, the story went. What in hell had Lynn Miles to do with Megan Tarantino and Hayley Welles? Hayley felt sick.

Jesus. She needed cleansing, that was it. She needed a kind of renewal, in the spiritual sense, as well as in the physical sense. Water was the great purifier. And so—

The moon lay on the surface of the pond, quivering in a kind of heavenly ecstasy. Hayley parted the leaves and looked at its shimmering reflection with bemusement. Why was she so uptight? The placidity of the moon's image, the smoothness of the pond's surface, the lack of tension or disruption—all these things combined to exorcise her own anxieties.

She stripped quickly, folding the expensive gown and underthings carefully and moving out into the moonlight, where she stood a moment before diving in gracefully. Hardly a ripple rolled out from the epicenter of her entry. She surfaced and swam to the shore, rose, and stood there looking down as the broken pieces of the moon slowly fitted together once again.

Her own body coalesced into view in the surface of the pond as she stood with the water rolling off her shining skin. The reflection gradually etched in the curves of her shoulders and her firm breasts, then her narrow waist, rounded hips, slender thighs, and tiny ankles appeared. With the rich auburn hair plastered to her head and swanlike neck, she formed an almost flawless picture of perfection in the naked female form.

Satisfied at her own elegance, exulting in it, she dove in again, letting the water slide around her, envelop her, possess her. She closed her eyes. All she needed now was a different kind of possession—a male essence, perhaps, a—

Suddenly she was not alone. The pond water shuddered, quaked, shook her. She stood to her neck in water, startled out of her wits.

"You got my message," he said to her as he flipped the wet hair out of his eyes.

The moonlight illuminated his face—which, along with his neck and shoulders, was all that showed above the water's surface.

"You're trespassing again," Hayley said.

"Sue me," Mead Brookhaven III dared her.

Now she flinched momentarily, and then relaxed. His hands were at work on her body under the surface of the water. He touched her breasts, and she was inclined to close her eyes and lean backward, but she did not. She watched his face. Warmth surged through her. Her breasts tingled. Her skin tingled. *She* tingled, all over. She could feel herself slowly coming alive inside—coming alive and falling apart at the same time.

He held her waist and drew her closer to him. She let her hands float on the surface of the water, touching his shoulders. The hardness of his body surged against hers underwater. She felt the manipulations of his hands as they moved down her body and caressed her buttocks.

"Hey," she said in a whisper.

He moved his hands to the front of her, touching her tenderly and probingly, and within seconds she could feel him inside her, his hips moving against hers. Then she did give in to her original inclination and let herself float backward. His arms were now grasping her tightly, and he was working himself firmly into her in the enveloping softness of the water. She enclosed him and felt him rise against her warmth and softness . . .

A hot tub was never like this! she thought drowsily as they lay on the edge of the pond, drying off.

"I plead guilty to trespassing in your woods," he said with a smile.

"Have my secretary make you out a permanent pass," she chuckled and turned to kiss him.

Wow! It had been a long time, she thought. Six months? But it was all over now. She felt renewed again, renewed and revitalized. It was almost as good as making a million dollars on an investment deal. Well, maybe it was *better*.

Abbey Martin could hear the frustrated cries and sobs from inside her Aunt Meggy's room, but she could not hear exactly what was being discussed. She had heard that Uncle Nicky's bank in Florence was in trouble—but that was all. Finally, when she saw her mother stalk out of the room with the green fire still glowing in her eyes, she knew it must have been a knock-down-drag-out battle between the sisters.

She wondered where her mother was going. On a whim, she followed. At one point, she thought she must have alerted Hayley to the fact that she was not alone in the woods, but her mother was obviously so involved in her own thoughts that she paid no attention to Abbey's misstep.

When Abbey became aware that her mother was going to the pond, she almost turned back. But it occurred to her that perhaps, if her mother happened to be in a pensive mood, she might be more accessible to persuasion from without. Abbey had a proposition to make. She wanted to go on her own vacation, probably to Europe.

She saw her mother strip, and was just about to come out into the moonlight to speak to her, when a rustle in the leaves made her freeze. She waited a long time, and there was more movement. It was difficult to see what was happening, but—

Then she saw and knew. She knew who was in the pond with her mother, and she watched, stunned and blinking back tears of rage and frustration, planted in the earth like a statue, while Mead Three and her mother—her own mother, goddamn it!—screwed each other like a couple of drunken eels.

She ran off, her outrage too deep and too personal to be measured.

With admirable restraint, Thérèse Maupin resisted the temptation to sneak into Beatrix Fontaine's bedroom and force her into some kind of resolution of their personal problem. Tessie was not going to stand for any rupture; but she knew how stubborn Beatrix could be, and she was afraid there would be fireworks.

She also knew that there were many hidden eyes in the Prescott mansion. And there were a million tale-carriers who would love to carry stories about Beatrix and her female lover. Now that the high level of the stakes had been made quite clear by the head of Welles Associates, Tessie knew that if she continued in her affair with Beatrix, she would have to be much more discreet than before—even in France.

Images! *Merde!* Yet business was business. And Mademoiselle Beatrix was definitely a businesswoman.

Tessie had left her door slightly open, so she could see the door to Beatrix's room, and when it opened some time near midnight, Tessie straightened in anticipation. She knew there was something cooking between Welles and Trish. By God, if she could somehow bring their involvement out into the open, she might have something to hold over Welles, in order to force him to let the Beatrix-Maupin connection continue.

In a moment she was in the corridor, following Beatrix, thinking how foolish she would feel if her boss was simply going down to the kitchen to whip up an omelette or something. But of course, Beatrix was not headed for the kitchen. She was headed for the next floor up. And that, Tessie knew, was the floor on which the Welleses were ensconced.

Sure enough, as she followed, glancing about every moment or so to make sure no one was observing her, she found that Beatrix was indeed on her way to a certain doorway in the corridor. Tessie watched as her lover paused in front of one of the doors, tried the latch, and opened it. With a cursory glance up and down the hallway, Beatrix pushed open the door and entered the room.

Tessie crept forward until she could hear what was being said in the room—and distinguish who was saying it.

Carney Welles was having a great deal of trouble getting to sleep. He lay there, tossing from one side of the bed to the other. It had been a good meeting—he felt certain that they were off on the right foot on the Beatrix thing—but somehow now he wanted a follow-up. He knew of the theory espoused by Napoleon, or somebody, that after a successful battle a warrior wants, and deserves, to screw somebody.

Of course, if it *was* Napoleon, he should know. He was French. Probably the whole thing sounded a little bit more adroit in the original French. But what the hell, he knew what Nappy meant.

He jerked the bedclothes off and tried sleeping without them covering him. He could feel the air playing over his naked body. He always slept in the raw. It was the only way to rest. But now he knew he could never get to sleep. He was too charged up about the Beatrix deal. It looked very good—probably the pinnacle of his career.

Where the hell was Hayley when he needed her? Well, of course, he had been the one to suggest separate rooms six months back. That was during the period he couldn't even get it up for her. And he was damned worried about everything then—his health, his marriage, and mostly his goddamned business.

He remembered the Gomez fiasco, that damned hotel caper. Welles's client, Carlos Gomez, had planned to expand his string of hotels in Central America. Right away, some left-wing revolutionary had blown the damned Gomez flagship hotel into bits and pieces. Worse than that, the media had proved that Gomez was financing a group of right-wing militarists to overthrow the government, so that Gomez would be in the catbird seat with the new military regime.

Carney had almost gone to the wall on that one. The U.S. media had just about eaten him alive. But he had lucked out when the military government itself had fallen. Gomez had been blown up in his limousine in front of the city's most famous whorehouse.

Now, Carney was on a roll—he *wanted* Hayley. She had brought in Beatrix, and this deal was going to be Big Stuff! Christ, he was even *ready* for Hayley. Startled, he looked down at his erection—one *anybody* could be proud of. Even Hayley, who had written the book on shafting. He sat up in bed and was reaching over to fling on his robe when there was a sudden rap on the door.

Hayley!

He grinned and turned on the muted lamp by his bed.

"Come in," he said. Wouldn't she be surprised at the old man's muscle tone. . . .

The door opened and Beatrix Fontaine appeared, closing it carefully behind her before turning to look directly at Welles. Meanwhile, he was so astonished to see her that he was unable to move a muscle.

Quickly he fumbled to throw a cover over his flaming tumescence.

"Did I interrupt something?" Beatrix asked with a sly sparkle in her eye.

"I don't usually—"

She moved quickly to the bed. "I had come to discuss *les images*, but I see I am needed for other considerations."

"Hey!"

She loosened her robe, dropped it, got into the bed beside him, and threw the covers over the two of them. "I was once a nurse. Disabled war veterans. I dealt in resolving great physical frustrations."

Carney sat up straight. She was grasping him in her agile hand and moving her fingers skillfully on him. Now both her hands were at it. He leaned back, closing his eyes. "Jesus."

"No talking," said the proficient ex-nurse, continuing to manipulate him expertly. Quickly, she curled up beside him, ducked her head down into the covers, and before he was able to protest, or even guess what was going to happen, he could feel her lips on him, and her tongue moving with amazing resourcefulness.

He stiffened and slammed his hands down on the mattress. He found his back arching, and suddenly he felt he could hold it no longer. She was working at him, and he could feel her long taffy-colored hair fanned out on his legs.

Then he felt her gone from him. He was gasping with stunned pleasure. Suddenly she was on top of him, her face looking down, her golden animal eyes peering into his, eyeball to eyeball, then her breasts—

round and petite, with lovely pink nipples—were presented to him.

He kissed her, and she lowered herself onto him, lifting her upper body as she worked onto him below, her soft thighs clasping his waist. She moved on him like an experienced jockey and tightened to him, egging him on and forcing him to strain and explode, which he did not once, but three times.

"Lovely," he gasped.

"If Beatrix la Belle goes under, I can always be a nurse again," she smiled.

He kissed her. Somehow the buildup was all backward. The big fireworks first, and then the foreplay. It was no way to build a public relations program, but a hell of a good way to get the sex back into his life!

What could he do now to cap that? Shake hands?

"Now, shall we talk about *les images?*"

Megan Tarantino was strolling about the mansion after midnight, trying to locate Nicky, when she heard a disturbance in a room ahead of her. She drew aside. After a moment, the door opened and a robed figure came out. It was the Frenchwoman, Beatrix Fontaine, the cosmetic queen. And the room—the room was Carney's!

Of course, the two of them had obviously been discussing the campaign for the new health spa. Like so much applesauce, they were, Megan thought, her eyes gleaming. Wait till she told Hayley in the morning.

But then she hesitated. Better than that, why not hang onto this piece of information and release it at a time when she could make more points with it? Like the next time Hayley had Megan in a cage, poking away at her with metal prods.

Then she'd spring it on her how her husband was getting it on with the Frog Princess!

Her eyes sparkled, and she almost laughed as she hastened back to her bedroom. There she found the *conte* asleep in the bed. How in hell had he managed to get in without her seeing him? She rolled over to him and grabbed him by the balls in a wifely way, but he only growled and flipped over, shoving his backside into her belly in a husbandly way.

CHAPTER FIVE

reakfast at Scobie Hills was an open-ended affair. There was a comfortable breakfast room just off the kitchen, with a wide picture window overlooking the Hudson River. Past the picture window, a kind of balcony, or terrace, could be accessed by a sliding glass door.

One entered the breakfast room, selected whatever fruit or dry cereal one desired, took it to the table where a pot of hot coffee and hot water for tea stood waiting, and ordered hot food from the breakfast chef.

Lynn Miles was the first one down the next morning. She and the senator had gone to bed early, and for some reason he had come on very strong with her, balling her as randily and as thoroughly as he had in the first days they had known each other. In fact, he was so totally engrossed in the action that he had dropped right off to sleep after the furor was finished— *inside* her, for God's sake!

She was just getting aroused. Sleep was beyond her. She tried to will it to come, but that had never worked anyway. Then she got up and did a series of aerobic exercises she had learned from her Japanese yoga instructor in Beverly Hills. Even that did no good. She lay down as bright-eyed and bushy-tailed as a seventeen-year-old.

Well, what the hell, she thought, and threw on her casuals—floppy sweat shirt, stretch pants, and open-toed sandals. Giving her hair a quick study, she shoved it into place and frowned. She needed a new tint job. The red roots were showing. Maybe she'd try purple this time. Blonde was all right, but hadn't Cher shoved it down their throats when she showed up at the Madonna-Sean Penn wedding in purple hair?

Early that morning, while she drank her coffee and ate her dry cereal on the terrace, Lynn glanced down at the paper she had pulled out of her pocket. Her nocturnal circuit of the estate had proved interesting, to say the least.

She checked the notes. Actually, the "notes" were simply figures, very much like a grocery receipt at the supermarket. The slip of paper showed a sequence of numbers:

1.13
2.06
3.23
8.23
11.13
12.13
13.02
13.20
14.20
20.13

Looking off into the blue hills that rose beyond the Hudson River, Lynn sipped at her coffee. A tiny frown appeared between her plucked eyebrows. She drew a line connecting 8.23 and 13.02. That made sense, she thought. There were plenty of rumors afloat about Welles Associates and about the Prescott treasury system.

Then, with precision, she drew a second line connecting 3.23 and 2.06. After a bit of thought she added another, connecting 13.20 and 14.20. The rest was easy. She linked 11.13 and 12.13 firmly.

Contemplating the figures, she frowned slightly. Had she forgotten any likely combination? There were two numbers left that were unlinked: 1.13 and 20.13. What were you supposed to do with them?

She considered drawing a line connecting them, but almost burst out laughing as she thought about what that meant.

"Erecting a horoscope?" a pleasant, slightly accented voice asked over her shoulder.

Lynn glanced up in surprise. It was the Frenchwoman—the young sharp one, the one that sent out such disturbing vibrations. Involuntarily, Lynn shuddered. She wouldn't want that creep running her fingers up and down *her* spine. She had never gone that route, except for one revolting trial in the past. It simply didn't pay off—at least, not for Lynn.

"Something like that," Lynn said offhandedly. But with that sharp bitch standing there breathing against her hair, her surface nonchalance collapsed under the strain of a relentless tension.

Thérèse Maupin reached over Lynn's shoulder and took the pencil from her.

"There's a mistake, you know." The eraser on the end of the long yellow pencil rubbed out the line between 13.20 and 14.20. Then, after a short pause, the graphite point formed a link between 14.20 and a new number written at the bottom of the list: 24.24.

The bitch! thought Lynn. She was sharp—in fact, even sharper than Lynn had thought. It took *somebody* to glance at a code like hers and break it *on the spot*.

"I wouldn't want you to have the facts wrong," the angular young woman said, sauntering gracelessly over to a nearby table and seating herself silently over coffee and croissants.

Piss on her! thought Lynn, crumpling up the note paper in front of her. What did *she* know, anyway?

After a moment, Lynn began to relax. She flattened out her notes and studied the numbers. The French bitch's additional marks made sense, all right. Lynn had seen that the count was as randy as a bull elephant. It was the countess who didn't know from diddley-shit about what went on. Apparently he had the talent for keeping her happy in the hay no matter what else he did on the side.

But as for the two Parisians, what was going to become of the cozy little arrangement between the big cosmetics queen and her girlfriend? Was it going to be dissolved? And if so—at what cost? Lynn knew that if she had Queen Beatrix in sexual bondage the way the ugly little woman had her, she would never let her off the hook without exacting maximum tribute. Max payoff! Max!

Lynn smiled. She bet the little slut would *get* max payoff. She was smart . . . to have spotted—at a glance—the game of "who's in bed with whom" that Lynn was playing the way *she* had? Sure, alphabet-position numbers was an old code, but not everybody was into codes.

Watch out for that Frenchie, she thought to herself. Watch out!

Carney Welles paused beside his wife's chair at the breakfast table and kissed her on the cheek.

"Morning, love."

Hayley looked up at him with a brief smile. "You're looking well."

"So are you, darling. An inner glow, I'd call it."

"It must be—*comment dit-on?*—catching?"

He stiffened at the stressed French phrase, patted her on the shoulder, and sat at the far end of the table, where he began chatting with one of the houseguests.

"Monsieur Welles, I hate to disturb you when you're at breakfast, but it *is* imperative that I speak to you."

Carney Welles glanced up at Thérèse Maupin and eyed her suspiciously. What in hell did this wavemaker want? She was obviously spoiling for trouble, and this appeared to be her way of preparing for a showdown.

"*S'il vous plait,* I have a commitment and must go to Mass."

Welles stared at her, uncomprehending.

"*C'est dimanche,*" she explained. "It is necessary for me to go to Mass. So must Mademoiselle Beatrix."

Light dawned. Catholic Mass! "Excuse my foggy-mindedness," Welles smiled. "I understand. But isn't it true that if you are on a visit to friends you can make up your obligations later?"

Thérèse smiled placidly. "Perhaps so, Monsieur Welles. Indeed, you speak the truth. But I am thinking about *l'image.*"

Welles blinked. "Image?"

"Respectability. It is Mademoiselle Beatrix I am concerned about. Would she—in the guise in which you wish her to appear—fail to attend church?"

Welles gave an almost imperceptible obeisance to the Frenchwoman's shrewdness. "Of course, you are right." He frowned. "I'll have a car for you in fifteen minutes. There's a proper Catholic church in the village."

Thérèse nodded, but did not depart.

"Mademoiselle?" Welles prompted her.

"I haven't yet brought up this matter to Mademoiselle Beatrix. Perhaps you would be willing to persuade her to conform to this new—image."

You loathesome little twat! Welles thought. Anything to drive a wedge between us. She *knew,* damn her eyes.

"Assure her that you are my personal messenger."

Thérèse withdrew. Moments later, in her bedroom, she faced a livid Beatrix Fontaine. The two of them went at each other in rapid-fire French until finally Beatrix calmed down, pondered the problem, saw no way out, and opted to comply. Besides, she thought, she and Thérèse had to face *their* problem, once and for all. It was definitely all over between them.

In the limousine provided by the Scobie Hills estate and chauffeured by a Prescott driver, Beatrix Fontaine finally announced her decision to Thérèse.

"I've been thinking about it, Tessie," she said, speaking in her hard-learned, fine-tuned, elegant Parisian French. "I've come to a decision that I know is best for both of us."

"*Eh bien,* let's not spar around, Trish. Suppose you let me hear it." Tessie's voice was larded over with sarcasm.

"It's over. All over." Beatrix's face was hard. Her eyes were watching the wooded Hudson Valley scenery flashing by as the limo headed down the hill. "I'll find you another apartment. You'll move out of mine as soon as we reach Paris."

"Lovely," said Tessie. "Just lovely."

"There's more," said Beatrix, turning to face her. Tessie couldn't help but notice how hooded and dangerous her eyes were. "I fully intend to carry out Monsieur Welles's orders. You'll be writing up my bio and working up the background material for the introduction of Beatrix la Belle in Nice. *But*—" here she paused deliberately "—you'll no longer be working out of our main office."

"You're canning me?" Tessie cried, almost in physical pain.

"People will be looking more closely at me. If they see you on the payroll—"

"I'll sue you for breach of contract!" screamed Tessie. "I've got a good case!"

"We don't *have* a contract," Beatrix said loftily, leaning back against the velvet seat of the limo and smiling slightly. "We'll make arrangements for payment of the money and your assigned piecework. On a free-lance basis."

"Trish!" gasped Tessie. "I can't *believe* what I'm hearing!"

"Oh, it's quite clear," Beatrix said as she pointed toward the door handle. The limo had pulled up outside a small church made of gray stone. "Out."

Mechanically, Tessie opened the door, got out, and turned to wait for Beatrix. Beatrix signaled the chauffeur to wait for them, then strode up the flagstone pathway to the church steps.

Together they walked in silently, did their proper

obeisances, and sat in a pew near the rear of the intimate little chapel. As the ceremony commenced, they sat in hostile silence, but once things were under way, Tessie leaned over against Beatrix and whispered in her ear:

"I'll leak everything I know about you to the tabloids, Trish. Believe me, I know *plenty!* I'll write up a bio that'll please your puppet master, Cornelius Welles—but I'll sell an *inside* exclusive about your real love life to whatever tabloid or book publisher bids the highest! And you can count on it!"

Beatrix gave Tessie a scathing glance. "Who'd believe you, Tessie? You? A disgruntled employee? Someone fired for incompetence? I can fight just as hard as you can. I can make it impossible for you to work *anywhere!* You'll need some kind of reference to get a job. Now, settle back and think about it. The best way is the way we're going to do it."

Tessie choked back a cry of rage.

"There's nothing personal about it," Beatrix said in a dry whisper. "It's just good business."

"Why, you flint-hearted, throat-cutting, tit-twisting bitch!"

"Isn't the choir doing a beautiful job?" She turned aside and glared at Tessie. "Since you dragged me out here to have it out with me, you're going to stay through the whole ceremony!"

Grinding her teeth, Tessie considered a rejoinder, but then swallowed it. There was nothing she could say, nothing she could do. It *was* all over. She was out.

But she'd come up with something. She knew that. She'd *ruin* the Queen Bee. *Ruin* her, damn it.

Abbey Martin knocked on the door to her mother's office and walked in. She could see Hayley over at her desk by the window, going though some papers in front of her. Even on Sunday, she was always at work. Abbey vowed not to grow up to be like her mother. It left no time for living life.

"Mom, we've got to talk." Abbey sat in a chair near her mother's desk and waited.

"Just a moment, dearest," Hayley said in a far-off voice, making marks on the sheet in front of her. "I'm busy."

"I had to catch you today. I can't sit around here all summer. You're going out to the Coast, and dad is going all over the world on the Beatrix thing. I want to go to Europe."

Hayley blinked and turned to look at her daughter. Abbey stared at her, once again astonished at the youth and vivacity in her mother's face. "Oh, you can't possibly do that, dear. It would cost too much."

Abbey shook her head, stifling laughter. She, who controlled billions of dollars—at least a full billion— had the gall to call an air flight to Europe too costly! That was a good one.

"Mother, I've saved up enough money out of my allowance—if *that's* what's bothering you."

"Actually, that's not the main thing," Hayley said softly, returning her attention to the sheets in front of her. "I want you home, here. It's dangerous over there, with those Irish Republican Army terrorists, and the Baader-Meinhoff gang—"

"Crap, Mom! Don't you think I can take care of myself? Don't you know I'm *aware?* Don't you trust me?"

"One of them almost got me, you know," snapped Hayley, stabbing at the paper with her ball-point pen to emphasize her point. "No. You're going to stay here."

"Is that an order?" Abbey asked, exaggerating her voice and making it sound like an actor in an armed-forces soap opera.

Hayley shrugged. "I guess so." She frowned at the sheet in front of her and made another emendation. "I'm trying to work out Aunt Meggy's problem," Hayley said in a slightly annoyed tone. "We'll talk later."

Aunt Meggy's problem! Abbey thought with disgust. What about Daughter Abbey's problem? What about the thought of dying on the vine at Scobie Hills while all the other Prescotts were flying, sailing, driving, or jogging to the ends of the earth? Why should *she* be the one always to get hung out on the line to dry?

"I deserve a little attention myself," she said stoutly.

"Oh, don't be silly, Abbey," Hayley said. "Now get along. We'll chat tonight." She offered her cheek for a kiss.

Abbey stared at her, wheeled, left the room, and within five minutes was in her room packing her flight bag.

Damn the woman! Carney Welles thought, still simmering over the cold-shoulder treatment he had gotten from Hayley during breakfast. There was more than a little guilt mixed in with his resentment. How the hell had Hayley *known* about Beatrix? Of course, it could have been a guess—but he knew Hayley well enough to know that she always checked her facts before she fired a verbal shot.

But that roll in the hay with Beatrix was Hayley's own fault. If she had been where she was supposed to be, Beatrix never would have wound up there instead. And what was *she* so high-and-mighty about, anyway? The Beatrix thing had gone good last night. You'd think Hayley would be proud of the way he'd pulled it all together.

"Oh, *here* you are!" a familiar voice said. Welles turned. It was Hayley. Speak of the devil. . . .

They were on the widow's walk, right out in the open. The sun was bright and the air fine. It was a lovely place to be—certainly one of the loveliest places in the area.

"Come to apologize?" Welles wondered, facing her and seeing for the first time the tightness and suppressed hostility in her expression.

"Apologize for what?" Hayley barked out, her voice rising uncontrollably.

"You treated me like some kind of goddamned *servant* during breakfast. As if you didn't know!"

"Oh, my goodness!" Hayley snorted in sarcasm. "Look who's annoyed! Don't you think *I'm* the one who should be on the attack?"

"Attack for what?" Welles was honestly puzzled.

"First of all, for the big bedroom farce you pulled with that Frenchwoman last night."

"*You're* the one who demanded separate bedrooms six months ago," Welles said smugly. "It wasn't my fault I was all alone when she smashed the door down to get at me."

"I was alone because you couldn't be a husband to me anymore! But I guess I don't have the proper French accent. Is *that* it?"

"That's a narrow-minded, racist thing to say," Welles retorted, just a hint of amusement evident.

"I don't give a damn about you bedding down that silly woman. I think she's only half there anyway. It's that utter fiasco you mounted last night for the Beatrix thing!"

"Fiasco!" yelled Welles, now truly angry. "What fiasco? I thought the thing went off one hundred percent smasheroo!"

"The hell it did. You pulled one of the biggest boners of your life on that one, Carney. I'm shocked at your incompetence. Not checking on that woman's background! Not *knowing* she was born out of wedlock! You were caught—caught with your pants down! Admit it!"

"So what?" Carney cried. "It'll all turn out for the best. We simply produce a first-class bio and—"

"And that prick kid from your office!"

"What's wrong with Mead?" Carney asked, realizing he was rising to the bait, but unable to haul himself in.

"He's wet behind the ears! He's stupid! I saw him sniffing around Abbey! I tell you this, Carney, I don't want that little bastard hanging around her!"

Welles was subdued. "Jesus. I didn't know that. Okay, I'll have a word with him." Welles was puzzled. If anything, he thought Mead was spending a great deal of extra time with *Hayley*. Maybe Hayley was right. Maybe he was losing his touch.

"It's mostly the Beatrix thing," Hayley said after a moment. "I thought you'd checked into her. There's *still* something odd about her, you know?"

"She's beautiful. She's bright. She's successful. Does that make her odd?"

"I gave you Beatrix," Hayley snapped, her voice rising again. "I expected you to go to work on her, to find out if she was a viable client before you plunged into that health spa thing. You didn't do it. You just jumped in. You pulled a boner! You could wreck Welles Associates!"

"It's *me* I'm wrecking, then," Welles yelled back. "It's not you. Now leave me alone!"

"The hell it's you!" Hayley screamed. "*I* put up the big money that made Welles Associates a first-rate organization. Besides, you owe it to me to do a good job on that person, anyway! She was my idea. What the hell is such a hot number about Nice? Christ, if all I could come up with to get people out to see a show was to play it in Nice, I think I'd quit and go back to writing obituaries!"

Welles knotted up with rage. He had started out his newspaper career writing obituaries. It was only after five years that he had finally been shifted to sports stories. He *hated* mention of it. That damned Hayley! She knew exactly where to hurt him!

"And that little lesbian. She was right, you know. She called you on every one of your mistakes. And you wound up letting Beatrix handle her dismissal."

"Listen, Hayley—"

"This is the first chance I've had to tell you what I think of the year's profit report at Welles Associates," said Hayley, switching to a subdued, snide, acid-dripping delivery. "Your profit-line is down, buster! Everybody else in the portfolio shows a profit-line gain—you show a drop! My God, Carney! What's it all about?"

"The damned books don't tell the real story," Welles said, his voice hollow. "I told you, part of that is the buy-out on the Gomez deal."

"Another Welles headliner!" sneered Hayley.

"Shut up, you intolerant bitch!" yelled Welles. "And you listen to me."

"No, Carney. You listen to me. Keep your nose clean with that French bed bunny, and keep your eyes on the ball at the office, or you're going to be .

one of those *retired* executives before you know it. And I'm the one that's going to retire you."

Welles was breathing so hard he could not form words. He reached out and grabbed Hayley by the arms, holding her tightly.

"Just shut up about your damned money and your damned genius! The Frenchwoman means nothing to me! I still love you, for God's sake! But you won't let me show it!"

"Huh!" growled Hayley, trying to struggle out of his grip. "Get your filthy hands off me!"

"I don't think much of your taste in guests, either, if you really want to know. That Senator Miles is one of the raunchiest loud-mouthed jerks I've ever met in my life."

"Still," Hayley said softly, "he does have a great deal of clout where it counts."

"Ah! He'll double-cross you the first chance he gets, even if he's promised to play ball with you!"

"You tend to your paramours and I'll tend to mine, Carney!"

"Your work, with the Prescott Foundation, doesn't stand up to public scrutiny either, Hayley. I'm talking about all that money you've got in South Africa now. The media is going to latch onto that soon, baby. And even *I* won't be able to help you. I'm warning you—"

Hayley slipped her arm out of her husband's grasp. He glowered at her. There was sweat on her skin now. She looked a trifle upset, if not shaken.

"I saw Abbey in tears a few minutes ago," Welles went on, digging in now. "I assume that's your work, too. My God, Hayley! You can't even keep a civil tongue in your head with your own offspring, can you?"

"Just keep your mouth shut about Abbey!" Hayley cried. "She's mine—not yours!"

"You're doing a great job of alienating her from you," Welles went on, riding the crest of a wave of anger that was building now, in reaction to his own humiliation. "If you don't look out, you won't even have her around here to kick in the face anymore!"

"What do you mean by that?" Hayley's face turned white.

"She's just as dispensable as your sister, isn't she? Oh, I heard some of the load you gave Meggy! Your own flesh and blood. I don't understand you, Hayley! You just ain't human!"

"She did a dumb thing," Hayley said defensively. "I had to tell her so."

"There are ways and there are ways, love," said Welles in a sarcastic tone. "And you just don't seem to know the ways that work!"

"Judgments sound great coming from you, Carney —a man who can't even do his own job right!"

"I'll admit you gave me Beatrix. But I'm going to be the one to put her over! Not you! Now just shut up about Beatrix la Belle and Welles Associates! I'll pull this one off as the best of my career—you wait and see!"

Hayley shook her head angrily. "You're too stupid to do the job right! I'm shocked at you, Carney! By God, if *I* were running that health spa thing, I'd show you!"

"Step right up, Hayley!" yelled Carney, his face red now, the perspiration pouring off him. "Show and tell!"

Hayley was so enraged she couldn't speak.

" 'Anything you can do, I can do better!' That's your theme song, isn't it?" Carney persisted.

Hayley stared at him a long time, her face screwed up and emanating hostility. Then she turned around and stalked off the widow's walk and into the mansion, leaving Welles out in the open air.

"I'll pull this thing off, the best of my career, or else—" Carney vowed, looking up at the sky for witness. "And then we'll see where the two of us are, my friend!"

BOOK TWO:
ALL POINTS

CHAPTER SIX

Hayley Welles braked her canary-yellow Lamborghini Countach and stepped out onto the asphalt pavement. Shithead, she thought, watching the goggle-eyed Mexican teenage valet stare down her blouse. Her face remained expressionless.

She was used to having her tits stared at, but the valet was standing just a little too close. The punk. He probably didn't even have a green card. Servants didn't know their places anymore.

She ignored him and breezed through the Santa Anita clubhouse. She could not wait for the stakes race, could not wait to watch the expression on the face of Austin Bush, her former spouse—her second, his fourth—when the great humiliation occurred.

He was easy to spot in the clubhouse, what with his white hair and his regal bearing, a glass of champagne in one hand, a *Daily Racing Form* in the other.

"Hello, Austin," she said phlegmatically.

He glanced up briefly.

"Hello, Hayley. Didn't know you were in town."

"Don't let me disturb you," she said airily. "On the Coast for business."

"What are you doing here at the track? I thought you didn't like horses."

"I came here for the stakes race." She looked around to see how many other movers and shakers of the great state of California were present. "I think you like horses more than you like women."

Austin returned to his *Daily Racing Form* and shook his head. "I'm not going to get into it with you today, Hayley."

She looked at the paper. "Horses. Are you into bestiality these days?"

Austin glared at her. "If I went to bed with you, I must be."

"Is that supposed to be funny?" Hayley said with mock indignance.

"I have a colt running in the stakes race, and I'm trying to find out the morning line—*if* that's okay with you?" He went back to the paper.

"Of course. What do I care? I'm only your former wife, not a horse."

She inspected the crowd, searching for Roland Graeme. He had promised to meet her.

Austin saw that she wasn't really leaving. "Do you want to bet on a winner?" he asked.

"I usually do—except in your case."

Austin ignored the marital barb. "Bet on Flap Doodle in the eighth."

"I didn't know you were a tout. Too bad you don't know as much about women as you know about horses."

"Here it is." Austin pointed at the *Daily Racing Form*. "Three to one. It'll probably go down to five to two."

Hayley yawned. "How exciting."

"He's *my* colt. He's a sure thing. I'm betting two hundred thousand."

"On *one* horse?" Hayley looked surprised.

"He can't lose. Look at the rest of the field." He read aloud the names of the competing thoroughbreds. "They don't have a prayer. Look at their times."

"That's a lot of money." She licked her lips. "I bet you'd hate to lose it."

"It's money in the bank."

"Are you betting across the board?"

"Of course not. I never hedge my bets. Two hundred thousand to win."

"What if he runs second?"

"Impossible. This is one of the best horses I've ever bred." Austin watched the odds changing on the tote board. "There, I told you. He's down to five to two. You can't fool the fans. Are you going to watch the post parade?"

"Oh, there's Roland." She smiled at a tall darkhaired man wearing a tweed suit.

"Who?"

"He owns a horse, too. It's also running in the eighth race."

"What's its name?"

"Sheet Lightning."

Austin glanced at the *Daily Racing Form*, then at the tote board. He chuckled. "Forget it. He's going off at twelve to one." He read Sheet Lightning's track time. "Do your friend Roland a favor and tell him to withdraw his horse. He'll save himself a lot of money. A minute fifteen for six furlongs on this track is pretty awful."

He placed his champagne on the bar and fingered the pair of binoculars hanging from his neck.

Hayley noticed a big-breasted blonde giving her ex a smoldering gaze. "Who's that out-of-work actress?"

"She's pretty, isn't she?" Austin, Hayley noted, was pleased with himself for his taste in women.

"Too fat in the ass. No wonder she can't get parts. Short legs, too."

"Are you jealous?"

Hayley laughed. "Your horses look better than she does."

"Maybe she'd like to join my stable." Austin ran his eyes down her figure.

"You missed your true calling in life. You should have been a pimp."

Disgusted with Austin, she walked over to Roland Graeme.

"Are you sure Sheet Lightning is going to win?" she asked him in a confidential tone. "If you're just imagining your nag is better than his—"

Roland smiled. It was a cute smile. Hayley felt herself, tighten, just the slightest bit. He had that bedroom look she loved. The first time she had seen that smile they had been in bed together, and she had creamed.

"Positive," he said.

"But Austin said *his* horse can't lose."

"Because he read the *Racing Form*?"

Hayley looked puzzled. "What does that have to do with it?"

Roland touched her elbow and escorted her away from the crowd.

"Sheet Lightning's bloodline on the *Racing Form* is wrong," he said in a low tone.

"So?"

"What do you mean, 'so?' "

"What difference does *that* make?"

"A thoroughbred is nothing without his bloodline. Without it, a thoroughbred is just a horse. Haven't you ever heard of stud farms?"

Hayley grinned and moved closer to him. "I'd like to."

"Is that all you ever think about?"

She shrugged. "You brought it up."

"I'm talking about Sheet Lightning."

"How do you know his bloodline is wrong?"

Roland lowered his voice so she could barely hear him. "I know a proofreader on the *Daily Racing Form*. I paid him to alter Sheet Lightning's bloodline."

"Won't somebody know?"

"How? This is the first time he's raced. Nobody knows anything about him."

"What about the people who watched his workout? They must suspect something's fishy."

Roland smiled crookedly. "I told my jockey to dog it."

"What if he reports you? I mean, this is obviously illegal."

"I told him Sheet Lightning's fetlock is weak, and to go easy on him. Anyway, he wants to win as much as I do."

"You've thought of everything."

Roland glanced at the tote board along the perimeter of the track. "And look at the size of the handle on this race. All those people betting should up the odds on my horse. I'm going to clean up."

Hayley glared at Austin, thinking with vindictiveness about all her quarrels and problems with him. "I'm going to bet on your horse, too. Are you sure he's going to win?"

"He was sired by Spectacular Bid."

"That's good?"

"Good! That horse is one of the fastest that ever lived. I've seen him race. Six furlongs is Sheet Lightning's best distance, and that's what he's running today."

"You'd better be right." She glowered at him. She was so close to putting something over on Austin—and she *needed* something to get charged up about. She simply *had* to have it come off right.

"I *am* right," Roland said serenely.

"Somebody else told me the same thing only a few minutes ago. You can't *both* be right."

"Austin? Sure, but he doesn't know what I know."

"Are you betting across the board?"

"Only chickens do that. I always bet to win."

"How much?"

"Fifty thousand dollars."

"That's not much." She gave him a little-girl expression.

Surprised, Roland said, "At twelve to one? That's six hundred thousand bucks. And the odds might go up by the time the pari-mutuel windows shut down."

"I have thirty thousand I want to bet."

"Bet it all on Sheet Lightning."

"You'd better be right." She was sounding like a broken record.

"You really want to win, don't you?"

"I really want Austin to lose," she said through gritted teeth. And lose to the guy who's getting it on with me, she added to herself.

"Some of the crowd might bet on my horse when they watch the post parade, because he's a fine-looking colt, so I paid my jock an extra grand to play a little trick.'' Roland smiled smugly, something like a cobra about to swallow a mongoose.

"Is this illegal, too?'' Hayley's eyes sparkled with excitement.

"No. I'm not going to drug the horse. For Christ's sake, what do you think I am? A crook?''

"What's the jockey going to do?''

He looked at her archly. "I'll tell you during the post parade.''

"You rat! Tell me now.'' She slapped his shoulder playfully.

"Go put down your bet. Oh, there's the trumpet. Hear it? The post parade's going to start. Bet now. Nobody'll be at the pari-mutuels.''

Hayley stood in line at a pari-mutuel window. The only reason she had come to this race was to see Roland's "foolproof scheme'' win the stakes race. She knew that Austin had his heart set on winning the race, and she had her heart set on watching him lose. In fact, it was she who had suggested to Roland he enter his colt in this particular race—so she could see Austin's face when he lost.

Her heart thumped crazily as she placed her bet. Not only would her machinations crush Austin and deprive him of his two hundred thousand dollars, but she would come away with something like three hundred and thirty thousand profit herself. Money—that was what it was all about!

If only she could *believe* Roland. Austin was a professional horse breeder. He should really know more about horses than Roland, yet Roland seemed to know what he was talking about, and he was a devious son of a bitch, no matter how you looked at it.

Whom could she trust? She did not actually know.

Her old anger against Austin finally decided her to go against him. It was very unladylike, but she ached to see him lose.

Palms sweaty, she stepped away from the window. The old cashier had not even blinked at the size of her bet. It wasn't his money. What did he care?

The out-of-work actress, whose name Hayley could not recall, brushed past her. "I'm sorry," she said fulsomely. "Are you Roland's new lover?"

"What business is it of yours?" Hayley snapped.

"He used to be mine."

"How you *do* get around."

What's-her-name grinned. "I can't really help it if I'm in demand."

"Everywhere except at the box office."

What's-her-name was taken aback at first, then beamed, "Oh, you *do* recognize me?"

"Yes. You come from the 'Silicone Valley.' "

So what if she wore a forty-inch D-cup, thought Hayley. They were fake like everything else in Hollywood. They had to be. God simply didn't make them like that.

"Jealous, honey?" cooed What's-her-name.

"Why don't you go out with Austin Bush? He likes cheap phonies."

"There's nothing phony about me."

"Just cover up those plastic surgery scars, so he doesn't find out the truth when he's rolling you."

"Your jealousy is going straight to your head. You've *got* to calm down. How do you like Roland?"

"Now look who's jealous."

What's-her-name laughed. "Of Roland? Does he still stuff a sock in his underpants to make his thing look bigger?"

"His *thing* works. Not like Austin's."

"I don't blame it for not working for you. You're not the most feminine of women."

"Am I supposed to strip every time a man sets eyes on me, like you do? Isn't that how you get your jobs?"

"Rich bitch."

They glowered at each other belligerently.

Roland spotted them and, figuring they might start pulling each other's hair, yanked Hayley away to watch the post parade.

"Have a nice day," said What's-her-name.

"Have a nice day yourself," said Hayley. If she had a knife, she'd . . .

"Come on," drawled Roland.

"How can you stand that slut?" Hayley wondered. "You should hear the things she said about you."

"I can't stand her. That's why we broke up. Forget her. She isn't worth it."

He practically dragged her to the stands to watch the parade.

"Her legs are much too short," Hayley observed.

"The horse's?"

"No. That actress's."

"Forget her. Look this way. There. Number Six. That's Sheet Lightning. Keep your eyes on him. See?"

He gazed through his binoculars, then handed them over to her.

"He's a pretty colt," she said, holding the binoculars to her eyes.

"See the lather on his neck?"

"Oh, *no!* I see it. That's a bad sign, isn't it?"

He stepped closer to her and whispered in her ear. She thought he was flirting at first. He said, "Normally it is, but it's not lather."

"Of course it is."

"I told the jockey to take a sponge soaked with soapy water when he rode in the post parade. Watch him. Every once in a while he runs his hand over the colt's mane."

"He's petting him."

"That's what it looks like. Actually, he's squeezing the soapy sponge. That's soapy water running down the colt's neck, not lather."

"How many other tricks do you have up your sleeve?"

"That should raise the odds on Sheet Lightning. At least it keeps them from going down. I'm not going to place my bet till the last possible moment, when the odds are the highest."

"Why did you tell me to bet my wad before?" Hayley was indignant.

"It's going to be a mad stampede to the pari-mutuels now. A lot of people get stuck at the end of the line and don't get a chance to bet before post time. I wanted to make sure you got down your bet."

"What about you? Why are you standing here? Shouldn't you be rushing to a window?"

"I already have somebody carrying my bet. He'll place it at just the right moment."

They found a seat high in the grandstand. It was the opposite of the theater. At the racetrack the most expensive seats were the highest and farthest away. The nearer you were to the track, the less you had to pay. Most of the poor stood packed in a crowd, hard by the track.

Hayley and Roland had their section to themselves with plenty of room to spare.

"What if he breaks his leg?" Hayley said, just to bug Roland.

Roland stared at her. "Why do you have to look on the bad side of everything?"

"You said Sheet Lightning can't lose."

"I can't guarantee it," he admitted irritably. "There aren't any guarantees. This *is* a horse race."

She took his binoculars and trained them on Sheet Lightning. She admired the colt's shimmering muscles, sleek and glistening under the afternoon sun. The horses entered the gate one at a time.

The actress suddenly blocked Hayley's view. She and Austin were standing just in front of her, one row lower. What's-her-name was thrusting her tits and butt out, squirming, to give Austin an eyeful. He ogled her low-cut blouse and tight jeans. How could she breathe in those things? Did she buy them at a garage sale? She was making a damned fool of herself. What some people would do for money! thought Hayley.

She turned away. She wanted Austin to lose this race now more than ever.

"They're off!" announced the loudspeaker.

The gates slammed open. In front of the backdrop of the purple San Gabriel Mountains, the colts galloped down the backstretch. Roland snatched the binoculars out of her hands.

"He's still at twelve to one," he said and jumped to his feet.

Hayley stood beside him. Everybody was standing and yelling. Tension vibrated through the crowd.

"I can't see," Hayley complained. "Which one is Sheet Lightning?"

"Look at his jockey. He's wearing pink and orange silks."

"I don't see him in front." God, she thought. What if this damned Roland was as phony as Austin?

"He's in the middle. About fourth or fifth."

"Where's Flap Doodle?" That was Austin's pride and joy.

"Second."

"Damn!" she muttered.

"Oh, no!"

"What?" Her eyes widened. She heard a noise like a gunshot.

"One of the colts broke down."

"That sound?"

"A bone cracking in the leg."

"I told you it was going to happen. I *told* you! Is it Sheet Lightning?"

"I can't tell— Yes! No! It was the colt beside him. He's pulling up lame at the turn. See him fall back?"

She watched one horse hobble uncertainly and drift back to last place. "Was it Flap Doodle?"

"No. He's first."

"Where's Sheet Lightning?"

"He's making his move in the homestretch. He's passed two colts, and he's challenging Flap Doodle."

Hayley closed her eyes. "I can't watch." Her hands trembled at her sides.

She glanced up at Roland. His knuckles, as he gripped the binoculars, had turned white. His body was still; he was not breathing. He reminded her of a statue.

"Jesus Christ," said Roland.

"What's happening?"

"Sheet Lightning's challenging Flap Doodle on the rail. Sheet Lightning wants to pass on the rail, but Flap Doodle is shutting down the gap."

"Is that fair?"

"Wait!"

"Now what? Christ, let's get this over with. I can't stand it anymore." She peeked down at the colts.

"Flap Doodle's lugging out. My jockey's going to his whip. Sheet Lightning's moving up on the rail! They're neck and neck. They're almost to the wire."

"I'm leaving." Her heart was pounding so hard it sounded like the crowd clapping.

"It's over."

"Who won?" she demanded, her throat dry.

". . . by a neck."

"I can't hear you! It's too noisy!"

"From here it looked like Sheet Lightning."

"We won? We won!"

They watched the number of the winning horse light the tote board.

"That's right," said Roland with a gusty sigh of relief. "What did I tell you?"

Hayley gloated triumphantly over Austin. Austin paid no attention to her. Face haggard, back hunched, he plodded dejectedly toward the clubhouse.

Hayley had never seen him look so awful. She almost felt sorry for him. She checked her pity. He did not deserve it—not after the way he had treated her when they were married, the way he had cheated on her with scores of women. Had he thought he was fooling her? She had recognized the signs: the long hairs on his jackets, the phone calls from throaty voices who supposedly had dialed wrong numbers when she answered.

She had even been forced to put up with the cheap boasts of women who bragged to her face that they had laid him. She had known most of them were lying to make her jealous, but not all of them were.

"Let's go to Ma Maison's to celebrate."

First, she would go over to Austin and rub salt in the wound just a little bit. She strode over to him jauntily.

"I didn't bet on your horse," she said brightly.

He regarded her mournfully. "Lucky you," he muttered.

"You see, you don't have all the answers."

"Why did you come over here? To make me feel worse?"

"I thought you would like to congratulate me for winning."

"You made my day." He turned away from her and continued walking.

"If you had asked me, I could have told you who was going to win."

Austin stopped, then faced her. "Is that your main joy in life—making everybody feel like hell?"

"Can't you understand?" she asked angrily.

"I understand. You want everything your own way."

He walked away from her and did not look back.

She returned to Roland. "That is one of the most horrible men I ever met. I hope he goes bankrupt."

"Austin Bush? It'll never happen. A couple of hundred thousand dollars is a drop in the bucket to him. Hell, you should know that. You were married to him, weren't you?"

"Regrettably, yes. A lapse in taste on my part."

"Hey, look!"

Hayley turned. Roland Graeme was pointing to a familiar figure.

"There's John Forsythe."

"He comes here a lot. He's an aficionado."

Hayley sometimes wondered what she saw in Roland. He was so *innocent*. Nouveau riche, too. As a rule, she looked down her nose at those hustling, bustling types. Roland had made his fortune off a chain of fast-food restaurants, which he had expanded from a single one. He had nowhere near as much money as she. Who did, for that matter? But she did not hold *that* against him. He wasn't sexy, but he was good-looking. He had absolutely no taste, knew nothing of the arts, and was a bore in conversation. Sometimes she wondered what she saw in him. And sometimes she *knew* that she saw nothing in him, that he was simply someone to fill up a gap.

Another thing that annoyed her was his curiosity about her husband's performance in bed. It was none of his goddamned business. Christ, she was tired of California. Even with the charge she'd just gotten out of shafting Austin Bush where it hurt the most—right in the fetlocks—she needed a change.

She'd bed down with Roland one more time, get out of him what she could get, and take a flight out of Los Angeles, right after closing up the Benedict Canyon place. She was only using it to crash in, anyway—as Abbey might put it.

That Abbey! she thought. She had lit out of Scobie Hills so fast, after the weekend party, that Hayley never had a chance to check out where she was going. Damned little fool. Why couldn't she stay at the mansion for the summer and—

Hayley laughed. Rest? Would *she* do that? Hell no! Maybe Abbey was kind of a chip off the old block . . .

Hayley was feeling restless again. She *needed* someone sexy. Someone sexy and *important*. Who the hell was important anymore? Carney was important—but he was balling that Frenchwoman. That was part of the image-making process. He'd done the same thing to her. The thing for Hayley to do was to get it somewhere else—and let him burn about it when he found it out!

Where the hell could she find somebody big enough to make a little extracurricular sack time *interesting?*

CHAPTER SEVEN

Abbey Martin met an interesting man in La Coupole Café in Montparnasse. He was thin, dark, in his twenties, and looked tough, but not stupid. It wasn't until she had gone out on the town with him a few times that she found out what his calling was. And then, even the unshakable Abbey was a bit disconcerted. No. Truth was, she was shocked.

One spring evening they drank Pernod together on the sidewalk in front of La Coupole, then they went downstairs and danced among artistic Parisian types: painters, prima donnas, poets, musicians, actors.

François Lucien got bored. He did not like the artists.

"Art is the opiate of the masses," he said.

"I thought that was religion," said Abbey lightly.

"They both are," François announced. "The capitalist bosses use them to convince the masses that they should be happy with the little they have. That way, the bosses hold onto their millions while the masses watch TV and go to church."

Abbey decided not to tell him her mother was one of the richest women in the world. "You sound like one of those revolutionaries."

François did not say anything. He stopped dancing, and they sat down at a small marble-topped table. They watched the café patrons dancing and drinking.

"They're all so phony," said François. "You see that guy over there?" He nodded toward a twentyish blond, who was languorously petting a model-thin redhead's arm. Her face was plastered with makeup. "He's from London. He's just out of Oxford, or some other blue-blood university, and he comes over here and pretends he's a great painter. Maybe he's done five paintings in his entire life. Six months from now, he'll be back in London going to law school or medical school with his banker father footing the bill."

"How do you know? Maybe he *will* become a great painter."

François sneered. "No, I've seen his type before. They're a dime a dozen in Paris. It's an act, a pose. As soon as he loses his room-and-board money, he'll run back to the fold and become a shyster, shaking the rich down with a glib tongue and no scruples."

"Where did you learn to speak such good English?" Abbey asked, in order to break the pattern of François's thought.

"I went to the University of California at Berkeley. Let's get out of here."

"Let's stay," Abbey responded stubbornly. "I like to watch the people."

"I have some joints at my flat. It's too crowded here."

"Who's that? He looks interesting."

A good-looking thirtyish man with an incipient beard idled past them, his eyes bloodshot, his steps uncertain.

François observed him superciliously. "That's what's called an *acteur-manqué*. He did one movie the critics liked, then made the mistake of having an affair with the producer's wife. The producer found out and blackballed him, called him an alcoholic and an unreliable hophead. It has destroyed his career—so far, anyway. The only reason the producer hired him in the first place was because he thought the guy was queer. The producer's wife has a reputation for being a nymphomaniac, and he hired this queer actor so she couldn't fool around with him."

"What happened to her?"

"She had a miscarriage. She's filthy rich, but she can't seem to have a kid. The word is, she's had half a dozen miscarriages. She blames them on her husband."

"That must be why she had the affair with the actor—to see if she *could* have a child."

"I don't know. I don't know what she's trying to prove. She doesn't have my sympathy. She has so much money she can spend all her time screwing everybody who wants a quickie. She doesn't have to work for a living."

"How do you know so much about her?"

"It's no secret. She comes here once in a while. She came on to me once."

"Is she any good in bed?" said Abbey, her eyes catty.

"I didn't do anything with her," said François, looking pissed-off. "I can't stand the idle rich."

"Maybe she turned you down, huh?"

"How did we get onto this subject?" François was still irritated.

"You gave me dirty thoughts."

"Sex again."

"What else is there?" Abbey grinned, her teeth perfect.

"Justice."

"How boring. You get that in a courtroom."

"That's the last place you get it!" he sneered.

"You ought to be a professor."

"Do you like professors?"

"No. But I went with a rock guitarist once. He gave me the clap."

"That'll teach you."

"Then I had an affair with a professional tennis player."

"You really get around."

"I had to get an abortion," she said dryly.

"You like living life in the fast lane, don't you?"

"I don't like being bored."

"If you ask me, you're living a selfish, aimless life."

"I didn't ask you," she said peevishly. "You sound like my mother."

"Does your mother give you joints and coke?"

"I don't want to talk about her. I want some Dubonnet."

"I want to get out of here. I told you I don't like these phonies."

"Drink your—what is it?"

"Absinthe."

"How can you stand that green stuff?" Abbey shivered. "It's too bitter."

François stood up. He looked hot and sweaty. "I'm leaving. Are you sure you don't want to come?"

"See, now you're the one with the dirty mind."

"Christ. Listen, I've got hash, acid, speed, downers, junk, black beauties, designer drugs—you name it."

"Yes, but why do you want me to go with you?"
She grinned, enjoying his discomfort.

"I want to straighten you out."

"On my back? This conversation is getting to be
X-rated." She giggled.

"You're wasting your life. You need something to
believe in. I know you're smart, and you can understand what I'm saying."

"I know what you're saying. You're trying to
seduce me."

"I'm leaving this goddamn dump."

"Oh, all right." She stuck her tongue out at him
in an obscene way.

"Good."

She stood up and pressed her hip against his thigh.
He tried to slip his arm around her waist, but she
stepped away. He made for the steps that led up to
the sidewalk. She came up behind him and brushed
her knuckles against his narrow round buttocks.

She walked unsteadily on her feet. She had not
realized she had drunk so much.

François tried to put his arm around her waist
again. She rebuffed him and ran onto the sidewalk.
The night breeze felt good on her face, puffy because
of the booze. At the corner, an old man with purple
lips ogled her and slobbered. What an ugly old man!
she thought. Like an old woman. Like her mother,
the deluded bitch in heat, running around with a guy
half her age, or less. Maybe that was why she had
sent Abbey away to all those private European schools:
to get privacy for herself at home, so she could fool
around with every man in sight. Abbey gritted her
teeth. How she hated mommy dearest, who totally
ignored her. Where was François?

She descended the steps at the Metro entrance,

stumbled, grabbed the steel rail, and made it to the platform. François caught up to her.

They rode underground to the Latin Quarter, then walked out onto the Boulevard St. Michael. Stars crowded the indigo sky and dripped light over Paris.

"Do you live here?" she asked.

"Over there." He made a vague gesture.

"Away from all the greedy rich on the Right Bank."

They headed down a narrow, crooked cobblestone alley, turned right, and entered a cozy bistro. In the back of it they climbed a narrow staircase to François's garret.

"This is nice," she said, looking around with interest.

"There isn't much room."

"I like its ambience."

He removed a glassine bag of coke from his desk drawer, dipped a miniature spoon into the white powder, and handed the spoon to Abbey, who lifted it to her nose and snorted.

She felt the rush. Her mind must really be screwed up, what with the booze and all, she thought. She watched François snort two spoonfuls.

"How about a joint now?" François suggested.

"I'm totally fucked up. Why not?"

"Now that we're alone, I can tell you about the revolution."

"Is that why you lured me here?" She sat down in an armchair and leered at him.

"Have you ever read Bakunin?"

"No."

"You Americans are all alike. You don't know anything about politics."

"Who is he?"

"He was a nihilist. We are nihilists. We want to destroy corrupt capitalism, so communism can supersede it."

He lit a marijuana joint wrapped in pink cigarette paper, inhaled the smoke, held it in his lungs, and passed the joint to her. She followed suit.

The room started to spin around her. She was glad she was sitting down. Had she ever been this polluted before?

"You're a terrorist?" she murmured.

"We don't flinch from using terror."

Abbey wanted to laugh. What if he found out she had a rich family? Would he kill her?

"I think I'm seeing double," she said.

"The only way to free ourselves from the greedy, sadistic capitalists is to terrorize them, so their society collapses."

"Are you the only member? I remember when I was a kid I invented a secret club. I was the only one in it." She giggled. Wisps of smoke trickled out of her mouth.

"Don't be ridiculous!" he snapped in anger. "We have many members. We call ourselves POW, People of the World."

She smiled, pointed her index finger at him, as though it were a gun, thumb raised, and said, "Pow! Pow, pow!"

"You ridiculous child! This isn't a game. I thought you were more mature than this."

"It's all these drugs you're giving me. I feel giddy."

She also felt a little nauseous. She wondered if she was going to be sick.

"Do you want some hash now?" he asked.

She exhaled smoke from the joint. "I don't know. Are you trying to turn me into a dope fiend?"

"I can give you skag if you want."

"What's that?"

"Heroin."

"No."

"I have a needle and everything."

"No. I don't want to be a junkie."

"You can sniff it if you want. Then you won't become a junkie."

She squinted at him suspiciously. "I don't believe that."

He looked malevolent to her now. Through the marijuana smoke, his black eyes seemed to be hatching plots to destroy her. She should have known. Men were all alike. They wanted to manipulate her, enslave her, put their cocks inside her, and then leave her to die, alone. God, she felt morbid.

It must be the dope working on her. Maybe. Her thoughts seemed to make sense though. It was scary. She needed someone to trust. She wanted to trust her mother, but *she* was the last person in the world she could trust. Mom must be out of her mind, running around in a push-up bra like Madonna, thinking she was sixteen. How could you trust someone like that? Next she would be doing centerfolds for *Playboy*.

Why wasn't François trying to take her pants off? He sure was slow on the uptake. She thought the French were supposed to be fast operators. She felt so dizzy. She might black out any second.

What was wrong with him? Wasn't he normal? All men wanted to do was fuck her. Fuck and run.

"We want you to join our group," he said.

"Where are the rest of you?"

"They're around. What do you say?"

"Why aren't they here?"

"We had to sound you out first. You could have been a spy, or a rich kid for all we knew."

"That's why you came on to me at the café? You'd already staked me out?"

"Something like that." He grinned.

"All right, I guess I'll join. At least you're not phony like most of the people I know."

And it was a good way to get back at her mom, she thought. That crazy woman. And she was supposed to be normal! If that was normal, what was abnormal? It was scary thinking about it. There were no measuring scales anymore that worked.

"Are you sure?" he pressed her.

"Of course."

She hated being trashed by everybody, especially men and mommy dearest. Mom would be sick at the very idea of her associating with terrorists. The scum of the earth, she would call them. Sleaze.

Abbey remembered her erstwhile lover, the tennis pro, with all his mistresses hanging around his neck. He would not like her terrorist friends either. He was a redneck Texan. To hell with him, too . . . for knocking her up . . . for pretending it wasn't his child . . . for being a goddamned liar.

She stood up and staggered toward the little window. She stuck her head outside. She could see the Seine on the right and a portion of a flying buttress on Notre Dame de Paris. To the left, she saw a wizened old man selling roasted chestnuts on the street corner. His hands, like lobster claws, hovered over the shallow pan, rolling the chestnuts around it with metal tongs.

She felt as though she was going to faint. She stumbled back to her chair.

"Nice ass," said François.

She did not say anything. What was she supposed to say? Thanks? Thanks for what? It wasn't *her* doing she had one. It was just there. Maybe she deserved part of the credit, since she didn't overeat.

She fluttered her eyelids at him. For some reason it seemed to take a lot of effort. Then she grinned and winked at him.

"You want to get fucked?" he wondered.

"You have such a way with words."

While he set to taking off his clothes, she began to unbutton her blouse. She fell asleep before she reached the last button.

She opened her eyes. The sun was out and had painted the little white curtain over the window gold.

She felt like hell. Why did she always wake up in the morning feeling depressed? The back of her throat was dry, her eyes sore, her muscles tense. She felt so lonely she wanted to scream.

The morning was the worst part of her day. It never failed. She wanted to keep on sleeping, but was too tense, and she could not. She rolled around under the covers searching for a comfortable position, finding none.

What had happened last night? She scanned the garret. She was alone in François's bed. How many other women had slept in it? Did he screw her? She couldn't remember.

She rolled over in bed again and hugged the pillow. She didn't not like French sheets. They were thick and raspy like sandpaper. How could the French stand sleeping in them? And they used wax paper for toilet paper. Why did they like hard things pressed against their flesh? She liked soft things: silk sheets, silk panties, silk peignoirs.

She wished she had an Alka-Seltzer. The inside of her stomach was bubbling like molten lava.

She realized she was naked. François must have undressed her. It figured.

A key turned in the lock. The door opened, and François entered, a fresh *baguette* in one hand, a jar of apricot jam in the other.

"*Petit déjeuner*," he said.

She grimaced. "Where have you been?"

"To get us something to eat."

"I need something to drink."

He retreated into the hallway and returned with a bottle of Perrier. "This is good for your digestion."

She sat up in bed and drank from the green bottle.

François retrieved a knife from his desk. He inserted it into the jam jar, dug out some jam, ripped a piece of bread off the loaf, spread the jam on the bread, and gobbled it down.

"We have to eat quickly," he told her.

"Why?"

"We have a job to do."

"A job?"

"We're going to knock over a bank," he said, matter-of-factly.

"What?"

"A bank. Have some bread and let's go."

She did not feel like eating. She kept drinking the Perrier. "Are you joking?"

"No. I never joke when it comes to the revolution."

"I don't know anything about robbing banks."

"We'll tell you what we want you to do."

Robbing banks, she thought. What next? Then she thought: who cared? Nobody. She might as well go through with it. Christ, it might even be a kick!

"I thought you hated the capitalists," she said.

"We do."

"Then why do you want money like them?"

"We need it for the cause. Get dressed. I'll meet you downstairs on the sidewalk."

François stuffed more bread in his mouth, then left the garret.

Abbey climbed out of bed, her head pounding, her knees wobbly. François was right. Millionaires were all a bunch of crooks, so why not rob their banks? Do unto others as they do unto you.

She struggled to get into her clothes. Yesterday's clothes. She needed *new* clothes.

Now she felt lightfooted. Odd. She practically floated down the steps to the bistro, then outside onto the sidewalk.

"Come on," said François.

They walked to the end of the block and got into a black Citroen parked at the side of the Boulevard St. Michel. Two young men with short beards, black leather jackets, and opaque black sunglasses sat in the back seat. They said nothing.

"We're going to hit the Crédit Lyonnais Bank at the other end of town," said François.

"What do you want me to do?" she asked.

"Drive the car. You can drive, can't you?"

"Yes, but I never drove one of these."

"Watch." François showed her how to work the gearshift.

"Can they speak English?" She nodded to the two in the back seat.

"No."

"I want to ask you one thing."

"What?"

"Did you fuck me last night?"

François smiled. "Don't you remember?"

"I can't remember much of anything that happened last night."

"Typical bourgeois concern over morality," he sighed. "No, I didn't."

"Why not?"

"It would have been too much like necrophilia. You were dead to the world. Let's trade places."

They climbed out of the Citroen. Abbey took the driver's seat, François the passenger's.

"Point me in the right direction," she said.

"This'll give you practice."

She pulled out into traffic on the Boulevard St. Michel.

"You do have a driver's license?" he asked.

She nodded. "An international driver's license."

"You well-heeled Americans. You have everything."

They crossed the Pont Neuf to the Right Bank and drove east. A *bateau mouche* sailed by them on the Seine toward Notre Dame. A barge with a dog loping across its deck sailed in the opposite direction.

They turned down the Rue de Richelieu.

"There. Park in front of that Crédit Lyonnais," François instructed her.

Abbey parked the Citroen.

François and his two cohorts pulled Beretta 9 mm. automatics out of their waistbands, checked the magazine loads to see that they were full, slapped them back into the butts, and returned the automatics to their waistbands, where they were concealed by their leather jackets.

Abbey eyed the automatics with surprise. "You're not going to kill anyone, are you?"

"We will if we have to," said François. "We cannot fail the revolution."

"Now what?"

"Keep the motor idling. As soon as we come back, drive us across the Seine and toward Montparnasse. We have another car there waiting for us."

"Okay."

"If a *flic* comes and spots the car exhaust, get out and pretend you're inspecting the engine. They get suspicious when they see a car idling too long in front of a bank."

François and his silent cohorts lifted empty brief-cases from the floor of the car, stepped onto the sidewalk, and made for the bank.

Abbey still felt skittish, faint. She had not eaten, and her hangover lingered. She admonished herself to keep on her toes until the completion of the heist.

What would her mother say if she could see her now? The thought brought a smile to Abbey's pale lips. Then she thought of François. Should she take it as an insult that he had not tried to make love to her last night? Men usually drooled at the very idea of getting her naked in bed. François had seen her in the raw and yet, apparently, had done nothing.

She would not want him to do anything while she was blacked out. But maybe he *had* tried something— and had failed. She wondered.

She regarded her face in the rearview mirror. Her reflection brought a gasp from her lips. She looked sickly pale—ghastly and half-dead.

She dug her hairbrush out of her purse and ran it through her hair. She would wash it after the heist. What was taking them so long?

The engine sounded as though it might die; she revved it up with pressure on the gas pedal. Christ, what if they had been arrested?

Her fingers nervously drummed a tattoo on the steering wheel. A pedestrian stood still on the sidewalk and stared in at her tits. She smiled at the geezer, so he'd leave her alone. At that age, he would not take her smile as encouragement to come on to her . . . she hoped. He could dream about her if he wanted, play with it in his pocket and have her in his mind. That was all.

He wandered away.

Three men pelted out of the Crédit Lyonnais; François and his two accomplices, briefcases and automatics in their hands. She swung open the car door for them.

They thrust themselves into the Citroen. "Go!" said François, his door still open.

Abbey accelerated.

Holding his bloody head, a bank guard charged out of the Crédit Lyonnais onto the sidewalk, a revolver in his hand. François shut his door with a slam. Abbey pulled out into traffic. A Peugeot behind her blasted its horn.

François leveled his automatic out the open window and loosed a shot at the guard, who clutched his chest in surprise. Blood leaked out through his fingers. He stepped back, fired wildly into the sidewalk, and dropped, where he made a twitching heap on the cement.

Bug-eyed, Abbey froze at the wheel.

"Let's move! Let's move!" cried François. He grabbed her wrist and shook it, his fingernails embedded in her flesh.

"You killed him," she muttered.

"He was trying to kill us!"

His screaming mouth yawned in her face, his teeth dripped saliva near her eyes.

She accelerated, shifted gears. The tires shrieked.

As soon as they crossed the Seine, François told

her to pull into an alley, then stop. Briefcases in their hands, they switched cars. François climbed into the driver's seat of a Fiat parked in the alley. The two leather-jacketed Frenchmen ducked into the back seat, Abbey into the front. The Fiat lurched forward. They drove down to the other end of the alley, then entered the Boulevard du Montparnasse, which they took to the Boulevard Raspail, François calm at the wheel.

He parked on the side of the boulevard and got out, along with Abbey. The two Frenchmen spoke briefly to François, took over the front seat of the car, and drove off, the loot stashed in the rear.

François caught up to Abbey and walked beside her toward the Dôme Café. She pulled away from him.

"Get away from me!" she said.

"What's wrong?"

"Nobody yells at me!" She strutted away huffily.

He strode after her. "I didn't yell at you."

"Yes, you did."

"I didn't mean to. I didn't want you to panic."

"I don't have to put up with this crap."

"You're spoiled rotten, that's what you are."

"And you're an animal. A killer."

He grabbed her arm. "Shhh! Hold your voice down," he hissed.

"Let me go." She freed her arm.

Two pedestrians glanced furtively and with some concern at them as they struggled with one another.

Abbey sat on a cane chair at a miniature round marble-topped table in the sidewalk café. François left her alone and browsed at a nearby bookstall. He looked up at her from time to time.

She ordered a Dubonnet. She needed *something*. Her nerves were shot. She figured a drink was the best thing to calm them, but she needed food, too. She ordered a croissant.

When she reached for the Dubonnet, she realized her hands were shaking. She leaned back in her chair. She enjoyed the sun warming her body and watched the pedestrians. She felt better now that nobody was ordering her around.

François flipped through several of the paperbacks piled on the tables set out on the sidewalk, then left that and approached her table. "Can I sit here?"

"Do I have a choice?"

"It's a question."

"If you apologize." Jesus! she sounded just like her mother!

"I told you I didn't mean it."

"Well, all right." He was a damned fool, either way, but suddenly it didn't matter.

He sat on the cane chair across from her. "You did a great job."

"Oh. No wonder you yelled at me." She crossed her legs defiantly and turned her face away from him. Let him work at it a little, she thought.

He ignored her sarcasm. "Anybody else would have panicked and crashed the car or something."

"Do you do this kind of job all the time?"

"Only when we have to." He leaned toward her, his voice low. "We can't say too much here in public."

"It's pretty thrilling, isn't it?" She felt warm and cozy somehow. What was *wrong* with her?

"And meaningful," he intoned in his lecture voice. "Better than brownnosing the corporate bosses."

"I don't know anything about that. I feel so tired all of a sudden."

She noticed his eyes seemed to be giving off sparks.

She liked to feel them caressing her body. Maybe she would fall asleep here, in his arms.

She laughed. What would her mother say if she knew she was sitting across from a bank robber and a killer—at least, *possibly* a killer? She wondered if he still had his foreskin. Did Frenchmen get circumcised?

She caught him looking at another table. She turned slightly and took in a brunette teenager staring at him and running the tip of her tongue along her lips in lascivious and blatant invitation.

"Is she trying to look cute?" Abbey asked.

"What?"

"Let's go."

She and François rode the *métro* to her Latin Quarter hotel on the Rue des Ecoles, not very far from François's bistro garret. The concierge in the lobby glanced up from his ledger at them, then returned to the ritual counting of his francs.

She and François mounted the lengthy staircase to her floor, found her room, and went inside.

"How about a joint?" said François. He withdrew one wrapped in yellow cigarette paper from his trousers pocket.

"You're full of surprises."

He lit up the joint and passed it to her. "I'm always prepared."

She inhaled the marijuana smoke, then exhaled.

"Are you prepared to get naked?"

She unbuttoned her blouse, which hung open to reveal her bra. He strode up to her. She removed her blouse. He circled behind her and unhooked the bra. Her breasts came free, but they were firm and did not fall far. From behind her, he cupped them, stroking the nipples, feeling them stiffen to his touch.

She threw herself on the bed. He jumped on it and started to remove his clothes.

She tilted her head up and cocked her ear. "What's that?"

"What?"

"Don't you hear it?"

He listened intently. "Yes. Now I do. It sounds like moaning."

"I heard it last week."

"It's coming from the wall."

"That's right."

He stood and walked to the wall. She followed him. They pressed their ears against the flowered wallpaper.

"I can hear it clearly," she said.

"So can I."

"She's moaning."

"Yes, it's definitely a woman."

"I know. She's the woman who lives next door. She's from Michigan. I've seen her downstairs eating *petit déjeuner*."

"She's not eating now." He grinned.

"She's doing it with someone. Can you hear?"

"She's moaning and saying, 'Do it. Do it.' "

"She just said, 'Oh, my God!' Did you hear? And the bedsprings are creaking."

"Did you ever see the guy who's with her?"

"No. I think she's a dyke."

"How do you know?"

"I met her at *petit déjeuner*, and she kept running her eyes up and down my body. It was creepy. She has very big black eyes, and thick eyebrows."

"Then there are two girls in there?"

"There must be, and they're doing it in the day-time like us. How do two girls do it?"

"I don't even know how two men do it, but I'll tell you one thing. I'm turned on."

"I can see it," she giggled. "So am I, but I wish *she* was doing it with a man."

He fondled her breasts again. "You can't have everything."

"Listen. She's going to have one any second now. Let's go back to the bed. It's time we had one."

She tossed off the rest of her clothes and crawled into the bed. He moved toward her and caught sight of a birdcage-shaped object with a cloth cover over it on the bureau near him.

"Do you have a parakeet?" he asked.

"That's a present from my last boyfriend."

His hand stretched toward the cover and pinched the top of it. "You shouldn't keep him covered during the day, only at night."

"I take my present wherever I go."

"I like parakeets. They have such bright, happy feathers."

Abbey was lying supine on the bed. François lifted the cover. What was revealed surprised him. It did not shock him at first—that came later—but it puzzled him.

Under the cover sat a pickle jar filled with fluid. The jar did not contain pickles, but a purplish object immersed in the fluid. It was definitely not a parakeet. Somehow it seemed familiar, but he could not place it.

"What is it?"

"My last boyfriend's present. It's a foetus."

"Christ! It's disgusting."

"I had to have an abortion, because my boyfriend pretended my baby wasn't his," she said dreamily, off in her own world, her eyes on the ceiling.

"That's *sick!*" He strode away from it. "Why don't you get rid of it?"

"You can't throw away presents. It's not polite." Her voice was distant, her eyes dim.

François hurriedly flung on his clothes. "I'm leaving. I'll see you later!"

"I thought we were going to make love—"

"I can't now. I don't like the way you sound, either."

He left the room.

Abbey stared vacantly at the armoire across from her and twisted a lock of her hair between her fingers. She wondered if she was abnormal. What did normal people do? Marry the first man who said yes to them and live happily ever after? That would be nice, but it simply hadn't happened that way to her.

What could you expect when you had a nympho for a mother? Like mother, like daughter—if there was such a saying.

From the ashtray on the little desk near the bed's headboard, she lifted François's joint and smoked it.

CHAPTER EIGHT

Staring glassy-eyed at the huge piles of brightly colored chips stacked on the green felt table in front of her, Megan Tarantino pinched herself to make sure she was not dreaming, and thought:

You're really on a roll now, Meggy!

She was winning—winning big. The blood coursed through her, the heat of excitement making her ears ring, almost shutting out the monotonous drone of the croupier's chant. Why didn't the fool say it in English? Grimly, Megan realized Hayley was right. She, Megan, *was* a fool. She had lived in Europe for seventeen years—and she *still* couldn't speak workable French *or* Italian. Hell, sometimes she couldn't even *recognize* the language being spoken.

"Place your bets," someone had told her the chanter was saying. Then, finally: "No more," which sounded like *ree-en de* something.

She split her groups, using the same rather idiotic system that had won her all the chips so far, and hunched forward to watch the wheel as it circled around and around, casting brilliant shards of re-

fracted light into her eyes—like a throbbing strobo-
scope.

As the wheel began to slow down, the clicks came
more and more slowly. Megan adjusted the Eva Gabor
stretch wig she had donned in her hotel room and
pushed the sunglasses back into position on her nose.
How anyone could see through glasses when they
slid down so easily, she had no idea.

God, is was hot inside that wig! She had felt like a
damned fool when she bought the thing, in that
dowdy back street in Pisa, but at least it covered her
head and face so nobody could recognize her. The
shades helped, too. When she had peeked at herself
in the dingy mirror of the hotel room in Monte Carlo,
she had been stunned; she looked exactly like an
over-the-hill French tart, plying her trade on the Mediterranean waterfront.

Two kibitzers stood at her elbows—both riding her
lucky streak by placing bets the same as hers. One
was a seedy Englishman, who kept saying, "Go,
love!" and the other was a fat Frenchman with a red
face and a waxed mustache. He kept muttering something in French. Megan wondered if he was proposi-
tioning her. If only she could understand the stupid
language!

"*Voilà*!" cried the fat Frenchman. She had won
again. The Englishman reached out and claimed his
chips. She pulled in her accumulation and stared at
the piles a moment. It was time to quit, she knew
that—knew it in her head. She had made a killing.
Although she had originally become interested in the
Monte Carlo scene when she had been told of the
shortages at Nicky's bank, she had not then been
obsessed with gambling as she was now.

Ten months ago she would have quit immediately,

while she was ahead. Now she simply could not, even though her head told her that she must. She pushed out the chips again, making the pattern she had planned in her mind, and listening to the chant of the croupier. Under the damned wig, she was perspiring freely. She was also stiff in the knees. She felt as if she had been sitting there for a full day. She promised herself she'd bring an inflatable cushion next time.

Christ, there *couldn't* be a next time. She had to stop this damned nonsense! What if Nicky should find out? *He* was the one with the original insane passion for gambling. She had cured him—apparently by picking up the disease herself! Some joke. And Hayley. What would her baby sister say if she found out Megan was tossing away Prescott money on the table?

She had to get out of this place!

The wheel slowed. Damn it. She'd lost!

Now she *couldn't* leave.

She played again.

Another loss. Now there was no one at her elbow on the left. The Frenchman had wandered off, letting the pile of chips he had won on her run of luck sift through his fingers, looking for another high-roller on a streak. Fuck him. Apparently he *hadn't* been trying to proposition her. Funny how everybody seemed to want a piece of you when you were on a roll, but when—

Another loss.

The Englishman smiled and faded away.

She was alone.

She won a turn, but then lost again. And again. And again. She was exhausted now, her bottom black and blue from writhing on the hard seat, her skirt moist against her skin. Damn!

Her glasses slid down the bridge of her nose, which was so damp with sweat she couldn't adjust them anymore. The stupid Eva Gabor wig was tilted now; she knew she must look like some kind of cock-eyed floozie.

Once more, Lady Luck. Once more.

No. Another bad roll.

She reached down to shove forward some more chips. There were none. She glanced about her. Where the hell were her chips? Had someone walked off with them?

"Madame?" The croupier was staring at her.

"Oh," said Megan. She shrugged.

The stiff-necked croupier muttered something in clipped French. Megan glanced around. Of course, he was telling her to move her ass, that someone else wanted to play.

If you don't like the heat, stay out of the kitchen, she thought wryly. She liked the heat, but she didn't have any more matches.

She flounced up and strode across the room, head high, sweat pouring off her forehead, her knees and hips stiff and sore from her long, sedentary activity.

It was darkest night when she stepped out of the casino into the street. How long she had been at the damned tables she had no idea. Obviously it had been hours and hours. She fumbled in her bag. She had absolutely no folding money left. It was a damned good thing she had paid her hotel bill in advance. She'd have to go get her carryall and start home. The Alfa Romeo Spider was parked in a garage near the hotel. She was cold sober—that was something anyway. At least she could drive safely.

Out of the shadows stepped a man, muttering something to her. She flinched away, realizing that she *did* look like a streetwalker. *"Via! Via!"* she cried. That was about the sum total of her street vocabulary. It did not occur to her that she was speaking Italian and not French.

The neon light was turned off on the hotel marquee, but the doorman, yawning and growling, let her in.

"I'm leaving," she told him loftily.

He shrugged as she entered the ancient elevator. He was sleeping sitting up when she came down with her bag and pushed open the door into the street. She turned the corner and approached the garage that she had selected because it was open all night. She had her claim ticket ready as she searched along the aisles of cars. At the end of the row, she paused and frowned. She remembered that she had definitely parked the car in that area. Where was it?

She retraced her steps, squinting at the hulking silhouettes in the darkness. She could not see it.

"The Spider," she told the attendant, a teenage French urchin, surly and unwashed.

He shrugged. They walked along the lines of cars.

"No Spider," the attendant said finally.

"Of course there's no Spider!" shouted Megan, now visibly upset. "That's what *I* told *you*. I've got the ticket! Where's the car?"

The teenager shrugged eloquently. "Is no here."

"I'll sue the shit out of you!" screamed Megan, now out of her head. These dirty bastards were all in it with the Mafia. The Spider was probably in some Riviera chop shop—in tiny pieces. "I'm a goddamned contessa, and I'll have your ass!"

"No my fault, madame," sulked the boy. "Somebody give me fake ticket maybe.'' His eyes brightened at the absolute genius of his remark.

"And maybe you split the money with the thief, you little French scumbag!''

"We get police,'' said the boy, a bit frightened now.

"We no get police!'' shouted Megan. Good God, if the authorities got into this, *everybody* would know she had been in Monte Carlo. And that would lead to all kinds of embarrassment. She didn't dare get the law into this!

She gripped her useless ticket. They'd *stolen* the damned car—and there was absolutely nothing she could do about it! Well, she *could* do something about it back in Italy. She could *report* it stolen. But she wasn't in Italy, and—she could feel the breath being sucked out of her chest—she didn't have any way of getting *back* there. She had no goddamned money left. She looked at the ticket in her hand and felt like screaming.

Instead, she cuffed the insolent kid on the side of the face and yelled: "You'll hear from me later, you lousy little goniff!'' Where had she picked up that Yiddish, anyway? "I'm a contessa, you shithead!''

The attendant cowered, but when he saw that she had turned from him and was on her way out of the garage, he was emboldened enough to follow her, countess or cunt or whatever the hell she was, yelling out threats in various languages, salting the threats with obscenities and scurrilities in totally unrelated street jargons.

By the time a very frightened Megan was marching with increasing cadence down the darkened street, he was standing in the shadowy entrance to the garage, waving his hands about and shouting at her as if it was all her fault.

On the sidewalk, a man dressed in the uniform of a French sailor stood directly in front of her, blocking her way. Megan glanced at him with impatience and stepped to one side to get around him. Instantly, he moved to confront her again.

She looked at him, stepped to the other side. Same thing. "Bug off, sailor!" she snapped.

"Ahah! Eenglish! I like Eenglish gorls!"

She swung her carryall at him, smashing it into the side of his head. It was a good roundhouse blow, and it took him by surprise. He had been reaching out to grasp her by the arm, and now he reeled back and fell against the side of a building. It took Megan by surprise, too. She had laid into the sod by instinct. Some countess she was, huh? She was, in fact, one damned *scared* countess.

She was running fast, headed for the street corner where she could see at least a slight glimmer of light. If she could get onto the main drag again, she would be safe. Well, safer.

Behind her, she could hear the sailor cursing at her and following. Then, finally, he yelled something loudly, and there were no more pursuing footsteps. Obviously he had given up the idea of enjoying her favors that night.

She was sweating and panting hard, stitch in her side, when she sank against the stone wall of a building. She was too fat and too out of condition to do the jogging bit. Somewhere along the way, she had lost the Eva Gabor wig. She had long ago put away the dark glasses. Her hair was a mess. It hung down over her face. She knew her makeup was ruined. She tried to brush the hair out of her eyes. Instead, she burst out crying.

Come on, Meggy, she finally told herself. This isn't getting you anywhere. Get a grip on yourself. What to do?

There was a café down the way, but she had no money. Yet it might be wise to go inside and at least get out of the darkness of night and all its attendant terrors.

She stepped inside. There were several figures seated at the counter, and one at a small table. She sank down at another tiny table near the unwashed window.

It was thinking time—the time Megan always dreaded most. Somehow the old brains never did perform the way they should. They seemed permanently enmeshed in cotton candy, with the bright and shiny *idea* she was blindly searching for always somewhere out of sight and out of mind.

Problem: She was over two hundred miles away from home, at least by the winding roadway that hugged the irregular seashore between Monaco and Italy. She had no money. Well, come to think of it, she *did* have a handful of coins in the pocket of the jacket she had thrown over her shoulders when she left the hotel.

Solution: She could telephone home and get Giardino, the majordomo, to telegraph her money for air fare home. Scratch that. Giardino would immediately get on the phone to Nicky in Rome and blow her cover.

Solution: She could purchase a train trip or a flight home by credit card. Scratch that. When the first murmur of bank irregularities had surfaced, Megan's attorney—a sleazy, grinning Venetian with astonishingly blond hair—had advised her to cancel her credit cards to prevent leaks. He had hinted that Nicky might drain off Prescott funds somehow. (It was a good point. If a panicked Nicky started to skim, she would have to make it up with her own personal fortune.)

Solution: She could wait until morning and get the cops on the car. Scratch that. Absolutely not. Then the press would get into it. The media would be blatting it all over the world—while the Cassa Fiorentina di Risparmio was hemorrhaging, one of its principal directors was tossing money away at the gaming tables of the Riviera.

Solution: She could call on her friends for help. Problem: Did she have any? It suddenly occurred to her that she did indeed have a companion of equal social standing in Marie Esterhazy, the widow of a very rich German industrialist, who now lived in a hotel suite in Monte Carlo! Marie was a flint-hearted bitch with claws that ripped—but perhaps she could be prevailed upon to advance a hundred or so for Megan's undercover escape back to Florence.

During her permutations of thought, Megan had ordered coffee and a croissant, and she now munched and drank as she tried to remember what hotel Marie had selected as her retirement headquarters. Then she had it. The Hôtel de Paris. The "el supremo" hostelry of Monaco. Or was "el supremo" even French?

Choking on the terrible coffee, Megan got up, purchased a *jeton* from the waitress with the last of her coins, and dialed the deluxe establishment just down the street. After a moment, a sleepy operator answered. Speaking her fractured French, Megan finally got connected to Marie Esterhazy's room. After a number of rings, someone answered in a very peeved voice.

"Marie?" Megan asked breathlessly.

"Who's zis?"

"It's Megan Tarantino."

"Wer zum Kuckuck?" There was a long pause. Then in English: "Oh. Prescott." So much for titles and Italian names, thought Megan with a sigh. The Prescott name still opened the doors.

"I'm in town."

"Congratulations," said Marie Esterhazy in her guttural accent. "What you call me for now?"

"I'm in trouble. I need help. Can I come up?"

There was another pregnant pause. "You *du Freund*. I help. Come oop."

The concierge at the desk of the Hôtel de Paris had seen many things in his lifetime in Monaco, and the appearance of Megan Tarantino, the Contessa della Camarra, at three A.M., her hair unruly and a frantic gleam in her eye, did not faze him terribly much. Besides, he had been instructed by Suite 19A to expect a visitor, and Suite 19A was loaded and bore marvelous gifts when Father Christmas came around.

Megan hugged Marie and Marie hugged Megan, and then they stood off and looked at one another critically. Marie Esterhazy, born Marie Elizabeth von Eckelin, had been exiled from the Fatherland, as a young woman, because of her father's obscenely close ties to the Nazi high command during Hitler's final years. But she had married a German untainted by such connections and had spent most of her life in Germany. On her husband's death, she had thought it expedient to move to Monte Carlo, where she entertained, and was entertained, by what remained of the aristocracy of Europe—including Megan *Prescott* Tarantino, the Contessa of whatever.

She was sixty; she was sharp; she was bright-eyed and nasty. She was ruthless, and right now she was *curious*.

"Tell me, *Leibchen,* of *die Sorge*—this trouble you have." Her bright gray eyes were avid.

"Somebody heisted my car! I was all ready to drive back to Italy—and they stole my car!" Megan was almost in tears again—with rage this time.

Marie made her sit down beside her on the rigid Louis XVI love seat in front of the electric artificial fire.

"We summon *die Polizei.*"

"No!" Megan's eyes widened in terror.

Instantly the older woman's face softened conspiratorially. "Ahah! You are here on some kind of private—how you say?—affair?"

Megan, who had been desperately trying to invent an appropriate excuse for being in Monte Carlo that had nothing to do with gambling, immediately saw the way out.

She cast down her eyes. "Please, Marie—"

The older woman leaned over and seized her by the arms. "I did not think you were *der Typ,* you cold-blooded Yankee, you American moneybag! But— hah!—you have the blood of *die Lusternheit*—how you say?—*lust* in you, too!"

She smiled craftily at Megan and nodded her head as if in acclamation of Megan's actions. "After what he do to you all these years, he deserve it," she said finally.

Megan frowned, not quite following the old woman's line of reasoning. Who was she talking about?

Then Marie's eyes clouded. "Hey," she said. "Why *der Liebhaber*—why the lover not help you?"

"I don't want to think about it," Megan said, lowering her voice. "We had a terrible row. It was the first time he ever laid a hand on me—in *that* way! I was terrified."

Now Marie's eyes sparkled. "Of course. It is the end of *der Liebenschaft*—the passion—and he throw you out. No. You cannot go to him. And you cannot go to your husband." She was looking into the distance. "Hey, how does Nicky let you wander away like this?"

Quickly, Megan explained that Nicky was meeting with bank examiners about problems at the bank.

"Ah! Somewhere I read about that. He had been fiddling with the ledgers?" Her face crinkled into a nasty smirk.

"It's all a mistake," Megan said lamely.

"And while he fiddles with the ledgers, you fiddle with the lovers, eh?" The old woman cackled like an aged chicken over an unexpectedly laid egg.

Megan laughed on cue. Fucking old bitch, she thought.

"We get you home safely," said Marie Esterhazy, looking carefully at Megan's clothes. "You *look* okay, even with your dress and jacket ruined. You need *die Maska*—how you say?—disguise." She frowned, then snapped her fingers. "My companion." The old eyes crinkled in an enigmatic smile. "In my old age, I *buy* friendship. Dominique is your size. She shops off the rack. Her tastes are cheap. We get you up to look like some *hausfrau* on a shopping tour."

"But—"

"The hydroplane, Prescott. She sail from Nice to Corsica, then she sail from Corsica to Italian coast near Pisa. You take bus home from Pisa. Be one of *die Mittleklasse* for a day." She giggled, happy as a clam at high tide now that she was involved in a romantic escapade. "I love to see you with a babouchka over the hair and a shawl over the shoulders!"

And so it was. Within an hour, Megan was in bed asleep, and in the morning, after a marvelous breakfast on the balcony overlooking the Mediterranean, she got into Dominique's truly tasteless dress and sandals, threw a babouchka over her hair and a shawl over her shoulders, and showed herself for Marie's examination.

"*Vollkommenheit!*" cried Marie. "Nobody know you!" She handed Megan the hydroplane tickets she had instructed the desk clerk to purchase for her, and then gave her folding money, held together by a gold clip. "We get together later this summer, no? The Beatrix la Belle party you are having at the Villa della Camarra."

"Of course!" cooed Megan. "I'd forgotten all about it! You *know* already?"

"The papers have notices every so often. Who is going to be invited. Who is going to be cut. All speculation. It is secret, but everybody know. To make it secret is to make it more known. Ha, ha. Your parties are *famos,* Megan—*das Stadtgespräch!* Talk of town. You know that!"

"You'll be there," Megan nodded. In fact, she had intended to drop the old bitch from the list, but now she couldn't afford to.

"Give Nicky kiss for me," she told Megan as they stood in the corridor of the elegantly appointed hotel.

On impulse, Megan hugged the old woman briefly and pecked her on the side of her withered face. "Thanks again, Marie."

*   *   *

On the hydroplane from Nice to Bastia, on Corsica, Megan sank into a kind of cataleptic trance and grabbed a catnap on one of the hard wooden benches. She was bushed from the night of excitement, frustration, and lack of restful sleep. Besides, she had suffered a really bad scare. Luckily, she had been able to fob off her folly by pretending to Marie Esterhazy it was a man who had done her in—instead of the damned roulette wheel.

She knew the German woman would talk, of course. But that was all right. Megan could rise above a rumored romance with a male. She couldn't rise above an obsession to gamble away the Prescott fortune—even if she had acquired the obsession trying to help her husband out of his own psychological trap.

She had to wait four hours in Bastia for the mainland hydroplane, but after it docked, she was soon off again. She slept, woke up, ate some food, and then almost lost it in the lurching, heaving ocean. Eventually, relieved, she landed at Pisa. Then she got on the bus to Florence and went to sleep for the first sound slumber she had enjoyed in forty-eight hours.

She cabbed out to the villa in the northern suburbs. As the driver waited impatiently at the foot of the wide, winding marble steps that led up into the well-landscaped estate, she summoned Giardino by the telephone at the gate to bring the proper money to pay for the ride. She refused to spend a cent of Marie's money. The old woman knew to the penny—or centime, actually—the amount she had handed over. And she had the amount of the hydroplane tickets toted up in her head, too.

Giardino pretended not to blanch when he saw his

mistress climb out of the cab in her disguise. He paid off the driver, and the cab vanished in a cloud of gasoline fumes.

"Don't stand there staring at me, you fool!" Megan cried out. "The Spider was stolen! Get the police on it! I didn't have a lira, and had to borrow money from a friend. You hear me? They stole my car!"

As they walked up the steps through the formal garden, past the reflecting pond, and into the foyer of the villa, Megan told him a disjointed and illogical story about driving along the roadway to a beach near Pisa, parking the car, and finding it gone when she came back to pick it up. Her original cover story for the Monte Carlo trip had involved Pisa and a friend who lived there; this was an extension of that earlier invention. Megan hoped she would not be required to repeat it. It was too full of holes to fool anybody but a moron.

Giardino listened, and his face resembled Marie Esterhazy's when Megan had explained the problem to her. The canny old slob, she thought. *He* thinks I've been in the sack with some stud, too. Well, why the hell not?

They were standing in the villa's high-domed central atrium when she finished. There seemed to be nothing more to say. Giardino considered a moment, seemed about to ask a question or two, then changed his mind.

Bowing himself away, the majordomo attended to the business of reporting the vehicle stolen. He found Megan again and told her about his conversation with the police. Megan was resting in the beautiful atrium of the villa, her eyes heavy with exhaustion. Now she rose, went inside to the family wing of the house, stripped off her dirty clothes, and fell down on the bed sobbing bitter tears. Then she relaxed in a tub full of sudsy water.

She was making up her face at the mirror of her sumptuous bedroom when Giardino rapped at the door with a message.

"A gentleman is waiting who says he is from the Vatican, signora. Something about the Holy Father's investment portfolio in the Cassa Fiorentina di Risparmio."

Oh good Christ, thought Megan. So Nicky's been diddling the Pope's accounts. She toyed briefly with the idea of fainting, but couldn't bring it off. She drew in a deep breath, touched up her frizzy hair, and marched out to face the firing squad.

CHAPTER NINE

The woman came awake out of a deep, impenetrable sleep—renewed, refreshed, and awakened by the cheerful morning that peeked in through her window. The sky, seen through sparkling panes of glass, was the kind of blue that promised a day of absolute perfection.

It was, in fact, the kind of day that made one want to get up immediately, bathe, and greet the morning with just the proper mind-set to plunge into a huge workload. There was a great deal on her mind, and—reinvigorated by a full night's sleep—she could solve all problems and move forward—

Problems? What problems? She knew there were problems, but—

She stared at the ceiling, helpless. The pattern was oddly familiar, and yet it was unfamiliar. It was, in fact, the kind of ceiling one saw in motels or hotels. Why was her bedroom—? Or, for that matter, *was* this her bedroom?

Full consciousness engulfed her like a heavy wave of surf, dropping her down into a whirling vortex of green tide and spinning darkness. Darkness! There was nothing there—nothing there where *she* should be. Her mind was a closet, sealed off from the world. Except for what she could *see* outside her, there was no physical presence.

Who was she? How had she come to be in this room? What had happened to her? Where was she going? What would she do? Where a moment before she had felt physically elated, now, quite suddenly and terrifyingly, she felt physiologically exhausted by tension that stretched her body painfully and filled her with frightening qualms of anxiety. She struggled in an impasse of absolute horror, and then deliberately relaxed herself, closing her eyes, trying to bring back the old familiar calm. Her heartbeat had increased until her temples were pounding and her heart was slamming against her ribs.

The waves of blackness began receding back into the distance, to be replaced by a vast grayness that flowed in on her inexorably, filling every corner of her mind. She tried to assume unconsciousness, but she could not. She opened her eyes involuntarily, hoping that she would find herself in familiar surroundings and not in this strange and inhospitable hotel room—

She was trembling with fear now, seated on the edge of the bed, her elbows on her knees, her head supported in her palms, her hair streaming down over her wrists, her filmy pajamas twisted around her body. My God! She did not know who she was. She did not know where she was. Slowly she rose and moved to the window. The windows were sealed, as any motel or hotel windows might be, to prevent the energy used by the air-conditioning from being wasted.

She peered outside and down. She seemed to be

high in the air, looking out over a beautiful park, with a pond beyond. Yet the pond was not the far limits of the landscape in view. Beyond the pond there were ugly buildings rising along a roadway, and railroad tracks. Industrial facility, the sight proclaimed.

How did she know this? she wondered. How could she think, and yet not know her own name?

Nevertheless, she could think and put words to things.

The problem was, she could not put an overall word to the outdoors as she saw it, and to herself as she existed in it. She turned to the bathroom door and—

There was a momentary hesitation. How did she know it was the bathroom door? That thought might be a hallucination as well. She approached the mysterious door, reaching out to open it, hoping on the one hand that it *was* the bathroom, which would prove that she was not completely mentally gone; and hoping on the other that it was *not* the bathroom, which would prove that her delusions were not real.

In the bathroom, she faced herself in the mirror. For all her confusion, she found that her reflection was that of a beautiful woman, a trifle puffy around the eyes from heavy sleep, but nevertheless lovely to look at. No makeup, of course. And her taffy-colored hair needed brushing.

Her eyes widened as she stared at herself. What about the other door? There was the bathroom door—the door that she had opened—and there was another door opposite it, opening into *the other room*.

She knew that, but she did not know how she knew that. She was able to distinguish these doors from the door out into the corridor.

Tension tore at her as she retreated from the image

of the perfect woman in the mirror and went to *the other door*. What lay behind it? She reached out, touching the knob. It was unlocked. She twisted it, and the door swung inward easily, noiselessly, effortlessly. She peered through the aperture of the doorway at another room just like hers, with a bed—and in the bed lay a man twisted in the covers, naked, breathing heavily and—

She had never seen him before in her life. She could see enough of his face as he lay on his side to know that. Yet the door between the two rooms was open and—

She felt sick. Suppose the two of them had been together before she went to sleep. Suppose they had made love. Suppose—

Did she make love for a living? Was this simply another reason for her to forget who she was? Was this the basis of her amnesia? And how, for that matter, was she even able to put the word "amnesia" to her own forgetfulness? She knew everything, apparently, except her own name.

Oh God, she thought, what if he turned and saw her, and smiled and said, "Hello—" and her name, whatever it was. At least she would *know*. But would simply knowing her name make her whole again? Would it fill the vast emptiness of her brain with knowledge about herself?

She was shaking now, palsied, breathing rapidly, her mind shuttered from reality.

Then she was in an elevator, dropping swiftly. Her stomach turned. She was hungry, but afraid to think about eating. The elevator slowed and stopped. It opened. She could see daylight and a wide street outside, with traffic passing by. She walked out of the elevator.

It suddenly occurred to her that she did not remember dressing herself. Was she in her filmy pajamas? Was she naked—?

She had on a lovely outfit, very new, cut to her size and silhouette by experts. She actually looked stunning. Why was she shaking so? As she moved from the elevator across a crowded lobby, a man in a pinstripe suit glanced at her and their eyes met. He smiled. He did not know her; she understood that he was flirting. Without thinking, she acknowledged his interest with a faint and supercilious gesture that said, "Thanks, but no thanks."

The birds were singing. It was a beautiful day. She was sitting in a park, with well-trimmed slopes of lawn rolling down to the lake. Lake? Pond? There were huge, sentinel-like trees everywhere—planted with respect for the overall landscape. How had she gotten to the bench?

Curiously, she looked down at the thick wooden planks out of which it was fashioned: no plastic bench; no old-fashioned iron bars. This was wood—real wood. Odd.

Why odd? she asked herself.

It was odd because she was able to question the fact that the bench was made out of wood, but she was not able to tell where she was or what she was doing there. Yet, now she realized that she had come from the immense building that dominated the area across the street from the park in which she sat.

A woman moved along the pathway that led into the park. The woman was walking a dog. The dog peed on the grass and then began sniffing at the trunk of a small tree near the bench. The woman sank down onto the bench and hooked the dog's leash over the end of one of the planks.

The woman sighed and turned slightly. She spoke amiably.

Words, phrases, conversation . . . inexplicable!

Now she was genuinely frightened. She could not understand a word the woman with the dog said! She could not make out *anything!* It was as if she were in a foreign country, with very familiar things all around her: men who flirted in hotel lobbies, women who had dogs on leashes—and yet she could put no meaning to speech.

Nevertheless, she smiled and shrugged her shoulders, implying one of several things: that she could not speak because of a speech impediment; that she could not understand what the dog woman said, because she was a foreigner; or that she did not want to speak because of any one of a million mysterious reasons.

The woman, fat and comfortable, shrugged in return, smiled brightly, showing a mouthful of rather bad teeth, and made sounds at her dog. The dog squatted and dropped his morning do on the grass.

Then she was at the water's edge, looking down into the mirrorlike surface of the pond. She saw herself; she saw her face—

The face was not the same as it had appeared in the hotel mirror. It was a face perhaps forty years *older*. The hair—gray and streaked—hung down in a careless, tangled mass around her throat, around her shoulders. Her clothes were filthy. She was screaming, her cheeks puffy, her eyes red-veined and horrible, her mouth open and revealing an absence of teeth.

"Crazy old bitch," somebody said in her ear.

They were talking about *her*. She wanted to die.

Crazy. Crazy. Crazy. Crazy. . . .

She was seated at a table in a small and crowded café. The people around her were chatting volubly in a strange tongue. Either that, or her brain had shattered and she was unable to understand a word she heard. She had managed to order a cup of thick coffee by gesturing toward what a couple at the next table were drinking. And she had also managed to get a small packet of cakelike refreshment to go with the coffee.

The words on the packet made no sense. She could not even *read!*

She drank, and the coffee was thick and strong. It made her shudder. All in all, it helped, and she found herself able to calm the shakes that had brought her into the place. Now she tore the plastic cover off of the snack and munched at the food. It tasted like nothing she had ever eaten before, but it went well with the coffee—if anything could.

Now, a bustling woman, dressed in an unclean apron and a dress that might have been a waitress's uniform, came over and tore off a sheet of paper with numbers on it. The check, of course. She reached for her bag.

There was no bag. She had not brought a bag with her when she had fled the hotel. What utter stupidity! What errant—

When she pantomimed her lack of funds, the thick doughy-faced woman took a long time trying to figure out what to do. Then she went into explosive fits, her face reddening, her hands moving about in agitation. Finally, she rushed back to the counter and chatted with a heavyset individual, who wore an ancient cloth cap and who had been reading a newspaper. He glanced at her where she sat, alone and cowering at her place. The shrewd black eyes narrowed, and the man rose from the chair and ambled over, his form approaching with an undercurrent of menace.

His words made no sense.

She began to weep.

Then she heard a specific word: "Police." Or something close enough to it to be "police."

She jumped up and ran for the door. The heavy man reached out and caught her and—

Everybody stared at her. The cloth-capped proprietor sat with her, gripping her by the arm, while the customers all pretended to continue their breakfasts. But they were rubbernecking, like a group of sadistic motorists at an accident on the throughway. She found that she was even unable to cry now.

Through the front doorway of the café strode a man in uniform, obviously a member of the local police force. He glanced about, acclimating himself briefly. He saw the proprietor, whom he apparently knew, and approached the table.

As he did so, she rose in hauteur.

The policeman directed his question to the man in the cloth cap. The man in the cloth cap chatted in return, gesturing toward her.

She was in complete control now. The waves of blackness had receded completely. She was irritated, if nothing else. Why this potato-face of a proprietor had not been patient enough to let her send for her identification papers at the hotel—after all, it was only across the boulevard!—she had no idea.

"I simply stepped out of the Inter-Continental Hotel for a moment without my money," she told the policeman in her well-accented Parisian French—always the best of international languages to use in

Europe (especially in Helsinki, Finland)—and he stiffened to attention.

"Obviously a mistake, madame," he returned, in a heavy, Balkanized French.

"Mademoiselle," she intoned loftily.

He bowed.

The cloth-capped proprietor was pale and nervous now. The instantaneous metamorphosis in this woman —from vacant-eyed idiot to haughty aristocrat—had undone him, leaving him gaping in total indignity. The whole thing had instantly become *his* fault. Where was that stupid waitress—?

"I'm Beatrix Fontaine," she told the officer carefully. "I am staying temporarily at the Inter-Continental across the street. Would you please convey to this person—" she indicated the cloth-capped fat man, who was visibly shrinking before her eyes "—that I shall send to him an envelope containing in full amount payment for this—" another pause as she surveyed the leavings on the table with nausea "—so-called coffee and—*eh bien?*—cake."

Again the official constabulary bow. "I shall, indeed, mademoiselle." And the officer turned to give the coffee shop owner a tongue-lashing in street Finnish.

Regally sweeping out of the establishment with the officer, Beatrix cast her eyes over the interior of the café with complete dignity, letting all the patrons suffer the lash of her most lethal glance.

Cornelius Welles rolled over and woke up at about seven in the morning. Shaking his head to get the cobwebs out, he ran his hands through his dark brown hair. He liked it combed back, but it always seemed to fall forward to hang down over his forehead. He was damned proud of his widow's peak and liked it to show. Hell, he was in the image business. The peak did as much for him as it had for Robert Taylor back in the 1930s.

Wrapping his robe about him, he went to the door of Beatrix Fontaine's room and listened. He could hear nothing. On impulse, he tried the door, surprised that it was not locked, and opened it.

"Trixie," he called. There was no answer. He moved into the room, glanced around, saw the bathroom door was open, and retreated to his own room, closing the door behind him. Weird bitch, he thought. After she had come on so strong to him in Scobie Hills, he had thought the rest of their relationship was going to proceed along the same course—and with equal velocity. But she had been uninterested last night, even after all the cocktails they had put down at the meal with Bertil Gustafssohn, the Swedish businessman whom she had selected to open the first Beatrix spa in Scandinavia.

He plugged in the shaver, glanced twice at it to make sure he was on the right voltage—in these damned European countries you never knew if you were going to blow out your motor or ground yourself to the earth's core—and began shaving off the bristles that had accumulated during the night.

In the middle of his chore, he paused and reflected. He'd have sworn he woke up in the middle of the night hearing screams from her room. They had stopped immediately, and he had put it down to imagination. Yet he had gone to the door anyway, and had tried the knob. It had been locked. Hearing no further disturbances, he had climbed back in bed, where he dropped off instantly. Obviously imaginations.

Now he wondered if he had not really *heard* the damned screams. Why hadn't she waited for him just now? They had intended to breakfast together, to compare feedback from their conversation with the irrepressible Swede, who appeared to Carney to be in complete control of his money, as well as his take.

But Beatrix's business sense was certainly impressive to Welles. She was as hard as nails when it had to do with outgo, and as soft as a kitten's fur when it had to do with income. She had this goggle-eyed Stockholm bagman completely in the palm of her hand by the time they had stirred their green liqueurs and said goodnight at Helsinki's swankest restaurant.

But now . . .

Welles shrugged. Women were peculiar. Beatrix had been all over him before, and now she slammed down the portcullis on him. The hell with it. Who cared? This was a business proposition all the way, and he was good at business. He was good at business in spite of what Hayley had said to him. God damn her soul. And he was good in the sack, too, though it seemed that this time the image-molding wouldn't include any more of that kind of performance.

Where was Beatrix, anyway? It occurred to him now, in a kind of delayed mental doubletake, that Beatrix could be in the hay—making hay—with the Stockholm entrepreneur. Not a bad idea, actually. Hell, *she* was the one who had to deal with him. Welles was only here to work out the public relations angle. Why not work on the money man? She knew how to work on *anyone;* he knew that now.

By now he was beginning to understand rich women, or at least he was *learning* to. Look at the woman he was married to. Christ! She was insatiable in the sack. First she had taken on that little wimp Carney had hired from Princeton; and then, the next thing he knew, his West Coast snoops had reported she was in bed with some seedy little entrepreneur he'd never heard of, some guy who'd made a pile on a fast-food chain. Showing off? Nah. Getting of. That was what Hayley needed. Somebody to neutralize that charged-up body and psyche.

More luck to him, Welles thought, not without a touch of resentment. Hell, you'd think she needed more than he could provide. He shrugged, putting away the razor and rubbing his hand over his face. He hadn't given her much lately; and that last weekend at home, Beatrix had taken everything he had.

But, shit! That little Princeton turd. You'd think—

Welles had to laugh. He had been a bit vindictive about it, all right, when he'd fired the little prick. But the kid deserved it, deserved it stuck in deep— damn it! No discretion, no cover, no style. Just straight, out-and-out "wham, bam, thank you, ma'am." *If* he even bothered to say thank you.

Just before he'd flown to Paris to pick up Beatrix for the Scandinavian meeting Carney Welles had called Mead Brookhaven III into his office.

He remembered how, bright-eyed and shiny, the Princeton yuppie had stood before his desk, expecting a raise, a brevetting, or at the very least a cushy new executive position. "Yes, sir."

"Mead," Welles began—although everybody at the office had taken to calling the kid "Three," or "Third," sometimes making "Third" sound like "Turd"—"you know I've had my eye on you from the first minute you started here."

"Yes, sir," said the kid, lowering his gaze modestly.

"You're a bright young man, upwardly mobile, as they say in today's popular jargon."

Mead smiled at the boss's joke.

"I've been remarkably impressed by your office

demeanor. You've been studying the files, looking over the reports, speaking with the old-timers, discussing upcoming projects with middle executives."

"Yes, sir," Mead nodded, happy that his activities were being scrutinized.

"As a matter of fact, you've been poking into a lot of things that don't even concern you."

The Princetonian was about to make some rejoinder about curiosity being linked to creativity, but Welles cut in.

"Like my wife, for one."

Mead blanched. The blood absolutely left his face. He stared at Carney Welles.

"Oh, hell, she's used to it," grinned Welles. "It's the nooks and crannies in the office that bother me more. I get the impression that you know more about what's going on here than anyone else in the place. Even me."

"I don't know quite—"

"That's why you seduced Hayley, isn't it?" he asked cheerfully. "So you could use her to get a handle on me?"

"Sir, I categorically deny—"

"She didn't tell me, Third," Welles said, his anger suddenly beginning to bubble. "These told me!" He slammed a thick packet of infrared photographs on the desk under the young jock's nose. Screwing in the water. Screwing on the sand. Screwing in the woods. Mead's face. Hayley's face. Jesus.

"She wanted me, Mr. Welles!" wailed Mead.

"She wants anything that's got pants on!" he snapped. "Kid, you're going out of here without anything. Without a recommendation. Without an evaluation. Without a damned thing! You understand?

*See that you don't surface anywhere that I might spot
you. Or I'll cut your balls off!''*

*Mead did the smartest thing he had done in months.
He kept his mouth shut.*

*"You're interested in public relations, so it says on
your application form.'' Welles tossed it over on top
of the infrared photographs. "I'd suggest you make a
change there, simply for clarification. Make that 'private relations.' It's more in your line.''*

*"That's—very good—Mr. Welles,'' Mead gulped.
"A* bon mot.''

*"Beat it,'' Welles said, looking out the window.
A faint smile softened his grim mouth. "That might
be a good motto for an unrepressed stud like you,
prick. Don't stick it—beat it!''*

Hell, Carney Welles thought now. It wasn't Hayley
who had him climbing the walls. It was the gall of
that damned kid. Once Mead was out, Welles had
gotten the picture clearly. The kid had been into
everything, asking questions, taking notes, storing it
all up in his head, sucking up to the clients—kissing
asses here, there, and everywhere. He was on his
way to take over the company someday from Welles
himself if he could! And he was bright enough to do
it.

Cheap little son of a bitch!

Of course, when Hayley learned about the kid's
fate, she had been a little annoyed. And that, actually, had led her to fly off to the West Coast, moving
into the Benedict Canyon house for a few weeks.
Ostensibly, she was out there to check into some
investment transactions, to raise money for Megan's
problems with the Cassa Fiorentina di Risparmio.
But Welles had gotten the real word about the trip.

She was messing around with some young stud—and seeing her second husband again.

Austin Bush was a decent guy, Welles knew. Why the hell would *he* like Hayley? It took some kind of nut to go for her. She was a real ball-breaker, he thought again—and noted that the appellation had been applied to Hayley not only by close friends, but by total strangers.

Christ. Where would she land next?

The room phone rang. He picked it up.

"It's me, Beatrix Fontaine," the voice said, cool but friendly. "I'm down in the coffee shop at the hotel. Bring my bag with you, please?"

"In a minute, Trixie."

He dressed quickly, and in five minutes was seated opposite her in the coffee shop. She gave a uniformed man an envelope with some money in it, told Welles it was for a cab fare, and laughed it off.

They shared a hearty meal, discussed their conversation with Bertil Gustafssohn the night before, had a few laughs over the bagman's boorish manners, and planned the rest of their stay in Helsinki. After that, they went back to their rooms, Welles opening his door with the key.

"I was worried last night," he finally said.

"About what?" Beatrix asked with wide eyes.

"I thought I heard you screaming in your sleep."

She laughed. "You must have had a nightmare yourself, my friend."

"Yeah. Who was that policeman downstairs?"

Her eyes, golden and glinting yellow at the centers, moved restlessly over his face. He could *feel* them. "I do not understand."

"There was a cop. You gave him money."

"I tell you already. A cab fare."

"Where?"

She quirked an eyebrow. "Please, my friend. This is none of your business."

"My business is your image, mademoiselle," he said, becoming stiffly formal once again. "I heard you screaming in your sleep. I wake up to find you gone. You have a cab fare that hasn't been paid. Did you entertain Gustafssohn? I don't care, really. But I'm thinking about the damage if such information should leak out."

She shrugged eloquently. "I am no common prostitute. I thought you knew that. If I choose to drive about the city on an early shopping tour, must you ask questions?"

"Shopping without money?"

She came over to him and pressed her body against him. "Please, my friend. Let us not discuss what does not matter one iota."

They were in his room. His bed had not yet been made up by the maid.

Her mouth was on his, her tongue probing his teeth and gums. Her arms were around him, and now his were around her. A warmth enfolded Cornelius Welles—the warmth of her body and the warmth of his memory of her earlier ministrations to him.

There was simply no way out of it now. They sank down into a vortex of excitement, of exhilaration, of sighs and moans and sounds that were not recognizable as human. They writhed naked on the unmade bed, together head to head one moment, together the opposite way the next, down and about, under and over, in and out. In was simply endless—the kind of thing that he'd sometimes daydreamed about.

If anything, this time Mademoiselle Beatrix Fontaine was truly insatiable in her demands and in her responses.

If Hayley could only see him now, Welles thought with a smirk. Jee-zuss!

CHAPTER TEN

Once in the Rolls Royce limousine, Hayley Welles relaxed and watched the London traffic flow by as they drove away from Claridge's down Brook Street toward Park Lane. She fumbled in her capacious bag and drew out the thick and prepossessing invitation, embossed umistakably with the gold insignia of Queen Elizabeth II of England.

"It's as thick as a board," Hayley observed with muted amusement, glancing at her companion.

"Not easily forged," smiled Sir John Huddlestone.

" 'The Lord Chamberlain is commanded by Her Majesty to invite,' " Hayley quoted, "and so forth and so on, 'to a garden party at Buckingham Palace.' Very much around the mulberry bush, don't you think?"

"Well, you see, nothing is right out in the open when one deals with English royalty," Sir John explained.

She put the invitation back in her bag, managing a sideways glance at her escort. Sir John Huddlestone was actually Lord Muirhead, if one went by his title.

He was one of London's most experienced and formidable investment counselors. It was for that reason that, years ago, Hayley's father had selected him to manage the Prescott Foundation's English portfolio, which involved millions of dollars' worth of stocks and bonds.

In his sixties, Sir John was lean and fair, with blue eyes, a hawklike nose, and a long, angular face that managed to maintain its innate dignity even when he was enjoying a good joke. Bright and witty, sober and austere, he was an interesting and somehow typical English combination of the repressed and the extroverted.

"I did drop your name to the proper contacts," he had explained when he first told Hayley about the garden party at Buckingham Palace.

"I'm surprised anyone there had ever heard of me."

"The Queen is a well-briefed and intelligent woman," Huddlestone had responded with a slight gleam in his eye. "Certainly she's aware of the Prescott fortune."

"I didn't mean—"

Huddlestone had interrupted with an upraised palm. "Of course not, dear lady."

Hayley now patted at her aquamarine-colored garden party dress—which had been airmailed to her express from Manhattan the night before, from her latest couturier, Gianfranco Ferré. If she did say so herself, Gianfranco had done himself proud. She would be a standout among scores of other standouts. It would be the first time in many months that she had worn a complicated hat—but this one had the effect of making her face seem softer and her eyes more afire.

She glanced out the window of the limousine to find that they were passing the Speaker's Corner of Hyde Park on the way to Buckingham Palace. Hayley had to admit to herself that her sudden decision to fly to London actually had nothing to do with the Prescott Foundation's business. She was restless—a continuing discomfort that had begun back at Scobie Hills after her infuriating confrontation with Carney Welles. The quick flight to California had done nothing to neutralize her jaded unsettledness. If anything, it had whetted her appetite for more Mr. Goodbars. Her fling with that conceited little yuppie from Carney's office had paid off her husband, tit for tat, but the romp at the racetrack, and around Southern California, with various bedroom escorts, had really not been too satisfactory. What *did* she want, anyway? It was hard to tell.

England had called out to her, because in England one could settle down in the company of civilized and intelligent people who did not seem to spend every waking—and sleeping—moment trying to outdo one another. And even when they *did*, they went about it in a slightly different manner. Once she had made up her mind to visit London, Huddlestone immediately arranged the invitation to the garden party— and now they were on their way.

"Here we are," her escort unexpectedly said, slipping out of the limo and moving to assist her, holding his walking stick gracefully out of the way.

Hayley glanced out, bewildered. "But where's Buckingham Palace?" She had stood many times in front of it, intrigued by the staid exterior and the brightly uniformed guards. The limo was nowhere near the palace.

Huddlestone allowed himself the ghost of a smile.

"Oh, no one in the know alights for a garden party at the East Wing."

"But where are we?" Hayley wondered, holding on to her escort's arm and climbing out of the Rolls. She could see a gate with high iron bars. She could see the familiar palace guards awaiting on either side of it. But as far as she could see down Grosvenor Place, there was only a high blank wall; and all along Constitution Hill in the other direction there was more wall, blocking out any view.

"This is the gate farthest from the palace. It's a rather nice walk."

As the Rolls Royce roared off, Huddlestone handed the invitation to one of the guards, who saluted and opened the gate for them. Ahead, Hayley could see several other guests proceeding along the winding walk that meandered through the garden.

And what a garden it was! The beauty of it—hidden away from the public eye—took Hayley's breath away. "Oh, Sir John!" she exclaimed. "It's enchanting!"

Huddlestone nodded. "This is a part of the palace grounds seen by few people."

Hayley shook her head as if to clear it of confusion. "It's incredible! You can hear the traffic zooming along on Grosvenor Place past the wall—but you can't see it. We're in a secret world, all our own."

"Fifty acres of it," Huddlestone murmured, sounding impressed in spite of his British reserve.

"But the palace isn't even *visible*," Hayley exclaimed, fascinated by the high trees that screened out the sky and created the illusion that the garden was buried somewhere deep in the English countryside.

Soon they emerged from the trees and were walking over a carefully kept lawn sloping down to a large, irregularly shaped pond. The lawn soon gave way to a dense, tangled growth of shrubs and hedges.

"That mulberry hedge was planted long before the American Revolution," Huddlestone informed her, pointing with his stick. "In 1609, to be precise. It still bears fruit."

They came upon a garden of magnificent roses, and then a plot of giant delphiniums and sweet peas. Hayley was so absorbed in the beauty of the flowers that she was almost unaware of the façade of the palace that now loomed up beyond the pond. When suddenly she saw it, she gasped.

"But it's nothing like the front! It's like a Cotswold cottage."

"The stone is actually from Bath," Huddlestone said in his refined and precise way. "It has that distinguishing honey-colored hue, hasn't it?"

That was the palace's original color, Huddlestone explained. In fact, when the first owner, John Sheffield, the Duke of Buckingham, lived in it, there were only three sections—a central block and two wings built around a courtyard. Later, the familiar East Wing, the front of the palace as it is seen today, was constructed of a more dreary gray stone, probably in conformance with Queen Victoria's conventionality and state of perpetual mourning for her prince consort.

Hundreds of guests were circulating about in the brilliant afternoon sunshine at the rear of the palace when Hayley and Huddlestone arrived. Martial music was being played by the uniformed band of the Irish Guards. Another band, from the Corps of Royal Electrical and Mechanical Engineers, awaited in the background for their turn.

Like Huddlestone, most of the men were decked

out in top hat and tails—some dark, some light. The women were glittering in all colors of the rainbow in their dresses and hats and matching accessories. Even bishops, in bright magenta robes, could be seen striding about the lawns.

"Ten thousand guests today," murmured Huddlestone in Hayley's ear.

"It does look that way," Hayley said.

Occasionally a couple would approach and speak to Huddlestone and Hayley, dropping small talk and greeting the visiting American millionairess with low-keyed British aplomb.

Amidst the swirl of color and formality, Hayley found herself lost in the total resplendence of the scene.

"Oh, dear," murmured Huddlestone, his grip tightening on Hayley's arm.

Hayley glanced up. She saw a remarkably attractive couple approaching. The woman caught Hayley's attention immediately. She was young, appealing, beautiful, with the strawberries-and-cream complexion that only true born-and-bred Englishwomen ever manage. Her eyes were hazel, her hair golden in the sun under a small hat tilted at a rakish angle. She was slender and supple and—well—succulent.

But the man with her was something else again— an absolutely gorgeous individual! He was six foot one, with a lean, graceful build. He had curly brown hair that was partially covered by a jaunty top hat, and his flawless face gazed out at the world with steady brown eyes.

"Sir John!" gushed the woman.

"Mrs. Prescott," Huddlestone said obediently, "I would like you to meet Meg Talbot, and Clive Argyll."

"How do you do?" Hayley said politely, unable to

keep her eyes off the man. There was something
electric about him, something that kept her eyes riveted to his face. His complexion was pale and almost
unhealthy in appearance, but his eyes were alive and
moving all over her. None of her body's secret places
seemed safe from his probing gaze. But instead of
being revolted, she found herself melting and tingling
under his gaze.

"The stage," Huddlestone murmured in Hayley's
ear. "*Nine Moons Wasted*," he continued. "The hit
of the West End."

Ahah! Hayley thought. Argyll was indeed the hit of
the season—starring in a play he had written himself.
She had read about it in the *London Times*. But what
amazed Hayley was the man's *presence* and attractive-
ness. He was the nearest thing to overpowering she
had ever *seen*. And the woman, of course, was his
co-star. Hayley remembered the name. They made a
most attractive couple.

Argyll was going through the usual murmuring of
greeting when he abruptly straightened. Hayley almost laughed; the gesture was a perfect double-take.
Of course, it was not unexpected. The man *was* an
actor.

"Prescott," murmured Argyll, his head tilted, his
eyes addressing a far-off cloud in the sky. "Not of
the bloodline of Robert Roy Prescott, called Rob Roy
of the Railroads, the Plunderer of the Old West, the
Reiver of the Republic?"

"Far removed," said Hayley gracefully, "but the
same."

Argyll turned to Meg Talbot. "The man had no
mercy. Nor, apparently, does the present generation
of Prescotts, judging from their holdings in dictator-
ships the world over, particularly in South Africa."

Huddlestone, gesturing toward the actress, interposed quickly, "Miss Talbot is a steeplechase rider of world class."

Argyll interrupted. "Miss Talbot is a magnificent personality on the stage, but a monstrous bore and sociological nonentity in real life."

Meg Talbot's elbow shot into Argyll's ribs.

"Her problem is not one of breeding," he went on. "She's spoiled, overbearing—and rich." Argyll was eyeing Hayley closely, studying her reaction.

"A fault with which many of us would love to be cursed," Huddlestone murmured.

"Oh, for God's sake, Hinny, will you shut up?" Meg Talbot snapped genially. "Pay no attention to him," she told Hayley. "The idiot once attended a meeting of working-class socialists and never got over it."

"I'm a *real* socialist," snapped Argyll. "As opposed to a limousine liberal socialist. And that makes me a natural enemy of anyone bearing the Prescott name."

"Oh dear," said Hayley, putting on a defensive smile. "Is that what your play is all about? The bastardly rich?"

"You haven't seen it?" Argyll asked, his face stiffening in disbelief.

"Sir, in spite of the fact that your play is apparently the talk of the town in London, I fear nobody in the States has ever heard of it. At least, I never did."

Huddlestone cleared his throat. Meg Talbot giggled.

"I'd send you a chit to attend," Argyll said stiffly, "but I'm afraid it's a bit over your head."

"You consider yourself on a par with Shakespeare?"

He was puzzled. "I was a Shakespearean actor for many years before I acted in the West End."

"No. I mean the title. From *Othello*."

"Of course, from *Othello*. Because I use the man's words, must I feel myself equal to him?"

Hayley smiled. "Perhaps I shall see it when it opens in New York."

Argyll glowered at her, his whole persona emanating waves of hostility. "You're an offensive woman, do you know that?"

"I simply said—"

"You *hinted* that I shall never make Broadway."

"Perhaps you need a psychiatrist. Most writers are paranoid, of course." Hayley searched for an invisible dust mote on her sleeve and let it drift invisibly to the ground.

"Not that I would *ever* settle for Broadway!" Argyll raved on. "They're going to have to come to Britain to see me!"

"You'd deprive the American people of the sight of the greatest actor-writer of the century?" Hayley was in open awe.

"It would be pandering to the Philistines if I *allowed* myself to think about Broadway or—"

There was a long pause.

Hayley smiled. "Or Hollywood?" she whispered, as if it were an obscenity.

"You'll never catch me selling out!"

"Perhaps nobody actually *wants* to buy you in the first place." Hayley gazed at him mockingly.

"Incredible!" snorted Argyll. "In-bloody-credible!" He took Meg Talbot's arm. "Come on, love. The conversation suddenly bores me. I can't stand talking with—with uncouth colonists!"

"Especially when the uncouth are ahead on points,"

Meg Tálbot laughed and winked at Hayley. "Good-bye, Sir John."

At that moment, there was an almost audible sigh from the crowd assembled in the palace garden. Huddlestone nudged Hayley, and she turned to watch where he indicated. At that moment, the royal party emerged from the Bow Room, a kind of extended entryway in the center of the West Wing of the palace, shaped in the form of a bow and topped by an interesting articulated dome, by John Nash, King George IV's architect and the original designer of the palace.

When the Queen, Princess Diana, the Duke of Edinburgh, and Prince Charles stood outside the Bow Room's glass doors, the band struck up "God Save the Queen." Then, after a very brief introduction to a group of dignitaries whom even Huddlestone did not recognize, the royal party strolled out into the garden to mingle with the guests.

Hayley studied the Queen, dressed in sky blue, and Princess Diana, who wore a suit of cream and tan. The Duke of Edinburgh and Prince Charles were dressed in light gray top hats and tails, and carried tightly rolled umbrellas, because of the mild threat of rain in the air.

Hayley was surprised at the piercing quality of Prince Charles's blue eyes. He was extremely tanned and looked very fit indeed.

Huddlestone waited for the Prince and Princess to pass by, but they did not. While she waited, Hayley found her eyes wandering over to Clive Argyll, who was now standing in the center of an admiring crowd of women. As she observed him distantly, she saw his face turn slightly and his eyes meet hers for one brief instant. Over a distance of thirty feet, she felt the dagger of hostility. She shivered, turning away.

A moment later, she was watching him move slowly through the crowd, several of his adoring acolytes following him. His head, with the top hat cocked at an angle, moved with an actor's grace through the assemblage standing on the emerald-green lawn.

That evening, while Hayley waited with Huddlestone in the hotel to enter the restaurant at Claridge's, she was struck with what she knew would be one of her "brilliant ideas." It was so overpoweringly on target that she was afraid to put words to it, and she did not mention it at all to her London representative. Nevertheless, she was thinking about it as she listened to the Hungarian orchestra playing gently in the background.

Finally, as their waiter, dressed in a red jacket with gold buttons, and velvet breeches with silk stockings, escorted them into the main dining room through the gilt and glass doors, she began to plan the moves involved in getting her idea off the ground. Even so, the chandeliers and elegant table setting made it difficult to concentrate on such mundane matters.

Huddlestone nodded to several people seated in the room as he and Hayley were ushered over to their table in the corner. Hayley was surprised to see Michael Caine seated at one of the tables with a woman she did not recognize. As Huddlestone glanced around the room, he turned to her and whispered:

"Penelope Keith, of course, over there with Peter Bowles. You recognize them from British television."

Despite the excitement of the afternoon and the elegance of the surroundings in the famed dining room, Hayley selected her English favorite for dinner, commonplace as it was: steak and kidney pie. She topped it off with figue royale. The grace and style of the Wedgewood and Royal Doulton china, with its intaglioed *C* for "Claridge's" incised in the green-and-gold border, occupied her attention as she ate and chatted in a desultory fashion with Huddlestone.

"Why, actually, did you come to Britain?" he asked her at one point.

"To see you," she laughed, putting her hand over his on the table in an affectionate way—just two old friends touching.

His blue eyes crinkled. "I know you better than that. Is it Cornelius?"

She studied him with a halfsmile. "I just needed a change, Jock." For years she had been calling him, "Jock," as he had told her to.

"How is Abigail?"

"Bored with school."

"Who isn't?" He smiled. "We can go over the portfolio, if you wish."

She shrugged. "Perhaps give it a token glance."

"There *is* something." He eyed her expectantly.

She faced him without subterfuge. "Let's go see a play, shall we? I haven't been for ages."

Huddlestone nodded. "Nor have I. The current crop hasn't been particularly fruitful. What would you like to see?"

"*Nine Moons Wasted*," said Hayley.

Huddlestone blinked. "But I thought—"

"Never mind what you thought. Can do?"

"For my most important client? As you Yanks say, can do."

It took some wangling in Claridge's luxurious, newly refurbished lobby, and some arm-twisting, but finally Huddlestone was triumphant, and he reported that the tickets would be waiting for them at the box office that same night.

The Rolls Royce picked them up at the Brook Street entrance to Claridge's, where an assemblage of flags hung over the marquee, and in minutes they were in the West End, picking up their tickets and making their way into the theater.

Hayley sank down in her seat and dared the play to entertain her. After some disappointments, it actually did. She found herself wrapped up in the story and rooting for the main characters—even if they *were* involved in putting down a rich old man who lorded it over the rest of them.

It was Argyll who overpowered her. She could *feel* the vitality of the man even from down in the audience. His presence crossed the footlights and entered into her—and into many other people in the audience.

At intermission, Hayley excused herself, passed by the groups of men and women consuming tea or orange drink in the lounge areas, and entered the lady's room.

Two London shopgirls were powdering their noses at the mirror.

"Ain't he the one, though! Oh, I could *feel* him, slipping it to me the way I like it best. And that *look* he gives the girl on the stage. You can almost see her creaming her knickers, can't you?"

"I wish George could do it the way *he* could. And when they're standing together kissing, I thought I'd *die*. Gracie was right when she told me not to miss this one! What a movie it would make—you know? Imagine him up there on that monster screen—bigger than life!"

"Wisht I could take him home with me."

The second act slowed considerably—but after

the tremendous beginning, it was not surprising. It was here that the playwright sowed all the seeds of socialism, not even bothering to disguise his lectures, playing with rhetoric like a full-fledged politician.

The third act picked up, and the drama was resolved in a modern way, without too much implausibility, and with considerable sincerity and honesty.

Hayley left Huddlestone that night with a suggestion. "Jock, I'd like to see you tomorrow. I've got something I want you to put together for me."

He nodded. "A new project?"

"Very new." She gave him a brief rundown of what she wanted. He was so stunned at the prospect that he simply stared at her when she had finished.

"Now close your mouth, you lovely man, and get some sleep. I want you bright-eyed and bushy-tailed tomorrow, as we Yanks say."

She pecked him on the cheek and closed the door to her suite. Once inside, she leaned back against the door, lifted her hands into the air, doubled them into fists, and yelled, "Yippie!"

Hayley had weekended at Lord Muirhead's country home, deep in the pastoral paradise of the Isle of Wight, several times before, and she never ceased to marvel at Jock's ability to bring back a way of life that was said to have vanished completely from Great Britain after World War I.

She knew that her weekend at the country home of the Huddlestones would be the high point of her trip to England. On Friday evening, after he had closed the office on Regent Street, Sir John ordered the Rolls to Mayfair and picked her up at Claridge's. Soon they were on their way down A3 to Portsmouth.

"That little project you gave me took some doing," Huddlestone told her as he relaxed in the back seat.

"I give you the difficult ones because you're so good at them," she told him with a yawn.

"Hard week?"

"I've been on the go twenty-four hours a day," Hayley admitted. "Still, I feel better for it." She turned to him. "The Foundation is in excellent shape, Jock. I've sorted out a few new directions we can take in the upcoming years. I'll tell you about them later."

He closed his eyes and stretched out his legs as the limousine picked up speed heading in a southwesterly direction from the city. Within a relatively short time, they were in Portsmouth boarding the Portsmouth-Fishbourne ferry for the surging, rocky trip across the Solent. It was quite beautiful seeing the sun set over the island ahead of them. They were at the front door of Muirhead Manor, the family home, before it had become really dark.

In the distance, to the west, Hayley could make out the ghostly silhouette of Carisbrooke Castle, one of the most famous castles in England, where Victoria had spent many years of her mourning.

Friday night was relatively calm at Muirhead Manor; since most of the guests were scheduled to arrive on Saturday morning. Hayley went to bed early, after a fine meal prepared by Jock's spectacular French chef and served with aplomb by Chantry, a butler right out of P.G. Wodehouse.

Hayley lounged in bed until very late in the morning—late for her, anyway. She eventually came down for brunch and then drove over to the western end of the island, to Alum Bay, in a car borrowed from Chantry. Under the colorful cliffs—almost every color of the rainbow was represented in the pale pastel shades of the sheer rock surface—she swam and suntanned at one of the finest bathing beaches around.

When she returned to Muirhead Manor, she could see by the line of cars in the driveway that the guests had begun to arrive. She took a bath and changed, then came down to join the guests in the marvelous terraced garden.

She saw several people she knew, and she chatted briefly with them. She was standing alone at the rear of the estate, gazing into the distance, when she heard footsteps stop dead behind her.

"My God!" said a voice. "It's the Lady Piranha!"

She turned. "Oh, hello, Mr. Argyll. I had no idea you would be here."

"Nor I you. But this week has been a busy one for me. I've been quite occupied."

"Treading the boards?"

His face lit up with triumph. "Of course, that. But something else!"

"Birth? Marriage? Income tax audit?"

"I've been picked up by Hollywood." He let this sink in. "Hollywood!" he repeated. "I've signed the papers already. My play. Me. Everything!"

"Gracious. Is that good or bad? Previously you were quite adamant about not—'pandering to the Philistines.' "

He winked smugly. "Lady, there's so much money involved here, I doubt I'll ever have to worry again."

"Congratulations are then in order?"

"Only if you *mean* them." His eyes glittered with vindictiveness. He was rubbing it in—in the worst way.

She shrugged. "I cannot tell a lie. I withdraw the congratulations and substitute condolences."

He came toward her, took her by the arm, and looked her in the eye. "What *are* you talking about?"

"Hollywood. You've sold out for money."

"You'd know about that, wouldn't you? Money?"

"I thought hating money was *your* line."

"Lady, I've not had it for so long, I'll know what to do with it when I've got it."

"Of course, you won't be your own man anymore."

"Clive Argyll has *always* been his own man. He will continue to be."

"Possibly. You mentioned piranhas. Hollywood invented them."

"I can handle them." He smiled crookedly at her. "You don't know me very well, do you?"

"Heavens, no! Nor do I have any intention of getting to know you 'very well.' "

He shook his head. "You know, I grew up hating the British because of their class consciousness. But you Yanks have a hell of a lot more class consciousness than anybody in these islands! Especially you American women!"

Hayley gazed at the actor a long moment before saying: "Mr. Argyll, do you realize that you are probably one of the most odious male chauvinists I have ever had the displeasure of meeting? It exudes from every pore of your body. You emanate hostility, envy, and vindictiveness in a male way until one can taste it."

He was furious now, furious and holding himself back with difficulty. "I came out here to be civil to you. Maybe I was about to apologize for being a little hard on you at the Queen's garden party—but

I'll tell you now, Miss Moneybags, I've got nothing to apologize for!''

"*Mrs*. Moneybags."

"I stand corrected. I know you've got too many millions for me ever to catch up—even if I'm as big a hit as the Beatles were in America—but I'm getting closer! Doesn't that give you a cold chill up and down your spine?"

Hayley sighed. "Perhaps it's the evening sea breeze."

"I've never met anyone like you," Argyll volunteered. "I don't know what it is, but you make me absolutely *ill*. It's surprising, because I like women. All women. Yet you simply turn me off cold."

"I would hate to turn you on hot," Hayley said with a shiver.

"I don't understand it. I've never felt more antipathy for anyone in my life. What *is* it?"

"Envy, perhaps. Envy of billions. Of status. Of clout. Of power."

Argyll threw back his head and laughed. "It may have been that at one time. But now I'm getting those things, and boy, I'm going to rub your nose in it!"

"If you catch me."

He grinned obscenely. "With the proper setting, who knows? I might have enough money to tup you right and proper, little lady!"

"Don't be absurd!" snapped Hayley. "I'm bored with the conversation. Good day!"

She turned and walked off.

In the darkness, Clive Argyll stood watching her, his feelings in turmoil, perspiration on his forehead, his heart pounding against his ribs. What kind of a ball-breaker was this bitch, *really?* he wondered.

As for Hayley, she was hurrying away from him, her own viscera tingling with warmth and anticipation. On her lips there was the faintest of smiles. His hatred was a palpable thing—something she could almost touch in the atmosphere between them.

And that made the payoff all the more satisfactory.

"Oh, yes," said Huddlestone as he sat opposite Hayley in his sitting room the next morning. He was dressed in a bed jacket; Hayley had on a thin, attractive lounging robe. "He signed with an absolute surge of glee."

"Good," Hayley said.

Huddlestone opened his leather case and drew out a sheaf of papers. "Here they are."

Hayley settled down to study them. She removed her reading glasses from the pocket of her robe and slipped them on. She had never bothered with contacts, and could usually get along without her glasses. She rarely allowed herself to be seen with them on, and then only by close friends.

Chantry Productions, she read with a smile. Lee Chantry represented the organization. He became sole proprietor of Clive Argyll and Clive Argyll's property, *Nine Moons Wasted*.

Her eyes gleamed as she folded up the papers and handed them back to Huddlestone.

"Love that Chantry Productions touch," she chuckled.

Huddlestone studied her pensively. "You sure about this?"

"Never more so in my life."

He shrugged. "All right, then."

She was gloating, her blood surging, her heart pounding.

"We've got him!"

CHAPTER ELEVEN

Lynn Miles had long ago learned how to play the game. Although anyone looking at her would have assumed that she was bored out of her skull, she was actually enjoying herself immensely. Her modus operandi was never to let anyone know that she really *liked* anything at all.

A thin, gaunt-faced, dark-haired clotheshorse, who might have been suffering from anemia or something worse, appeared on the small stage, pirouetting and showing off the apricot cocktail dress she wore with all the flair one would expect of a model in a Parisian house of haute couture. Behind her lidded blue eyes, Lynn's brain was toting up the number of gowns she had already bought. This one was a beauty. It would show off her own more than generous curves in an eye-bulging display.

"Night wear, next," said the high-strung female designer who was standing at the side of the stage directing the promenade. "Madame?" Her avaricious, sparkling black eyes glistened at Lynn.

"I've had enough," said Lynn. She made a move to get up out of her comfortable chair.

"If madame is unable to find—"

Lynn shrugged. "Numbers fifteen, eighteen, twenty-four, and thirty."

The designer's lined face relaxed, and she managed a smile of feigned ecstasy. "Of course, madame!"

"Send them to my suite at the Georges Cinq," Lynn intoned, sweeping to her feet and starting out of the showroom. Christ, she thought. Wait till Miley sees the bill! She'd already gone through at least fourteen thousand dollars just getting the business of her fall wardrobe organized. Today's foray made it an additional two, maybe three, thou. Still, he liked her to look good; it was the thing she did best. He had always agreed that he needed the proper setting for his little diamond. Actually, she had told him that to begin with. And he'd never argued.

At least she had finally learned how to shop for clothes in Paris. When she had first come over, the year before, she'd bought her clothes off the god-damned racks in the haut couture joints on the Champs Elysées. Then, one day, she'd overheard an old bag at the hotel telephoning ahead to one of the exclusive shops to open up the showroom for her, and Lynn had simply followed suit. Why not? To her surprise, she'd been ushered into the privacy of some of the best designer boutiques in town, and had been given free private showings at each of them. Once, of course, they'd checked to make sure she really was one of *the* Mileses.

Fantastic! All you did was take down the numbers and order them when you left. Of course, you had to give them your special measurements ahead of time, but what the hell? It saved all that time standing around with swatches in her hand and tape measures draped across her body.

As she approached the door, to exit the inner showroom, a Frenchwoman opened it from the other side and strode in. She was an angular, scrawny, rather emaciated woman—younger than Lynn—and yet, somehow familiar. As a matter of fact, the moment the other woman saw Lynn, she paused, startled, and blinked. Then she looked away and hurried on.

"Hey!" Lynn called after her.

The young woman froze, then turned.

Now Lynn's mind linked the face with the event. "You're the breakfast girl. On the Hudson."

The Frenchwoman hesitated, as if considering whether to ignore Lynn's statement, pretend she did not speak English, or admit who she was.

Thérèse Maupin smiled. The reaction relaxed her taut face and gave her expression a softness that it did not always possess. "Madame Miles. The wife of the senator."

"That's it. You're the Cosmétique Queen's gofer."

A faint smile. A shrug. "You are shopping?" Tessie said rather awkwardly.

"*Oui*," said Lynn, using one of the few words she had in French. "You're shopping, too?"

A quirked eyebrow. "Me? I do not wear expensive clothes. It is not proper. Besides, I no longer am Beatrix Fontaine's—how you say?—gofer. I labor on my own time."

"She fired you?" Lynn chuckled. "Figures."

The Frenchwoman's expression turned furtive. She glanced around to make sure no one was listening to what they were saying. "Please. I have hurry-up appointment. But I would like to meet later. For coffee? A snack?''

"You name it," Lynn said. "It's time we let our hair down a little.''

Again Tessie Maupin shrugged. "Les Deux Magots. On the Boulevard de Saint-Germain. Very famous.''

"Three o'clock?''

Thérèse nodded and hastened into the rear of the establishment. Lynn watched her go, wondering if the Frenchwoman now worked for this designer—or, in fact, what she was really doing there.

Promptly at three o'clock, Lynn was seated at a sidewalk table at Les Deux Magots, watching the Parisian street theater being played in front of her. The program was a cliché of everything she had read about Paris street cafés. She had ordered a licorice-flavored pasti from a lean, weary, and surly waiter with a greasy apron tied around his middle.

As she sipped it, she watched the tired old men around her, puffing as if their lives depended on the smoke from their drooping Gitane cigarettes. A young Frenchwoman nearby wore jeans and a shirt, with the jeans tightly fitted at the ankles, and white stockings and red shoes with big bows. An older Parisian woman strolled by, showing off her hair, dyed a bright and repellent orange.

"I come," announced Tessie Maupin, taking the seat opposite Lynn. "You have been waiting long time?''

"Nothing to worry about.''

Tessie ordered a citron pressé from the waiter and sank back into the hard-backed chair to rest a moment.

"You are here with the senator?'' she asked after a moment's silence.

"He's in Paris on a fact-finding mission. Translation: junket to Paris.'' Lynn giggled. ''It keeps him out of trouble. And it gives me a chance to buy a few clothes.''

Tessie's eyes glanced briefly at Lynn's tight-fitted waistcoat and flared skirt. Tasteless but expensive, her appraisal read. But Lynn wasn't interested in the subtle interpretation of other people's expressions.

''She sent you packing because of the roadshow Cornelius Welles is organizing, didn't she?''

The eyes were bleak and expressionless. No answer.

''Come on. It's obvious, isn't it?''

Tessie nodded. ''Please. I do not want to destroy Mademoiselle Fontaine's fortunes. I go peacefully.'' Her eyes narrowed.

Lynn leaned forward just a bit, almost as if she were engaging in conspiratorial dialogue with a fellow traveler. ''Friends of enemies are friends,'' she said slowly. She was watching the Frenchwoman's eyes. There was a moment of sympathetic response. ''Ahah! I thought so! You want to get her good, don't you?''

Tessie sipped at the citron pressé silently. ''I do not think I answer.''

''The Cosmétique Queen is on a high roll. You understand?''

Tessie smiled.

''The fortunes of Carney Welles go up as Beatrix Fontaine's fortunes go up. Right?''

''*Mais oui.*''

''About him, about her, I couldn't care less. It's the wife.''

Tessie's eyes narrowed. ''Madame Welles? The Prescott heiress?''

''Exactly.'' Lynn worked at her pasti. Christ, the

taste of licorice was overpowering. "If one falls, they all fall."

"Friends of enemies are friends," Tessie quoted Lynn, nodding her head in understanding.

"You said you did not want to destroy Mademoiselle Beatrix. What would change your mind?"

Tessie made a moue. "It would not take much."

Lynn burst into laughter. "I've got the money."

"It is a known fact."

"We work together." Lynn reached out to take Tessie's hand in hers. "Agreed?"

"Why you want to hurt Madame Welles?"

"Who said I wanted to hurt her? I just want to see her fall down a level or two."

"There is, perhaps, a reason?"

"I do things on impulse."

Tessie stared a moment, then in turn grasped Lynn's hand. "We work together." Her eyes moved about at the tables nearby. "I have found out interesting things about Mademoiselle," she admitted softly.

Lynn's eyes crinkled at the corners. "I knew you were onto something! I just *knew* it!" She leaned forward. "Is there any way I can help?"

"*Peut-être*," murmured Tessie. She leaned back in her chair. "It is *difficile*. Your husband—"

"Forget about Miley! He doesn't know anything about this. Even if he found out about it, he wouldn't do anything. He hates her guts, too."

"Mademoiselle's?"

"No, no. Hayley Prescott's guts. She snubbed him all her life until he got into the Senate. Now they're buddy-buddy. But he needs her. She needs him. There's a move on to tax nonprofit foundations. It'll cost the Prescotts millions if it goes through. You scratch my back, I'll scratch yours."

Tessie nodded. "I do not work anymore. I have no job."

Lynn understood. "You need money? You've got it. And we do a job on Mademoiselle Fontaine."

"Okay," said Tessie.

"Now tell me what you've got."

Senator Kirby Miles blew up when Lynn told him what her plans were.

"Provence? What in hell's in Provence? I didn't know they sold Parisian clothes in Provence! If you want to go, go right ahead. I, for one, certainly won't cry over missing *that* trip."

"It's just that I'd like to broaden my horizons a little, Miley. I thought it would be the right time to see some part of France that wasn't Paris."

"Uh huh," said the senator, eyeing her shrewdly. "How do you plan to get there? Tour bus?" His face wrinkled in the parody of a knowing grin. He knew his wife. She wouldn't be caught dead on a tour bus.

"Miley!" cried Lynn. "Of course not! I've hired a Citroen for the trip."

The senator nodded thoughtfully. "It sounds like you've already made up your mind. Don't say I didn't warn you. They've got dust there that you wouldn't believe. It's like the Staked Plains of Texas, or the Panhandle during a dust bowl. They've got a wind that comes up called a mistral that sucks the guts right out of you. In the midst of the heat and the sunshine that wind can freeze your balls off. Christ, people have written poems about that damned wind!"

"How come you know so much about Provence, Miley?" Lynn understood enough about her husband to reason that she might take some of the edge off her husband's curiosity if she could get him to talk.

"Hell, my sister Frannie bought a goddamned castle there about ten years ago. She was married then to that Englishman with the title. Lord Middlesex, I think. Dumb name, huh?" he grinned. "She'd keep dragging all the Mileses up there during the summer for a couple weeks 'in the country.' Actually, the local wine isn't bad—but it's not a *great* wine. There's plenty of fruit—melons, peaches, apples, strawberries. But the people there are nuts."

"Come on, Milcy. You're just kidding."

"Yeah? One of Frannie's servants got caught in the castle's hay rick with a local milkmaid. His wife, Frannie's cook, put a knife through her husband's dong. Son of a bitch bled to death. Hell, he had nothing to live for at that point, anyway. Gendarmes all over the place. Big news in *Le Provence*—that's the local rag. About two weeks later, we all got laid up sick as dogs from some tainted goat cheese that Frannie's four-star chef bought from a second cousin. We put the castle on the market three days later. It's that goddamned wind, I'm convinced of it!"

Lynn giggled. "It sounds quaint as hell. I've got to go, Miley!"

"You're not going alone, are you?" the senator said, more as a statement of fact than as a question. "It's that French kid, the one that used to work for Mademoiselle Fontaine, isn't it?"

Lynn felt her blood run cold. "How'd you know?"

"That frumpy wife of Senator Woodward—the woman we all call 'Woodwork,' short for 'out-of-the' —saw you and this one at some outdoor café. By the description, I figured it was the Maupin dame for sure."

"How'd you remember her name?"

"Kid, I may not be too smart where it counts

academically, but there's three things I remember. Faces, bank statements, and names." He was still eyeing her. "So what's it all about? She found some sensational, *merveilleuse* couturier for you in the Massif Central?"

"It's not clothes, Miley!"

"If it ain't, I'm worried. But at the same time, I'm relieved. You've already gone through fifteen grand right here in Paris. God knows what you'd do down in Provence."

"She's an interesting person, you know." It came out all defensive and mea culpa. She cursed herself for not having better control over her lying.

"Uh huh."

"It's some nice things for the house. Tessie says there are flea markets down there that have really valuable and unusual antiques."

"And it just so happens her grandfather runs one, huh?" Miles was grinning again. "Anyway, I'll agree about the fleas. I'm still scratching from the time I went to the last one down there."

"You're so—uncouth!"

"How'd you happen to look her up?"

"I didn't look her up. I ran into her." Lynn was watching her husband's face, and she saw the sudden glint of intelligence.

"You 'ran into her'?"

"At one of those designer boutiques on the Champs Elysées."

"Honey, there ain't no 'ran into.' Not in Paris. This is the headquarters for Interpol, and for good reason. There is no plot or scam or bit of skullduggery in the world that wasn't invented in Paris. You were *made* to meet her."

Lynn blinked, staring at the senator in bafflement.

"I don't believe it! Nobody knew where I'd be. I'd just seen a private designer showing. How could—?"

"Baby! Everybody in Paris knows you're into designer shows! My God, there was a notice three days ago in one of the gossip columns."

Lynn's mouth hung open.

"I read it, damn it!" the senator emphasized.

"I didn't know you could read French!"

"I can't *read* it. But I can sure as hell *communicate* it!" He laughed. "Honey, I'm a bullshit artist. That's how I make my way. A bullshit artist doesn't have any brains for the finer things, but he can sure make sense out of words. Even if they're in a foreign language. Hell, the notice said you were making the rounds of all the most expensive boutiques. It didn't take any talent on my part to translate that!"

Lynn was subdued. At one point, she had paused to think it over and had been struck by the coincidence of Tessie Maupin's arrival at just the proper moment at that showing. But why—?

"What are you two up to in Provence?" Miles asked quietly. "And how does it tie in with Beatrix Fontaine?"

Lynn sank back in her chair in defeat. They were eating breakfast at the Georges Cinq, just finishing their breakfast coffee, and she now felt utterly drained. She also felt like a fool. Maybe Tessie *was* leading her down the garden path. She had said she needed money to continue her search for the truth about Beatrix—but maybe it was all going into her pocket.

"It's that campaign of Cornelius Welles's, isn't it?" the senator prompted. He would have made a pretty good trial lawyer, Lynn realized. You just couldn't put anything over on him.

"How do you know about that?" Lynn asked in startled shock.

"Welles is no dummy. He's been placing little announcements here and there for weeks now, all to build up to a big flashy introduction of Beatrix and her system of beauty spas."

Lynn sighed. "It's fake. Beatrix's life. She was born out of wedlock."

"Wow!" said the senator dryly. "*Quelle scandale!* So what, kid? It gives a little edge to her personality!"

"Maybe. But Tessie thinks there's more to it than that."

"More to it? What more? That Beatrix has had a lesbian affair with that Maupin creature for a year or so? That's the point of Carney Welles's campaign. To purify the image so that at least it *looks* good in print."

"It was Tessie who wrote up the Beatrix biography. I mean, from scratch. It's all a pack of lies."

"Like any film actor's bio." The senator shrugged. "So?"

"Tessie did a little research, trying to make the facts that were invented dovetail with the real facts."

"Sure. That's known as manufacturing the big lie out of little bits and pieces of the truth."

"There's something funny about Beatrix's roots."

"Funny, ha-ha?"

"Funny, kinky."

"What does it matter to Tessie? She's written her handout, hasn't she? I've seen parts of it printed here and there. Something about Beatrix's real father being an Indo-Chinese aristocrat, or something exotic like that."

"There's some secret Beatrix is trying to cover up," Lynn went on stubbornly. "And that's why

Tessie wants to go to Provence. To a place called Grignan.''

"And that's where the ghost of Beatrix's father stalks the bloody tower?''

"You're such a clod, Miley!'' Lynn was suddenly so furious that she brought her hand down hard on the table, upsetting her coffee cup and sending both cup and saucer onto the hard floor. There was a crash and clatter, and every head in the sedate and swanky restaurant turned toward them.

The waiter hastened over. The senator slipped him a large bill to take care of the mess, and quiet was finally restored. The conversation continued in a hushed, intense tone.

"It's not Beatrix you're after, is it?'' he asked in a tight whisper. "It's Welles! Or it's Hayley!'' His eyes suddenly lit up. "You've been going on about Hayley for years, haven't you? You were so excited when we got invited to Scobie Hills. It was Hayley Welles you wanted to meet. I got all that. And yet, when we finally arrived, you hid out from her. What is it all about, Lynn?''

"Shut up! Shut up!'' sobbed Lynn, furious tears springing into her eyes.

"I don't think much of the little bitch myself, kid,'' the senator went on offhandedly, "but I can certainly do without whatever kind of mischief *you've* got lined up for her. That's why you're going after Beatrix, isn't it? Because when she goes down, Welles looks like a jerk, and so does Hayley.''

Lynn kept her fists clenched and out of sight, tight to her thighs. Her fingernails were biting into her palms.

"The word is that it was really Hayley who spotted Beatrix as a potential client for the Welles organization. She brought the two of them together.''

Lynn's eyes widened. "I didn't know that!"

"You never look past the end of your nose," the senator said absently. "I'm involved in this Beatrix thing, you know. I've promised to be one of Welles's VIPs at the Nice thing—typical example of the Beautiful People." Kirby Miles gazed at his wife for a moment. "You and me, babe. It might be a good idea if you did take a look at what's stirring in Beatrix's background—if there is anything. I don't want to take the fall because of something she did before this beauty spa project was born."

"Darling!" said Lynn with a quick release of pent-up breath. She reached out and hugged her husband over the table. Once again, everybody in the Georges Cinq Restaurant turned around and shook their heads, with whispered comments about "ugly Americans"—even though the majority of them were Americans, too.

She felt it first as they were driving the Citroen through the winding roads of northern Provence, gazing out at the purple wildflowers on the hillsides, the green grapevines clinging to the slopes, the huge sunflowers opened wide in the gardens.

Funny. It came from the north. The heat lay all about them, with no motion evident. And then, suddenly, this wind from the north.

Spooky.

"Mistral?" she asked Tessie.

Tessie, hands gripped on the wheel of the car, sweat beaded out on her forehead, turned slightly. "Huh? Oh, *oui*. Mistral. Fever weather."

The Citroen bumped over the less than smooth

roadway, raising dust as it descended into a quiet valley with tiny ancient houses clustered together like old-fashioned villages. The terra cotta tiled roofs gave the scenery a definite Mediterranean flavor.

Other than the brief mention of ''fever weather,'' Tessie said nothing, becoming remote once again and concentrating on her driving. Weird dame, thought Lynn again, recalling her husband's similar appraisal.

The plan was to make Grignan, hole up in a hotel there, and use Grignan as headquarters for other forays into the countryside in the search of the background of Beatrix Fontaine.

On closer questioning, Tessie had volunteered a bit more information. Lynn suspected it was because Tessie was afraid the Miles money source would dry up if she didn't reveal something of the raison d'être for the Provence trip.

Beatrix Fontaine had been born in Paris. Her birth was recorded properly in the city archives. Her father was listed as Valentine Fontaine, her mother as Ursule Fontaine. Of course it was known by close associates that there never was a Valentine Fontaine in Paris, and it was presumed that perhaps there never was a Valentine Fontaine anywhere. Perhaps the name was simply a myth.

After writing up a fanciful biography of Beatrix Fontaine, inventing an aristocratic Eurasian forebear, and weaving together a story of her romantic origins, Tessie had searched out people who had known Ursule Fontaine during Beatrix's very early years. She had then lived in what Lynn understood to be a very seamy section of Paris, which was beginning to undergo redevelopment and rejuvenation in postwar France. Beatrix was born in 1955, just when postwar Europe was coming alive again. Tessie discovered that Ursule had arrived in Paris only a few months before the birth of her daughter.

Where had she come from? No one seemed to know. Ursule was handy with a needle, and she had managed to make enough money to bring up her child. She had the help of several people whom she had befriended while she lived in the dilapidated quarters she shared with another working woman. From this most unprepossessing start, against all odds, Beatrix had educated herself and become a brilliant chemist in the main outlet of one of France's most important cosmetic firms. From this company, she had begun to develop several "lines" that were later to become the mainstays of Beatrix Cosmétique, which she founded when she was only twenty-five years old! She was definitely a prodigy in chemistry and science.

Her own company had caught on immediately, and she became rich almost overnight. By that time, she had severed all connection with her birthplace in the stews of Paris. After a while, no one cared. She was rich and she was respected.

Tessie had not given up when the trail to Beatrix's past seemed to pinch out. She searched for other people who might have known Beatrix when she was small. And she struck paydirt eventually. A teacher of Beatrix's—the one who had recognized her ability in mathematics and chemistry—recalled that Beatrix's mother had visited her once or twice to discuss the possibility of scholarships for Beatrix.

It had occurred to the teacher, who was interested in languages and in accents as a hobbyist, that Ursule's accent was one of Provence, in southern France, rather than Parisian—athough, of course, Ursule had taken on the Parisian manner of speaking after a while.

To check out this tiny clue, the teacher had once asked Ursule directly if she knew the Drôme country, and Ursule had shrugged and mentioned only Grignan. Then, the moment she had said it, she changed the subject. When the teacher brought up Grignan again later on, Ursule pretended never to have heard of the place.

Mentioning Provence and Grignan to people who had lived in the same neighborhood in Paris with Ursule, Tessie found that there were other indications that Ursule might have come from Provence. She loved goat cheese, for example, a specialty of Provence. And she cooked a tender *confit* of guinea hen and lentils—what one woman said was called *pointade aux lentilles,* a favorite in Provence.

When Tessie had written to the authorities in Grignan asking about the Fontaine family, she had drawn a blank. There was simply no record of any Fontaines at all. She was at this point in her search when fate interposed and put her together with Lynn Miles.

Lynn had never tried to ascertain whether or not Tessie had set up their meeting. She really didn't care. It was enough that the two of them were on the same wavelength in regard to Beatrix. That is, both wanted Beatrix to come crashing down, one way or another.

They were winding their way along the twisting roads into Grignan in the Massif Central when Tessie turned to Lynn for the first time in many hours of driving.

"There is another factor," she said slowly.

"About Beatrix?" Lynn asked eagerly.

Tessie nodded. "I am unable to confirm everything. Physicians do not like things to be repeated."

Lynn was instantly alert. "Beatrix was seeing a doctor?" Of course! Lynn thought. She was pregnant! What a story! What a twist—and, of course, Welles was the father! Marvelous!

Tessie smiled nastily. "Not a doctor of *médecine*. A psychiatrist."

Lynn's face fell. "Hell, everybody has a private psychiatrist." Well then, she *wasn't* pregnant. Damn!

"But this was a man who specialized in one specific type of disease."

"The *mind* doesn't catch diseases, Tessie!"

"He would tell me nothing, you understand. But this man treated Beatrix. He is a specialist in Alzheimer's Disease."

Lynn frowned. "But there's nothing wrong with Beatrix! You'd be able to spot *that* in a minute."

"Unless," said Tessie, her eyes gleaming, "it *wasn't* Alzheimer's Disease, but only *resembled* it." She sat back with a satisfied smile.

Lynn mulled that over, thinking of all the recent articles she had read about the disease in newspapers and magazines. "You mean she's crazy?"

Tessie shrugged. "There was no indication from anyone that Beatrix had any mental problems. This trip is important because we have to find out about Beatrix's father. Maybe *he* was nuts! The mother wasn't. But if we can link the *father* and the daughter—"

Lynn's face clouded. "It's kind of nasty, isn't it? I mean, here we are trying to prove that someone is flaky—"

Tessie said, "Here we are. Chez Lousteau."

Lynn looked out the window. They had come up

to a very small inn by the side of the narrow road. All around them were tiny buildings with tiled roofs crowded in together on both sides of a cobblestoned one-way street. They were in the center of Grignan, Tessie explained.

They took their bags into the hotel, which they had telephoned the day before to make reservations, and Tessie drove the car around in back where there was an ancient stable attached to the inn, now serving as a garage.

When she returned, she was frowning and shivering. "Bitter cold! It is the mistral."

Together the two of them unpacked their bags, and Lynn pulled herself into a warm sweater. She felt the penetrating cold as sharply as Tessie did. It *was* cold. The sweater warmed her.

They ate dinner at the inn itself. The food was, just as Miley had warned her, unappetizing. Lynn was hungry after spending half the day driving and the other half sitting in the passenger seat of the Citroen, and she made no fuss. Nor did Tessie. She seemed preoccupied, occasionally glancing sideways at Lynn.

By the time the dessert had come—it was a plate of figs in sweet sauce—Lynn was definitely uncomfortable. It was Tessie's glances that were getting to her. Tessie seemed to be occupied with Lynn's sweater, her bust, in fact. Tessie *knew* Lynn was not gay. Why was she acting this way? If this broad made a pass at her, Lynn swore, she'd tear her face off.

Finally she had had enough. "What in hell are you staring at?" Lynn demanded.

"Is expensive sweater," said Tessie, shrugging. "I am envious of the warmth."

Lynn felt like a fool.

When the proprietor came to them at the end of the meal, Tessie restrained Lynn with a slight pressure on her wrist and drew the hotel owner into a conversation that proceeded in rapid colloquial French.

Lynn tried to keep from yawning as she listened to the rapid-fire talk, and when the proprietor's wife joined in with her own offerings, Lynn simply leaned back and dozed with her eyes half shut.

It was a half-hour after they had finished eating when they finally made their way up tthe stairs of the ancient inn. Lynn was leaden-eyed with fatigue—plus the soporific effect of the cheap table wine the innkeeper had plied them with. She could hardly wait to get into the bed after taking a most unsatisfactory shower in a sheet-metal shower stall located at the end of the hotel corridor.

"It sounded like the inside of a shooting gallery during target practice," Lynn groused, remembering her father's shooting exercises when he had been keeping himself in trim for his security job.

Tessie had stretched out in the bed and was laughing at Lynn. "You Americans!" she chuckled. "Always the bath or the shower."

Lynn ignored the Frenchwoman's sarcasm and got into her pajamas, turning her back to Tessie as she did so. Lynn was aware of Tessie's eyes on her as she adjusted her pajamas.

"Studying the price tag?" she asked wryly.

Tessie shook her head. "You have the good figure."

Lynn flushed. "Okay. So what?"

"I admire good figures."

"That's as far as it goes, Tessie. Admire but keep the hands off the merchandise." Lynn was climbing under the rough covers and keeping her back to Tessie.

"I do nothing if you no want."

"I no want."

Lynn leaned over and turned off the light. The switch mounted on the plastered wall was something out of a 1930's movie—a black knob on a ceramic device, resembling a solid black nipple on a woman's white breast. Lynn thought it was a rather odd and somewhat unfortunate omen.

Darkness sank over them. Lynn could still feel the intensity of the mistral. It seemed a live thing in the room with them, something out there trying to get inside her body, trying to invade her secret places.

"How do you know you don't want, unless you know what is?" Tessie asked in a soft voice.

"Down, Tessie! I told you. I'm no dyke! I don't go the gay route."

Tessie sighed. "Americans. They know everything without knowing nothing!"

"I'm just a person who prefers men."

"Because a man can get his big thing in you and make you do what he wants you to?"

"Because it feels goddamned good!" snapped Lynn. "Now shut up and let me get some sleep."

The bed creaked. Lynn flinched. Nothing happened. She shut her eyes and tried to doze off. Sleep would not come. Twenty minutes before, she had been unable to keep her eyes open, and now she was wide-awake and staring.

The bed creaked again. It was ancient enough to have been built for a straw mattress. Now Lynn felt warmth, sudden and ingratiating, enveloping her. Then, with a start, she realized Tessie's hand was on her thigh.

"Will you stop that?" Lynn cried, thoroughly aroused. "What in hell do you think you're doing?"

"Is it unlawful to touch?"

"I don't like it."

"Um."

Lynn lay back again, trying to close her eyes against the sudden excitement caused by the pressure of Tessie's hand. She lay on her back, fighting the bumpy curves of the bed. She shifted and the bed creaked.

Tessie giggled.

"Shut up!" snapped Lynn. She tried to burrow into the mattress to get her body a place to rest.

There was silence.

Lynn felt relaxed. She felt warm now, warm and comfortable. She was in a kind of cocoon. There was softness and warmth and security. She found herself breathing more deeply and more slowly.

She came awake drowsily. Her breasts were tingling and her body was alive. It was as if—

"Christ!" she yelped.

Tessie was fondling her breasts and had her in a kind of scissorlock, one leg thrown over her thigh and the other under her. She had no pajama top on. Somehow Tessie had snaked it off.

"Ooooh!"

That was nice, Lynn thought. Tessie had put her face down by Lynn's right nipple and was working away at it softly and thoroughly. Lynn caved in. She could feel the needles of pleasure all over her body . . . in her breasts, in her abdomen, in her crotch, and even in her toes. Wow!

"I told you, I don't like—"

A hand closed over her mouth.

Ooooh!

Skilled fingers were moving over her mons veneris, bringing her to a throbbing warmth. Then, without a wasted motion, the fingers entered her and penetrated her and after a moment brought her to a sudden shuddering orgasm.

She arched her back as Tessie took her lips off her breast and covered her mouth with them. The tongue darted in and out, forcing Lynn back onto the rough surface off the pillow. Her thighs caught Tessie's hand and squeezed hard.

My God, she was coming again! She let herself go and felt the presence of the Frenchwoman flow over her like warm olive oil.

Then the tongue was on her nipples again—nipples that were erect and aching for more and more. Tessie's teeth, sharp and pointed, suddenly closed over her flesh and she tried to scream in protest, but no sound came.

She lay pinioned in the bed, the Frenchwoman suddenly upside down over her, her tongue moving in and out of her in a way that Lynn had never imagined a tongue could move. Better than a man's any day, she thought, suddenly understanding the reason some women went in for this kind of thing.

Wow!

Her legs locked like a vise around the Frenchwoman's neck, the coarse hair flowing over her skin like a kind of human stretch pantry. Good, good, thought Lynn. My God!

Without quite understanding how it had happened, and puzzled a bit about the anatomical implausibility of it, she found her face crushed up against the Frenchwoman's pudendum, the pubic hair rubbing coarsely against her nose.

I'm not doing this, she thought as she plastered her mouth over the other woman's genitals. I'm not here at all. I'm a block away, coasting down the road on my roller skates.

The mistral, she thought. The goddamned mistral. If only Miley could see me now! He was right. There was nothing like the mistral. It did you in. Completely.

Lynn was lying there, absolutely drained of all tension. My God! It was like being a car and going through a car wash. Or maybe being a chicken and plucked for roasting.

Clever Miley, she thought. He was right. A dumb thing to do, to go to Provence with this confirmed lesbian. Now the damned weirdo had something on her—something she could blackmail her with.

And where the hell was Tessie now, anyway? she wondered as she drifted off.

Shit. She had never thought—

Oh, my God! What have I done?

BOOK THREE:
BEVERLY HILLS

CHAPTER TWELVE

Hayley Welles sat in the VIP lounge of Heathrow Airport sipping at a lemon Perrier as she watched a morning television drama courtesy of the BBC. The story had to do with a girl testifying at a trial, and while the plot was interesting, Hayley's mind refused to attend to it.

She was thinking of her daughter, Abbey.

That in itself, Hayley realized, somewhat startled at the idea, was something out the ordinary. For years now she had simply accepted Abbey's presence as something that was part of her, without really thinking too much about it.

Abbey was gone. That was the long and short of it. Abbey had decamped, had run away from home. A dumb nineteen-year-old girl, and she had simply run off somewhere.

Why?

Just to show off! Just to make her mother and father miserable. Father? Carney wasn't her father. Pete Martin was her father. Hayley's number one mistake. But Pete didn't care. He never sent her anything. Claimed his presents would be scorned, not only by Abbey but by the Prescotts, too.

There was something of the truth in that.

Where had the damned kid gone? That was the question. Was she trying to prove her independence? Hayley had an idea that independence was part of it. But there must be more. What was there about Abbey that Hayley didn't know? Was she into drugs? Was she into the counter culture? Was she in a commune, for God's sake, if they still *had* them? Why in hell didn't Hayley know more about Abbey?

It was Carney Welles who had first told her about Abbey's disappearance—since that was what it had turned out to be. Hayley had been in California at the time. She had considered it simply a means to annoy her. She was sure Abbey had simply packed up and gone to a friend's house to stay a few weeks or so—in spite of Hayley's warning about kidnapping!

She tapped the half-empty glass of lemon Perrier against her bottom teeth and narrowed her eyes. It was so damned easy to panic. When Carney's low key, deliberately unanimated voice had come over the wire, Hayley had immediately thought of the possibility of a kidnapping. She had bitten her tongue to keep her concern from sounding in her voice. When it turned out that there had been no indications of kidnapping—no ransom demands—then she had relaxed a bit. Certainly, if Abbey had been taken for ransom, there would be demands made.

So she and Carney had chatted about this and that, with Carney's voice finally curling back a bit—like a pair of lips against bared teeth—to give just the slightest hint that he knew she was screwing around on the Coast to get him ruffled. And when Carney had broken the connection, she had been quite sure

Abbey's flight was simply another attempt to bother her.

But that was weeks ago! And since then, there had been absolutely no communication from her! She certainly wasn't one to sit down once a day to pen a postcard home, but, Christ, she could phone or something. She hadn't even been using her credit cards, it seemed. They could be used to trace her whereabouts. Obviously she didn't want to be found.

The damned kid! She'd probably show up just before the September semester started at Smith and—

Hayley strode over to the do-it-yourself bar and poured herself another lemon Perrier. How that kid could get to her! All children could, of course. But somehow, Hayley felt that her own flesh and blood could do it better than anyone else.

The television drama droned on. Now a young man was on the stand, talking about meeting a girl in Piccadilly Circus. Hayley considered her own problems. Perhaps it had been a bad move to contact the Prescott Investigation Group. But then again, maybe not. Abbey was *somewhere* in the world. She would leave some kind of trace.The PIGs would find her!

She remembered how her own father had sneered and railed at *his* father for creating the PIGs. Actually, the Prescott investigation arm had originally been formed to keep surveillance on the activities of various governments throughout the world, so that Prescott money wouldn't be funneled into the wrong countries—to be impounded, nationalized, or whatever, by emerging nations.

But the group—composed of ex-OSS agents—had turned up other nasty little facts, as well. For example, when the price of gold made its dramatic ascent into the stratosphere in the early 1970s, the PIGs had warned Hayley's father, who was managing the Prescott billions then, that gold was heading for a fall. The Prescotts got out of gold just in time and made a packet by acting just prior to the break. The mechanics of the deal had never been clear to Hayley, but she knew it was the PIGs who had spotted something and issued the right warning signals.

When Hayley's Aunt Millie had been anxious to divorce her first husband, Otto, the PIGs had provided accurate information about his amours in West Germany, where he had held an ambassadorial post. And so on.

So far the PIGs had come up with an absolute zero on Abbey. But then, they had only been working on the case for three days now. Still, they were paid enough to find out important things immediately.

The sudden blare of the loudspeaker overrode her thoughts. The Concorde for Kennedy Airport in New York was ready to load, the tinny non-voice said. Hayley picked up her carry-on and departed with two other people—a man and a woman—who had also been waiting in the VIP lounge.

As she walked down the long corridor, Hayley suddenly smiled. Not all the news she had gotten lately had been bad. Her sister Megan had written her a very funny letter about a visit from a representative of the Vatican.

The joke, of course, was that Megan would be the last person in Europe to be worried about the Vatican or anything the Vatican did. A Protestant, she was impervious. In fact, she was, if truth were told, an agnostic. To her, religion was something someone else had—like the measles.

To think of the proud, earnest, intellectual member of the Vatican seated with Megan in that sunny and

scrumptious Florentine villa, trying to discuss in a
serious manner the strange disappearance of a great
many church lire, tickled Hayley's funnybone—even
though it was *not* a funny thing.

The upshot of the whole affair was that the Vatican
rep had simply been chauffeured off in his enormous
custom-made Fiat to brood in private about the seem-
ing loss of the money. At least there was no proof
that Nicky had put the stuff in his pocket. The mess
seemed more and more to be a simple ball-up in the
bank's computer records.

Hayley would have given a day's interest of the
Prescott billions to have heard that conversation. She
laughed aloud now and stepped into the accordion
passageway that connected the airport with the plane.

She was savoring that amusement and thinking
about getting home to the townhouse apartment on
Fifth Avenue as she sank into her seat on the Concorde. Several of the other passengers had also been
seated, and she was looking out the window at the
activity of the airport when someone sat down in the
comfortable seat next to her.

There was a contented sigh, a shifting of the body
to settle into the contours of the carefully engineered
seat, and a slumping down to await whatever was to
happen next.

Hayley turned.

The man next to her on the aisle was Clive Argyll.

Argyll's mouth dropped open in a comical reaction
of almost total disbelief.

"Ms. Prescott!" he intoned, unable to conceal his
sardonic disapproval of the Women's Lib term even
in his surprise. "Of course!" He regained his aplomb.
"It *would* be you on the Concorde!"

"One learns to appreciate intimate groups," Hayley observed. "The simple things in life."

He relaxed, stretching his big body as far as he could, turning up the toes of his feet, and putting his arms up above his head in the most boorish way he could manage.

"I simply cannot be annoyed, even at meeting *you* here, Ms. Moneybags. Life is too good!"

"The masses are rising—and I haven't heard about it? When do the tumbrels drive up to take us away?"

He eyed her in a raunchy way. "Oh, stuff it, tootsie. I absolutely refuse to let you ruin my trip!" He smiled, turning his head sideways and almost winking at her in his obviously ebullient glee.

"You're very good looking when you smile," Hayley said evenly. "You should try it more often."

He guffawed. "I allow people I loathe and detest one smile a year, no more, no less. I have given you my quota. Begone! I shall see you in a twelve-month."

"The words are there, but somehow you just don't seem to get the melody right," Hayley laughed.

"You can't darken my day, madame. Cease and desist."

Hayley smiled and relaxed. She snuggled down into her seat in emulation of his obvious self-satisfaction.

"I'm on my way!" he crowed. "I did it on my own. Nothing can stop me now."

Hayley nodded, said nothing.

"You obviously don't care a bit about my good luck. But I'm damned if it's going to bother me."

Hayley looked out the window. The Concorde was beginning to move out into the traffic pattern, and the attendants were going through their take-off ritual.

Once they were airborne, Argyll sighed and finally

surrendered fully to his unending animosity for the rich and titled.

"You can't *possibly* care about anyone else's luck, can you?"

Hayley turned from the window. "I beg your pardon?"

"Here I've got the best crack at fame and fortune in my thirty years—and you just don't care!"

"I care."

Argyll raised his eyebrow at her in a theatrical manner. "But you haven't congratulated me yet!"

"I was ordered to cease and desist," Hayley said softly.

"A jest," he said broadly, "offered in a moment of true affection. Don't you understand humor? I was imitating the Bard."

"Ah! I see."

"In a manner of speaking," Argyll said airily.

"But only in a manner of speaking."

"You just lost me."

"The Bard was notoriously a gentleman."

Argyll frowned. "What in hell is that supposed to mean? That I'm not a gentleman, just because I'm not rich? I mean, that I *wasn't* rich?" His eyes gleamed maliciously.

"Indeed, nothing of the sort. The Bard was always beholden to his patron."

"Ahah! The Earl of Southampton."

Hayley nodded.

"But there's no Earl of Southampton now." Argyll grinned. "We don't have patrons today. We do it on our own!"

"So you say." Hayley looked out the window.

She felt a tap on her elbow. She turned.

"Lady. There is Clive Argyll." He pointed at his

chest. She looked at his jacket. He had purchased a brand new Savile Row suit. She recognized the tailor. "This is me. Nobody else. I did it."

"Modesty is obviously not one of your main strengths."

"No, it isn't. I'm a working man. A professional. I do the best I can at what I do. I have been rewarded for my skill in stagecraft. Period."

"Again I bow to your excruciating logic."

There was a long silence.

"You're implying that I *didn't* do it on my own," he said after a while.

"I implied nothing of the sort. I was discussing William Shakespeare."

Argyll sank back in his seat, glowering ahead of him. Finally he reached inside his jacket pocket and pulled out an envelope. He removed several sheets of paper from it and studied them a long time in silence.

He handed them to her. "It says here that I did it on my own. I wrote my play. I acted in my play. The essence of the business proposition elaborated in the contract is that I alone am responsible for my success."

Hayley leafed through the papers.

"It says here that Lee Chantry is purchasing your play for adaptation to a screenplay. It also says that Lee Chantry is hiring you to turn your play into a screenplay. It says further that Lee Chantry is casting you in the lead of your own screenplay."

He took the papers back. "Exactly."

"I know who Clive Argyll is. Who is Lee Chantry?"

Argyll smiled loftily. "I have not met the gentleman. He is obviously a person of discernment and good judgment. He has, in fact, selected me as a—" Argyll frowned. "How do the newspapers put it? 'Hot property.' "

"Does Lee Chantry then own you?"

"*Own* me?" Argyll sat up straight. "Hell, no! He's simply hiring me! He—"

"But you signed a contract with him . . ."

"Hell, yes! Pages and pages of it! Had to initial every goddamned item! Tons of garbage."

"Is Lee Chantry alone in charge of your work?"

"He's got a huge organization, they tell me," Argyll said. "Maybe *he* won't be in charge of the details, but somebody close to him will."

"I see."

There was a long silence.

"You upset me," Argyll grumbled. "What in hell are you trying to do? Ruin my triumph?"

"How *could* I?" Hayley asked.

"I don't know. But I'll bet you could figure out a way."

"What a nasty thing to say!" Hayley giggled.

Argyll pulled the envelope out of his jacket and tore out the papers again. Carefully, he went over the words and pursed his lips.

"Sod the bastard!" he said finally.

"Sod whom?" Hayley asked politely.

"I thought this Lee Chantry was a representative. You know, like a kind of agent. Sure, he arranged the purchase of the play, and my contract. But it says—and right you are—that Lee Chantry and/or his associates purchased my play *and* control of me. The son of a bitch does own me! Lock, stock, and barrel! Ain't that a kick in the head?"

"Free enterprise, rather," said Hayley vaguely.

"Free exploitation!" snapped Argyll, getting back up on his soapbox.

"But you're rich. You don't need to put up with anything now."

"I've been had," said Argyll, wadding the papers into the envelope and thrusting it into his pocket. He sank down into his seat and brooded a minute or two.

"I had no idea Lee Chantry was such a bad man," Hayley observed.

Argyll turned toward her. "You know him?" He frowned. "Of course you know him. Hell, your husband is Welles Associates, isn't he? He'd know this Chantry."

"Chantry's not an American," said Hayley.

Argyll blinked. "Huh?"

"He's an Englishman."

"But the papers—"

"Oh, he's the front man. I'm sure that's the way they did it."

"A front man? Then who—?"

"He works for Sir John."

"Who the hell is Sir John?"

"Sir John Huddlestone, Lord Muirhead."

"The bloke who had me out to his place on the Isle of Wight. Where we—"

"He's a very good lawyer, Sir John," said Hayley. "Don't worry about it. I'm sure your contract is air-tight, water-proof, and, in two words, in-destruc-tible."

Argyll licked his lips nervously. "Why didn't my goddamned agent warn me I was getting into some very high finance here?"

"Brooks Bogard?"

Argyll shot her a glance. "You know Bogie?"

"I read something in the columns about him."

"Chantry. Chantry. Where the hell did I hear that name before?"

"It's not a common name." Hayley frowned. "I

think Sir John's butler is named Chantry. Yes, I can hear him now. 'Chantry, won't you—' ''

"The bloody butler!" shouted Argyll. "It's Sir John's fucking butler!"

"He was probably a stand-in for someone else," Hayley said, trying to be helpful.

"I've been jobbed!" he yelled.

The stewardess hastened down the aisle. "Did you call me, sir?"

"No, I didn't bloody call you, but now that you're here, bring my seat partner and me two champagnes—*if* you please!" Argyll was simmering. The stewardess, flushing at his overbearing attitude, spun around and vanished.

"You know, I'm beginning to sense a slight stench in the atmosphere, something like the scent of the air when Hercules cleaned the Augean stables."

Hayley bowed her head. "Charming simile."

"Wait a minute! Wait a minute! Do I detect a fine Italian hand here? The artful Ms. Hayley Welles? I mean, you *do* have money in that Welles organization, don't you? You *do* arrange deals for him. I heard about that Beatrix la Belle deal—that was your baby, really, they say. Did you put him up to *this?*"

"If I did, how would it strike you?"

"If you did, *I* would strike *you*, lady."

She shrugged. "I did not, on my honor, set up a deal for my husband."

His hot brown eyes were boring into hers. He began sloshing the champagne around in the glass, and Hayley shook her head. "It loses its fizz if you jounce it."

He tugged at it, almost breaking his teeth on the rim. "Lee Chantry. Sir John. It's too coincidental."

She sipped at her champagne, relaxing handsomely next to him.

Then his face was close to hers, his breath hot, his skin sweat-glistening.

"You?"

"Mr. Chantry was happy to act for us. Yes. Sir John was actually not quite so impressed with you or your play as I was, but he agreed to handle the transaction. In a purely legal sense, of course."

"It's not Welles Associates?"

"Oh, dear me, no," said Hayley. "This is one of my own little projects."

"You?"

"Me," she smiled brightly. "Hayley Welles."

"You're going to produce my movie?"

"Actually, no. I have a production company lined up."

"And you're Lee Chantry?"

"I'm Hayley Welles. And you'd better be nice to me, Mr. Argyll."

"I'll break the contract somehow," he muttered.

"Not one of Sir John's, you won't." She smiled.

He guzzled down his champagne loudly.

"So you're my patroness, huh?" The prospect seemed to age the British actor as he thought it out.

"In no way, Mr. Argyll. A patroness simply sponsors. You're a different kettle of fish. Or, really, you're *in* a different kettle of fish. Buster, I *own* you!"

There was a stunned silence.

"It's illegal! It's not the democratic way!"

"No. It's the capitalistic way. It's the Prescott way. Lock, stock, and barrel, as they say, Clive *honey*. And you do what I say, or you wind up with zero money and multiple lawsuits!"

Subdued, he waved the empty glass in his hand at the stewardess, who hastened over to him and refilled it immediately.

"You set the whole goddamned thing up," Argyll sulked.

"I saw talent. I appreciate talent. I decided to purchase it. My husband isn't the only image-maker. I'm one, too. You're my male version of Galatea."

"Oh, shit!" gasped Argyll, taking a belt of the expensive champagne.

"Immediately upon landing in New York, photographers will be taking publicity pictures of us together," Hayley said, assuming her managerial manner.

He sank lower into his seat.

"These photographs will be the last that will be seen of you until the grand entrance."

"What?"

"That will be weeks, perhaps months, from now."

"But, lady, I've got to get to work on the screenplay! I've got to—"

"You will be sequestered where no one can see you. Indeed you *will* be working on your screenplay. But you will *disappear* from view, not to be seen until the big party at which you will be introduced to the Hollywood movers and shakers."

"I'm no secret. I'm an actor! What kind of dumb—?"

"Image-making *par excellence*," Hayley said. "The party that brings you into center stage—"

Argyll groaned unhappily.

"—will be held at the Prescott mansion in Benedict Canyon. There, everyone who is anyone in Hollywood will be present, waiting to see the newest star in the firmament. At the present time, all publicity about you will cease immediately. You will be effectively blanked out from the public memory.''

"I've never heard of anything as asinine as this!' Argyll cried. "An actor has to be on stage in order to be seen—and heard! This is nuts!"

"We recreate the image," said Hayley with a faint smile. "Nothing but the name remains."

"Everybody knows I came from an honest working-class background in Scotland. Everybody knows—"

"In America, nobody knows," Hayley shot back. "America loves to pretend it hates the upper classes. In truth, it *idolizes* them. It dotes on the rich. You, sir, are to be the new British-American idol of the age. I can see it now. A blue blood, an English nobleman, with a title dating back to the Norman Conquest, a title that has been hidden from the public for centuries for political reasons. You have a degree from Oxford— "

"Christ, lady! I never even matriculated from fourth form!"

"Details, details. Don't fret. Actually, you won't have a thing to say about it. The media will eat it up. I'll hire a publicist who'll do the work. Meanwhile—"

Argyll waved his empty champagne glass feebly at the stewardess, who came trotting over.

"He doesn't want another champagne," Hayley snapped at the stewardess. "He wants a bottle of Perrier."

"Now wait just a minute, Ms. Welles! You're not going to tell *me* what I drink!"

"I'm sorry," Hayley told the stewardess. "That was rude of me. I'm sure Mr. Argyll will be glad to tell you himself what he wants."

"I want a champagne—"

"That will cost you exactly—" Hayley closed her

eyes and toted the figures in her head "—one million, eight hundred thousand dollars, minimum. Plus court costs, possibly."

Argyll turned pale.

"Do you get my meaning, Mr. Argyll?" she asked sweetly.

He held out the empty glass, his eyes cast down.

The stewardess glanced at Hayley, and the two exchanged a meaningful look. The stewardess smiled and brought back the British actor's Perrier water.

"I don't want you sozzled and bibulous in front of those cameras at JFK," Hayley said.

"I'm cold sober," he muttered as he settled down with his sparkling French liquescence from Mother Earth. "Cold bloody sober."

"You'll be the bright new talent of the era," said Hayley with a brilliant smile. "And you'll be all *mine*."

CHAPTER THIRTEEN

It was a problem in aesthetics, in logic, and in individual preference. Which was the most beautiful? The city of Rome as it basked in this weatherman's gift of perfect cloudless weather; or the woman who stood at the intersection of the Via Vittorio Veneto and the Via Pinciana just opposite the Borghese Gardens?

Quite probably, to most observers, the beautiful woman would win out, simply because she looked exquisite, fine, and desirable. As for herself, Beatrix Fontaine felt that certainly Rome's beauty surpassed her own because of its dramatic presence, its perfection in taste, and its classic grandeur.

She breathed in deeply as she stood there looking down the familiar Via Veneto, her favorite spot in one of her favorite cities. A Parisian, she naturally felt Paris was the jewel of all metropolises. But perhaps Rome was second. New York, with its dynamism, and London, with its elegance, would vie always for third place.

Rome on that day was decidedly the most beautiful

place in the world, set as it was against the total perfection of a cloudless sky and sunshine made for basking in. Beatrix had been promised by her mentor this stroll down her favorite avenue before she must appear at the apartment of the Count and Countess della Camarra in Rome's exclusive Ludovisi Quartiere surrounding the Via Veneto.

It was Sunday, and the street was jammed with slowly moving traffic: Rolls-Royces, Jaguars, Renaults, Alfa Romeos, Mercedes, Fiats, Seats, Volvos. She crossed the street to move down what she always considered, with her Parisian background, to be the Left Bank of the Veneto—the eastern side of the street. She walked in front of the Flora, one of the city's plushest hotels. Its basement grill, she recalled, served the best charcoal-broiled steaks in Italy. Beatrix had once sat very near the King of Sweden while dining there.

Even with the perfect Roman weather, it was a trifle chilly, and Beatrix pulled her neckerchief tighter around her throat. She had never felt better, but she did not wish to risk laryngitis or the flu during this most important part of Welles Associates' "buildup" of her new image. People stared at her—not a simple passing glance, but a total ogling gape. She was that beautiful.

Besides, she had visited Via Condotti the first of the week for a private showing of Signor Alberti Gianconi's newest creations. And she had purchased three—the prize being the cocktail outfit she now wore: skirt, blouse, jacket, hat. Perfect!

That was what people were staring at, as much as at her. But in her secret heart she knew it was she who was causing the gasps of excitement. She was beautiful and she knew it. And since that was the way Welles Associates wanted her, the perfect symbol of health and beauty, she was pleased and happy that she could oblige.

Besides, she had not suffered another blackout since the Helsinki experience. Carney Welles was no longer suspicious. He had worried in Finland and was still worrying when they left for Holland. But now he seemed quite satisfied with the way things were going. Right now, in fact, he was at the swank apartment of his sister-in-law—five minutes' walk away—supervising the hired photographers who would be shooting supplemental film for the big spread in *Paris Match* and Rome's *Oggi*.

"Federico Fellini!" she murmured *sotto voce*. What was *he* doing in town? Beatrix stared, then jerked her eyes away. He was seated where most of the motion picture bigwigs sat when they were in Rome—at the Caffé Doney, probably the most famous establishment on the Via Veneto.

More people were pointing her out as she continued on, and she was finding it difficult not to blush. Her sudden fame was obviously due to Carney Welles's skill at publicity. Pictures of her taken as if at random, had appeared again and again in various publications. The photos accompanied stories of various parties and openings that she had attended in Rome during the past week. She was now known as "Beatrix la Belle," rather than simply "Beatrix Cosmétique," or "Beatrix Fontaine."

Hayley Welles had not exaggerated when she had promised Beatrix over a year ago that she would get the best buildup possible if she signed on with Hayley's husband, Carney Welles. She wondered briefly what had happened between Hayley and Carney to cause the estrangement between them. It had been to

Beatrix's advantage, of course. Carney was a man she felt she could trust—in love or out of love.

The true landmark of the Via Veneto rose massively on her left as she continued down the esplanade —the Hotel Excelsior, one of Europe's best-known hostelries. It had almost five hundred rooms, making it the largest in Italy.

She passed the American Embassy and waited to cross the street. By now she was bored with all the people staring at her and talking about her. She gazed straight ahead and pretended she was not really there at all. She moved over to the "Right Bank" and then turned to continue on her way toward the address of the Countess della Camarra's penthouse apartment.

Poor Nicky, she thought. He had trouble at the bank. She had heard about it during her visit to Scobie Hills in the summer. But now, it was more fully reported in the papers. Some bad investments, some bad advice, some bad accountant work. . . .

Beatrix had known Nicky years before she had met Hayley Welles, of course; had known him without even meeting Hayley's sister Megan. A bit dim in the skull, but he was very nice in bed. Definitely a Marcello Mastroianni type. Too bad about the money. Maybe Megan could bail him out with the Prescott fortune.

It was ironic. Here Beatrix had been a lover of Hayley Prescott's second husband, as well as a lover of Megan Prescott's *only* husband. And, of course, she was now a lover of Hayley Prescott's third husband. She was almost part of the Prescott family!

From the balcony of the Countess della Camarra's penthouse, Carney Welles followed the course of Beatrix Fontaine's progress through the Sunday afternoon pedestrian crowds, shifting the focus on his Zeiss fifty-powers as the distance between lens and subject varied.

At least, he thought, she was smiling and radiant, head up, famous bosom out. Her passage, planned meticulously in advance, was paying off exactly as he had known it would. People were ogling her, pointing at her, talking about her. The expensive publicity inserts in the newspapers had certainly been worth it. Getting her talked about and noticed was his job. But getting it done in the right way was even more important.

He let the glasses hang from his neck a moment and leaned against the balcony rail. He was worried about her. He had never really figured out what had happened to her in Helsinki. There was no point in questioning her repeatedly about it, but he had done so, again and again. Nothing out of the ordinary had occurred in Holland. In fact, they had renewed the intensity of their affair in Holland, after that strange rejuvenation of it in Helsinki at the Inter-Continental.

Welles was certain of one thing: there was *something* just the slightest bit off-key about Beatrix Fontaine. Hopefully, he could get her health-spa network launched before whatever it was imploded on her. The fault, dear Brutus, lay not in the stars, but in herself.

He was convinced of it—by instinct, nothing else. He had no pretensions to psychiatry, but he knew something was fishy there. It wasn't the lesbian thing. She had shucked off that kinky little creep who had been at her, without a thought. Tessie Maupin had vanished into limbo, and good riddance. She was dangerous. Wow!

He flipped the glasses to his eyes again, trying to

catch sight of Beatrix as she wound her way through the crowded street that led up to the apartment. Where the hell was she? Frantically, he panned the glasses up and down the street. She was gone! Damn. She had disappeared. . . .

No. There she was. She had paused to look in a window. A man spoke to her. She snooted him. Good! That was just right! Carney's blood pressure lowered. He began enjoying the sight of her presence on the street, and the obvious excitement she aroused in the passersby.

The guests had been arriving at the countess's apartment for the past hour and a half, and it was getting noisy inside. Carney put up the glasses again and turned. He gave a sudden start. Nicky Tarantino was standing in the open doorway to the balcony, leaning against the doorframe, watching him.

The Italian grinned. Welles was always astonished when his brother-in-law showed his teeth. They were such great store-bought jobs; they were unbelievable. Capped, of course. The teeth certainly gave his tanned and swarthy face the proper contrast. And they highlighted the general evenness of his features—something not all Italians possessed.

"Observing Rome on a Sunday afternoon?" he asked in his accented but very slick English.

"She's a beautiful woman, Rome," Carney responded.

"So there will soon be one of the Beatrix health spas in Rome."

Welles nodded. "Ostia. Outside Rome, of course, but definitely a *Roman* spa."

Nicky smiled lazily. "Everybody talks about it."

"That's what I'm here for," Welles laughed. "To plant the clues. To get people talking."

"You are very good at it."

Welles inclined his head.

"I could use a little less talk about me," Nicky admitted.

"Another problem entirely."

"Not one you are expert in?" Nicky asked a bit ruefully.

"Public relations works both ways." Welles frowned. "You worried about a run on your bank?"

Nicky shrugged. "It is an evil situation. All the talk is bad. I would like good talk."

"People always talk bad when investments go sour."

Tarantino watched Welles silently.

"So you wait until the losses are analyzed and you go back to work building up a good image."

The count nodded. "If you say so."

"Is there something else?" Carney asked, suddenly sensing that the bank problem might be rooted in more than simple investment errors.

"No." Nicky was too quick to answer.

Welles remembered Hayley's enlightening remarks about Nicky's gambling.

"Horse racing? Roulette? Twenty-one?"

Nicky's tongue passed over his upper lip. He frowned and was about to speak.

"Nick-kee!" A shrill voice assaulted them. It was Megan. She came running over to the balcony, waving her hands at her husband. "Come here, dear! It's the mayor of Rome! I want you to take care of him until Beatrix gets here."

Nicky hurried off. Carney Welles stared after him, wondering what exactly was behind the bank problem that was disturbing Nicky *and* Megan. But mostly, as he now realized, disturbing *Nicky*.

Hell! If only Hayley were here. She could find out

more about it. But then, he and she had their own little problems—mainly, where was Abbey? She still hadn't surfaced, after all these weeks. And even Hayley's PIGs couldn't find a trace of her. The kid was *really* underground.

That was an example of what Nicky wanted: publicity in reverse—to disappear from the public eye.

Senator Kirby Miles gripped the cold glass of scotch and soda in his hand and let a deep draft of it seep down his throat to warm him a bit. He had barely come alive that morning. The hangover from his night out on the town with that sweet pizza-for-hire at the Excelsior had really lowered him deep into the pits.

"Hi-yah, Megan honey!" he called out to Megan Prescott Tarantino, the Countess of Whatever. "How's the countess?"

"Fine," Megan said with a strained smile. "Where's —uh—Ginny?"

"Linny," mocked Kirby Miles with a grin. "It's Lynn, Megan. She's not here, actually."

"I thought she'd be dying to attend a little get-together like this."

Miles guffawed. "Little get-together? This bash is the biggest thing going on in Rome this week!" He gulped down more of his drink and reached out for a refill. "One hell of a Sunday soirée, I'll say that!"

"I thought Lynn was with you in Europe," Megan said, sharp-eyed and alert.

Miles looked at her. Yeah. That was what everybody else thought, too. They were *all* trying to get something on *him*. What a coup if they could find out his wife had walked. Trouble is, *he* didn't even know where the hell she was! Last he had seen her, she had been rattling on about that flaky lesbo who had been sucking off Beatrix. . . .

"Lynn had never been to Provence," said Miles, taking more sustenance, saluting it. "Good stuff! Good!"

"From our Florentine wine cellar," said Megan with a touch of sarcasm.

"Yeah. The kid decided to take a closer look at southern France. We were in Paris—I'm on this important fact-finding mission—and—"

Megan put her hand on the senator's arm and excused herself. A moment later, he saw her ushering in Beatrix Fontaine. Miles's eyes bulged. My God. That French broad looked good enough to eat. To drink! Whatever your preference. What had Carney Welles done to her? He had sure shaped her up somehow. Or maybe it had all been there and had just needed bringing out.

Welles? Nah. Who *was* she sleeping with?

And, by the way, where the hell was Hayley Prescott Welles? She was the one with the clout. As if in a phantom answer to his question, Carney Welles emerged from the crowd of babbling people and came over to him.

"Hi, Carney," said Miles.

They shook hands.

"Where's that beautiful wife of yours?"

Welles thought a moment. "London, last I heard."

"Ahah! In London, to see the queen?"

"As a matter of fact—" Welles grinned.

"Don't *tell* me!" cried Miles. "You mean, she *did?*"

Welles burst out laughing. "One of those flukes. Yeah. Some garden party. I never did get the details, but you know Hayley. In fact, I read about it in the *London Express*."

Welles looked the senator in the eye. "Lynn around?"

"Could be. Seeing Provence, she tells me."

"We've got a daughter somewhere over here in Europe, too—we think."

"Think?"

"Abbey. She talked about doing Europe this summer, but we haven't heard from her. You know kids."

"Women," said Miles, slugging down the rest of his scotch and soda and reaching for another.

"Rich women," agreed Welles.

The crowd was so boisterous now that Megan could hardly hear herself think. She was exhausted, running about the confines of the apartment, introducing people, making sure there were enough canapés and drinks, watching to see that no one fell clean off the balcony, rushing to supervise the cleaning up of a broken tumbler and spilled liquor on the expensive oriental carpet . . .

She *had* to sit down a moment. Moving quickly to the rear of the apartment, she edged into a small writing room to get away from the noise. With the door closed behind her, she sank into an easy chair. It was then that she realized someone was around the corner, in the alcove, talking on the telephone.

She listened. It was Nicky! He was speaking cautiously in a low voice, so as not to be overheard—but he need have no fear of that, at least from her! He was talking in Italian! Drat him! She listened, but could not make out any more than a word here and there.

The bank examiners had been at her again and again, and they had laid out the problems they had found—mostly having to do with bad investments. But there was a large amount of money that simply did not appear anywhere. Something did not compute.

Was Nicky now talking about that money? Was the damned fool in league with the Mafia, or something? Was he back onto the gaming tables? Or was it a woman . . . ? She felt like a fool thinking this way—but certainly *something* was not kosher.

The conversation continued, low, intimate, charged with a kind of intensity—unintelligible to Megan, but obviously important. She decided not to eavesdrop— even if she *could*. It just wasn't done. She opened the door cautiously and then slammed it loudly shut.

Immediately Nicky switched to English. "We talk later. *Ciao,* signor."

A moment later, he appeared from the alcove. He looked properly startled. "Meggy!"

"Yeah," she said. "Who's your friend?"

Nicky's eyebrows rose. "I have many friends."

"The dame on the phone."

Nicky put on a mask of injured innocence. "Me? Dame?"

"Come on, you're Italian, aren't you? Who is she?"

"Honestly, Meggy—" He put his arms around her.

She tried to wriggle away. "Stop it! You're crushing my dress!"

He kissed her loudly, then laughed. "Jealous? Meggy? Come on!"

She pulled away, looking at him grimly. "You don't get enough from me? Is that it? You want it from every hooker on the street?"

"Meggy!" He pulled her down on the daybed beside him. "There's no one but you, *carissima*. You know that."

His hands were moving over her breasts now, feeling her up through the expensive material of the cocktail gown for which she had paid way too much money in order to give herself some distinction at this party of trend-setters.

"Cut it out, you dumb guinea!"

He was laughing now, pulling her dress up from her knees and running his hands up her thighs. She began weakening and, finally, giggled as he pulled himself over onto her and shoved her down into the softness of the bed.

"Woops!" Megan gasped, and then thought with panic—my goddamned dress! You're ruining my dress, you oversexed stud! "Nicky!"

Oooh!

And again—

"Nicky," she whispered. "Oooh. Ummmm."

Ten minutes later, she floated out into the party again and found it going swimmingly. She was smiling all over from her head to her toes. There was, in fact, a kind of glow on her—the glow of love, of acceptance, of satisfaction.

Jesus, she thought. If only he could add figures like he could fuck.

Beatrix Fontaine became the center of attention at the Countess della Camarra's apartment the moment she entered. She had picked up a newspaper at the corner and used it as a prop to project nonchalance as she entered. Immediately, she was taken over by Carney Welles. She laid the paper down on one of the tables and forgot about it as she began circulating with Welles to say hello to all the guests, who had come from Rome and its environs, north, south, east, and west.

She was a hit. She knew it. She felt good—never better. Welles was putting her up on a pedestal, and she was enjoying every minute of it!

When asked, she gave out the details of the spa that was going to be built and opened in Ostia, near the point where the Tiber River flowed into the Mediterranean. She was bubbling over with information that had been force-fed into her by Carney Welles days before.

Reporters were taking notes. Photographers—the famed paparazzi that always found their way into every party in Rome—snapped shots again and again. So did a group of hired picture-takers whom Welles had instructed beforehand.

She posed against the balcony balustrade with the Vatican in the background. She posed at the window, with the Colosseum in the background. She posed under flowers, beside statuary Welles had rented from a museum; she posed beside celebrities from Rome. She posed with anyone and everyone.

Megan relaxed. The party was a big success. Hers always were. The next would be in Florence. There the focus would be the spa that would open in Milan. Beatrix would be there, too. So, she hoped, would Hayley.

Strangely enough, a chair was now unoccupied. Megan sank into it, stretching her legs to take the strain off her aching calves. A newspaper lay draped over someone's empty hors d'oeuvre plate. She picked it up and glanced at the headlines. Even though she couldn't read Italian, she did know a few key words.

Flipping through the newspaper, she looked at the

pictures. Christ! She shot up in her chair as if she had
been electrocuted. It was Hayley! Hayley never had
her picture taken! Certainly never published! Megan
squinted at the caption. It was a bunch of Eyetie
blather. Then her eyes moved back to the man beside
Hayley. He was a tall man, with a regal look. It was
that actor! She knew him! Cliff Arkette, or something like that. No! Cliff Argyll! That was it—*Clive*
Argyll! She read the caption. Right. It *was*. But what
in hell did Hayley have to do with him?

Megan surreptitiously signaled one of the girls she
had hired to help with the serving.

"What's this say?" she asked, pointing to the
caption.

The girl struggled with the words a moment and
then said, finally:

"He is actor, Signora Contessa. He go to Hollywood to make movie. Woman is—to produce—*cinema*
—motion picture. She is—how you say?—*discover*
actor. I think? Yes."

Hayley, a movie producer? A talent scout? An-
other Welles Associates? But, of course—that was it!
She was one-upping Carney Welles! That was just *like*
Hayley!

Megan snatched the paper from the girl, and the
girl hastened away.

Where had Hayley *found* this guy? Megan had met
him several years before, during a few days spent in
Devon with some titled Briton Nicky knew. Hayley?

She looked at the picture more closely. They were
holding hands, for Christ's sake! That meant one
thing. This was another of Hayley's conquests!

Jesus. Did Carney know? If he did, he couldn't do
much about it—not all tied up with Beatrix as he

was. And if he did, so what? A little bedside fisti-
cuffs had never stopped Hayley before.

Megan wasn't going to let this one go by without a
fight. She wanted a piece of him! No! *All* of him!
Why not?

The memory of Nicky's soft voice on the phone,
electronically caressing some Italian bimbo's ears,
returned in a flash, arousing instant envy and hostility. Everybody was having fun but her. She'd get a
piece of that British star or know the reason why!

Handsome brute, huh? Look at those—biceps?

Beverly Hills. He was going to be introduced in
Beverly Hills—as Hayley's masterpiece! At the Prescott place in Benedict Canyon, Megan bet. Well,
she'd be there, too!

CHAPTER FOURTEEN

With a Pernod before her on the marble-topped table, Abbey sat with François on the sidewalk in front of La Coupole. She gazed across the boulevard at the Rotonde Café farther up the street. Nothing was happening there now.

"Why do we have to keep coming here?" François asked. "You know how I hate these phonies."

"That's why I like it. I like to see you suffer."

"Sadistic little—"

"Now don't get nasty," Abbey cut in. "Tell me about that homely woman over there, the one who keeps glaring at you."

"Her? I almost feel sorry for her, but she's too obnoxious even to waste pity on."

"She dresses badly."

"She's homely. She can't help it. We talked once. Basically, she's a man-hater."

"Then why did she want to talk to you?"

"She overheard me in conversation with a friend about a lousy movie, then she introduced herself and told me she used to be a reader for a talent agent in Hollywood."

Abbey sneered. "I know some Hollywood people. A more hateful bunch I never met. They all eat each other up in that business."

"How would you know movie people?" François asked, an arch glint in his dark eyes.

"Never mind," she said shortly. She did not want to reveal to him yet that her parents were rich, her stepfather the head of a huge talent agency. She thought it would ruin their relationship.

"That girl was a reader," François said finally, "but she really wanted to be a writer. She didn't write much. She spent all her time criticizing the movie scripts her boss gave her to read. She did a hatchet job on every screenplay written by a man."

"Why?"

"Most screenwriters are men, so she did her damnedest to see that none of the screenplays by men got by her."

"Maybe she had a point."

"Blaming everything on men?"

Abbey sipped her Pernod. "Well, look at it this way. The men were the ones who rejected her scripts, so why shouldn't she reject theirs?"

"She only wrote one script, which nobody wanted. She never had the courage to write another one. She vented her spleen in her criticisms and sat around feeling superior to male writers."

"Probably with good reason."

François scowled. "The men weren't getting their scripts produced simply because they were men. Do you really think every man who writes a screenplay is going to get it produced?"

"A man has a better chance than a woman."

"Maybe so, but why blame every man you meet for that?"

"I'm not. I'm saying I can see her point of view."

"It goes deeper than that with her."

"Oh? Does she have a secret?" Abbey leaned closer to François.

"Her girlfriend told me. Our reader friend over there had no scruples when she tried to get her start as a writer. She was willing to do anything to sell a script. She saw writing as no different from acting. And you know what actresses will do to get a part." François's eyes gleamed, a crooked smile briefly on his lips.

"Ye olde casting couch? This is getting juicy."

"At all the Hollywood parties she attended, she let it be known to the producers that she was available. The only problem was, she was such a dog none of the producers wanted anything to do with her, in bed or out." François sniggered.

"How cruel. How can you be so cruel?"

"The upshot is she became frustrated, full of bile, and blamed her failure as a writer on men."

"Why is she in Paris?"

"I think she's writing hatchet jobs for a French cinema magazine. Readers love her acid tongue, especially women. She churns out one hit piece after another. It's her big thrill in life."

"She looks intelligent to me."

François scoffed. "She's a fool. She blames all her problems on the gender gap when she should be blaming them on capitalism."

"You and your revolution!" Abbey said petulantly.

"We welcome everyone: men, women, even bulldykes like her." He held out his arms as though embracing the world.

"You noble macho pig."

Taken aback, François retorted. "What's eating you?"

"You hate women."

"Let's face it. The only reason *she* hates men is because she couldn't get into bed with one—one of her rich producer friends."

"That's the stupidest thing I ever heard."

"I got news for you. She doesn't like *you,* either. Look how she's glaring enviously at you."

Abbey turned and took in the woman's hard, beady blue eyes; her sharp, thrusting chin; wizened, embittered lips, a permanent sneer etched on them.

"I don't even know her," Abbey said meaninglessly.

"She hates beautiful women as much as she hates men."

"I'm sick of this conversation. Let's talk about something else."

"You're the one who wanted to come here. I told you I didn't like this circus."

"You're worse than her, you hate *everybody.*"

François did not say anything, merely drank his absinthe.

Abbey watched the woman walk, with abrupt angry steps, away from the café. Nothing seemed natural about her, everything forced. Her feelings of spite appeared to be held tensely under rein. In some ways she reminded Abbey of her mother, but whereas the script-reader was repressed and bitter, Hayley was overweening and domineering.

"I feel sorry for her," Abbey said finally. "She really is pitiful. How sad."

"Sad and lonely."

Abbey nibbled at her canapé, spread with *pâté de foie gras*. "This is delicious."

"I'm tired of gossiping. Let's go back to the Boul' Mich'."

"To your place?"

"Right. We'll blow some hash."

"I know what *you* want," she said suggestively.

"No, you don't, but you will soon enough."

"How mysterious!"

Instead of going directly to François's garret, they walked onto the Pont Neuf, stood against the railing near its center, and with their faces in the breeze sweeping over the Seine, admired the Gothic arches and twin towers of Notre Dame on the Ile de la Cité in the river. A bruised cloud scudded across the blue sky.

"Nobody can hear us here," said François.

Abbey's dress fluttered caressingly about her legs. "It's a nice view."

"We need more money." François stared off into the distance.

"But you just robbed a bank."

"It's not enough. We need more. The revolution has huge expenses."

"You sound like a corporate executive."

"Are you willing to help us?"

"What do you want me to do—rob a bank for you?" she asked incredulously.

"No."

"Then what?"

François faced her. "Let's stop beating around the bush. We know you're Hayley Prescott's daughter. We know she's one of the richest women in the world."

Abbey could not believe what she was hearing. She stood motionless and simply gaped. She seemed to have lost all capability of functioning.

"How long have you known?" she whispered finally.

"From the start."

Her pulse raced. Fearfully, she remembered François's hatred for the rich. What was he going to do to her? Would he kidnap her? Push her off the bridge? Was that why he had brought her here?

She looked furtively about her. There were no witnesses. All he had to do was lift her over the railing and give her a shove. The police would report it as another suicide leap. Should she run? No. Maybe she could talk him out of it.

"Why didn't you tell me you knew me?" she asked.

"Why didn't *you* tell me who you *really* were?"

"It's not something I go around bragging about."

She realized the joke was on her. All along, she had thought she was fooling him about her rich-girl status, when in fact, he had been fooling her by feigning ignorance of her identity.

"Can you help us?" he asked.

"All right, you've had your fun. Now let's get out of here."

"What are you talking about?" François was honestly puzzled.

"Your little joke. It's over."

"This isn't a joke. When are you going to grow up?"

He embraced her tightly.

She shivered. Was he getting ready to hurl her over the bridge into the water? She pounded her fists against his chest.

"What's wrong with you?" he snapped.

"Don't kill me!"

He relaxed his hold on her. "I'm not trying to kill you. I thought we were in love."

She drew away from him. "I thought so, too, until now."

"What's changed?"

"You lied to me."

"I didn't. You wanted to go around incognito, so I played along."

"All you really want is my money."

"That's not true. If that's what I wanted, I could have kidnapped you easily."

"Maybe," she said and folded her arms stubbornly.

"If you don't believe me, leave. I'm not stopping you."

Abbey sighed forlornly. "It doesn't matter anyway."

"That we're in love?"

"The money. I can't get any for you. It's all locked up in a trust fund. I can't have it till I'm twenty-one."

François frowned, eyes intent. "Then how do you pay your bills? Credit cards?"

"No. My credit cards have low credit lines. I also avoid using them when I don't want anyone to know where I am. I live on a small allowance I get from my mother."

"How can you stand her? She's living the life of a queen while you have to live like a charwoman!"

"I hate her! I don't want to talk about her. I get sick thinking about her."

"Isn't there some way you can get your money from her?"

Abbey shook her head. "Not that I know of. She has about a thousand Harvard lawyers who do nothing but think of ways to keep her money out of everybody else's hands. Those shysters would tie me up in court till I was ninety. Besides, *she's* a lot sharper than her lawyers are.''

"She sounds like a hideous bitch."

"If only you knew."

François gazed down at the dirty river and thought for awhile. "Maybe we can help you get your money."

"If you can, I'll help POW."

A sudden upsurge in the wind blew Abbey's dress up around her chest, revealing her white lace bikini panties and a fringe of bush.

"Damn," she said and slapped the billowing dress down.

François laughed at her embarrassment.

"What's so funny?" she asked testily.

"Somebody got a free show."

"You can really be a bastard."

"Don't worry, you didn't show everything," he said, a fatuous smirk on his lips. "I know girls who don't wear panties. They would have bared all if they stood here instead of you."

"They sound like whores. I hope you don't have one of their diseases."

"At least I don't have AIDS."

"Don't tell me about the dirty things you did with all of them. I don't think I could stand hearing about them."

"Methinks she doth protest too much."

"Don't fob me off with your fractured Shakespeare."

"Methinks I should stick to Bakunin and Engels."

"Don't tell me even one dirty thing you did with them. I can't believe the things they do if you pay them enough. Is it true they . . . ?"

"What?" He was amused.

She held her hands over her ears. "I don't want to hear it."

"I'm in the mood for it now. What about you?"

"Sure, we'll do it right here on the bridge, so everybody in Paris can see us. They'll throw us in jail!"

Her mouth watered. That was the terrible thing—in spite of all her pretense, she *wanted* to do it here with him. It would not take much to convince her. What a horrid thought. She had to put it out of her mind.

Maybe she truly was in love this time, and they could have a pretty baby. Was he the right man? How could you know for sure?

Then she could have her own family and get as far away as possible from her tyrannical mother. Abbey pulled a face at the idea of her mother, then thought how a baby would give her something to live for, a meaningful life, in which she would not have to take marching orders from her mother. It was a nice thought.

CHAPTER FIFTEEN

Lynn Miles awoke to a room in disorder, with the bright morning sun shining in through the ancient and warped glass windowpanes. She stretched and yawned, not fully aware of where she was or what was expected of her.

Suddenly, however, she *remembered* and shot bolt upright in bed, clutching the rough bedclothes to her chest. Where was Tessie? She promised herself to have a final showdown with her—no more of this kinky stuff at night!

But Tessie was gone. Lynn climbed out of bed, shivering, and stumbled out into the hallway. No sign of her in the bathroom at the end of the corridor. Breakfast? Was she at breakfast? Or did they even *serve* breakfast at this out-of-the-way inn?

Quickly, Lynn got into her clothes and ran a brush through her hair, slapped some lipstick on and started for the door to go down to the dining room. At that moment, the door burst open of its own accord before she reached it.

Tessie entered, her face glowing with excitement.

"Where have you been?" Lynn snapped. "You and I have a lot of things to talk about!"

"Later!" cried Tessie. "I'm leaving now."

"Leaving?" Lynn repeated, her mouth agape. "What about breakfast? I'm starved!"

"I've located Valentine!" Tessie rummaged excitedly through her things for the keys to the car. "I must find him!"

"I'm coming with you," Lynn announced, standing at the doorway.

Tessie shook her head. "No. It is complicated. I tell you later. I must do this alone."

"Oh, no you don't!" Lynn protested, now in front of Tessie as if to block her exit. "You're not going to run out on me!"

"Not to run out," Tessie argued, frowning. "What you think?"

"Come on," Lynn said. "We *both* go after Valentine."

"Is impossible," Tessie said, her accent thicker in her obvious anxiety. She pushed past Lynn, but Lynn reached quickly and grabbed her by the wrist. Tessie twisted and pulled out of Lynn's grip.

"I tell you," Tessie cried. "I must go alone!"

Lynn hesitated.

Immediately, Tessie slammed the door in her face and ran down the hallway. Lynn tried the knob, but it was jammed. Cursing and fighting with the ancient hardware, she finally got it open, but when she emerged from the room, she could not see Tessie, who had apparently run down the stairs and vanished.

Bewildered, Lynn ran down to the lobby of the hotel, but still there was no sign of Tessie. She went out into the narrow street in front of the inn. There were a half-dozen kids playing in the dirt, throwing an ancient ball around. Tessie was nowhere in sight.

Now Lynn remembered the car. Tessie had said she parked it at the rear of the inn, but she had not told Lynn how she had gotten back from the converted barn to the inn itself.

Damn! Lynn tried to find some passageway between the buildings, to lead her to the garage. There was no such passageway. When it finally occurred to Lynn that Tessie might have used a rear entrance in the kitchen of the inn, it was too late. Indeed there *was* a rear entrance, shown to Lynn by the proprietor. But when Lynn got to the barn, it was too late: the Citroen was gone.

Lynn climbed the stairs to her room again, puzzled and somewhat discouraged. Tessie, she reasoned, must have discussed the problem of picking up the trail of the Fontaines with the proprietor. In fact, it was rather obvious: Tessie had gone down to breakfast alone in order to get the jump on Lynn. But why had she then insisted on doing the investigation on her own?

It didn't make a great deal of sense. Lynn finally realized she was hungry and needed something to eat. She put on her sweater and climbed down the rickety stairs. The breakfast she ate was far from superior, but she did get some hot coffee—or something thick and dark and syrupy *resembling* coffee. Whatever it was, it made her feel better.

Lynn went back up to the room to wait for Tessie to return. If Tessie didn't show up in another half hour, Lynn determined to go down and walk around the little village to kill time.

She was bored out of her skull sitting in the dingy little room. After she had risen to pace to the window at least a dozen times, to see if she could spot the Citroen, she finally sank down on the bed and leaned back for a moment. Unmade, the bed was as uncomfortable as a rack of nails, but Lynn was exhausted from the previous day's driving and riding; almost immediately she fell into a shallow sleep that rapidly deepened.

It was noon by the time she was startled awake by the entrance of a humpbacked little woman in scullery clothes carrying a thick stick broom and a bucket. Lynn was unable to produce any kind of communication between the two of them, but she knew the woman was obviously in to clean and make up the bed.

She staggered over to the ancient bureau to pick up her wallet and credit cards. Realizing it was high noon, she thought it would be a good time to tour the village to see what Grignan was really like. If she liked it—

Now Lynn's throat constricted. Where *was* her wallet? She had mislaid it somewhere. No. She was positive she had placed her credit cards on the bureau. She went through everything carefully again, pawing through her bag, certain now that she had left her things in plain sight on the bureau.

She was unable to locate her wallet. She stood there, frowning, and as she stood there, she happened to see her own face in the dim mirror, whose silver backing had almost completely flaked off. The reflection, however imperfect, was the startled face of someone who had been had.

She, Lynn Miles, wife of Senator Kirby Miles of the United States Senate, had been done—by a second-rate, kinky, unwashed Frenchwoman!

Tessie Maupin! Tessie had somehow learned that

Lynn had a hate on for the Prescotts. By hurting Beatrix Fontaine, Lynn could hurt the Prescotts indirectly. She had played on that—and she had engineered this whole scam! She had set Lynn up, set her up for a fleecing. And Lynn had been too stupid to see through it. There was no big story that Tessie was searching out. There was no *mystery* about Beatrix Fontaine. *That* was a lie.

The idea was to get Lynn out into the boondocks, somewhere in the backwoods of France, to roll her, take her credit cards and cash, steal everything she had—and vanish. How could Lynn blow the whistle on Tessie Maupin, when Tessie had something to blackmail Lynn with? A night in the hay with a scheming French lesbian!

Lynn frowned. That reasoning didn't really add up. All Lynn had to do was to make a phone call and immediately her credit cards would be certified as stolen. Tessie couldn't really *use* them.

Why had she stolen them? What was Tessie *really* trying to do?

At half past two o'clock in the afternoon, Lynn Miles sat hunched over a Pernod on the back terrace of the Chez Lousteau Hôtel, presumably Grignan's poshest hostelry. Nothing had been proved yet, but it certainly appeared that Mademoiselle Thérèse Maupin had vanished.

But why?

The hotel proprietor—whose name was Gatien Lousteau—and his wife, Chloris, had both talked to Lynn, trying their very best to make themselves understood in what little basic English they had.

No, they did *not* know where Mademoiselle Maupin was going. No, she had *not* checked out of the hotel.

She had eaten breakfast, had chatted with them, had talked about interesting places around Grignan—sites that tourists might like to visit.

And, no, they had indeed *not* talked about a man named Valentine Fontaine. They had simply pointed out to Mademoiselle Maupin the neighboring towns and spots of interest on her Michelin road map. No, they could not remember any specific points that might have appeared to hold a special interest for Mademoiselle Maupin.

With the help of Gatien Lousteau, Lynn was able to inform the local police of the disappearance of the automobile she had rented—along with the disappearance of her personal credit cards. The license number was noted, having been taken down by Monsieur Lousteau when Lynn and Thérèse had signed for their rooms.

One of the two policeman spoke a broken variation of English, of which he seemed very proud. He assured Lynn that every effort would be made to return the rented car and madame's personal effects. Discretion, of course, would be observed, so as to attach no stigma to madame's companion, at her request. And, of course, there was always the possibility that something had happened to her to *prevent* her return to the hotel!

Lynn was mulling over that very idea now, even as she sat fuming to herself. A telephone call had alerted American Express about the disappearance of her Amex card; someone on the other end had assured her that she would be issued a new number soon. So far, no one had tried to use her original card.

Perhaps, for that matter, Tessie had not run off; perhaps she had indeed gotten into some kind of trouble. She had appropriated Lynn's personal effects, but to what purpose? She must have known that the credit cards would be useless to her.

What Lynn did *not* want to happen was for the senator to be informed of the situation, no matter *how* it all turned out. He had warned her not to indulge in this tour of the hinterlands of France, and he had been right, damn him!

"Madame Miles!" spoke a heavily accented French voice. Her name sounded more like "meals" than "miles." *"Violà!"*

It was the first policeman, the one with the barely workable English. He was standing in front of her, his right hand gesturing through the inn wall toward the street out in front. Lynn could make out nothing, of course.

"L'automobile est arrivée," he explained proudly.

Lynn stared. The automobile? By God, the gendarmes had *found* the rented car! Was Tessie in it?

When she asked that pertinent question, the policeman's lugubrious expression returned. *"Hélas, non!* The mademoiselle is not found."

"Where's my stuff?"

"Hélas, encore," sighed the policeman, spreading his hands in a Gallic gesture, "there has been no discovery of madame's effects, either."

"My credit cards?" flared Lynn.

"Exactement," murmured the policeman, bowing and suffering with Lynn. "They are disappear. Poof!"

Lynn bit her lip in frustration. It wasn't his fault. He was trying to help her. Why was she so sore at him?

"Where did you find the car?" she burst out, unable to contain her surging anger.

"Eh? *Escusez-moi, madame. Je n'ai pas compris.*"

Oh, too fast for him, thought Lynn murderously. "*Où est* the damned car?"

"Ahah! *L'automobile!* You see it out in front. It was parked in a side road many kilometers out of the township. In fact, it was located in another town."

Lynn stood up. "Take me there, if you please."

The policeman bowed. "*Oui*, madame."

He led her out of the inn and into the sunshine. Curious villagers—a mix of people from six-year-olds to eighty-five-year-olds—stood about staring at the shiny Citroen. Next to the car stood the other policeman and several men dressed in business clothes.

Skillfully, the policeman helped Lynn into the car, then he drove it through the winding narrow streets of the town and finally out into the countryside, where the road wound between gently sloping hills covered with wild flowers, vineyards, and thick grass. The policeman with no English sat in the back, mute and erect.

On the way, the talker explained that his name was René du Lac; his rank was sergeant; and his status was father, married, and mortgaged. His partner was named Pierre Entient; his rank was corporal; status, unmarried.

Eventually, the car drove through a low sloping valley that became dotted with farmhouses and then more low-roofed houses grouped together. This village was not half so large as Grignan. A church spire dominated the tiny settlement.

Du Lac steered the Citroen onto the verge of the roadway and turned off the key.

"*Ici*, madame," he said.

"You found the car here?" Lynn gazed about her in astonishment.

"*Oui*, madame."

"Perhaps she is in this village? Mademoiselle Maupin?"

"We questioned the people. They saw a woman get out of the car. She then walked across the village to the intersection with Highway 20."

"Where does Highway 20 go?"

"To the Riviera."

Lynn frowned. Tessie was obviously safe. But what was she doing headed for the Riviera?

"And to Paris."

Of course, there were *two* directions possible! Lynn realized. Anyway, there was one other option. Maybe it *wasn't* Tessie.

"The person who got out of the car. Was she large and fat? Or thin and short?"

"The villagers do not describe her carefully."

"Did she pick up a ride on Highway 20?"

"It is not known, madame."

"Jesus," whispered Lynn. It could have been someone else who abandoned the car and walked through town. Maybe Tessie *was* in trouble. How would Lynn ever find out?

They drove back to Chez Lousteau in Grignan. Lynn half expected to find Tessie seated at a table, waiting for her with some outlandish story—but no one was there except for the proprietor and his wife.

Gatien Lousteau commiserated with Lynn over the disappearance of her companion. He then discussed in more detail exactly what Tessie had been trying to find out. It had nothing to do with Valentine Fontaine, as had been established. It had been something else entirely.

According to Lousteau, Tessie had told him at dinner, the previous night, that she was a journalist for a Parisian magazine, on the track of an important story that had to do with underground activities during World War II. She was writing about a member of the French underground and an Englishman who had been killed near Grignan. Could there be, she asked, graveyards around in which such people might be buried?

"Graveyards?" Lynn repeated, trying to focus in on this crazy story of Tessie's

"*Oui.* So I tell her that there is the official graveyard of the town of Grignan near the main church, with several others nearby in other churchyards. But for some reason, she seemed more interested in a tiny burial ground *outside* of town, near a small monastery, far out in the country."

"Can you take me there?" Lynn asked, a sudden excitement tingling up and down her backbone.

"I do not drive," Lousteau explained.

"I drive!" said Lynn. "You show me the way."

"But I must turn over the inn to my wife."

After an interminable wait, Lynn finally coaxed Lousteau into the Citroen and started driving slowly through the winding streets of the small French village. She followed the directions Lousteau kept giving her, winding through sloping fields and up and down over rolling hillsides. In the rearview mirror, she could make out in the vague distance the village of Grignan, clinging to its spot on the side of the hill, its terra cotta tiles red in the Provençal sunshine, its whitewashed walls glistening, its tiny threads of smoke climbing into the clean blue country air.

All signs of the mistral of yesterday were now gone.

"*Halte!*" said Lousteau.

Lynn applied the brakes. The car rolled to a stop

by the side of the road. They were parked under a huge and graceful chestnut tree. The spot Lousteau had selected was beautiful, bucolic, and calm.

"The monastery," Lousteau said, pointing it out.

Lynn could see a cluster of ancient buildings nestled beneath a stand of shagbark oaks by the side of a tiny silver stream that wound down the valley, perhaps three quarters of a mile away.

"It is a school and hospital, madame," said Lousteau.

"And the church?"

"No church. But there is a graveyard attached to the school and hospital."

Lynn smiled. "Hospital to graveyard in one easy move."

"I beg your pardon, madame?"

"Nothing. Can we speak to the monks?"

"Is run by nuns, not monks."

"But I thought you said it was a monastery."

"Originally, *oui*. Now the sisters run the hospital and the school."

"Can we speak to the nuns?" Lynn corrected herself.

Lousteau shrugged. "Quite possible vows of silence, madame."

"What does *that* mean?"

"Impossible to converse with nuns. They maintain their vows of silence."

"But how do they teach school?" Lynn asked, curious.

A Gallic shrug.

Lynn sighed. "Let's go back to the inn. Thank you very much for showing me the monastery. And you say there is a graveyard nearby?"

"Attached to it, madame."
They drove back to Chez Lousteau.

The news at the inn was unchanged. It was now
late afternoon, and still there was no word on the
whereabouts of Tessie Maupin. A messenger had
brought an important-looking envelope to the inn,
and it was now delivered to Lynn by Chloris Lousteau.
It was a new assignment number for her American
Express card.

She went up to her room and sank down on the
bed, exhausted, frustrated, and annoyed with herself
for being taken for such a jerk. But as she sat there,
she suddenly realized why Tessie had invented such a
weird cover story in her conversation with the
Lousteaus. She did *not* want either of them tumbling
to what she was after—the name of Valentine Fontaine. Her crazy tale had been a veil to hide what she
was really looking for—him. And, according to her
hurried conversation with Lynn—she had found him.
Or, what she meant, probably, was that she had
found a *trace* of him.

And, of course, since she was looking back into
the past, she would be trying to track down the name
through records—which she had already done in the
Grignan town hall, as she had explained to Lynn—
and through other means of recognition. A gravestone?

Within minutes, Lynn was in the car again and
driving through the winding streets to the highway,
down by the monastery. It didn't matter, really, that
Tessie had pulled a fast one, and run out on Lynn.
What mattered was to find out what she had discovered about Valentine Fontaine.

If it was *bad*, it was obvious what Tessie must
have done. She had vanished, leaving Lynn stranded

in Grignan. Tessie knew her way around. She was a born conniver. Blackmailing Beatrix would be almost second nature to her. And, for God's sake, why *share* a tidy blackmail income? Why not simply cut her ties with Lynn and go after Beatrix Fontaine *alone*? Then she'd have *all* the money! It would not have occurred to Tessie that Lynn wasn't in it for money.

But there was also the theft of the credit cards. Lynn still couldn't figure out why she'd made off with them. She'd obviously taken Lynn's wallet for the cash. Lynn always carried a roll of mad money— force of habit from her raunchy early years. With that cash, Tessie would be able to get back to Paris *tout de suite*. Once there, she could begin her campaign against Beatrix.

That was it, all right. It *had* to be.

But what was it she had discovered?

There, ahead of her, was the oak tree. It was getting dark now, with the sun behind the hills and the dark blue of the late afternoon turning into purple and black. She pulled up at the side of the road under the oak tree and shut off the engine. For a moment she sat there, gazing down the sloping hill toward the tiny settlement below. She could see flickering lights inside the buildings now; it looked as if the monks— nuns, rather—lived by candlelight or oil lamp rather than by electric lights.

She shivered. What a life!

She got out of the car and started down the hill- side, glad that she had brought good walking shoes with her on this so-called tour of Provence. Even so, it was hard going, with many small ravines cutting through the terrain.

A cold breeze had sprung up by the time she got

down to the stream. She could barely see the graveyard attached to the school property, but as she neared
the trees, she could see the dull glow of the white
stones against the stygian darkness under the trees.

Sure. Gravestones. That was what Tessie was after: information on a gravestone . . . a trace of Fontaine . . . a trace of Valentine.

A low stone wall separated the graveyard from the
school and from the fields around it. She climbed
over the wall after searching for an entrance. None
existed. Skinning her knee, she cursed softly, but
continued on. It was getting *really* dark now. She
could barely see the names.

But here and there she could spot an English name,
and a German one. Tessie certainly had her cover
story correct. A lot of these graves were apparently
those of men who had died in combat during World
War II.

Lynn paused. One of the graves . . . she knelt
down. Yes! The dirt was freshly turned! A *body*
might recently have been buried here! or—

Or, for that matter, it might just as easily have
been dug up!

Whose body was buried?

Tessie Maupin's?

Because she had found out too much?

Found out too much about *what?*

Or was Lynn simply indulging herself in fantastic
Gothic dreams?

Lynn now felt the cold wind of the mistral in her
vitals, even though she knew the night breeze was
not a mistral. She felt a tingle run up and down her
backbone, what the French called a *frisson*. She rose,
backing away from the freshly turned grave, stum-

bling over a tombstone that had been tipped over behind her.

She tried to get to her knees to rise when there was a muffled noise behind her.

She turned, terrified.

Yet, at the same moment she turned, her mind registered the writing on the tombstone that had been tipped over.

She knew her search was over.

At almost the same moment of discovery, she saw the shadowy hulk over her—the powerful shape of a man.

CHAPTER SIXTEEN

*   *   *

EXCERPT FROM NEWSPAPER COLUMN BY "SUZY":

Question of the week: Where is big West End drama hit Clive Argyll—playwright, Shakespearean scholar, actor? Arriving Stateside recently to launch big career in H'wood, Argyll appeared in photos for a *People* spread, then—*finito!* Star does disappearing act! Very odd for hot property bought up by none other than Hayley Welles—she's *the* Prescott, of *the* Prescott billions, and don't you forget it!—suddenly to go poof. Where? Rumor says terrorists have kidnapped him to hold him for big ransom. Incidentally, the Argyll play, *Nine Moons Wasted*, is still doing very well in the West End with an understudy playing Argyll's part. . . .

EXCERPT FROM WEEKLY *ENQUIRER*:

Rumors continue surfacing in regard to the whereabouts of English actor Clive Argyll, recently signed on by Hayley Welles Productions to transform his hit West End play into a smash U.S. motion picture.

Argyll was in fine fettle aboard the Concorde from London, in company with Welles, but once in Los Angeles, the actor vanished from the sight of human eye.

In an exclusive interview with Dr. Robin J. Forsythe, a British research scientist renowned for his work on especially difficult medical problems, *Enquirer* reporter Tom Titt has uncovered an important clue to Argyll's "disappearance."

Forsythe says he was approached by a colleague in medicine, also a Briton, for the latest information on research into AIDS. The colleague confessed he wanted the information for a "patient."

Argyll was, at one time, a patient of Forsythe's colleague, who now threatens reprisals if named. Forsythe would not allow himself to be quoted for publication in the *Enquirer*, and he was noticeably upset during the interview conducted by this newspaper.

When approached in a telephone conversation, Hayley Welles refused to make any comment whatsoever. In fact, she told reporter Tom Titt to "Bug off, buster." Intimates of Ms. Welles indicate that "buster" is a familiar term in her vocabulary. She has used it many times in reported arguments with her husband, Carney Welles—also a packager of talent and properties.

Carney Welles could not be reached for comment at all. A spokesperson in New York indicated that he was hard at work introducing "Beatrix la Belle," a worldwide network of health and beauty spas created by Beatrix Fontaine, one of France's most glamorous cosmetologists.

The Welles duo has been reported frequently in the *Enquirer* as being in serious marital hot water. Speculation by a former associate of the Welles organization indicates that perhaps the trouble stems from a medical problem. AIDS? The informant would not specify.

"It would be presumptuous of me to make any statement at this time," said the former employee, a Princeton graduate.

EXCERPT FROM TRANSCRIPTION, *JOHNNY CARSON SHOW*:

CARSON. Lori Lee Banion, ladies and gentlemen —a stewardess on the Concorde, and probably the last person to see Clive Argyll in the flesh. Isn't that true, Lori Lee?

BANION. Well, sir, in the flesh, yes, but he *was* fully dressed, Mr. Carson—

CARSON. (Smirking) Figure of speech, Ms. Banion! You told us he was on a roll at the start of the trip, drinking champagne, laughing it up with Ms. Welles.

BANION. Oh, yes! He was happy, buoyant, *up!*

CARSON. Did he seem to you on the verge of vanishing from human sight?

BANION. I hardly *know* the man, Mr. Carson. But I'd say he had it made, and he was waiting to go out and show the world!

CARSON. But you told me things—that things, oh, changed?

BANION. Yes. He was talking to Ms. Welles—

CARSON. (Leering) Hayley *Prescott* Welles, ladies and gentlemen. That's not George Washington you see on the dollar bill, it's Hayley *Prescott* Welles.

BANION. And he changed. Oh, he changed. He

was broken up. *She* did it to him, Mr. Carson! She began bossing him around— she told him he couldn't have a drink of champagne. She told him he couldn't do anything unless she *permitted* it!

CARSON. (Mock concern, making face at audience) Down, Ms. Banion! We get the point.

BANION. I think she's got him tied up in a room somewhere! (Very excited) She thinks she *owns* him, Mr. Carson! She's torturing him, probably—

CARSON. (Flinching comically) Uh. The legal department is looking me right in the eye, Ms. Banion. Let's just hold it right there, please?

BANION. But you *asked* me—

CARSON. (Waving his arms and bringing camera in on his face) Miss Lori Lee Banion, ladies and gentlemen! An unusual insight into people—a brand new feature of the *Johnny Carson Show!* Thank you, thank you. The problem still remains, of course. Where *is* Clive Argyll? (Suggestively) And what is he up to? (Smirking) And if not, *why* not?

EXCERPT FROM *TIME* MAGAZINE:

Since British actor Clive Argyll signed a contract to write and star in his own motion picture version of the hit West End play, *Nine Moons Wasted*, he has become a riddle wrapped in a mystery inside an enigma. After the usual publicity handouts detailing the signing of the contract between the actor and Hayley Welles Productions (she's married to Cornelius Welles Associates), Argyll simply dropped out of sight.

Friday last, in Benedict Canyon, Beverly Hills, California, an enterprising free-lance photographer snapped a picture of a man closely resembling the

British actor at the window of the large mansion
owned by the Prescott family and frequented regu-
larly by Hayley and "Carney" Welles. The photograph shows a man, seemingly in good health, standing
at the window, stripped to his jockey shorts, exercising in the sunlight streaming in through the window.

"I don't know what you're making all this fuss
about!" snapped Hayley Welles upon being questioned at the Beverly Hills office of the Prescott
Foundation. "Mr. Argyll is simply sequestered—
and *not* in my Benedict Canyon home—to get his
screenplay in shape. He's paying a large rent and
seems to be a reasonably quiet tenant where he is.
Why all the fuss?"

Questioned about the rumors regarding Argyll's
health, Welles sniffed in contempt. "Tabloid para-
noia," she termed it. As to the persistent rumors that
have surfaced around town about the richest woman
in the world, that she is holding her bought-and-paid-
for star in sexual bondage as a love slave in the
early-1920s mansion, Welles simply waved her hands
in dismissal. "I'm a happily married woman. Mr.
Argyll has his own circle of friends."

OVERHEARD IN MA MAISON:

"You *haven't* gotten your invitation to the party
yet?"

"No, goddamn it, and I'm furious! Joan got hers
yesterday. You got yours Monday. What does Hayley
think I am? Some kind of pariah?"

"Don't worry, Jackie. You'll get it soon enough. I
swear she told me you're on the list!"

"Don't give me that all-knowing smirk, you little
bitch! *I* know when I'm being jobbed!"

"You thinking what I'm thinking? That this is going to be the big unveiling of Clive Argyll?"

"I thought he had AIDS and was dying."

"*I* thought he was with her in some secluded love nest."

EXCERPT FROM THE *LOS ANGELES NEWS*:

(By Sebald Donovan—Exclusive)

Clive Argyll is *not*—repeat, *not*—living in the Benedict Canyon mansion of Hayley Prescott Welles, as has been intimated by faked photographs published in a weekly news periodical.

I know, because I explored the mansion inch by inch last night and found—absolutely no sign of him. I have signed an affidavit to this effect and have registered it at City Hall prior to filing this story.

Using mountain-climbing equipment, with which I am familiar in my avocation as a mountain climber, I entered the chimney that leads into the fireplace of the mansion's huge living room. Descending by the simple method of rappel, I was able to enter the interior of the mansion proper, after which I made a detailed search of the place, encountering only the night watchman and a live-in house-sitter.

"There never was any Clive Argyll here," said the watchman, who refused to divulge his name. "Mrs. Welles [Hayley Prescott Welles] comes in once in a while. But never anybody named Argyll."

"I don't believe there *is* a Clive Argyll," said the woman, who lives in the house and is in the personal employ of Mrs. Welles. "I think those pictures taken at JFK are fakes."

There *is* a Clive Argyll, contrary to her opinion.

He is reported to be somewhere in the United States. He is *not*, I now know, at 1235 Benedict Canyon.

EXCERPT FROM *THE HOLLYWOOD REPORTER*:

(By Patricia Patton)
Do you have your invitation to Hayley Welles's party yet? If you don't, leave town immediately, sign into a health spa or religious order, and never come back. Those who have been asked are in. Those who haven't are out.

Here are the facts:

Hayley's bash—called ''Hayley's Comet'' by the *cognoscenti*—will be *the* affair of the North American continent this year. The poop says the party is being held to cement relations between Hayley and husband Carney Welles, to prove to the public that they are still a pair of lovebirds.

The poop is fluff, invented by Carney and Hayley, who have proved themselves to be experts at flummoxing the public with half-truths and half-lies. The truth is that the party will introduce to the American public a British actor, Clive Argyll, who is now at work on a screen version of his famous West End play, *Nine Moons Wasted*.

Where is Argyll?

No one knows. The poop, further, is that he will be there, at the party—with more data on the upcoming screen version of his play. In other words, all this is public relations hype—the so-called disappearance of Argyll, the story of his sequestration by Hayley Welles, his supposed ''affair'' with Hayley Welles, the supposed ''escape'' from the mansion. All hype.

See you at the party!

*   *   *

Hayley Welles leaned back in the chair of her office on Beverly Drive near Rodeo and scanned the folder of newspaper and magazine clippings. Not bad, she thought, not bad at all for an amateur. The interesting thing was that the media had not considered her as an amateur at public relations. They apparently thought of her as a professional.

Whatever. Her concept of *non*-plants had proved to be just as effective as deliberate publicity plants in the newspapers, magazines, and journals. In fact, the non-appearance of Clive Argyll was every bit as intriguing as the actual appearance-to-be *would* be. Well, not really. But at least it built up the public's appetite for a glimpse of him.

That story in the newspaper, about the mountain climber hired to go into the bowels of the mansion to locate Clive Argyll, had turned out to be an even better idea than she had anticipated. Of course, the whole thing was strictly fiction. It was easy to buy the services of an out-of-work sportsman who had once written a book on mountain climbing, and to plant his ghosted story in a not-unwilling paper. The truth was that Clive Argyll had really been at the mansion for six weeks, laboring on the script for his picture. Hayley had been in contact with him at least once a day, telling him about the progress of the story of his "disappearance." Although he had not been very tickled with the idea at first, he had begun to appreciate her technique once the stories began to appear.

Also, it was obvious that interest in Argyll was growing out there in the real world. *That* was important to him, more than anything else. As she got used to him, Hayley realized the man was not the fool and boor she had originally taken him for.

He seemed a thoroughly decent sort—a trifle macho, of course, and a trifle serious, but that kind of
role suited him. He had the build and the temperra-
ment for it. Nevertheless, she knew that he still held
it against her that she had put one over on him in
signing him up the way she had. *Buying* him, as it
were.

At first Hayley had anticipated a physical reaction
on his part. He had played so strongly at being
enraged over her contract with him that she had
thought he would *do* something about it: rape her,
make a phoney pass at her, humiliate her. But so far,
he had done nothing, absolutely *nothing*. In fact,
they had begun to get along quite famously with one
another.

The invitations to her party—"Hayley's Comet"
as the media called it—were all out now. The party
would take place in three days. All the movers and
shakers of Hollywood would be there. It was a perfectly orchestrated public relations campaign—rather
in the grand manner—but imprinted with Hayley's
own individual stamp of creativity.

She was going out to see him in the afternoon. He
had almost finished the completed draft of the script,
and she wanted to look at the ending. Of course, she
was no cinematic genius—she would leave the details
to the director and producer—but she had an eye for
a good thing. And if it was good, as the rest of it
was, it would be something to be proud of.

Nevertheless, she wondered what was keeping him
from coming on to her. Was she losing her touch?
She shrugged. Not that it mattered. With money,
who needed looks, too?

As she sat there projecting her thoughts and

daydreaming, the telephone rang. She reached over and lifted the handset. . . .

In the deck chair beside the swimming pool at the Prescott mansion in Benedict Canyon, Clive Argyll gave a contented sigh, much like a satisfied and happy animal just finished with dinner. In truth, he was *not* satisfied, nor was he particularly happy—but he was sinking into a kind of ennui caused by the marvelous sunshine and temperate weather of the West Coast of America. No wonder all the kooks wound up in Beverly Hills, he thought. What a place to laze around!

It was that damned Hayley Welles who caused perfect contentment to elude him. It wasn't her confinement of him on this marvelous estate, to finish up his manuscript. That, which had at first disturbed him no end, was a real plus. He had been able to work long hours each day, trying out things from a literary standpoint that he had never had time to try out when he had created the play version of his story.

Creatively, he was hitting on all eight cylinders. It was in the other department that things were not up to par. Hell, he didn't mind not having a woman around. Sometimes the sex thing got to be a bit of a bore. Well, not *really* a bore, but kind of expected, and thus not . . . unexpected—to coin a pleonasm.

She bothered him. When he had first met her, he had reacted socio-politically to her presence. That is, the fact that she was money, and the fact that she was power and clout, overrode in a negative way his *personal* and positive reaction to her. That conflict had continued in their subsequent meetings, culminating in their confrontation on the Concorde bound for New York.

Once he realized what had happened, Argyll decided that he had been had, but in a most ingenious and imaginative way. And he had secretly admired the manner in which she did him in. It was impish; it was clever; and it was outrageous.

Naturally, when she had instructed him about his living at the huge estate in Benedict Canyon, he had thought of himself the prisoner of a madwoman—and had told her exactly that. But her good humor had disarmed his own rage and irascibility. Eventually, he had simply pulled out his portable, plugged it in, and started to work. He usually drank a beer or two with the groundskeeper at night, and sometimes he chatted with the old woman in charge of the house.

Hayley had taken to dropping around every evening for a short visit and chat. When the stories had begun to appear in the newspapers and magazines, Argyll had been honestly intrigued and fascinated. It was *working!* And he had never given it a chance.

But there was something else. He now found himself looking more and more closely at Hayley Welles. She was, he decided, a most intelligent and independent woman. In addition to that, she was classy and had excellent taste. The clothes she wore were expensive, but they also *suited* her perfectly. Being an actor Argyll *knew* good taste; she had it, and in spades!

Also, she carried herself the way an aristocrat should. Sure, Argyll hated aristocrats, but that took away nothing from their form and manner. It was the elegance of the aristocracy that made the upper class what it was; not the arrogance and the selfishness. Whether she was aristocracy or not—and of course, America simply did not have an aristocracy—Argyll knew he was watching something akin to what the English knew as royalty.

When he realized he was beginning to watch her more carefully and feel closer to her—in fact, to get just the slightest *itch* when she was around—he immediately tried to ignore her effect on him. It worked for a couple of visits. But then, as she continued making her low-keyed, almost androgynous appearances, he began to enjoy hearing her talk, and the sound of her laughter began to produce tingles on the surface of his skin.

The entire situation had degenerated the night before, when Hayley Welles had stayed with him after a small supper out by the swimming pool. The sun had sunk in the west, and the quick darkness of Southern California had settled immediately over the estate. There had been so sign of smog during the day. The air was wonderful. It was very quiet in the hills.

And Clive Argyll threw away his sacred key to socialism and made a pass at the richest woman in the world. It had been coming for a long time. He knew she was waiting for it. And he knew how deliberately he had held off for many days. He knew it; she knew it.

Yet when he had his arms around her and reached over to kiss her on the mouth, she stiffened in his embrace and pulled away.

He was startled. "What's the matter?"

"I never mix business with pleasure," Hayley said, almost as if she had made it up on the spur of the moment.

"You've been giving me the look every night since I've been here!" Argyll cried out.

"Perhaps you misconstrued kindness for lasciviousness," Hayley responded bitingly.

"Oh, come on now! Don't tell me you're not interested!"

She eyed him boldly. "There is interest, and there is interest," Hayley told him. "I *would* like to find out what kind there is here—but not until *after* we make our millions!"

"Shit!" cried Argyll, getting up and stomping around on the deck of the pool. "Look at that, you've got me all worked up! For *nada*! See? I'm even talking like these Angelenos!"

Hayley was cool. "No fault of mine. I never led you on one bit, Clive."

"The hell you—" He bit his lip. He came and stood over her. "What's this going to be? A contest? See who's the strongest holdout?"

"Oh, no fear of that," Hayley said softly. "If you go into your caveman act, I simply call for Cecil, and you go into the pool."

Cecil was the groundskeeper. Cecil Innes. Good man. Big man. He could do it, all right, given a chance.

"Is he always your keeper?"

"Only when I want not to be kept," she said lightly. "Now let's get to work. I want to see what you've got for me . . . on paper."

He was slow in cooling down, but eventually he had realized he would have to. He had smouldered all night at the treatment she had given him. Damn her! She really knew how to do a number on a man! And so, during the day, as he finished the pages that wound up the script, he had been thinking with one corner of his mind how he was going to get back at her. He had Cecil on hold. He had given him tickets to a concert in Los Angeles—Cecil was an avid cello aficionado—and in so doing, Argyll had discovered that Hayley had been bluffing all along. There *wasn't* any secret signal, or call or anything, to alert Cecil to trouble.

So Argyll would do it tonight when she showed up. What? *Some*thing.

What he was going to do was to humiliate her. She had pulled that tease deal on him the night before. He'd turn the tables. He would take her down—one, two, three—and rape her, in a gentlemanly fashion, of course. It would serve her right. She thought she had tamed him! He'd show her the truth!

He rose now and dove into the cool, soft, marvelous water in the pool. He swam the length and back again, enjoying the feel of the water against his body, the churn of his muscles through the froth, the exertion of his flesh against the buoyancy.

He swam back and forth for fifteen minutes, and when he climbed out, he was breathing hard, but steadily, and he was feeling simply marvelous. Let that silly woman show up and he'd take her right out here on the deck!

He lay down to dry off in the slightly chilly evening air as the lights automatically came on above the pool. He was lying there, letting exhaustion take over completely, when he heard the rear door of the house open.

He looked up and saw her standing there. The outside pool light cast her in shadow. He rose then, almost the way a panther might, and approached her. Would it be now? Why not? She'd be surprised. Maybe she wanted it, and if she did, he'd oblige her. He was not about to put up with another refusal like last night. She didn't know what she wanted, anyway. He had a theory that no woman *really* did.

As he approached, the water sliding off his body, she stepped out into the arc of the light.

"Goodness!" Her mouth formed a little *O*, and she smiled at him coquettishly.

What in hell—? It *wasn't* Hayley Welles! It was somebody else! Now who in hell *was* it? He had seen her before—somewhere!

Then he had it. It was Hayley's sister, Megan. The countess! Lah-di-dah!

"Sorry," Argyll drawled in that west country accent he had perfected on the London stage. "I was expecting Mrs. Welles."

"Mrs. Welles has been detained," said Megan with a wide smile. "I've just left her. She wanted me to come out to convey her regrets."

The goddamned bitch! Argyll thought. Just like that! She *knew* what he had planned. He'd bet that. Yet, how could she know? Damn her! She had radar—human radar!

His eyes were traveling up and down the form of the woman in front of him. She was a bit plumper than Hayley, actually, not at all bad looking, for that matter. In fact, she was closer to his age than Hayley was, when you came right down to it. Of course, no one *knew* how old he *really* was.

"Devonshire," Argyll said, with a snap of the fingers. *"That's* where we met."

"Right on!" Megan squeaked, ecstatic that he recalled her. "You remembered!"

"Hard to forget," he grinned, the water dripping down his skin, causing him to tingle all over. "You're that Countess Something-or-other. I was playing Shakespeare in the provinces."

"That's right," Megan giggled.

He was staring at her. Her clothes were cut very

well, a little tight, but there was nothing really wrong with that. In fact, she bore a strange resemblance to Hayley, a resemblance and at the same time a slight difference and—*vive la différence!* There was a kind of softness where Hayley was sharp-edged, a kind of relaxedness where there was tension in Hayley, a kind of comfortableness that had never existed in Hayley.

"So where's the count?" He sauntered over to the deck chair in which he had been lying.

She followed him. "In Florence."

"Lucky Florence." Argyll spoke smoothly and quickly, delivering it like a punchline.

She colored prettily. *"Firenze,"* she said, trying to get the sound right, but failing as usual. "He has banking troubles."

"Don't we all?" Argyll lifted the bath towel crumpled on the deck and began drying off his upper body. He kept his eyes on Megan, who sank down into an upright chair nearby. He saw that she was watching him as closely as he was watching her.

"Lee is talking to a woman who thinks she saw Hayley's runaway daughter in Paris."

"Lee? Who's—? Oh. Hayley."

Megan nodded. She went on to explain that the informant would not reveal anything more than the fact of the sighting to the Prescott family's detectives. The informant wanted money for the disclosure. "Beaucoup bucks," Megan explained. However, no one knew whether or not this woman was simply trying to squeeze money out of the Prescotts, or if she really had something. Hayley was now flying over to Paris to dicker.

Argyll finished drying himself and strolled over to Megan. "Drink?"

She looked up at him. For a long moment, they watched one another. Good Christ, thought Argyll. She's as charged as Hayley is. And, the damnedest thing—I'm charged, too! What the hell is happening?

"I'm not particularly thirsty," Megan told him, still smiling, still with her eyes locked on his.

He felt suddenly gone inside. He knelt down slowly beside her chair, knees spread, sitting on his haunches, and touched her cheek with his finger.

"You hate the working class, too? Like your sister?"

Megan looked him over carefully, his bare chest, his straining muscles, his wide shoulders, his dripping thighs. She shivered involuntarily.

"I don't know. I never thought about it."

He threw back his head and laughed uproariously. "You don't hate demonstrators? Marchers? Rioters?"

"Gosh, no. I guess I'm just not too bright politically."

"Meggy," he said, having heard Hayley once call her that, "you're coming with me." And he reached over to take her by the shoulders and lift her out of the chair. She came up to him willingly, light as a feather.

"Where are we going?"

"For a little orientation. It's called bedroom politics."

Marvelous! thought Clive Argyll, stretching and yawning. She was breathing softly beside him, her mouth slightly open, her naked body twisted in the sheets. He laughed aloud. What would Hayley think? Or had she set this up?

Who cared?

What puzzled Argyll was the situation between the count and the countess. If *he* were the count, he'd never let this live one out of sight. But then he remembered all he had heard about the count, and he turned to stare at Megan beside him.

She opened her eyes. They were clear. Her skin was glowing. She had that bed-damp look that very few people honestly get during sex. She certainly did glow.

"Serves him right," Argyll said.

"Who?" she whispered, moving slightly, so that he took her in his arms and kissed her again.

"The count."

"Nicky?" She blinked her eyes. "Poor Nicky!" Her face turned red.

Argyll laughed again. "Oh, come now! Don't pretend."

"Pretend—what?"

"Pretend you don't know!"

"I *don't* know," Megan said, baffled. She looked so innocent and puzzled that Argyll grabbed her and went at her again, and she conceded defeat and lay with him once more.

"Nicky's little pleasure palace."

"Our place in Florence?" She was drowsy and half-asleep.

"*His* place. Come on, Meggy. Everyone in Italy knows. The inmate at the Villa Bella Maria."

Megan's eyes opened wider. She said nothing.

Argyll was so tickled at her expression that he rolled over on top of her and they were at it again.

In a way, the party—"Hayley's Comet"—was pretty much a letdown, both to Hayley Welles and to Clive Argyll, at least after the fantastically successful and appealing buildup. But it went over very well with the members of the media, who were everywhere with their cameras and tape recorders and pencils and pads.

At precisely ten-thirty P.M. Hayley Welles walked to the center of the main living room of the mansion and raised her arms for quiet.

"Ladies, and gentlemen—the man you've been waiting to see!

"They seek him here, they seek him there!
"The media seeks him everywhere.
"What's his pose? What's his style?
"That damned, elusive Clive Argyll!"

On cue, he appeared on the stairs, smiling and waving, to descend and mingle with the movers and shakers of the entertainment world.

"Senator, would you tell us where your wife, Lynn, is? There are rumors—"

"Come on now, boys! You're not trying to make me do some off-the-cuff stuff, are you? Hell, Lynn's somewhere in Paris. I had to get back here for a big do in Beverly Hills—not this crazy party—but a political meet. She's just not ready to return to the States. You know, fellows—nothing to wear!"

"Oh, sure, senator—"

"You betcha, and if you print a word about her and me splitting up, it's going to be your ass, boy!"

"Well, Madame Beatrix, what do you think of Hayley Welles's new celebrity? How do you like Clive Argyll?"

"I would like to see him at one of my new health spas."

"You think he needs your treatment?"

"I think I need his treatment."

*   *   *

"Your wife seems to have done a superlative job on gearing up the public for tonight's presentation of Clive Argyll. Do you have a comment on that, Mr. Welles?"

"Hayley knows her way around."

"Can I quote you on that?"

"You do and I'll sue."

"There is a rumor, Mrs. Welles, that your daughter has been kidnapped by terrorists, and that a ransom has been asked for her safe return. Would you please address yourself to this question?"

"There is no truth in it at all. Abbey is simply enjoying herself in Europe."

"Specifically where?"

"*Specifically*, wherever she can."

"We understand your husband has been indicted by a secret jury in Rome. Is that a fact, Countess della Camarra?"

"There's not a word of truth in it. Besides, it's still a secret."

"Excuse me, Madame Beatrix. Telephone call for you."

"Thank you."

Beatrix Fontaine was tired, but somehow, at the same time, she was invigorated. The excitement of the party, at which Clive Argyll had been introduced to the world of the media; the laughter and the infighting; the booze and the shouts—all had made her light-headed and remote from the strife and agony of the real world around her.

"Hello," she said into the telephone, assuming the speaker was an American.

She listened, and then pushed the handset closer to her ear. She frowned, concentrating, and as she did so, her face turned ashen. For a long time she stood there, frozen in a kind of idiotic stance that was a weird combination of shock and despair.

Slowly, she hung up the telephone and started to move through the crowd toward the door.

It was twenty-four hours before Carney Welles discovered that Beatrix Fontaine had checked out of her suite in the Beverly Hills Hotel. She had left no note as to where she was going. She had contacted no one—not even Welles. She was simply gone.

BOOK FOUR:
THE RIVIERA

CHAPTER SEVENTEEN

Abbey Martin did not know *what* to do. She felt a magnetic attraction for François, and had felt it ever since the first night she had seen him at the café. "Oh, my God," she had said to herself. His dark eyes had stared at her in a way that made her feel moist and ready between her legs. "Oh, my God, is he looking at me?" And then the tingling sensation—could you have an orgasm just by having a guy look at you?

Nevertheless, he frightened her. He had shot a guard in cold blood. He robbed banks. He would do anything to attain his revolutionary ends. And now . . .

She glanced down at the copy of *Le Monde* lying on her bed. She had just read one of the headlines in French, and it had startled her. The truth was, François was *more* than a bank-robber. The guard at the bank they had robbed had died. François was now a *bona fide* killer.

She sat there in her hotel room and rubbed her head, puzzled, indecisive. If she left François, where would she go? Back to mommy dearest, the tyrant

315

who threatened to suppress her every desire, her every attempt to enjoy life?

She shook her head abstractedly. She wanted a life of her own, not the slavish life of a daughter doting on a mother of whom she did not fully approve. But maybe François wanted to enslave her, too. Would he kill her after he got her mother's money? There was always *that* terrifying possibility!

All she wanted was to be free, to live life as it came. Yet it seemed impossible. Everybody wanted to entrap her, to make her a slave.

She left her room, double-locked the door, descended the stairs, and walked out onto the sidewalk— where the odor of fresh bread baking across the street permeated the morning air. Then she headed down the steps to the *métro*.

Now she was pretty sure what she would do. She would leave her luggage behind at the hotel and let François think she was still living there. She would buy new luggage and new clothes, and then she could escape. All she needed was her passport, which she carried in her purse. She had plenty of traveler's checks.

Head spinning, she inserted her yellow cardboard *métro* ticket into the turnstile, passed through, and climbed onto the next train.

She got off at the Champs Elysées, climbed the steps to the boulevard, and strolled down it. She liked to shop along the fashionable Champs Elysées.

It was different today. There was a huge crowd marching down the center of the boulevard, where usually there were hundreds of hurrying cars. Some kind of demonstration, she could see.

She read a twenty-foot-long banner held above the

crowd by demonstrators. It was an antinuke parade. She stopped to watch the noisy gathering.

After a while she heard a voice at her side. "Are you against nuclear weapons?"

"Yes," she said, turning—and saw François. "Oh! What are you doing here?"

"I'm here for the demonstration."

"You just happened to be here when I'm here?" she asked suspiciously.

"Not really. One of our group followed you here and telephoned me." He had that crooked smile on his face.

"You have gang members *following* me?"

"We don't want you to get lost." François seemed amused.

Abbey did not like the idea of people tailing her. It was the same as being a prisoner, even if only in a psychological sense.

"I'm not *lost!*" she protested.

"When I found out you were coming here, I hurried over. You're against nuclear weapons?"

"I already said so. Yes."

"Then you're one of us. We're in favor of unilateral disarmament."

Abbey realized later that François's question was a loaded one. Of course she was against nuclear weapons. Wasn't everyone? But that did not mean that she was in favor of unilateral disarmament. She found, to her surprise, that she was having a lot of second thoughts about things ever since she had read that the bank guard François had shot was dead.

To be honest with herself, she had always supported liberal causes because it was the chic thing to do. All her friends did it. Hollywood actors and actresses did it; trend-setters did it. Everybody wanted peace, and so did she, but now François and his political gang wanted more from her than a signature on a petition—they wanted her money. And maybe they wanted more than that. Maybe they wanted her, as well. Certainly they wanted the publicity of her famous face and name to use for propaganda on their side.

It was becoming increasingly complicated and scary for her. She could not figure out what François *really* wanted, but he seemed to need more from her than love. Sometimes she felt manipulated, like a puppet.

Why couldn't *anything* be easy?

"Want to join in the demonstration?" François asked.

"All right."

At least she was against nuclear weapons, and anyway, she could not have escaped from François now, even if she tried.

They stepped onto the boulevard and marched with the procession.

"What did you do before you started your gang?" she asked François.

"I used to teach political science at the Sorbonne."

François's breath reeked of garlic. Ironically, Abbey felt a sudden pang of hunger.

"Why did you quit teaching?" she asked.

"It was useless, accomplished nothing. I was telling my students the same lies my teachers had told me—*and* I was getting paid for it! That's what teaching's all about."

"I know what you mean. My mother tells me to obey whatever she tells me, so I do, and where does it get me? Nowhere. Trapped at home. A nobody."

"Exactly. Parents and teachers are very similar.

They only give you orders so they can control you, not for your own good.''

''How do we get away from them?''

''Only one way. We have to take over. You're right to distrust your mother. She's a capitalist. Capitalists only care about money. Every order she gives you either makes money for her or saves it for her.''

''No wonder I hate her so much.''

''When POW takes over, you will be the one giving the orders.''

''What if we can't take over?''

''We have to try. We can't sit on the sidelines. That's the same as endorsing our enslavement. The only way we can become free is by throwing out our fat-cat masters and taking their place.''

''Just like that?''

''It won't be easy.''

''I want something to eat. I haven't eaten all day. There. Let's go to Fouquet's.''

She made her way through the crowd toward the café. He followed her. She glanced over her shoulder, saw him, and ran away from him. She giggled. Even on an empty stomach, she liked to flirt.

He ran after her and caught up to her. ''Let's go to bed,'' he suggested.

''It's too early for that.''

She wondered what the French equivalent was for, ''I want to jump your bones.'' That's what guys told her Stateside. This was better than being cooped up at home, she thought.

She laughed.

''What's so funny?'' he asked.

''I don't know.''

Now he was staring at her with those oh-my-God eyes. How she loved to flirt, to make men drool with desire. That was her power. She exulted in it. Mommy dearest could not take that away from her. François would become the head of the new government, and she would control him between the sheets. She knew the way men ogled her, and François was a man like all the rest. He could not resist her charms.

Ernst Roedeker waited in François's garret for his return. Ernst, erstwhile member of the Red Brigades in West Germany, graduate of Patrice Lumumba University, twenty-nine-year-old son of a prosperous attorney, heard a key turn in the lock of the front door. He tensed.

The door opened and, key in hand, François entered.

Ernst scratched his closely cropped brown hair. "What took you so long?"

"Guess."

"You're alone, aren't you?"

"You mean without that prick-teaser?" François snorted. "She's back in her hotel room."

Sniffing the tobacco smoke in the garret, François shot a dirty look at the crushed cigarette butts on the floor beside Ernst's feet. "Didn't you ever hear of an ashtray?"

Ernst shrugged. "I couldn't find one."

"Thanks."

"What about the poor little rich bitch? Is she in on it yet?"

"She's coming along. Somebody's watching her hotel at all times now. I don't want her getting any ideas."

Ernst sighed. "I still say she isn't worth the trouble."

"She's the key to seeing her mother!" François protested.

"Who needs the mother?" growled Ernst. "Why don't we just hold the cock-teaser for ransom?"

"It's not the money, Ernst, it's the *publicity!* We're nothing if we don't let the public know we exist."

"I hope it doesn't backfire. Getting in is one thing. Getting out is going to be tough. All this *publicity* is going to make it even tougher!"

"As long as the girl is with us, we should be safe. They're not going to want to risk *her* life just to take us."

"We crash the party," Ernst spat out. "Then what?"

"POW becomes a household word. The capitalists broadcast our organization's name all over the world. We get prime-time coverage on television. They do hour-long specials on us. We hold a big press conference at the chic party. Abbey denounces her mother and her mother's greedy friends to the media and espouses our cause in front of the world press. The public sees the naked self-interest of the rich and rallies to our side."

"What party are you blatting on about?"

"I'm talking about the gala opening for yet another capitalist venture to milk the bourgeoisie for all they're worth. Some spa and health club called 'Beatrix la Belle.' "

"How did you get onto this?"

François motioned for Ernst to toss him a cigarette. Ernst complied. François caught it against his chest.

"It's all over the media," he said. "Haven't you seen the ads? Magazines, movies, newspapers—how could you miss it?"

"I don't pay much attention to ads," Ernst said

with disgust. "I go to sleep during those commercials that precede the movies at the theaters."

"I just saw an ad for the club in *Paris Match* the other day."

Ernst lifted his eyebrows apathetically.

"The whole world will be watching," said François. "This is what we *want*."

"Manipulation of the media." Ernst blew smoke thoughtfully upward.

"Exactly. It's much easier than you think, because they *want* to be manipulated. Papers sell more copies and television ratings skyrocket when they cover a sensational story, which is what we're going to give them."

"It sounds like a circus."

"More like a soap opera. Listen, and give me a light for this cigarette."

From his leather jacket, Ernst withdrew a book of matches, which he tossed to François. "Why am I the one who always buys the cigarettes?"

"Listen. Don't you remember the Beirut hijacking? The jet. It was a great media event. Every day, the media would cover a new development in the soap opera. The public watched, glued to their TV sets, waiting for the next plot twist, sitting on the edge of their seats. Every day, a few more hostages were released. Some of them were ill and needed special treatment at a hospital. At our gala, every so often we'll fire our submachine guns for menace, to get the adrenalin pumping in the audience. Our actors will be the beautiful people, the rich and famous."

"It sounds like we'll make the top ten on American TV."

"Now you understand. Like everybody else, we have to sell ourselves, our project. It's not enough to have an idea, we have to publicize it and do it dramatically, so people will listen to us.''

''As long as we don't end up on a slab in the morgue; like Hans.''

François growled in his throat. ''Hans was grandstanding. I *told* him he could never get into the Prescott estate and kidnap Hayley Prescott. He was born half out of his mind.''

''He did manage to pilot that Ultralight of his onto the estate. I never thought he'd get even that far.'' Ernst shook his head in dismayed approval.

''We'll never get to Hayley Prescott. We've got her daughter. She's just as good, if you ask me.''

''What does the rich girl think of our project?''

François exhaled cigarette smoke like an old-fashioned movie idol expressing nonchalance. ''I haven't told her.''

Ernst gaped at François in astonishment. ''Well, you'll have to tell her *sometime*.''

''I'm not sure she's ready yet.''

Abbey sat at a sidewalk café in Montparnasse watching a gypsy strum a guitar and sing off-key, then stagger drunkenly between the marble-topped tables and pass his hat for coins. She tossed a few francs into it.

He was pretty dreadful, but he looked hard-up, so why not help him out? She felt happy today.

He smiled through his three-days' growth of beard, nodded, and weaved his way through the remaining tables.

François caught her eye as he entered the café, his pants as tight as ever. He sat down across from her.

''Did you hear the news?'' he asked.

"What news?" she rejoined airily, full of Parisian *joie de vivre*.

"Your mother is helping to start up a new health club called 'Beatrix la Belle.' "

Abbey's expression soured. "Oh, that's my stepdad's baby, really. I hope it falls flat on its face."

"We can make it do exactly that." François leaned closer.

"Sure. And you can squeeze blood out of oranges."

"You think we can't?"

"My mother never fails. She's an American success story. She succeeds at everything she tries. If she's behind it, this jerky health club will make millions. Believe me."

"Not when we're through with it."

"This I have to see."

"You sound like you don't believe me."

"Mommy dearest is invincible."

Amused, François ordered an absinthe. "You must really hate her."

"You don't know the half of it. Whatever mommy wants, mommy gets."

"I have a surefire way you can get back at her."

"I'll believe it when I see it."

François and his politics, she thought. She was sick of politics. Corporate politics. Sexual politics. "Ism" politics: capitalism, communism, et ceteraism. Everything was politics. Her mother was the consummate politician, the consummate manipulator.

François leaned over the tabletop and whispered to her. "We're going to disrupt that gala at Nice. We want you to come."

"What can I do?"

"You can tell the whole world how horrible your mother really is."

"The world would throw up if it heard the truth."

"That's the spirit!"

"You've never locked horns with her. You'll need an army to best her."

"We'll have better than that."

"What?"

"We'll have her husband handle our public relations."

"Stepdaddy? He won't help you. He doesn't want to lose any of the Prescott money. He'll always take mommy's side."

"He'll do it because he *has* to. We're going to manipulate the media, and they will have no choice but to obey. They will champ at the bit to cover his downfall, because it's a terrific story, and because the public will be dying to see it."

Abbey kicked off her shoe, rubbed her foot gently against François's calf, and looked coy.

"I bet I know what you're dying to do," she said. She would not mind peeking under the table at the bulge in his crotch.

"I'm serious."

"So am I." She put her finger on her lips.

"We need the Prescott millions backing us."

Abbey giggled. "Forget it. My parents hate communists. They're dyed-in-the-wool reactionaries."

"I thought they were liberals, the way they swap bed partners every week."

"Reactionaries fuck as much as liberals. Reactionaries try to keep it secret. That's the only difference."

"Your mother doesn't keep it secret."

"How can she? There's always a photographer for the *Enquirer* or some other rag lurking in the bushes, ready to jump out and snap a candid shot of her and her partner of the moment. It's not easy being rich."

"She's got it rough." He pulled a long face.

"Do you want it rough?' she asked, winking and smiling.

"I'm trying to focus your mind on the injustice in the world."

"I'm trying to focus yours on the pleasure."

"There isn't much when you have to serve the rich."

"You're boring when you get on your soapbox. Let's party."

"Nothing can stop us. If we have to die for our cause, we will."

"Will you die for my pleasures? Swear you will die for me."

"Of course."

"Then I will help you destroy Beatrix la Belle." She paused. "Now, stand up and let me see how firm your oath is."

"My oath is hard and fast."

"Good. Let me see."

"If I do, I'll be arrested."

"Then it must be a good oath, and I am flattered."

"We can't make light of the work we have ahead of us."

"Is it hard?"

"Yes."

"Then I look forward to it." She giggled. "And it looks forward to me."

François looked surly.

"I'm sorry," she said. "I can't help it if I'm a healthy girl who wants to enjoy life."

"We all want to enjoy life, but a lot of us can't afford it."

She jerked her head away. "That's not my fault. Why are you such a spoilsport?"

"I'm not. I simply want you to understand our cause, so you can be sure you're one of us."

"I'm sure. But we can't be all business and no pleasure. I can't live like that. Even Karl Marx laid his maid."

She wondered if she would ever settle down, ever have a family. Could she ever limit herself to one man and be satisfied simply being a mother? Other women did that. Would it ever happen to her? She wasn't sure she wanted it to. It was more exciting like this, being free to go out with different men. The problem was insecurity; she could not trust any of the men she met.

She did not want to think depressing thoughts. She drained her Dubonnet. Christ, she only wanted a little happiness. What was wrong with that?

"I want to be happy," she told François.

"You want to be happy, but you don't want to pay the price."

"You're starting to sound like my mother."

"That's a cheap shot."

"Then don't lecture me."

She was tired of slumming. She felt like going to the Champs Elysées and buying mink coats. It was fun to buy beautiful things: clothes, jewels.

"Are you going to Nice with us or not?" François wanted to know.

"Of course. Nice is beautiful. I love to travel."

"Not as a tourist. You know what I mean."

"I'm going to Nice. Now let's party before I'm out of the mood. Oh, look who just walked by!"

François turned around to look. "I've seen him before," he said dryly.

"It's François Truffaut. Does he have a lot of girlfriends?"

François stood up. "Let's go."

"Okay. I want to see if your oath is as hard as you say it is."

CHAPTER EIGHTEEN

ayley Prescott Welles glanced out the Fifth Avenue window of the Prescott penthouse apartment in the East Seventies and surveyed Central Park with an inattentive gaze. She was still furious at the total incompetence displayed by the police of two continents, and at the absolute inability displayed by the private intelligence arm of the Prescott family.

Seated in a chair near the window, Carney Welles cleared his throat and was about to utter some oracular observation, when Hayley cut him short with a wave of the hand.

"Two failures!" raged Hayley, now moving away from the window and toward the center of the luxuriously appointed sitting room. "Not one, but two! It's impossible to believe! Not with all the money we put into your pockets, monsieur!"

The person to whom Hayley was addressing her cutting remarks sat uneasily in a lounge chair placed near the center of the room. He was a tall, rather swarthy man with a clipped mustache and a well-barbered head of hair. He had a hawklike nose, piercing black eyes, and a mobile mouth, which now, uncharacteristically, was closed and pursed in frustration.

"Well?" prompted Hayley, standing in front of him, the full fury of her rage focused directly on him.

Boissy Goriot touched his mustache with the forefinger of his right hand in what Hayley had come to recognize as a habitual gesture when the man was nonplussed. Good, she thought. At least we've got him worried!

"Everything you have said is so true, madame," he responded finally, smiling only a tiny bit, to assure those who watched him that he was not amused at the situation, however much he might be amused at his own inability to *control* the situation.

"Too damned true," snapped Carney Welles from his lounging position near the window.

Hayley turned to him curtly, moving her hand in the air. It was the most obvious and patronizing kind of dismissal. Welles watched his wife carefully, one eyebrow quirked.

Boissy Goriot spoke. "Let us take up the two problems one at a time—if madame will permit me."

"Madame will goddamned well permit you, monsieur. Now let's cut out this horseshit and—"

"If one may presume to disagree with Madame," Goriot said in a steadily more confident tone. "We at Prescott Investigation Group feel quite positively that her own precipitate introduction of herself into the negotiations with a possible informant was a tactical error that may have the most unfortunate and irreversible consequences."

"Why shouldn't I contact that miserable little

bitch?'' Hayley cried. ''You—none of you—were doing a damned thing about Abbey's disappearance. And I include Interpol and all the European police forces in that statement!''

''Here we have a possible lead to the discovery of the whereabouts of your daughter, madame, and the informant disappears! How is this possible? *Impossible*, truly. Except, of course, that quite likely others interested in the whereabouts of Abigail Martin *discovered* the informant's intentions when you—a well-known personage—suddenly appeared in Paris, quite possibly to lead them straight to the informant before she could contact you!''

Boissy Goriot bounced out of the chair and faced Hayley on the expensive oriental rug. Hayley's face was suddenly crimson.

''You've got the gall to blame me?'' she shouted.

''You did a foolish thing,'' snapped Goriot, his accent thickening. ''The approach to this woman—whoever she was—should have been attempted through faceless entities. Not, *parbleu*! through the most famous face on two continents!''

''But she *came* to me! She wanted to talk! She wanted money. Hell, I didn't care about the money—I wanted information about Abbey! Sure I agreed to meet her. But—''

Goriot broke in. ''—but Mademoiselle X did not appear at the appointed rendezvous.''

Hayley heaved a sigh and sank down onto the empty couch. ''No. She didn't appear. She was obviously followed, intercepted, and *prevented* from making the contact.''

''Or, possibly, intercepted and *killed*,'' Goriot suggested softly.

Hayley bit her lip. "You're saying I've got her blood on my hands now—is that it?"

Goriot was still standing. He spread his arms in a slightly stylized Gallic gesture. "No one can be sure. I have gone over the Parisian morgue lists for that week, and I simply have not been able to put a name to anyone who might have been your supposed contact."

"Forget all this crap," snapped Carney Welles. "What do we do *now* about Abbey?"

Goriot looked at Welles for a long moment, considering. "We continue our search for her. That is all we can do, monsieur. Right at this moment, there is no way we can pick up a lead on the woman who chatted with Madame Welles on the telephone."

"We do know Abbey is in Paris," Hayley said in a soft, crushed voice.

"Do we?" Goriot swung around to face her. "Perhaps yes, perhaps no. I am not impressed with the odds. If *I* were someone seeking a great deal of money as an informant, I would certainly not arrange my meeting *near* the object of any possible search. I would set it up somewhere else, so as not to tip off the possible payer of the information money. Your informant may have been a German woman, an Italian woman, a Spanish woman, an English woman—"

"She had a French accent," said Hayley firmly. "But she could speak English pretty well."

Goriot spread his hands. "A profile of millions of women on the continent of Europe, madame!"

Hayley sank into silence, glowering.

"We have these facts," Goriot said, his voice resonant and aggressive. "One. A woman, claiming to have information concerning the whereabouts of Abigail Martin, telephoned Madame Welles in California. Two. The woman desired to meet in person with Madame Welles in Paris, at Fouquet's Restaurant, at two P.M., within two days. Three. She had a French accent, but spoke fluent English. Four. She gave no specific information that might prove she was not simply an adventuress trying to squeeze money from the Prescotts. Five. Madame Welles was at Fouquet's at two P.M. on the agreed-on date, but no contact was made.''

Silence.

"That, madame, monsieur, is it!"

Hayley stalked moodily to the window and looked out at Central Park. It was just getting dark, and some of the lights were appearing on Central Park South, in the windows of the big hotels and the posh apartments. She shook her head slightly and clasped her hands behind her back.

Jesus, she thought. She was really worried about Abbey now. Damned worried. She had never really realized how much she loved her daughter. Oh, she had known it in an intellectual way. But this concern was getting to her in a deeper, emotional way. She had lost her appetite, and she thought she was dropping a little weight. She didn't really *need* that. What she needed was action. Action, damn it!

Sure, Abbey was in France somewhere—or on the Continent. The records showed that she had entered France. That was recorded at passport control when she had flown in. But since that moment, she had simply vanished from sight. She was apparently using some other name—but what that name was, no one could guess. The PIGs weren't doing well at all, Hayley thought. Just flubbing around.

And now, with this Beatrix thing—

"Now we talk about the disappearance of Beatrix

Fontaine," Goriot was saying, resuming his stance in the middle of the room. "Problem number two." Hayley shrugged and sank down into her chair again, promising herself she'd remain silent through this discussion. It had a lot to do with her, but nowhere as much as Abbey's whereabouts.

"You say, Monsieur Welles," Goriot intoned, "that Mademoiselle Beatrix simply checked out of the Beverly Hills Hotel and—*disappeared?*"

"There's no other way to put it," Welles said, sitting up straight and looking at the investigations chief. "Vanished from sight!"

"What you mean is that she did not inform you where she was going."

"Exactly. There's a great deal of money depending on her presence and on her person. I am anxious to know where she is."

Goriot rubbed his mustache lightly. "You suspect kidnapping?"

"I suspect nothing," Welles admitted, looking at Goriot with a frown. "But since keeping in contact was certainly part of our arrangement, I am surprised that she has not done so—no matter where she may be."

"The success of the Beatrix la Belle enterprise, which you have exhaustively described to me, is dependent on her active communication and participation with you—that is the truth?"

Welles nodded. "Look. She's scheduled to make at least a half-dozen important appearances at various spots on the Continent in the next few weeks—before her grand appearance in Nice during the Festival of Flowers."

"The records show her boarding a flight from Los Angeles to Paris—a polar flight that arrived at Orly

Airport on schedule. She too, like Abigail Martin, has been reported last seen on French soil.''

"You suspect a connection?'' Hayley asked lazily.

Goriot shrugged. "It certainly appears to be a coincidence—if there is not a direct connection.''

"Or indirect connection,'' Welles said thoughtfully.

"Was Mademoiselle Fontaine in a good mood when last you saw her, Monsieur Welles?''

"She was in excellent spirits,'' Welles said. "That's why it surprised me so much when she turned up missing. Sure, when she left the party in Benedict Canyon, I thought it was odd. But it was certainly not a serious matter. Then, when another day passed without my hearing from her, I began to be somewhat worried. And now—nothing. A full week—and nothing!''

Goriot pulled a crumpled notebook from the pocket of his expensively tailored jacket and leafed through some notes. "Now, we know one thing. She received a telephone call during the party. Shortly after that, she left the Prescott estate and returned to the hotel by cab, packed, secured a flight to Paris, and left.''

Welles nodded. "That's all we know.''

Goriot took in a deep breath and moved over to the window, where he stared out, exactly as Hayley had done before him. There was a prolonged silence in the Prescott apartment. Finally Goriot turned, still standing at the window, and looked first at Hayley Welles and then at her husband. His eyes narrowed slightly and he moved his lips as if pursing them involuntarily.

"I do not like it,'' Goriot said softly. He folded his arms on his chest and leaned back against the window sill, fitting his buttocks comfortably against the ledge. "I do not like any of this, Madame and Monsieur Welles. I do not like it even if you have the money to pay me to like it."

Welles frowned. He was quicker on the uptake this time than Hayley. "What the hell are you trying to say?"

"I am trying to say that I do not like to be a party to a fraudulent operation like this one, monsieur!" Goriot stiffened as he spoke, as if in anticipation of a spirited response.

"What?" cried Hayley, half rising from her seat, in a sudden and angered reaction. "Fraudulent? You don't *believe* us?"

Goriot swung around on her. "I am quite aware of the psychological importance of public relations, madame," he said slowly. "I am also quite aware that the two of you are master and mistress of manipulation of the media."

"What's *that* got to do with the disappearance of my daughter?" Hayley blazed.

"Everything!" Goriot snapped, continuing his folded-arm stance at the window, somewhat like a lecturer berating a college class. "I have been mightily impressed, madame, by the clever way in which you yourself managed to procure press coverage in your clever buildup of that British actor, Clive Argyll. You managed to achieve twice the dramatic impact of a simple public introduction by making everyone believe the man had *vanished!* Clever, clever."

"But that's just promotional technique!" Hayley protested. "It has nothing to do with reality!"

"What *is* reality?" Goriot asked with a slight smile. He turned to Welles. "No, Monsieur Welles. I cannot accept the fact that Mademoiselle Beatrix Fontaine has in truth 'vanished.' Quite certainly, as I see it, she is—how you say?—'in the wings,' waiting to reappear at the proper moment, like the actress she actually is, acting in your play. Building up the expectation, I suppose you might say. Eh, Monsieur Welles?''

Hayley's face turned pale. "But Abbey—"

"Cleverer and cleverer," Goriot said softly, turning back now to face Hayley Welles. "To have the daughter missing, her picture in the papers everywhere—"

"But we haven't *done* that!" shouted Hayley. "We didn't publicize her disappearance *at all*, because it would give ideas to people who might *use* it against us, against her! It isn't that way at all! Don't you see?''

Goriot shrugged elaborately. "But what a neat plum to pluck from the public relations tree—to have Beatrix Fontaine and Abbey Martin reappear, happy and united, just before the grand opening of Beatrix la Belle in Nice! Beatrix, the discoverer of a wandering, or possibly *kidnapped* and *molested*, Abigail Martin! The *reason* for the coincidence that both disappeared in France? To foreshadow that final denouement of their reappearance, perhaps? Oh, it's neat, it's beautifully formed, professionally sculptured.''

There was a stunned silence in the apartment. Welles bounded from his chair at the same moment Hayley bounded from hers. They stood in front of Goriot, both shaking with anger.

"There's no truth in that allegation!" cried Welles. "She really disappeared! *Both* have really disappeared!"

"To think you'd suspect we were *using* you!"

Hayley cried. "If we wanted to pull some cheap trick like that, we'd set it up differently! Better!"

"Nevertheless, however you 'might' have done it, you have done it the way you did, madame, monsieur." Goriot unfolded his arms and stood in confrontation with the two of them. "And now, if you are quite unprepared to admit the truth, I believe it is time I took my leave of you."

"You go out of this room now and you're *fired!*" snapped Hayley.

Goriot turned and looked at her, his eyes moving up and down her scathingly. "Madame," he said softly, "I've enjoyed working with the Prescott Group for twenty years now, leading it for the past ten. But so far, no one has tried to make us look like fools, working to bring off a public relations ploy. I am happy to submit my resignation, as of this moment, if you wish it. In writing? Is that the way you would have it?"

There was a moment of stunned silence.

"That attack by the POW outfit!" Hayley said in a shocked voice. "You think *that* was a setup, too? If so, for what purpose?"

Goriot seemed taken aback. "But *that* is an entirely different proposition, madame! Two individuals were killed then. It was *not* an imaginary confrontation at all. It was *not* in the mind, in the psyche. It was of the real world."

"You didn't find *them*, either!" Hayley was flushed and trembling as she tried to stare down the Frenchman.

Goriot shook his head in silent admission. "They exist. We know that. But whether they exist in France, or Germany, or Italy, or Yugoslavia, or Greece—or wherever you can name—we do not know."

Finally, Welles spoke in a subdued tone. "We

don't want your resignation. We just want you to believe we aren't trying to set you up.''

Goriot remained firm. ''Good night, madame, monsieur. We meet again when we are in a better frame of mind for objective discussion.'' He broke from them and strode across the room to let himself out of the apartment.

When he had gone, Hayley turned to Welles with a defeated expression. ''What are we going to do now?''

Welles shook his head. ''I don't *know*. What *happened* to Beatrix, anyway? Why hasn't she called me?''

He reached out and gripped Hayley's hand. She squeezed his in return. There seemed, at that moment, to be nothing they could do to resolve their parallel problems—except wait . . . and hope.

CHAPTER NINETEEN

The woman adjusted her wraparound sunglasses, patted the tight bun of hair on the top of her head into place, twisted her loosely fitting, rather creased, and somewhat tatty blouse so that part of it hung out of her skirt, and walked into the sunshine outside the cheap country motel in which she had stayed the night.

The eagle-eyed proprietor paused in his morning scan of *Le Figaro* and noted the fact that she was getting into the battered Renault in which she had come, then lost interest as she gunned the engine in a cloud of black exhaust. She had paid for two nights' lodging in advance. *Tomorrow* he might worry, but not until then.

The Renault lurched forward, settled down into a loud whine, and bumped along the ill-paved road toward the east. Soon the little motel was lost to sight in the rear-view mirror.

She had spent little time in the deep countryside of France, and she felt alien to the constant sunshine, the early morning quiet, the endlessness of space around her. Frankly, she would take Paris any day; she did not wonder that her mother had fled to the big city just before she was born, having left the countryside for, obviously, more reasons than just one.

Beatrix Fontaine glanced down at the slip of paper in her hand and checked once again the instructions that she had transcribed onto her Michelin road map. The road map did little good, since it failed to include the side roads and byways that were listed in the verbal instructions she had received.

She had lost so much time! It had been days and days since the party in Beverly Hills, when she had answered the telephone and heard the voice on the other end outlining the facts of her case—facts that she might once have suspected, but which were really so ugly and unbelievable that she did not even want to *think* about them now.

And those facts dovetailed perfectly with the earlier communication she had received, from Tessie. Tessie's threat to reveal the truth about Beatrix Fontaine's birth was formless and phantomlike, yet it throbbed with conviction. Beatrix knew Tessie intimately—knew how her mind worked. And when Tessie had threatened to reveal some "very disturbing facts" about the background and roots of Beatrix Fontaine, she *knew* she had to pay the blackmail money Tessie demanded.

She had paid, and Tessie had crawled back into the woodwork where she belonged. Beatrix knew she would make an approach again, for more money, but that was simply the way it would have to be. She did not *want* to find out whether or not Tessie was exaggerating the seriousness of the situation; and so she had accepted the fact that things were serious and had paid up the demand.

Tessie had never mentioned Provence or hinted at the specific area where she had unearthed the facts that could ruin Beatrix la Belle—through the disclosure of details that would make Beatrix and everything she touched unacceptable to the great middle class of the world.

Beatrix had lived for awhile with the specter of Tessie hanging over her head waiting to pounce again. So the telephone call at the party in the Prescott mansion in Benedict Canyon had been, in itself, only a nasty intrusion, and no surprise at all.

She shuddered as she steered the Renault through the rutted road and turned to the right onto a much more bumpy and rutted side road. There were rolling fields around her now, with hills in the near distance, and a shade tree here and there dotting the horizon. Crops and grapevines that looked dusty and undefined lay along the road on both sides. There seemed not to be a human being anywhere around.

The voice on the telephone—she thought she recognized it, but she had been unable to put a name to the voice—had outlined facts that Tessie had never mentioned. And the facts were sickening and absolutely irrefutable. They *seemed* irrefutable, anyway, because the hideous picture that those facts painted made immediate sense to Beatrix when she applied it to her own fears about the series of blackouts and patches of amnesia she had suffered in silence for so many years.

She would *not* think about it!

The voice on the telephone did not want money to suppress these injurious facts. Nor had the person hinted that she might demand money in the future to suppress the truth. She simply wanted to *inform* Beatrix Fontaine about the truth. In a way, the voice was pulling the rug out from under Tessie, who had not told Beatrix the details, but who had extorted money nevertheless, on the simply veiled threat of revelation.

There was a name mentioned, and a place, and an area in France: Provence. That made sense to Beatrix. She knew her mother had come from Provence—from Grignan, for that matter, or near there. She had once made an attempt to trace her family through records, but the search had failed; no records were available. Her curiosity was not so intense that she had pursued the matter any further. Somehow she had instinctively known that a search for the truth would lead her only to misery.

And now . . .

The roads were becoming steep now, and even bumpier. More trees appeared, some hung with fruit of one kind or another, others dusty and suffering from lack of moisture. An occasional farm appeared near the road, dilapidated, unpainted, and forlorn. The road followed the curve of a small valley full of vineyards now, rising toward some elevated peaks in the distance. A tiny stream tinkled by, below the level of the roadway. Birds sang in the trees, scattering as the Renault made its noisy approach. She saw a woman walking in a field, then another, and another.

The farms were closer together here. She came to the crossroads mentioned in the telephone call and slowed. She should make a right turn, pass two farms, and turn in at the third. There she would encounter Monsieur Jérôme-Nicolas Châtelet: at least, so the telephone voice had said.

Mon dieu! But she had lost so much time!

As soon as the anonymous telephone call had been

completed, Beatrix had quickly summoned a cab to the Prescott mansion in Benedict Canyon to take her to the Beverly Hills Hotel. There, she had telephoned to request a flight to Paris as soon as possible. Able to obtain a reservation immediately, she had taken the polar flight the next morning. Once in Paris she had begun her plans to go to Provence, but—

As usual, when she was least prepared to cope with those disastrous bouts of darkness in her mind, she had suffered a massive blackout. This one was so fierce and so sudden that she had been in no way capable of handling it. She could now remember *nothing* of what she had done for at least nineteen days. Nineteen days!

And when she had recovered, she had found herself in a cheap hotel somewhere in Bordeaux. Cleverly, in her clouded state of mind, she had apparently assumed an entirely new identity—that of a Madame Gentil Michaud—complete with new hairdo, dark glasses, and the dreariest wardrobe Beatrix Fontaine had ever seen.

Her subconscious mind had seemingly perpetrated this change of identity in the knowledge that the real Beatrix Fontaine would wish it. And her subconscious had been right. Beatrix Fontaine had vanished from the eyes of man. Oddly enough, there seemed to be no mention of her disappearance in the newspapers, which she read carefully from day to day. Yet newsdrops about the upcoming presentation in Nice of the Beatrix la Belle health and beauty network continued to appear.

What must Carney Welles think? she wondered, shivering with shame. More than that, what would Carney Welles think if he discovered the truth—if, of course, what had been revealed on the telephone *was* the truth. She would have to contact him as soon as she learned the details. Then they would face the facts together and try to put it all in the best possible light.

There it was. The small, rather tumble-down farmhouse of Jérôme Châtelet. She drove the Renault into an almost indistinguishable driveway and turned off the ignition. The car belched to a stop. In the sudden silence, she could hear birds singing in a tree near the house.

No one appeared.

Beatrix climbed out of the Renault, tried to twist the wrinkled blouse into a more presentable shape, adjusted her skirt to her hips, and walked up to the front door. It wasn't much of a door at all. Nor were the windows on each side of it very good windows. She could see nothing inside, and knew by the absolute darkness within that there was no electric power in the neighborhood.

She banged on the door, but there was no response.

Giving up after three tries, she began to walk around the side of the house to the rear. The fields stretched away behind the house, down toward a small stream. There were truck garden crops here and there. Obviously, Châtelet did not live alone. There was a woman out in the fields with a white cow.

"Madame?" inquired a voice.

Beatrix stopped in her tracks. She saw a man, a hulking giant of a man; with a large, round face, clean-shaven; with dark eyes and a mass of thick pepper-and-salt gray hair standing up on top of a low forehead.

"I am looking for Monsieur Jérôme-Nicholas Châtelet," she said in her elegant Parisian French.

"You are looking at him," said the giant. He was

dressed, she saw now, in well-worn trousers and shirt, with ancient mud-spattered shoes that were huge and ungainly on his feet. There were wine stains on his shirt and nicotine stains on his fingers. He smelled bad: He smelled of the barn that she now saw out in back of the house.

"May we talk?"

"If it is important." The big man smiled slightly.

"It is important," said Beatrix. "Madame Michaud. Gentil Michaud."

"*Oui*." They shook hands.

"Let us sit," suggested Châtelet after a moment's silence. He indicated two rickety chairs under a wide-spreading apple tree that grew between the barn and the house.

"Thank you." Beatrix drew her skirt about her legs and sat primly. Châtelet sank into the other chair and pulled an ancient and smelly pipe out of his shirt pocket. He began probing it with a pipe cleaner.

"I am in search of information about Valentine Fontaine."

The giant paused, fingering his pipe and reaching into a pocket to pull out a pouch of tobacco. "So does everyone seem to be."

"I was given your name, monsieur."

"Perhaps I *can* help you. He is dead, of course."

Beatrix realized that, although he may have looked the fool, Châtelet was no such thing. He spoke an accented but literate French; his thoughts seemed clear and straightforward. This was the man who had furnished the telephone voice with the information Beatrix would give her life to cover up.

"They say you knew him."

"Valentine and I worked for the Allied Underground during the war," Châtelet said, striking a match on the leg of the chair and puffing on the pipe furiously to get it going.

"You knew him well, then?"

Châtelet nodded, watching her.

"Did he die in the war?"

"No, madame. Valentine was—" he shrugged "—crazy. Oh, very brave. He did things no one else would do. Unfortunately—" he tapped his temple "—he was mad."

Beatrix was shaking inwardly.

"Like his sister," Châtelet continued. "They were both *fou*." A cloud of smoke puffed up. "It was the mother. The father was a fine man; but he was killed by the Germans at the beginning of hostilities. And that turned Valentine and Ursule to the Underground. We worked together."

"But you said Valentine's mother—"

"—saw visions," Châtelet explained. "Disappeared for days at a time. Claimed she could not remember who she was." He shook his head. "That's where the kids got their crazies." He used a kind of country slang.

Beatrix stiffened to keep tears from flowing. The amnesia, and the syncope—all the details added up to what *she* had. Was it, as the physician had suspected, a type of Alzheimer's Disease?

"What happened to Valentine, then?"

Châtelet grimaced. He looked off into the fields where the woman struggled with the cow.

"It is not a pleasant story."

"I must know. I have promised important people. It is necessary."

Châtelet shrugged. He had told the story several times. One more time would not hurt.

"The old woman went crazier and crazier. When the war ended, she shut the kids up in the house—wouldn't let them out. You understand, we were young then—not adults at all. Children can't be shut up that way. They—" He stared at Beatrix.

"Of course."

"One would occasionally escape. But when he or she returned, the mother put the locks on again. She kept the children in the house always, secluded. They lived some distance from the village, or the authorities might certainly have done something about her."

"And?"

"The girl became pregnant. Ursule. She was eighteen, perhaps."

"But how—?"

"No one could have entered the house. The mother didn't want anyone to know about it, but there were signs. And once, Ursule escaped and went running about the village, where she was seen and her condition noted."

"But who—?"

"Then Valentine went mad. One could hear the screams and the yells. The authorities were summoned by neighbors. When the authorities finally arrived, Valentine was gone. The old woman was dying in her bed, stabbed with a kitchen knife. Ursule lay in a heap on the floor, her eyes sightless, and her body limp. Valentine was nowhere to be seen."

There was a long silence.

"Two days later, his body was found at the foot of that rocky cliff," Châtelet said, indicating a prominence in the distance up the hillside. "He had fallen in the night—of his own free will."

"Good God," whispered Beatrix. "The mother?"

"Died soon after being found in her bed."

"Ursule?"

"With the nuns, madame. I understand she later left the convent and went perhaps to Marseilles."

"And Valentine? Where is he buried?"

"Where else, madame, but in an unconsecrated grave? A murderer—*and* a suicide?"

"But you never said—"

Châtelet shrugged. "One does not have to stretch one's imagination much to understand what happened."

Beatrix could barely speak. "Incest?" she whispered.

There was no answer, only an intense gaze from the black eyes.

"There is, however, a gravestone," Châtelet said. "Near the tiny church school and hospital in the valley below."

Beatrix closed her eyes. Of course. The voice on the telephone had indicated that. She would have to go to it to see for herself. Valentine and Ursule. Beatrix's father and—and her mother.

Then she was driving the Renault again, bumping over the dirt roads and choking on the dust the car raised as it bounced along the countryside. Where in the devil was the little settlement, the convent where her father was buried? Where . . . ?

The clouds of darkness were flowing down over her mind now, and she strove to remember the directions he had given her. Up a hill, down a lane, through some trees—

From the road, she saw the huddle of structures. She parked the car under a tree and got out. She was hardly attired for hiking, but she managed to cross the field, and she found the stream and the graveyard just as he had told her she would. She was able to climb over the low stone wall into the graveyard.

A brief search soon rewarded her. There was the tombstone, tipped over, as if moved by vandals or grave robbers—although why anyone would rob a grave like this one, far removed from civilization and humanity, was a mystery to her.

Yes. She read it slowly. The words had been carved by someone far from skilled with a hammer and chisel. VALENTINE FONTAINE, it said, quite simply. 1925-1955. Her father. She sank down beside the stone, staring at it with a strange mixture of loving and loathing.

In spite of the strange and disagreeable story it told, the tombstone marked the remains of her own flesh and blood—even if her father *had* sired Beatrix by his sister. Strange are the ways of God, thought Beatrix, but even stranger, the ways of man.

For some reason, she had hoped against hope that the proof of Valentine's name, the proof that her father and mother were brother and sister, was false, and would be proved false by her trip to this remote spot. And yet, of course, it had not worked out that way at all. The opposite was true. She now had evidence that she was the issue of an incestuous relationship.

Wouldn't that be just fine for Beatrix la Belle? Oh, she could imagine the joy and ecstasy with which Carney Welles would greet *that* bit of information!

She was quite aware, too, that there were good solid biological reasons why those as close in kinship as brother and sister or father and daughter should not mate. The scientific study of recessive genes told the story quite accurately and quite frighteningly. Any weakness or negative quality would be reinforced by such a mating. And so, with not one but two parents who had showed strains of madness—or perhaps in the case of the Fontaines, Alzheimer's Disease—it was evident that Beatrix Fontaine was doomed as well as they.

She sank against the coolness of the rock that lay on top of the mortal remains of her father, and closed her eyes.

It was just as well. The darkness descended on her, covering her like a blanket and lapping at the edges of her consciousness until there was nothing there at all—just blackness and oblivion and infinity.

Sister Marguerite, from the school and hospital next to the graveyard, found her there late that afternoon, slumped against the tilted gravestone, eyes closed, body limp. Slaps on the wrist and ministrations to the hands and face failed to revive the woman, whom Sister Marguerite did not recognize.

With the help of Sister Nicole and Sister Anaïs, Sister Marguerite was able to carry the now semi-conscious woman into the small hospital operated by the convent sisters. There they put her to bed, where she fell into a deep sleep that lasted for over twelve hours.

When she awoke, Sister Nicole, whose watch it was, asked her if she was hungry, but the woman did not respond. She simply turned her back on Sister Nicole, faced the wall, closed her eyes, and feigned sleep. Soon, Sister Anaïs was able to establish communication of sorts and brought in food that the woman ate without a word, and with apparent disinterest.

On the second day, it became obvious that the woman was not going to communicate with her saviors. The sisters discussed the situation among themselves and wondered whether their patient might not be deaf and dumb. Some said she was; others said she was perfectly normal. No one knew for sure.

A physician summoned from Grignan was also unable to establish communication with the patient, but told the sisters that she was indeed normal and, apparently, was willing herself not to respond to any attempts at communication. The case was, he intimated, a mental problem rather than a physical one.

"Do you wish to continue attending her?" the physician asked Sister Marthe, who was the Mother Superior.

"Certainly, Doctor Rigauld! We are prepared for such a situation. It is our mission in life."

Doctor Rigauld shrugged. "Then keep her here. She is apt to come out of this voluntary catalepsy immediately, or she may stay in it for years. Or, perhaps, for the rest of her life." Doctor Rigauld hesitated. "She has apparently decided that she does not wish to continue in communication with people. I do not know anything about her past medical history, or her past personal history, or I might be able to hazard a guess as to why she has opted to become mute. Nevertheless—"

"Thank you," said Sister Marthe and she ushered him out.

In the tiny room where Beatrix Fontaine lay on the bed in self-imposed silence, Sister Marthe stared at her for a long time, thinking it ironic that someone from the outer world should impose upon herself the same vows of silence that certain sisters of the cloth did for the sake of God.

"We shall simply have to pray for you," she told the silent woman, with a resolute air. "Perhaps that is the best thing to do at this juncture. You seem to have arrived at an impasse in your life. Perhaps our prayers will help you.''

The woman stirred slightly, opened her eyes, gazed at Sister Marthe a moment, then closed them, turned slightly, and continued breathing steadily and slowly.

CHAPTER TWENTY

It was a remote, picturesque part of the Florence suburbs that Megan Tarantino had never seen before. She cruised around a curve in the foothills rising from the River Arno and saw spread out in front of her a panoramic view of the entire Florentine area. She felt tempted to stop the Alfa Romeo Spider— which the police had recovered from a Riviera parking lot where its thief had apparently abandoned it—and take a long, relaxed look at the beautiful scenery, just like some kind of goggle-eyed American tourist. But she knew she didn't have the time to waste today.

In five minutes, she had found the road, a shaded, winding street with impressive villas backed up onto the hillside, snuggled beneath Lombardy poplars and small maritime pines. She stopped the Spider in front of one of them and sat there, triumphant, but victorious only in a Pyrrhic sense. "Villa Bella Maria," the small sign proclaimed, the post supporting it buried in the rich Arno Valley loam.

The villa was painted a delicate pink, and rooted

into the hillside in a complacent posture, it over-looked the slope down to the river. It was low, rambling, and comfortable, with a typically Mediter-ranean look about it. Not quite so big as the Villa della Camarra—but damned near! Megan could feel her blood beginning to boil. On impulse, she gunned the Spider, turned into the driveway, and shot up the incline to the turnaround, where she slammed to a stop.

In a moment, she was out of the car and up the stone steps to the wide verandah. A servant appeared when she pressed the button to activate the chimes. His eyebrow was quirked superciliously; there was a put-upon air about him.

"I'd like to see your—*mistress*," snapped Megan, her voice midway between a growl and a screech, and the impression of the hesitation before the word was one of condescension and reproach.

"*Non capisco*," said the servant, almost on cue.

Megan was not about to be put off by a servant who obviously understood English as well as anyone. "Get her out here! *Pronto!*"

The servant's eyes narrowed, but he lacked the gall and the authority to challenge his guest. He backed away obediently. "*Un momento*," he mut-tered between his teeth.

Megan fumed on the doormat, glancing about at the plush, manicured surroundings in which the villa was ensconced. The goddamned son of a bitch, she thought. He's fixed up this shack job with a bloody *casa* better than my own!

The woman was tall and muscular with broad shoul-ders and a powerful torso, thick legs, and just the hint of a mustache on her swarthy, yet somehow feminine, face. Her thick black hair was coiled in an intricate knot on top of her head, covering her ears and giving her an interesting Oriental look. Her snapping black eyes were half hidden by huge eyelids. Her mouth was heavily made up with a too-bright shade of thick cheap lipstick.

When she spotted Megan, she gave a somewhat uncontrollable start, but quite soon regained her aplomb. *"Si?"*

"Don't *si* me, honey," Megan said. "Let me in. You and I have got to talk."

"Io non capis—"

Megan shoved past her, pushing the muscular, tough body to one side. The woman involuntarily moved to resist, lifting a hand to strike Megan, but thought better of it and followed her somewhat meekly into the comfortable foyer.

"What a layout!" Megan said with a rueful smile.

"Who *are* you?" the woman finally asked in broken English.

"You know damned well who I am, baby." She almost said "buster," after Hayley. "I'm the Contessa della Camarra. And you're Nicky's *amante*—or should I say *meretrice*?"

The woman colored deeply, her eyes flashing fire. She let out a long line of abuse in a Florentine dialect, some of its street-words familiar to Megan, but not wholly translatable. Nevertheless, the floozie kept her hands to herself.

"Name?" Megan snapped, hands on hips, head lowered in an attitude of attack, waiting for a response.

"I am Maria Elena Patrucci," the woman said, straightening in pride. She had at least two inches on Megan, Megan could see, much to her annoyance. She certainly had a huge pair of boobs. To Megan's horror, she conjured up a sudden picture of Nicky

attached orally to one of them—a picture that almost
brought a lusty laugh roaring up out of her throat.

"Maria," Megan said deliberately, setting her jaw
in the familiar line her servants knew when she became *La Tarantula* instead of *La Soave*. "It's talking
time." Megan glanced around. She pointed to a chair.
"Sit."

The hostess of the Villa Bella Maria hesitated,
then almost docilely took the chair and waited for
Megan to settle opposite her. At that moment, a door
opened at the far end of the room, and a boy about
five years old bounded in and saw Maria Patrucci
seated with a guest. He ran across to her, babbling
something angrily. Megan had no idea what he was
yelling about, but she was stunned. The kid absolutely looked like Nicky—a perfect miniature version. A spitting image of Niccolo Tarantino, the
Conte of Camarra!

The woman responded angrily and quickly, and
the kid turned around, gave one baleful gawk at
Megan, and slunk from the room. Boy, Megan
thought, I wish I had that kind of control over *my*
two!

"That answers my first question," Megan said,
pointing to the door after it had closed behind the
retreating youth. "You're running a little family unit
here in direct competition to my own family unit at
the Villa della Camarra, aren't you?"

Maria Patrucci muttered something about not
understanding.

"Oh, come on now! That kid's a good five years
old. How long have you been working this scam?
How long has Nicky been keeping you here?"

"Ten years or so," said Maria Patrucci, magically
gaining control of her English. "Perhaps twelve." A

slight smile. ''I tend to forget the exact moment it all started.''

''I'll bet!'' growled Megan. She drew a sheaf of papers out of the capacious bag she wore on her shoulder and waved them in front of the dark-haired woman who was her husband's lover. ''Here are the papers that show when. It was exactly fourteen years ago that Nicky bought you this place, after the previous owner's mortgage had been foreclosed. Fourteen years ago! And since that time, you've been draining money from the bank to keep this joint running!''

Maria Patrucci shrugged. ''I do nothing. It is Nicky—Nicky who—''

''Fuck Nicky!'' yelled Megan. ''He's out of this. That's *my* money you've been using. It's bank money—money from the Cassa Fiorentina di Risparmio,'' she said distinctly, so the woman could not mistake her meaning.

''What you want me to do?'' the woman asked after a moment.

That stunned Megan. What, indeed, *did* she want Maria Patrucci to do? The woman had the house. She had the kid. She had Nicky's ''other life.'' It wouldn't do Megan any good to acquire any of that—except possibly the house. And yet, what would *she* do with a damned villa? Sell it? Megan had found out about her, once she had started looking in the right direction, and that was what really mattered. The woman's previous history hinted that she was not about to give up *anything*—not without a vigorous battle. Indeed, it was a kind of ironically amusing impasse.

''I'll tell you what,'' Megan said, leaning forward suddenly, letting the papers flop down onto the exquisite ceramic-tiled floor under her feet. ''You're going to become Maria Patrucci Tarantino, the Countess della Camarra. That's what you're going to do!''

Maria blinked in astonishment. "But I—"

"Sure!" rasped Megan. "You thought I was going to break up this little twosome you've been running with Nicky, didn't you? You thought I was going to forbid Nicky from coming here. You thought I was going to buy you out, pay you off, and fatten your purse with payoff money—didn't you?"

The woman's cold black eyes narrowed defensively. "I am sorry—"

"Fat chance! Fat fucking chance!" yelled Megan in glee. "I'm going to give you just what you pretended you wanted! Nicky *and* a title! You're going to get what I've had for years—full time! A stupid, sulking, dumb-ass spoiled aristocrat who takes pampering, coddling, and humoring twenty-four hours a day! And for that you get ten minutes of sex a week—if he's feeling like it."

The woman's face blanched slightly. "But I love him," she said. "Why should I *not* want him here?"

"There's something else, honey. What I've given you is the bad news. What I'm going to give you now is the *worse* news. He's going to be here at your side all the time, whimpering and asking to be stroked, and he's going to be *broke! Broke*, baby! Stone, cold broke! That's without penny one! *Lira una*, you Florentine fishwife!"

"Together we make a good life," said Maria stoutly.

"Not bloody likely!" shouted Megan. "Not the good life. The threadbare life. The fucking conte is going to be a *clerk* at the bank he now runs."

"But—" The woman seemed to be considering a swoon.

"I run that bank, Mistress Maria! *I* run it. And I

say who does what, where." Megan looked around at the expensive furnishings and smiled slightly. "You may have to lower your standard of living a bit, *mia meretricina*, but I'm sure you can do it. After all, you've had *practice!*

That was a low blow, even for Megan. Her investigations had shown the woman to have come from a family of store clerks in Florence. Tacky, Meggy, she told herself. But somehow justified. *Justified!*

"I love him," Maria repeated in a low, rather subdued voice. Megan sensed that the woman might have been repeating the thought in order to convince herself. Love didn't usually have much to do with the kind of arrangement Maria had with Nicky. Not *really*. Or at least, that was the way Megan looked at it.

"Then you'll be pleased to settle down with him while the two of you pay off the mortgage to the bank for the money that went into this house." Megan smiled sweetly. "It's been refinanced, sweetie, to put the money back where it belongs."

Maria Patrucci suddenly rallied. "Is nothing unusual about this thing in Italy," she said stoutly. "Is *usual* thing with important man like Nicky—to have a close friend."

"Yeah," said Megan, her voice dripping with scorn and sarcasm. "So I'm told. The double standard is standard in Europe. But I happen to think about it a little differently, honey."

The woman shrugged.

"I think of you as nothing more than a full-time whore."

The woman now leaped from her chair. *That* word, in English, she did understand. "You insult me—in my own house!"

"There's some argument about *that*," Megan said with a faint smile. "About *your* house, that is. It belongs to the *bank*—until you pay for it. I thought I'd made that clear."

"Via! Via!" Maria Patrucci advanced on Megan, her eyes smouldering, her chest heaving, her hands clenching into fists at her sides.

"Eventually," Megan said slowly, standing firm.

"I am no *prostituto!*" The woman choked on the word, tears suddenly coming to her eyes.

Megan straightened. Now she was reaching into this woman; she was touching her where she lived.

"Not on your terms, maybe. On mine, you're nothing but a part-time lover, a professional lay."

Maria Patrucci exploded quite suddenly and shockingly. She grabbed at Megan's hair and yanked her head downwards. Megan was startled, but was suddenly released from any physical inhibition that might have been holding her back. When she felt her head jerked downward and felt the pain of the ripped-out hair, she swung her fists at her assailant's chest, battering the huge breasts. Then she got a grip on the woman's upper dress, tearing and ripping as she did so.

The bigger woman had Megan in a wrestler's hold now, and the two of them were rolling on the floor. Megan clawed at the woman's face, feeling the tough skin give and start to bleed. Now Maria had Megan in her clutches and began to bang her shoulders and head against the tile floor.

Megan screeched and twisted over, getting herself on top of the other woman. She cuffed her on the face a few times, then grabbed her right arm and began to twist, the way she had seen wrestlers do on the television shows. Now Maria began to cry out.

Megan slammed a fist into Maria's face. Then, suddenly, before Megan could see a thing, she was thrown backwards flat on her ass, and sat stunned on the tile floor.

The servant who had let her in was standing over her, holding off Maria, who was struggling to get her torn dress over her huge bared breasts, and waiting for Megan to rise. Sheepishly, Megan clambered to her feet, holding her left eye, which was swollen and throbbing, and picked up her papers carefully, putting them in her bag. Then, while the servant watched, clutching Maria by the arm, Megan slowly made her way out of the villa.

What an ass I've made of myself! Megan thought—but she grinned hugely at the same time. Christ, but it felt good!

A stately building on the main street in Florence housed the Cassa Fiorentina di Risparmio. To her surprise, Megan found an empty parking spot right in front. She glanced in the rear-view mirror, patted her hair into place as best she could, and looked at her bruised eye, which was swelling up, but which had not yet turned dark gray. She smoothed down her blouse and skirt and stalked across the sidewalk to the entrance of the bank.

Yes, Il Conte, Signor Tarantino was indeed in his office at the moment, she was told. However, he might have a special appointment, and it might be inappropriate for La Contessa, Signora Tarantino, to see him just at this moment. Could she perhaps arrange an appointment—?

Megan punched the clerk in the chest and pushed past him. The clerk, a young man in his twenties, proudly wearing the stiffly cut European jacket and trousers of the rising junior executive, complete with flowery tie and silk shirt, reeled back against his desk, too astonished to punch back. He had never been assaulted by a woman before—not one like La Contessa.

It was easy sailing, and Megan soared through the door and into the plush little office of Il Conte della Camarra, president of Cassa Fiorentina di Risparmio. Nicky was on the telephone, frowning and swinging importantly back and forth in his swivel chair; but when the door slammed open, hitting the wall, he swung back and, alarmed, held the handset away from his ear.

"Hang up!" Megan snapped as she reached around and closed the door with a shuddering jolt. "We talk."

Nicky looked at the handset and then at Megan, thought briefly about a rejoinder, but then decided against it.

"I'll call you back," he said in Italian into the handset, and he hung up. "Yes, Meggy?"

Megan had settled into the huge chair Nicky used for important clients. "I just talked to your tart, Nicky."

Nicky blinked and turned gray. "Tart? What tart?"

"You're stand-in wife! That little cunt out in the Villa Bella Maria!"

"Oh," said Nicky, deflated. "What you talk about?" His accent was thickening, Megan saw. Good! She had him on the ropes.

"We talked about *you*, Nicky! We talked about what a marvelous jock you are!" Megan was on a verbal roll now. She was making it up out of thin air, and Christ! but it felt good. "We talked about European history and how the Tarantinos are probably the most randy, willing, and able clan in the history of the Continent! We talked about me, Nicky, and about what a stupid idiotic bitch I am—never to have guessed you had her set up there for fourteen years!''

Nicky's face cleared. He straightened—his body, his tie, his thoughts. "It's common practice in Europe, honey,'' he said softly, his accent now totally vanished. "We have a social standard that is somewhat different from your puritanical Protestant ethic in America. Please let me explain—''

Megan slammed her bag down hard on the table and leaned on it, glowering across at her husband. "Don't you give me that bullshit, Nicky! I may be in Europe, but I'm not a European! I'm a Prescott, damn it, and don't you forget it! A Prescott believes in marrying only one man or woman—at least, one *at a time!*''

"So do I, Meggy,'' Nicky spread his hands, looking more like Marcello Mastroianni all the time. "Happily married for eternity.''

"Ten years ago, I would have said dump her and come back to me, Nicky,'' Megan said, her voice rising and becoming stronger. "But today is today. I sing a different song to a different tune. Love.''

"A mistress is acceptable practice here,'' Nicky muttered rather emptily, watching her steadily and warily.

"Today, I say out you go, Nicky—on your tail. Out of the Villa della Camarra forever, Nicky. You can live with your lover there in the Villa Bella Maria—Christ, it's almost as good as the family estate, isn't it? And built on my goddamned money! You rotten bastard!''

Nicky licked his lips, frowning.

"But you're going to buy it back from the bank—

which has now attached it, Nicky." Megan fumbled
with the papers in the bag and pulled one out. "Here
are the papers, already drawn up. I had that slinky
little Venetian bandit Alessandro Biondi—my lawyer, Nicky—make it out. There's one good thing you
can say about lawyers. They're *happy* to do anybody
in—for a fat fee."

"The Villa della Camarra is *mine*, Meggy," Nicky
said with an ingratiating smile. "It's been in the
family for centuries."

"Sure. And I'll bet through the years there's been
a maximum of screwing around in that manse. But it
doesn't belong to you anymore, my friend. It belongs
to Megan Tarantino, née Prescott."

"It does not, in no way, belong to you!"

Megan fumbled with the papers and threw another
on the desk. "I bailed you out when we were married, you simpleminded shit. You forget that? The
villa and its property are in *my* name. It was the way
we paid off the debts you ran up after your parents
died. It's mine. You can have the Villa Bella Maria—
after you pay for it!"

"Meggy, you wouldn't do this to me!" Nicky
gaped. "After all, I'm your husband! I have my
rights!"

"Here's the third piece of paper that slinky Venetian creep drew up. Divorce proceedings, Nicky.
You may think your wedding was drawn up without
a loophole, but it wasn't! I'm not a Catholic, Nicky,
and the way I think about marriage is this way—
when it's over, it's over! And this one is definitely
overdue over. I'm sick and tired of being lied to,
cheated on, laughed at, giggled about, and humiliated!"

Nicky was speechless.

"I want your junk out of the house within twenty-four hours. And I mean everything! All those moldy family heirlooms—those that aren't mounted to the walls—take them with you. And get everything out of there by tomorrow, including yourself, or by God I'll have you removed physically by the Florentine police.''

"But, Meggy—"

"Is that clear?" yelled Megan, standing there gripping her papers and bag in her hands and glowering across the desk at her husband . . . ex-husband-to-be.

"*Eh, bene—*"

"This is the last time I have to look at you, Nicky, and while I'm unhappy in one way, I'm so extremely happy in another way that I could almost scream with joy! *Scream!*"

She wheeled swiftly around and stalked to the door. As she stomped through the outer office, she saw the clerks and secretaries all staring at her in astonishment. It was obvious that they had heard everything, and even with the language barrier, certainly the tone of voice must have communicated the nitty gritty of the confrontation.

Nicky was following her. She could hear him running, calling out her name.

"Meggy, for God's sake, I love you! Meggy!"

"It's over, Nicky!" she called back, not even turning. "I've had it with you. Two ways, Nicky. Being screwed by you! And being *not* screwed by you!"

Now she was marching through the main banking area, where customers, startled in their lines at the tellers' windows, turned to watch.

"You're my wife!" Nicky cried out.

"Not any more, sweetie!"

"Marriage is made in heaven, Meggy! It's an eternal bond!"

"Tell me all about it at the divorce proceedings, darling," Megan snapped, turning on him and baring her teeth. "Or, tell my lawyer. He'll be representing me!"

"*Carissima!*" Nicky called out, rushing to close the distance between them and grabbing her arms. "You can't go! Who will take care of you?"

"Let me go, Nicky." She pulled away from him as he clumsily tried to kiss her. "It's worked for all these years, but it doesn't work anymore."

She rushed out into the street as Nicky followed, yelling and waving his arms.

"You can't do this! You'll ruin your life!"

She climbed into the Spider and started the engine.

"Meggy! Let's talk!"

"We just did, Nicky. And for the first time in my life, I'm having the last word. And, *carissimo*, I love it!"

Giggling ecstatically, she pulled out into the traffic, while passersby stared at her, and at Nicky, who stood on the sidewalk in his elegant banker's clothes, watching his wife disappear in a cloud of exhaust.

"Christ, but it's great to be rich—and free—and *in love!*"

She shouted the words out in English as she sped through the heavy traffic toward the bridge that spanned the River Arno. The sun shone in the heavens; the sky was bright; and Clive Argyll was waiting at the airport in England for her imminent arrival.

Something about meeting his mother and father.

CHAPTER TWENTY-ONE

ornelius Welles stood in silence at the rear of
the huge, 2,500-seat Apollon Auditorium that
was the main feature of the immense Acropolis Entertainment Complex in the heart of Nice, France. It was here that Beatrix la Belle would be introduced five days hence—on the massive stage, nearly 13,000 square feet in area, that dominated the super-theater.

What a show! Welles thought.

What a show, indeed—a show without a star. Unless, of course, he located her pretty damned quick.

He ran his fingers through his hair, as he had many times in the past few weeks, in total distraction, trying to pull an answer out of the air somewhere. What could he do? How could he bluff it out? Who could stand in for Beatrix Fontaine, the missing cosmetologist? How could he pull it off, anyway, without making himself the laughingstock of the entire public relations industry?

The original plans to kick off Beatrix la Belle with the opening of the flagship spa had, of course, been superseded when he and Beatrix had agreed to use the splashy new Nice entertainment complex, with its built-in ability to handle worldwide media, as the site for Beatrix's introduction to the public. The spa openings would follow within weeks and would feature multiple debuts—simultaneously in six different countries—in time, hopefully, to get people into the spas to help pay off the tremendous cash outlay used for the construction of the initial facilities.

In Nice, the debut of Beatrix herself was scheduled to run at the height of carnival festivities—with everyone in costume, abandoned to the excitement of the general merrymaking and jollification.

Everything was great, Welles decided, except for that one "minor" detail. With Beatrix gone, who was going to star in this million-dollar production?

Shaking his head, Welles walked slowly out of the huge auditorium and into the afternoon sunlight, which shone down on the ancient vacation-town of Nice and was reflected by the water of the Mediterranean.

Within minutes he was on the Promenade des Anglais. The marvelous open esplanade bordered the beach and afforded a view of the Baie des Anges to anyone on foot, with Cap d'Etretat to the west, and Cap Ferrat to the east, hiding Monte Carlo and Menton from view. To the north, the hills of Nice sloped quickly up toward a blue sky. To the south, the sea was flat and calm, with sailboats and yachts visible in the distance.

Almost immediately the Hotel Negresco appeared, rising from the palm-dappled width of the Promenade, with its white dome, its pink roofs, and its almost tatty—but not quite—Art Nouveau decor.

Welles's pace began to quicken. Hayley was in the suite, waiting for some word from Boissy Goriot. Perhaps she had heard something—about Beatrix, or about Abbey. There were so many things that were not right; it was only natural, somehow, that Hayley and he should more or less come together to try to work out their problems. Oddly enough, under crisis, Hayley seemed a better woman than she was when everything was going along all right. For some reason, she accepted him under stress more naturally than not. Odd.

A huge jet sailed overhead for touchdown at Nice Airport, one of the busiest airports in France—second only to Orly in Paris. More arrivals for the debut of Beatrix la Belle? Welles wondered wryly. Hey, have we got a surprise for you!

He hastened into the swank lobby of the hotel, greeted the desk clerk, who like all the rest of the hotel personnel had been liberally papered with high-figure American greenbacks to insure top-drawer performance, and hastened to the elevator. He rose quickly to the fifth floor and let himself into the suite at the end of the hallway. Bright sun shone in from the beachfront.

Hayley looked up from a small writing table where she was going over some papers. She was always going over papers. Welles was almost shocked at her appearance. He had been with her now for several weeks, but somehow had failed to see the degenerative physical effect that constant worry was having on her. Her normally smooth skin was dry and limp. She appeared haggard. Her eyes were sunken, and her hair seemed lank and dry. Tiny lines around her eyes, which usually would not have been visible, were quite plain now, especially in the brilliant light that shone in from the Mediterranean.

"Any word?"

"Goriot will appear this morning," she said languidly. "I just had a telephone call from Paris."

"Any news?"

She shrugged. "I didn't go into all that."

Welles slumped. Five days. My God, if he didn't hear something before Tuesday, when the Festival of the Flowers opened in Nice, there would be no Beatrix la Belle introduction, no opening, no network of spas *anywhere* in the future—

He walked over to the window and stared out at the Bay of Angels. Damn it! There had to be *some* way to cover this situation. His people in New York had searched for a Beatrix lookalike and had located at least three who could pass muster, but so far Welles had made no commitment. It was a shoddy trick at best, one some wise member of the media would certainly unmask. After all, they were convinced now that Beatrix's "disappearance" was a fraud—the type of PR hype that Hayley had used in the Clive Argyll presentation. They would *sense* a substitute, damn it—no question about it.

If he had to, he would run with it, of course. A man had to do what he had to do.

The telephone rang. Welles turned. Hayley picked up the handset. "Send him right up," she said in a dead voice. "Goriot," she told Welles.

Welles focused his eyes on a sailboat in the bay. That's where he should be . . . on a sailboat, in the distance, fading into the sunset. Goodbye, cares and woes.

"How's the setup at Apollon?" Hayley asked listlessly.

"*Magnifique*," Welles smiled. "It's the perfect setting for my non-jewel."

She made a face.

Goriot entered after a sharp rap and stood glancing from Welles to Hayley and then back again. "No news on Beatrix," he said in a soft voice. Then he turned to Hayley. "For Abbey, there is good news—and bad news."

Hayley came up out of her chair. "Well? Well?"

"Which first, madame? Good or bad?"

"Both at once, you fool!" snapped Hayley.

Goriot tried a smile that didn't quite fit. "She's been located, we think. She's with a known criminal."

"Shit," said Hayley. "What *kind* of criminal? A pickpocket? A parking-ticket scofflaw? Come on! What?"

Goriot looked at Welles and then at Hayley again. "Sit down, please," he told both of them. Hayley took the couch, Welles an easy chair. Goriot paced back and forth a moment, getting his thoughts in order.

"We think the woman who called you on the telephone, Madame Welles, *did* have information about your daughter, Abigail Martin. We think that it was an honest call."

"Where is this woman now?" urged Hayley.

"On a slab in the morgue, madame," Goriot said calmly.

Hayley closed her eyes tightly. "God! Go on."

"She was a Parisian reader for a Hollywood talent agent. Her job was to report on French movie scripts, or books and stories published in Paris, for possible motion picture adaptations."

"How did she die?"

"By drowning in the river Seine, madame. The police fished her out several days ago."

"And that's why she didn't meet me?"

Goriot nodded. "That seems to be the reasoning of the police, based on excellent evidence."

"But how do you *know?*"

"In searching through the things in her room, we found the name 'Abigail Martin (Prescott)' in among her personal effects. With the name, was scribbled the word: 'Mont.' We theorize 'Mont.' stands for Montparnasse. That's a section of Paris in which artists and young people tend to congregate."

"But you said there is a *criminal* connection?" Welles interrupted.

Goriot nodded. "Among this woman's friends—her name, incidentally, is—was—Seline Beauchamp—were several cheap street criminals with records. Unfortunately, Seline had also been known to cohabit and associate with a group of professional—uh—terrorists."

"Oh, my God!" wailed Hayley.

Welles was up out of his chair, standing directly in front of Goriot. "Where are these people now?"

Goriot shook his head. "We do not know, Monsieur Welles. We have put out an invisible dragnet in Paris, but feel that the group may well have left the area. We have no idea what they're up to but we suspect Abbey is with them. One member of the group is named François Lucien, wanted for armed robbery and homicide. Another is Ernst Roedeker, wanted for aggravated assault."

"Right," sighed Welles. He turned to Hayley, gripping her hand in his. "There's nothing we can do right now. Maybe Abbey will be able to get away from them."

Goriot considered, staring directly at Hayley. "If, that is, she *wants* to leave them."

Hayley flew into a rage. "*Wants* to leave them? Of course she *wants* to leave them! They're holding her under duress! Do you think my daughter—?"

Welles raised a hand to silence his wife, and she stopped immediately. "What you're saying is that she may have *joined* them? The Patty Hearst syndrome?"

"I don't believe it!" cried Hayley, her face red.

"The possibility exists, Monsieur Welles," said Goriot.

"Then what can we do?" Welles wondered.

Goriot shrugged in his Gallic way. "We wait, Monsieur Welles."

Hayley was up and walking back and forth in agitation now. "I don't *feel* like waiting, Boissy!" she snapped. "I want action!"

"There is no other course to pursue, madame," Goriot advised her.

She paused in front of the window, staring out, unseeing.

"What about Beatrix?" Welles asked after a moment. Before Goriot could answer, the telephone rang. Welles was nearest, and he lifted the handset. He looked across the room at Hayley and held out the handset. "For you."

Lynn Miles sat on the deck of the Miles family yacht, *Miles to Go*, anchored in the Bay of Angels and stared at the picturesque panorama of Nice against the backdrop of the hills. She was still recovering from the incident in the graveyard. People were bathing on the beach, and others were strolling up and down the Promenade. Lynn had a glass of bourbon on the rocks in one hand, and the handset of the ship-to-shore telephone in the other.

She waited and finally heard the voice she recognized.

"Hi. This is Arlene Garnet, Hayley."

There was a stunned silence. *"Who?"*

Lynn smiled. "Come on now, Hayley. You've got one of the best memories in the world. Just think back about twenty years. We used to speak to each other then, you know."

"You're Charlie Garnet's daughter!" Hayley burst out in genuine surprise.

"Gotcha, huh?"

"We thought you'd died! Does Charlie—?"

"I'm calling about Pete Martin, Hayley, not about my father. I *can* call you Hayley, can't I?"

"What *about* Pete? He was my first husband."

"You've forgotten how you met him, Hayley."

"Met him at a party at Scobie Hills, if it's any business of yours! What *is* this, anyhow?"

"He was *my* date, Hayley."

There was a moment's silence, then a soft, "Was he? Oh—at one of those parties we used to throw for the help."

"That's it, Hayley. I brought him, and you married him. You took him away from me."

Hayley burst out laughing. "You aren't trying to make me *believe* that, are you, Arlene? That's the most foolish thing I ever heard!"

"You were rich," said Lynn, her voice rasping. "You bought him! And left me with nothing."

Hayley's voice changed. "If you're serious about this, Arlene, I don't know quite what to say. My marriage to Pete Martin was over many years ago."

"Uh huh. But you owe me one, Hayley."

"Exactly what is the purpose of this telephone call?" Hayley's voice was now hard and strung out with tension.

"I left home because of you and what you did to me," Lynn said in a far-off voice. "I changed my name. I had my leg fixed. You remember that ugly limp from poliomyelitis? Then I sang in a group. I got a job in a movie. I turned into someone else. But I remembered you, Hayley.''

"Go on!"

"She's in a convent in the remote countryside of Provence. Take this down. Grignan. Outside Grignan on the road south. That's all.''

"Abbey?" shrieked Hayley. "Abbey Martin is *there?*''

Lynn stared at the handset. "Hell no, you creep! Beatrix! Beatrix Fontaine!''

She slammed down the handset and picked up her bourbon. She put her bare feet up on the metal table bolted to the deck. Soon, Hayley would know the truth about Beatrix Fontaine. . . .

A moment later, Senator Kirby Miles, stripped to the waist and wearing a pair of properly ragged bathing trunks, emerged from the interior of the craft.

"What are you doing, hon?"

"Making a few phone calls, Miley. Reestablishing some old contacts.'' She grinned at him, her spirits soaring.

He cocked an eye at her. "I worry about you when you're in this mood, baby.''

She giggled. "Come on, Miley. We're going to have great fun at this big Cornelius Welles bash in Nice. You said it yourself! It's going to be the greatest opening in history! Beatrix la Belle!'' She burst out laughing.

"Christ, kid. Sometimes I think you've got a screw loose.''

She reached up her arms and pulled him down on her. "Speaking of such . . .''

"Right here on the deck?" he asked after a moment.

"Can you think of a better place?''

*   *   *

In the back seat of Boissy Goriot's powerful
Mercedes limousine, Hayley Welles told her husband
and Goriot as much as she could about Arlene Garnet
and the weird accusation Arlene had made on the
telephone that morning. Hayley simply could not
understand how Arlene Garnet had nursed her hatred
of Hayley for so long without getting back at her
before this. And why had Arlene really run away
from home the way she had? Did Charles Garnet
know she was still alive?

For years, Charlie Garnet had considered Arlene
dead. She was one of those missing kids you hear
about all the time and see on milk cartons and on
posters in grocery stores. Charlie had given up hope.
There had never been any contact made between
Arlene and her father. Nor had any of the other
Garnet children—all grown up now—heard from her.

And what an odd way to get back in touch with
Hayley!

Was there, in fact, any truth to the story about
Beatrix's presence in a small convent outside Grignan?
Hayley wondered aloud as she discussed the matter
with the two men. And if it were true, what was
Beatrix doing there, anyway?

"We shall soon see," Goriot commented and
plunged into a silence that lasted for a long time.
Welles himself seemed to be totally indifferent to the
discovery of Beatrix. Hayley was annoyed with him
for his listless attitude. She called him on it.

He roused himself once and shrugged. "Look.
You said it yourself. There's something a little wacky
about Beatrix. If she's in a convent with a bunch of
nuns, that certainly bears out the fact that she's some
kind of nut. Who would wind up in a convent on the

eve of a media event that would make her name
world-famous?''

Hayley frowned. ''Is there something *wrong* with
her?''

Welles thought about it a moment and finally nodded. ''I think she suffers from blackouts. You know,
short bouts of amnesia. I don't want to go into
details, because I can't, but I think it happened to her
in Helsinki. Maybe it's happening now.''

''If the woman in Grignan *is* Beatrix.'' Hayley
shrugged.

Welles nodded morosely.

With the help of a local police official, Boissy
Goriot found the small convent settlement in the
valley south of Grignan and led Welles and Hayley to
it. In moments, they were in the building that housed
the hospital, clustered around the bed in which Beatrix
Fontaine lay, eyes open and staring at the ceiling.

''She won't talk,'' Goriot said after listening to
Sister Marthe's detailed and somewhat voluble report. ''She hasn't said a word yet. Nor can she get up
out of the bed. But she eats and sleeps and, other-
wise, is an entirely normal person.''

''Good God!'' Welles murmured. ''Will she come
out of it?''

Sister Marthe was trying to be helpful. ''She has
been this way for days now, monsieur. I do not know
when or if she will recover her ability to communicate. Or if she really *wants* to.''

Welles pushed forward. ''Let me try,'' he told
Sister Marthe, who understood a little bit of English.

Sister Marthe backed away obediently.

Welles knelt by the bedside and took Beatrix Fontaine's hand in his. It was flaccid, cool, and totally

unresponsive. It felt as if the person whose hand it was had no control over its movements.

"Beatrix," he said softly. "It's Cornelius. Can you hear me?"

There was a moment of dead silence. Everyone in the room was intently watching the woman on the bed. With a slow and graceful movement, she turned her head and looked directly into Welles's eyes.

"Of course I can hear you," she said in that musical voice she could assume so well when she wanted to.

Sister Marthe raised her hands to heaven, closed her eyes, and crossed herself.

Goriot leaned forward with interest. Hayley quirked an eyebrow and stood back, watching.

"The sisters have been worried about you. You wouldn't talk, they said. Are you all right?"

"So many bad things, so many bad things," she muttered, blinking her eyes and staring once again at the ceiling.

Welles gripped her hand, as if to drag her back to him. "We've been worried about you," he said deliberately. "Why haven't you tried to get in touch with me?"

"So many bad things," Beatrix whispered, tears sliding down her cheeks as she blinked rapidly.

"But there are *good* things," Welles said quickly. "We must get on with the opening in Nice! You remember Nice?"

"I remember," Beatrix said, closing her eyes tightly. "I want to go. I *try* to go. But I cannot."

"Cannot what?" Welles asked, tightening his grip on her hand.

"Move," said Beatrix. "I cannot *move*. I try so

hard! I want to walk to you to make you see I am all right. But there are so many bad things.''

"You've been eating and drinking," Welles said, glancing over at Sister Marthe for confirmation. "What do you mean you can't move?"

"Please. I want to get up and live my life. But something holds me back. I cannot go forward. And yet I *must!*''

"Have you tried to stand?" Welles asked, somewhat puzzled over Beatrix's problem.

Sister Marthe moved forward. "She has tried that. She simply collapses on the bed. It is true. She is unable to *will* herself upright.''

"I pray to God," sobbed Beatrix. "I ask to walk, to be myself again. Nothing happens.''

Welles glanced at Hayley. "Too much pressure." He turned back to Beatrix. "The opening is unimportant. *You* are what is important. You get well first, and *then* we hold the opening, just like we planned.''

"I must open the spas!" she cried miserably. "Now!"

"Later," Welles said resolutely. "We'll postpone the opening until later.''

"Now!" whispered Beatrix in agony. "I *must* appear. I am Beatrix!''

Welles hesitated.

She turned to the wall then, doubling her knees up against her chest in the classic foetal position.

Hayley gripped Welles's shoulder and pulled him back. "Let me.''

Welles stood, frowning in frustration at the woman in the bed.

"The bad things," Hayley asked softly. "What are they?"

Beatrix turned and studied Hayley. "Many, many things. Impossible to make them go away."

"The bad things are powerful? Powerful enough to keep you from getting up and opening in Nice?"

Beatrix nodded her head tearfully.

"Tell me."

The woman in the bed wept silently and copiously. Then she began to talk.

It all came out: The truth about her blackouts. The truth about her treatment for suspected Alzheimer's Disease. The truth about Tessie's blackmail attempts. The truth about the mysterious telephone call and her trip to Grignan to find the man who told her the story of the Fontaines.

They stood in that room, in various stunned postures, listening to an endless stream of hideous revelations coming from the lips of the beautiful woman lying there, and there was no sound but the sound of her soft voice.

Finally she was through, and she lay there, exhausted.

"My God!" Welles whispered.

Sister Marthe crossed herself again and raised her eyes to heaven in silent prayer.

Goriot stood against the wall, arms folded, his eyes narrowed to slits, thinking hard.

Hayley stood up and faced her husband. "It's your move," she told him, a slight glint in her eyes.

Welles blinked. "It's best we cancel our plans," he told Beatrix after a long silence. "We'll come back when you're better."

"I am never better!" cried Beatrix. "I *must* open now, or there will be no Beatrix la Belle ever."

Welles bit his lip. She was right, certainly. After all the buildup, a cancellation now would doom the project. It would *never* get off the ground.

"But you can't walk. You can't stand." Welles frowned. "How can you appear?"

"I am Beatrix!" she told him, fury in her eyes. "If I am Beatrix, *I open the spas!*"

Welles breathed hard. Perhaps a miracle would occur and Beatrix Fontaine would suddenly get up off her bed and walk around, the way she used to. Perhaps. There *had* been miracles. But if she couldn't do it . . .

There was also the problem of Beatrix's background to consider. The absence of the key person in the Beatrix la Belle network would naturally raise questions that would spur investigations by members of the media, as well as members of the competition. If those prying eyes found out what Welles and Hayley and Goriot had just learned, there would be so much negative publicity that the entire affair would be doomed. A living and responsive Beatrix would at least be able to *defend* against any allegations—and possibly obviate any attack by her presence at the gala. Her presence would insure a lot less poking about for dirt—there was no question about that.

"Let's go ahead," Hayley whispered in his ear. "If she *doesn't* come out of it well enough to appear, *then* we pull out."

"But her health—"

"It's one way or the other," Hayley told him. "I'd opt for the green light."

And so, Welles made his decision. Once he had done so, Beatrix turned to him with a warm smile and reached out to grip his hand. "I get up now!"

But when she tried to rise, she fell back limply on the bed, crying out in rage and frustration.

After much arranging, Goriot finally got together an ambulance to drive Beatrix Fontaine down to

Nice, where hospital facilities were made ready for her. She was admitted to the Sisters of Mercy Hospital under the name Jeanne d'Arcy.

After seeing her wheeled into her room, they went back to the hotel, where Boissy Goriot bade Hayley and Welles goodbye and was driven in the Mercedes limo out to the Nice Airport. He took a commuter jet back to Paris, promising to return in four days to set up the security for the coming Beatrix la Belle opening.

"Keep me informed about Mademoiselle Beatrix's condition," he instructed Welles with an almost-grotesque grimace of doubt.

Hayley and Welles had dinner sent up to their room, where they ate it slowly and without relish.

"She wants it so badly; I'm going to try," Welles said at one point in the meal. "But how am I going to pull this off with her lying there like a paraplegic?"

Hayley looked at him with sympathy, shaking her head. "It's beyond me!"

"I'll have to wire the office in New York to send over the best lookalike they can find, as backup. But I'm worried about the truth leaking out. We can get away with this kind of cover-up for a while, but when the media finds out that I've manipulated them, they're going to pull the plug on me."

"Call the opening off?"

Welles tried to smile. His face felt as if it might crack apart. "I was bluffing when I suggested that to Beatrix. After all the hoopla? No way!"

"Tell the truth?"

Welles sank back in his chair, leaving the food on his plate untouched for a long time. "That would seem to be the right way to go. But do you realize what that would mean? What kind of an image is that—the daughter of a brother and sister who engaged in incestuous sexual relations! The father a suicide and matricide! It would make the eleven o'clock news, all right—but for all the wrong reasons! The health spa network would go down like the *Titanic*! And I'd go right along with it!

"There's more. I can't even get away with a half-truth. She may be a psychotic of some kind, *or* the victim of Alzheimer's Disease. For God's sake—you can't have the symbol of a health and beauty spa be a victim of insanity or Alzheimer's!"

Hayley sighed. "It's a difficult problem."

"It's a difficult and *insoluable* problem!" Welles raged.

"Don't get mad at me!"

"I'm not! I'm just blazing away at the world! At the universe! Sleeping sickness! Isn't that the living end?"

Hayley drank her coffee.

Welles rose and put his hands behind him. He was pacing rapidly now, back and forth across the room, frowning, smiling, making faces. He was thinking deeply, moving his lips but saying nothing.

"Something?" Hayley asked. She had seen him before when he had been suddenly struck with an idea.

In true Wellesian form, he held up his hand for silence and resumed his rapid walk.

"That's it, of course!" he said after a moment. "That's *it!* Now where in hell can I get a half-acre of crystal?"

CHAPTER TWENTY-TWO

On its way to Nice, the jetliner flew over the floury strands of the Côte d'Azur. In her passenger seat, staring out the tiny window, Abbey Martin drank in the breathtaking view, the blue water, the sun-drenched, smooth sands below.

She was going to love her stay in Nice, she knew that. It was carnival time in the ancient city, which, according to a guide book she had read, was called Nicaea in Roman times. For centuries, this had been the playground of the rich and the super-rich. Tourists flocked to the cafés and beaches in order to watch the annual Battle of the Flowers, a boisterous and rollicking carnival parade known worldwide for its pageantry.

Visitors partied, drank, and celebrated through the night and into the next morning, and on and on, till the end of festivities.

What a city! It was better than Paris—so they said. Abbey would find out soon enough.

Maybe, if she liked it, she would stay in Nice forever. She could easily persuade François to remain. You would have to be out of your mind to want to leave this place.

Too bad they had to go to her stepfather's obnoxious gala. She would rather party in a café during the night and walk beaches in her string bikini during the day, soaking up the good sun.

A baby girl across the aisle set up a bawling screech. Abbey stuck her fingers in her ears to shut out the clamor. Kids could *really* be a swift pain in the ass. She blotted the horrible sounds out of her mind and watched the coastline below.

She was going to have a good time here.

Nice. The word itself sounded—well—nice.

They touched down at the Nice-Côte d'Azur Airport, and Abbey could not wait to disembark.

All Tuesday, the flower-decked floats crammed the Promenade des Anglais along the Mediterranean coastline. Abbey, and the terrorists with her, watched the bobbing figures and capering celebrators from the sidewalk in the brilliant sunshine. Later, Abbey tried to talk François into going to the adjacent beach.

François had other plans. He leaned over in a conspiratorial manner. "Let's go."

"What?" said Abbey. "We just got here."

"We have a job to do. Don't you remember?"

"We have to work out the details," Ernst explained in his obnoxious, quasi-practical manner.

"We can do that later," Abbey said. "This is too much fun to miss."

"We're going to have more fun at your mummy's party," said François smugly.

"It's my stepfather's party," said Abbey absently.

"Your mother's putting up the money," François reminded her.

Ernst sniggered and ducked his head.

"You're sick," Abbey said.

"You and your parties," François sighed. "When are you going to grow up?"

"Adults have parties, too."

"The rich can have parties all their life," sneered Ernst. "They don't have to work for a living."

"You don't know anything," Abbey responded. She had disliked Ernst from the first moment she met him.

"You're the one who doesn't know anything," Ernst shot back. "Locked away in your private mansion, you've never seen how awful the world really is."

"I'm trying to have some fun in my life. What's wrong with that?" Abbey asked.

"Nothing," François said. "You can get away with it, though. That's what's fucked-up."

"You're jealous!"

François gave a leer. "You hit the nail right on the head."

"Then it's *your* problem," Abbey responded angrily.

"It's going to be your parents' problem pretty soon because they're the ones who are going to *pay* for it!"

"You're right. That's why I'm here," Abbey said in a softer voice.

"Good. Then listen," said François. "Welles is having a costume party at the gala. In fact, the gala is the peak of today's carnival parade. It's going to be a costume party at the Apollon Theater, where he's going to introduce Beatrix la Belle. That's perfect for us."

Ernst grinned. "We'll wear costumes, and nobody

will know who we are. We should be able to walk
right in.''

"Easier than that.'' François smiled in a broken
way. "We'll dress up as terrorists!''

"Of course!'' Ernst's dead eyes lit up, his usually
impassive face brightened. "They'll think the ski
masks on our faces are costumes and the submachine
guns in our hands are props. The fat-cat guests will
die laughing.''

"You must be a genius,'' Abbey said sarcastically.

"Watch your lip, bitch,'' Ernst growled.

"I can be as sarcastic as the next person.''

"Ernst, you'll be the only one in a conventional
costume: a sixteenth-century French aristocrat, with a
domino over your eyes.''

"I like it!'' chortled Ernst.

"You'll be lookout, just in case of trouble.''

The screaming and cheering of the carousing mob
nearly drowned out the terrorists' voices as they continued to discuss their upcoming operation.

By evening, the entire village of Nice was bedlam.
The usual intensity and excitement of carnival time
had been augmented by anticipation of Cornelius
Welles's big show at the Apollon Auditorium. Since
it had been decided in advance that anyone in costume could enter—on a first-come, first-serve basis—
any semblance of order had perished in advance of
the show.

Charlie Garnet was weary and nursing his sore
feet. He had been on his feet all day, keeping the
marauders at bay outside the Apollon, since the plan
was to keep the place secure until late afternoon
when the guests—everybody who could come in—
were to arrive. The "big names"—Senator Kirby

Miles, the President of France, Clive Argyll, several
members of England's royalty, and the Countess della
Camarra—were to sit in roped-off seats, which the
PIGs were keeping empty.

Garnet was in walkie-talkie contact with Boissy
Goriot, the head of the Prescott Investigations Group;
between the two of them, working under the Nice
security force, they had the Apollon pretty well under
control—as much as it could be in the free-for-all
envisioned.

He was thinking mostly about his aching feet when
he saw a battered Fiat approach and disgorge a group
of young men and women. They were laughing and
talking loudly in French and slapping one another on
the back. Garnet smiled vaguely. They had certainly
selected a current and popular costume-theme for the
event: they were disguised as terrorists.

"Interesting costumes," one of Charlie Garnet's
men said next to him.

"Uh huh," said Garnet.

His eye lit on a young member of the group. It was
a woman dressed in men's clothing, also acting the
part of a terrorist. Her stance seemed familiar. The
group moved quickly into the inside of the auditorium, and just at that moment Garnet realized he
knew the face.

It was Abbey Martin!

He flicked on the walkie-talkie button. "Security
Central. Security Central! Garnet, here. I've spotted
Abbey Martin."

After a moment, the accented voice of Boissy
Goriot came on. "Hold her there!"

"She's gone now," Garnet said. He described the
group.

Goriot sighed. "There must be a hundred groups

of 'terrorists' here tonight. It's the thing to be—the easiest kind of costume to wear! I'll pass the word about Abigail Martin.''

God, his feet ached, Charlie Garnet thought, reaching down to rub some circulation back into his ankles.

Abbey and the terrorists gazed about at the vast auditorium, with its 70mm, 35mm, and 16mm film projection equipment, and its eidophore system for teleprojection. International-television news cameras were placed at strategic spots throughout the auditorium.

François rubbed his hands together gleefully. There was even an infrared light system that provided simultaneous translation of every word spoken, into six languages. Ernst gripped his automatic pistol in his hands and gave a half-hearted smile at the extent of the media coverage involved.

Nobody paid any attention to the guns or the costumes. The guests thought the guns were props for the outfits, and the ski masks and black commando shirts costumes for the roles they were playing.

"Perfect," whispered François, eyeing several of the movie cameras. "We couldn't have asked for more!"

"Now what?" Abbey asked in a small voice. She was uncomfortable. She didn't want to be seen by her mother or her stepfather. In addition to that, she thought she had seen Charlie Garnet outside. Certainly, he would recognize her, even if she *had* changed her makeup and hair.

"We wait for Welles to mount the stage and give his sales pitch. We wait and we watch. *Then* we act."

They stood in the crowded aisle among a crush of

international movers and shakers. A sheik in his burnoose glided past them, spritzer bubbling in hand.

Backstage, Carney Welles and Hayley Prescott huddled together in close conversation.

"She's here!" Hayley said, with excitement lighting up her eyes. "Abbey!"

"You think she'll come to you?"

"Why not? Maybe it's her way of surprising me."

Welles tried to smile. "Beatrix is here, too. I wonder if those cynical media types are going to accept this."

Hayley shrugged. "You're going to have to find out the hard way. Good luck. I'm going to circulate in the auditorium and try to locate Abbey."

Taking a deep breath, Cornelius Welles stepped out into the brightness of the auditorium in front of the closed curtain.

"There have been all kinds of rumors," he said into the microphone, "rumors about Beatrix la Belle, about Beatrix Fontaine, about this entire network of health and beauty spas. Those rumors have sometimes been nasty—fomented by competition, fomented by the press, fomented by people who love to tear things down."

There was silence in the huge auditorium.

"Let's *see* her, Welles!" someone shouted out.

Welles smiled faintly. "Beatrix Fontaine is one of the most beautiful women in the world," he went on. "It is fitting that she be the one to let all the rest of you women in on the secret of beauty and grace. The surprise is that she was not really born that way, but worked her way into beauty through a very simple method. You too, ladies of the world, can be just as beautiful, just as healthy, and just as exciting.

"In a moment, Beatrix Fontaine! But first, let's just think about this new venture—Beatrix la Belle. When you see her, you will know that you, too, will achieve her beauty once you join her new health spa. That simple? you ask. Yes! Anybody here can be as beautiful as Beatrix Fontaine herself!

"How? That is the really amazing secret of this method of health and beauty care. The real beauty of the Beatrix la Belle health spa is that you don't have to exercise if you don't want to, and you can eat whatever you want, in limited amounts, of course. Most of your time will be spent simply getting rid of fat. What could be better than losing weight while you sleep? No sweat, no tears. And in the end, no fat!

"Sleeping away fat? Yes! That is the secret of the Beatrix la Belle method of gaining health and beauty. You eat in moderation; you exercise in moderation; you have fun in moderation—and in the end, you reduce while you sleep. You become, at Beatrix la Belle, a Sleeping Beauty."

There was a long silence.

Welles turned in profile and gave a signal to the backstage crew. The curtains slowly parted.

"Ladies and gentlemen—Sleeping Beauty herself. Beatrix Fontaine!"

And there she was!

A gasp of astonishment, then shocked silence, and finally approbation cascaded over the assembled multitude, and the applause was deafening.

- Partly it was the lighting, partly the staging, but most of all, it was the audacious approach of the presentation that did it.

In the center of the brightly lit stage stood a platform on which was constructed a large glass case, with aluminum edges holding the plate glass surfaces together. Inside this brilliantly illuminated glass case stood a bed covered in silken drapes, upon which Beatrix Fontaine lay, as if asleep, dressed in a gaily designed sleeping gown.

As she lay there, the audience could see her chest rise and fall slowly as she feigned sleep.

Only then did the eye of the viewer notice that the background of the stage was lined with trellises, laden with flowers of all kinds, colors, and shapes, from which the reflected glory of ten thousand petals added to the beauty of the woman in the crystal container—the legend of Sleeping Beauty brought to life by Beatrix la Belle.

Lynn Miles gripped her husband's arm as the audience around them riveted its attention to the stage.

"The son of a bitch has brought it off!" Lynn said quietly.

"He has, that!" grinned Miles, gripping her hand. "Wonder when she's going to get up and make her spiel?"

"I don't quite think she is, Miley," grinned Lynn. She shook her head. Damn that Welles; damn Hayley. In spite of what had happened to Beatrix Fontaine, they had pulled it off! How in hell—?

Abbey Martin and her group were lingering at the back of the auditorium. She was staying behind them, so her stepfather and her mother could not see her. She would be seen soon enough. She did not want the meeting with her mother to be premature. If Hayley or Welles spotted her and talked to her it could jeopardize the whole plan.

On the stage now Welles waved a hand.

"I'm now going to ask a spokesperson for the Beatrix la Belle spa network to come up on the stage here and tell you more about it. Step right up, Donny."

A frail, anemic-looking cosmetician mounted the stage.

Welles moved down off of the stage and walked toward the back of the auditorium. He seemed shaken, although he was hopeful that everything would continue to work out.

François eyed the cosmetician who was talking some nonsense from the stage. "Who is that ass-licker?"

"Never saw him before," Abbey said.

Ernst gave a sign. The rest of them began sauntering toward the stage during the cosmetician's talk. Ernst, in his domino, remained at the back of the auditorium, his handgun hidden in his waistband.

"Okay," said François, and he waved his people toward the steps and up onto the stage. Abbey followed dutifully.

Megan Tarantino, née Prescott, soon to be Argyll, turned to the British actor at her side in sudden excitement.

"It's Abbey!"

Argyll leaned down toward her, frowning. He had never seen Abigail, but he knew she was Megan's niece, and he knew that the family was looking for her.

Megan pointed to the steps that led onto the stage. "Who are those ruffians with her?" she asked Argyll.

"I have no idea!" Argyll said.

A ripple of amusement went through the crowd in the auditorium as Abbey and her companions took

over a corner of the stage. There was laughter as
François moved quickly across the stage toward the
cosmetician and pushed him away from the microphone.

The cosmetician's twerpy expression—one of frustrated rage and indecision—got a real laugh. Some of
the people in the audience intuitively sensed trouble,
but most simply rolled with the action.

The cosmetician, Donny Albright, grabbed at the
mike stand, but François rammed the butt of his
machine pistol into the man's jaw. Albright staggered
forward and fell off the stage into the orchestra pit,
grabbing at his broken and bloody jaw.

Several people screamed.

A middle-aged man stood up near the front of the
auditorium. "You're going too damned far, Welles!
Come on. Enough's enough! Let's hear from Beatrix,
and the hell with this phony melodrama!"

"It's fake blood!" cried a woman in sudden delight. "It's a typical Welles PR stunt. Oh, well done!"

Clive Argyll knew enough about show business to
realize that this action was unrehearsed and very real.
When Megan Tarantino had told him she recognized
Abbey Martin, he had seen that she was obviously
with the group masquerading as terrorists. But he
could sense her tension. Were they really only
masquerading?

He moved quickly toward the side aisle to gain the
stage steps. But the instant he reached the aisle, with
Megan following and clinging to him, he was blocked
by Cornelius Welles, whom he had met once, and
only knew vaguely.

"No," said Welles. "It's Abbey, all right. I don't
want her hurt. If you do anything—"

Now Hayley joined them. "They've got her! Boissy was right! What can we do?"

Welles turned, exhibiting only a very cool and controlled attitude to the assembled audience. Those around him began to relax. He was looking for Boissy Goriot, and he saw him in the distance. Quickly, he flicked his hand, and Goriot knew what to do.

In an instant, the PIGs were moving quietly and briskly through the back of the auditorium toward the front.

Ernst Roedeker, the lookout, spotted the movement immediately and pressed a beeper he had hidden in his trousers pocket. A receiver, in François's pocket picked up the signal instantly.

Onstage, François jerked the bolt back on the machine pistol and prepared to fire it. He could see Welles halfway to the back of the auditorium, and he swung the weapon in Welles's direction. Their eyes met. Welles held up his hands to signal for the security guards at the rear to stay out of the sight of the men on the stage. François did not see Goriot; he thought Welles had simply caved in.

François grabbed the microphone stand. "We are now in command! Ladies and gentlemen, we are members of POW, People of the World!"

There was silence, and then ribald laughter from one corner of the room. A rich Texas wildcatter named Houston Smith swaggered out of his seat in the first row and started to mount the stage steps. He was a heavy man, wearing sloppy, expensive clothes.

One of François's men covering him swung around and fired at him, blowing the side of his skull off. The Texan fell back dead. There was blood all over the side of the auditorium.

Panic broke out. Women screamed and men cursed. Immediate chaos ensued as people got up out of their seats and began running. The crowd was soon milling about. Some of the people in the rear ran out into the night.

François blasted away at the ceiling of the stage, creating a tremendous racket as the shots were amplified by the microphone. The fleeing guests froze in their places.

"Joke's over!" yelled one guest.

"Shut up!" François said into the mike. "Don't move! Anyone!"

A brunette woman with a pageboy haircut hysterically broke for a side exit. One of the terrorists on the stage leveled his machine pistol at her and loosed a burst of shot that stitched a seam of red blood across her back. She fell on her face, ripping her diamond necklace apart.

"Bring the cameras closer!" ordered François, now in control. "We have an important announcement to make. Do you see this woman with me? She is Abigail Prescott, one of the richest women in the world! Part of the Prescott fortune! She has a statement she wants you to hear!"

There were murmurs from the crowd. Women were sobbing and crying.

"She is going to denounce the Prescott family for what the Prescotts really are: greedy robber barons who plundered America and will lie, cheat, steal, and stoop to any crime for money. Cornelius Welles is the biggest tightwad chiseler ever born, his wife nothing more than a high-class whore who fucks anyone for a profit!"

A tall man stood up and shook his fist in the air. "Get a job!" he shouted.

François reacted with rage. "You're as crooked as all the rest of them!"

"Get a haircut!"

"Bum!"

The crowd seemed about to react against François. He knew he had to do something to regain control. One or two of the guests still thought it was an elaborate PR gimmick, part of the Sleeping Beauty campaign. They were outraged, not able to believe Welles would go to such lengths to sell a product.

"Using violence to sell a product is bad enough," one of the guests shouted, "but that blood looks too real. I thought I could hear bullets shattering that woman's ribs. This guy Welles needs a psychiatrist!"

When the woman died, Abbey Martin panicked. The gunfire and the bloodshed unnerved her. She knew it was real; she knew it was no sham. Nevertheless, she did not fall apart. She had seen François kill a bank guard. She knew what was going to happen. It was going to get worse, not better.

Besides Abbey, there were three terrorists with François on the stage. One of them now donned a mask of Cornelius Welles's face. Out of a suitcase he carried he withdrew a black ball and chain. He locked the ankle of one of the other terrorists to the chain, removed a bullwhip from the suitcase, and pretended to whip the terrorist wearing the ball and chain around his leg.

The enchained terrorist slouched over toward the center of the stage where the crystal case enclosing the Sleeping Beauty stood. He opened the glass case and entered it, leaning down over Beatrix Fontaine where she lay, still, apparently sleeping. The terrorist pretended to be working very hard at lifting her off her bed, but nothing happened.

The man in the Welles mask cracked his whip, and the other terrorist pantomimed an attempt to frisk Beatrix as she lay there. He made a mime of removing money from her, displaying it to the Welles look-alike. He then handed the money over.

The masquerading Welles laughed uproariously and snatched the money.

"How did you like our little playlet?" François asked into the mike. "As Shaw once said, 'In real life truth is revealed by parables and falsehood supported by facts.'"

There was no reaction from the spectators in the auditorium. Then someone called out, "What's your real scam, buddy?"

François turned then and stared into the lights. "Throw your wallets and jewels into the aisle. All of you!"

"You're as greedy as everybody else!" called out a voice.

"Do it!" François waved the weapon in his hand threateningly.

"What gives you the right to tell us what to do?"

"This!" screamed François, becoming a little upset. He fired the machine pistol over the heads of the audience. Glass shattered and a chandelier fell heavily.

Now the guests began to toss their jewelry and money into the aisle.

"You too, Mother Whore Hayley Welles," François called out, spotting Hayley in the side aisle.

Appalled, Hayley did as he told her to.

"Tell her what you think of her, Abbey," said François. "It's your turn to speak."

*   *   *

Abbey Martin cringed when she heard François call her mother a whore. She hated her mother, the bitch, but she did not like hearing other people call her names.

No one who came in contact with her stood a chance. She smothered people. She would not let anyone exist as an individual. You could only exist if you followed her orders.

But there was more to it than that. François, in his own way, was just as bad as her mother. Worse, even. If you did not agree with him, he shot you. Abbey now eyed him as he stood in front of her on the stage, the machine pistol in his hands, his movements tense and jerky. A cold shiver of fear ran down her spine. He would kill anyone who crossed him. Would he even kill her?

The attack was getting out of hand. She had not expected anybody to be shot. Already, three bloody, mutilated bodies lay on the floor below her. How many more would follow? These terrorists were fanatics. She knew that. Human life meant nothing to them. They would murder in cold blood for power, for publicity—for money, the thing they pretended to hate so much, for God's sake!

Her mother was obsessed with power, too, but at least she did not kill for it.

Abbey knew François wanted her to denounce her mother over the microphone, but she doubted she could do it. Not now. Not with all the blood and gore around her.

While François was talking, she had tried to back furtively away from him so she could climb down the stage steps to the floor. What happened next made her give a sudden start.

The cold steel muzzle of a machine pistol jabbed

into the small of her back. The fourth man on the stage had no intention of letting her get away from them.

Now fear built inside her vitals, fear like a block of ice.

Why did they have to insult her whole family in front of the world? She knew Carney was a no-talent tightwad who, for some unknown reason, was full of himself. But why did François have to tell the world about it? And now he wanted her to tear down her parents in public. Her family was her private business, nobody else's. All their warts and moles, as well.

"Tell them!" cried François, his eyes flashing.

"No." She could hardly get the word out.

"What do you mean, no?" His face turned red. "You said you would, you little traitor!"

"You didn't say you were going to kill anyone!"

"It was self-defense."

"That's what you always say when you kill someone. You said it when you killed the guard at the bank."

"We don't have time for your whimpering. Get up there and talk, or I'll kill you now."

White-faced, she stared at him. She could not believe her ears. "Who do you think you are?"

He trained the Uzi machine pistol on her stomach. "Move!"

"You tricked me, liar. You don't love me."

"How could anyone love a rich bitch? You're all whores. Spoiled little whores. Now talk into the mike!"

The look in his furious eyes terrified her. She had no faith in him at all anymore. He was capable of doing *anything*.

She reached out and took hold of the microphone, trembling. François's face relaxed into a grin of triumph.

"Listen, everybody," Abbey began. "These people kidnapped me and brainwashed me and—"

The sharp jolt to her kidney forced a gasp out of her. Without looking around, she knew it was the steel muzzle of the machine pistol that had jabbed her. The pain and the shock of the blow made her stagger forward. She blundered blindly ahead, fell to her knees, and then rolled over on the stage.

Then all hell broke loose.

From his position near his new boss, Senator Kirby Miles, Mead Brookhaven III could see that Lynn Miles was very much upset, although he had no idea why. He was along on the trip simply because the senator wanted him to handle any press conferences he might set up. He had been reluctant to make an appearance, since Cornelius Welles had, in no uncertain terms, said he never wanted to see him again. But the senator had assured him that Welles was a nice guy who would get over all that soon.

He was sickened by the overblown show that Welles was putting on. Mead assumed that most of the terrorist thing was a scam of some kind, with Abbey Welles assigned a certain role to carry out. Now he was not quite so sure about that. Maybe she *was* in the grip of these morons.

He *liked* her, damn it! When she had staggered forward and fallen on the stage, he had felt it deep inside him. He found himself running, breaking away from the senator and his wife and heading down the aisle. He could see Welles ahead of him, and Hayley—

* * *

Boissy Goriot saw Welles give the signal to move, and he waved his men on. Abigail Martin was safely out of the way now; at least, there was no one threatening her immediately. Perhaps she had been badly injured; perhaps someone would shoot her. Hopefully not, but no one knew what would happen.

It was a grand old military charge, submachine guns blazing away at the men on the stage. With the girl out of the line of fire, the sweeping horizontal patterns of fire cut the four men almost in two. One guard, at Goriot's signal, threw a stun grenade onto the stage. The explosion blinded and deafened the terrorist still visible. Slugs flew throughout the room, from both sides of it.

One young television cameraman in blue jeans continued manning his camera and recorded the gun battle as it blazed away.

The smoke from the stun grenade dissipated on the stage. The terrorists all lay in bloody heaps. The bullet-shredded flowers on the trellises behind the stage dripped blood. Bits of petals from the orchids and roses fluttered down onto the corpses and the shattered glass case that had contained Beatrix Fontaine.

And near it, but out of the way, Abbey Martin lay motionless and prostrate on the stage. Boissy Goriot waved his arm.

"Hold your fire!"

There were a few shots, then silence.

"Monsieur Welles! Please! Stay away!"

Cornelius Welles spotted Abbey's still body and bolted up the steps onto the stage, disregarding the shouts of Boissy Goriot.

"Carney!" he heard Hayley scream behind him. "Be careful! Some of them may still be alive!"

Welles disregarded his wife's cries. He choked on the acrid smell of gunsmoke as he knelt over Abbey's body and looked down at her.

"My God! Abbey!"

He reached down and held her in his arms, and said, "What have I done?"

"Is she all right?" asked a voice at his side.

Welles turned. It was Mead Brookhaven III. Welles frowned. How had *he* gotten here?

"She's got a pulse," said the young yuppie. "It looks good."

Charlie Garnet arrived with Boissy Goriot. He stepped over and leveled a handgun at the terrorists spread out on the stage, his teeth clenched in rage. He kicked at the bodies to see if they responded.

Now a hand touched Welles's shoulder. "It wasn't your fault," Hayley told him. "You did all you could do."

"I shouldn't have signaled the guards."

"The terrorists would have shot her anyway."

Mead Brookhaven looked up at Hayley. "She's not dead. Let's get her out of here, quickly."

Boissy Goriot was on his walkie-talkie. "Are there any more of them?"

"I don't see any," Charlie Garnet said, scanning the crowd that was beginning to dwindle away now.

"Shoot on sight if you see one," snapped Goriot. He set his jaw, glowered, and scrutinized the guests, his eyebrows knitted.

"Somebody call an ambulance," snapped Garnet. "Clear a space. Help those people here. Someone. Help over here!"

Most of the guests were moving up and down the aisles to collect the jewels and money dumped there.

Welles pressed his finger to Abbey's throat. He, too, could feel a faint pulse.

"She's alive," he said, confirming what Mead Brookhaven had said. "Hurry! Get that ambulance here on the double!" With Mead's help, he laid Abbey's head down gently on the stage, leaped to his feet, and seized the microphone. "An ambulance! Get an ambulance!"

Mead grabbed his arm. "I'll take care of her, Mr. Welles. You've got other problems here."

Welles stared at Mead. "Okay, kid. Take off!"

Then he turned around and tried to make out what was happening on the rest of the stage.

Lynn Miles was petrified with fear. She hid her head when the shooting started. There were people screaming everywhere. The senator held her tight, or she would have collapsed on the floor.

"Miley, my God!" she kept saying.

"Rougher than the last Democratic Convention," he said to her at one point, trying to make her laugh.

She was sick instead. But once the bullets stopped flying and the glass stopped shattering, she stood up and looked up on the stage. The big glass case that Beatrix Fontaine had been lying in was utterly destroyed. Pieces of glass lay all around.

She and the senator began moving toward the stage. Now that they were closer, Lynn's eyes focused on Beatrix Fontaine. She was lying there—

Lynn stumbled up the steps in panic. She stumbled over the bodies of the four terrorists and saw the plate glass pieces on the stage floor, covered with blood. Then she was standing over Beatrix's bloodspattered body, looking down at her glassy eyes, her frozen face, all now rosy-colored from the veneer of blood coating her body.

Lynn Miles restrained herself from vomiting. She dry-heaved a few times and wheeled away from the glass coffin. She felt faint. She knew she had been the partial cause of Beatrix Fontaine's ultimate fate— her death—

She staggered and felt someone's arms about her. It was not the senator. It was one of the guards. It was, fatefully enough, Charlie Garnet.

"Pop!" she wailed. "Pop! Oh, Pop, it's—"

She fainted dead away.

"Arlene!" she heard distantly. "Arlene!"

As she lay on the stage, Abbey Martin felt as though she was dying. She could not stand being alive any longer. How could *anybody?* If this was life, why did people go on living? Why did they have kids?

She had felt this bad only one other time: when she had had her abortion. She did not go to a regular hospital, she remembered, because she feared the doctors would report the abortion to her parents. There was a state law that minors had to have parental sanction before hospital doctors would perform the operation.

She did not have enough money of her own to bribe the doctors into keeping their mouths shut. Besides, with a name like Prescott, even if it was only her middle name, she knew word would get around.

She had no intention of telling her parents someone was laying her. Christ! Could you imagine the tantrums they would throw if they found out? She did not even know if they would allow the abortion. They had mixed feelings on abortion. Her mother was almost puritanical when it came to other people's sex lives, but when it came to her own, she was an alleycat.

Abbey had to have an abortion on the sly. It was so godawful; she shuddered to think about it. It had to be done, though. Her tennis-pro boyfriend refused to admit he was the father. That meant she would be an unmarried mother, which was about as low as you could get.

A friend of hers, a former high-class call girl at the 21 Club, told her the name and address of a doctor who performed abortions on call girls who became pregnant.

She found her way to the seedy dive in the dead of night. The runty doctor, who had a goatee, shambled across the room, the black eyes behind his spectacles fixed to the floor. The sight of him made her flesh crawl.

He made her strip, lie down on the cold table, put her feet in the stirrups, and keep still. She watched the cold fluorescent striplight above her throughout the ordeal.

The quack only gave her a local anesthetic, said it was all she needed—the liar, the fake! Before he started cutting into her she considered leaving the place, but then what would she do? Where would she go? What would she do with the baby?

If the other girls came here, he could not be a total charlatan. They would not keep coming to him if he botched his operations.

The instrument inside her burned like a hot poker. She almost fainted. To this day she did not know why she had not lost consciousness. Then she heard a horrible scraping sound. It did not sound as though it was coming from her, but she knew it was.

It was the sound of the obscene doctor removing the foetus and scraping away the afterbirth inside her womb: a relentless scraping, like a hiss . . . and it was coming from inside her!

She nearly died.

She lived, and she refused to let him flush away the foetus. That would have made the operation too foul for words. It was bad enough as it stood.

That same nauseating feeling of being on the verge of death passed over her again as she lay on the stage. She wanted to die and get it over with.

It was all because of François. First it was Phillip the tennis pro. Now François. They were all phonies. They tricked her into believing they cared for her. Then, when they got what they wanted, they left her.

Like Mead Brookhaven III. He had never done that to her, but he *had* left her. She thought she could see him now when she tried to open her eyes. But she knew it was just a mirage, just a hallucination. Funny thing. She kind of liked him.

Men! They were no damned good. You couldn't trust a man. It would be a mistake ever to do it again.

She slipped into unconsciousness as a voice said, "Abbey! Good luck!"

Ernst Roedeker drew a nine millimeter automatic out of his shoulder holster and deliberated for several seconds, sizing up the situation on the stage, where his comrades now lay dead. He figured his only ticket out was a hostage, so he approached Hayley Welles and stuck the automatic's muzzle into her breast.

"See this?" he whispered.

Her eyes bulged in fear. He lowered the automatic out of sight so nobody else could see it. He pressed it against her kidney.

They headed out of the auditorium.

On the stage, Cornelius Welles stared down at the remains of Beatrix Fontaine and felt himself going limp all over. There was nothing he could do about it now, he thought. He was ruined, sure enough. Completely.

He happened to look around, and he saw Hayley leaving the auditorium. But she was not alone.

"Hayley!" he called out, his voice hoarse.

She looked at him, but said nothing. He did not like the look in her eyes. She seemed terrified of something. Of what? The terrorists were all dead. Where was she going?

He saw someone next to her, someone who—

He bounded down the steps, made his way across the length of the auditorium, and followed her. A man in a domino was walking very close behind her and a little to one side. Was he another of her shack jobs? Welles's ears burned red at the thought. She could not wait to get screwed, could she! Even with Abbey more dead than alive, Hayley was off for a quickie with yet another stud! Was she born with her snatch on fire?

Welles had to put a stop to it. He trotted toward them. Why did she look so frightened? She was walking stiffly, her face drained of blood. What was really going on?

He caught up with the man in the domino in the lobby of the theater, and, with his finger, tapped him on the back. The man whipped his head around, and in that instant, from his vantage point, Welles caught sight of the cause for Hayley's alarm. A gun!

Christ! What was he going to do?

Frenzied thoughts flashed through his mind in a

fraction of a second. He had to disarm the man. How?

He was no kung fu expert. He had never even served time in the army. He had no idea how to fight, except for what he saw on television.

He kneed the man in the groin. Welles knew that had to hurt. The blow, and the pain, caused the man to jerk the automatic away from Hayley and fire. Welles grasped the man's gun-hand and tried to wrestle the gun away from him.

At the sound of the shot, the PIGs swarmed toward Welles, noted the gun, charged the man in the domino, disarmed him, and flung him to the floor.

Welles grabbed Hayley around the waist and dragged her away from the fracas.

"I thought he was going to kill me," she whispered.

"He won't now," Welles said. "Who was he?"

"I don't know. All of a sudden he was sticking a gun in my ribs and telling me to leave with him."

"He must be another one of these scumbag terrorists. He'll rot in jail for the rest of his life!"

Welles stepped toward the man and, between the PIGs, kicked him in the ribs, then returned to Hayley. He felt good about kicking the man when he was down, and for some reason, he had absolutely no remorse about it.

"I'm just glad it's all over," Hayley said.

EPILOGUE

The body of Beatrix Fontaine had been removed from the stage, and the cleanup men were working at hauling away the broken glass and pieces of junk. Another crew was trying to wash up the blood and stains made by the shootings in the posh auditorium.

Cornelius Welles and his wife Hayley Prescott were standing there, staring down in disbelief at the carnage.

"The bastards ruined everything," Welles said softly. "They ruined Beatrix la Belle and they ruined me. I'm finished. I'll be the laughingstock of the world." He clutched his head miserably. "What am I going to do?"

"This was supposed to be the grand event of the year, bar none," Hayley said, shrugging.

Welles pulled himself together at the glimmer of an idea. "We may not be dead yet."

Hayley glanced at him suspiciously. "What do you mean? The gala's a disaster."

"By God, we might be able to pull it off!"

411

"What are you babbling about?"

There was a glint in Welles's eye. "Remember all the cameras covering the gala?"

"Of course. We'll never be able to live it down. The massacre will be in every scandal sheet in the world. They'll probably call it the Nice Massacre—play on words. Get it? Another Nice mess you've got us into, Stanley! You know what a sick sense of humor newspaper hacks have. What are you smiling about?"

"The more coverage we get, the better."

"You're out of your mind."

"The media coverage will serve as public relations."

"Public relations for what? Terrorism?"

"For the movie our talent agency is going to produce." Welles's eyes glittered.

"What movie?"

"The 'Nice Massacre.' "

"You *are* insane."

"No, I'm not. The movie's already shot. We have tons of film footage. We'll give the film audiences the inside story of what *really* happened here today."

"You're too much, Carney."

From her tone, he could not figure out whether that was a compliment or an insult.

"It's the only chance we've got to salvage our company's reputation," he said.

"What if it backfires?"

"How could it be any worse than it already is? This is the only way we can snatch victory from the jaws of defeat."

"It's ridiculous," Hayley said, but her voice was soft and her eyes were narrowed.

"Do you have any better ideas?"

After a while she said, "No. I wouldn't be surprised if the company goes under."

Stirred by adrenalin, Welles paced around restlessly. "I'll show you. I'll show you. We'll pull it off yet."

"It'll take a miracle."

"Then a miracle we'll get!" Welles rubbed his jaw. "Let's see. We can always get Clive Argyll to narrate—maybe even appear in a segment or two as himself. And James Garner—he was here. Cary Grant showed up. This is real-life stuff, Hayley."

Hayley threw up her hands and started to laugh.